W9-BNE-288

manhattan
on the rocks

janice harayda

SOURCEBOOKS LANDMARK™
AN IMPRINT OF SOURCEBOOKS, INC.®
NAPERVILLE, ILLINOIS

Published by Sourcebooks, Inc.
P.O. Box 4410, Naperville, Illinois 60567-4410
(630) 961-3900
FAX: (630) 961-2168
www.sourcebooks.com

Library of Congress Cataloging-in-Publication Data

Harayda, Janice.
   Manhattan on the rocks / Janice Harayda.
      p. cm.
   ISBN 1-4022-0119-2 (alk. paper)
   1. Manhattan (New York, N.Y.)--Fiction. 2. Periodicals--Publishing--
Fiction. 3. Fashion editors--Fiction. 4. Women editors--Fiction. 5.
Supervisors--Fiction. I. Title.
   PS3558.A558M36 2004
   813'.54--dc22

                                                          2004013217

Printed and bound in Canada
WC 10 9 8 7 6 5 4 3 2 1

In memory of
William Gantner Harayda
August 31, 1950–May 14, 2004
Brother, friend, and sportsman,
who said in the last week of his life,
"I don't know where I'm going to go
or what I'm going to do,
but I know it will be an adventure."

1
Nightmare

Laura waited at the back of the church in a purple satin gown. Beside her stood five identically dressed women who looked like eggplants that had been fed Miracle-Gro until they assumed grotesquely human proportions. Nobody but Laura seemed to see anything unnatural about their appearance. As the organist launched into "Jesu, Joy of Man's Desiring," she recognized her cue and began moving down the aisle. She had taken only a few steps when her knees buckled, and she crashed to the floor as three hundred wedding guests watched in horror.

The nightmare woke Laura up. Ever since her cousin Tina had asked her to be a bridesmaid after not speaking to her for two years, deciding that the time had come to bury the hatchet in a bouquet of tea roses, she'd dreaded the wedding. Now her fear was disrupting her sleep. Laura wished she could get a little sympathy from Nick, who would never have to wobble down an aisle in a pair of heels that resembled purple golf tees. But Nick was staring at his computer across the room, and she hated to disturb him. Lately she'd found that "Good morning" could elicit anything from a brusque "Easy for you to say" to an irate lecture on the need not to interrupt an artist at his work.

After several years as a writer for the largest-circulation magazine in Ohio, Laura understood the fragility of the creative process. But she was beginning to wonder how hard Nick was working in the hours he spent brooding at his computer. For months he'd been suffering from a writer's block the size of Antarctica and just as impenetrably frozen into place, a problem that baffled her. They'd met while they were working for the student newspaper at Notre Dame, and back then Nick wrote trenchant film reviews as easily as their classmates invoked the sacred memory of the Gipper. When they drove home to Ohio together for vacations, Laura admired the way he could write on a laptop in a minivan, a skill she had never mastered.

The trouble started a few years after college when they'd rented a drafty one-bedroom apartment in an arty part of town that everybody called "the Greenwich Village of Cleveland." Nick could hardly conceal his disdain for this description of a neighborhood that had two restaurants, one movie theater, and fewer gay men than the locker room of the Minnesota Vikings.

"The 'Greenwich Village of Cleveland'?" he said incredulously, when Laura repeated the rental agent's description. "That's like calling the Polo boutique at Dillard's 'the Rodeo Drive of the Midwest.'"

But Laura pointed out that the neighborhood was one of the few in Cleveland that attracted young people and that their low rent would allow them to save up enough to move to New York or Los Angeles. To pay his share of their expenses while keeping his days free for writing his screenplay, Nick had taken a job as the night manager of the movie theater down the block. By then Laura was a staff writer at *Buckeye Magazine,* where she got bylines every month while he waited to see "Nicholas Peters" roll by on a list of credits. He had never quite forgiven her for her better luck, and his resentment had erupted into open hostility two weeks earlier when she had accepted a job at a new magazine in New York, thinking that a bit of distance might help their romance.

As she tried to figure out how to pacify Nick on her last day in town, Laura saw a spot of hot-and-sour soup on the sheet beside her. Ever since getting the call from *Cassandra,* she'd had no time to drive to the Laundromat with pillowcases stuffed with their laundry, and Nick had stopped helping out after he began planning an annual summer film festival at his theater that the management called "the Sundance of Northeast Ohio." Their wicker hamper was overflowing, and she was almost relieved to be leaving town before somebody had to come in to fumigate the place.

Laura stretched her legs under the sheets and felt her big toe hit a plastic soup spoon. She reached under the covers to retrieve it, wondering why she lived with a man who could remember the address of every film agent in Hollywood but not the general direction of the wastebasket. When she surfaced from under the tangle of the sheets, Nick was sitting beside her on the bed, tugging at her Land's End nightshirt, reminding her of one of the reasons.

***

An hour later, they had lost the postcoital glow that, when they were students, was practically radioactive. Nick was sipping coffee made from the rich Tanzanian beans that he had started drinking in the hope that a stronger pick-me-up might cure his writer's block. Sitting across from him at a chipped white enamel table, Laura felt a pang of nostalgia for the life she was leaving. An eat-in kitchen was one of the things that she would have to give up when she moved to New York. Nick, she hoped, would not be.

Even after straggling out of bed, he looked like a man who had failed to make the cast of *Baywatch* only because he couldn't maintain a tan in the feeble sunlight that Cleveland got for ten months of the year. Tall and broad-shouldered, he had tousled blond hair and intense, delft-blue eyes set off by a rumpled white T-shirt and black jeans. He had such conspicuously Aryan features a professor had joked that only his un-Teutonic slouch kept him from passing for "a poster boy for the Hitler Jugend."

But the force of his gaze—which had thrilled Laura whenever she saw him crossing a leafy quadrangle at Notre Dame—was unnerving when he was angry. And Nick hadn't calmed down since he'd learned that she had taken a job as a writer for *Cassandra,* the latest magazine started by a television star hoping to become the next Oprah or Martha. "You're going to end up just like David Justice!" he ranted. "After the Indians traded him to New York, he was never the same again." Nick made it sound as though the ballplayer had wrapped his car around a street lamp in the Bronx and spent the rest of his life as a vegetable. She couldn't figure out whether he was more upset that she was leaving Cleveland or that she was moving to the hometown of the Yankees.

Laura glanced at the daisy-shaped clock on the kitchen wall that their landlord had received as a wedding present thirty years earlier, and saw that she had to survive only seven more hours until her plane left for New York. Hoping that Nick wouldn't start arguing when she had to pack, she tried to lighten his mood with an upbeat story about her final assignment for *Buckeye,* a profile of a retired schoolteacher in Sandusky who collected airsickness bags and wanted to find a showcase for them that would rival the Hoover Vacuum Cleaner Museum in North Canton. The woman had more than two hundred bags, many from extinct airlines like Braniff and Eastern, and loved it when carriers went belly-up and enhanced the value of her holdings. On the day of the interview, she had been praying for a swift end to the financially troubled Aer Lingus. Laura was talking about the Sabena and KLM bags when Nick exploded.

"Stop!" Nick slammed his coffee mug down on the table so hard that he added another chip to the aging white enamel. "You're doing this just to torture me. You're trying to rub it in that I'm staying behind with the airsick lady in Sandusky while you go off to a city filled with people who have their own Gulfstream jets."

Laura blinked, not expecting this line of attack. As far as she could tell, New York wasn't filled with people who owned Gulfstream jets but with people who ate salami sandwiches on the IRT.

"You know that's not true," she said. "In any case, I'm sure some people here have private jets, too." Laura tore through her memory, trying to remember any stories she'd read about rich Clevelanders who went into anaphylactic shock at the sight of a Continental departure lounge. "For example, I'm sure the Jacobs brothers—"

Nick gave his mug a shove, and it skidded toward Laura like a hockey puck. She caught it just before it slid off the table.

"I don't understand why you need to leave Cleveland," he said testily. "A true artist can work anywhere." Laura chafed under the implication that her move was a sign of weakness but said nothing as Nick spoke passionately of the many geniuses whose talents had prevailed under worse conditions than the Lake Effect, the meteorological phenomenon that helped to explain the perennial cloud cover over Lake Erie. He began with Mozart's poverty, moved on to Tolstoy's disastrous marriage, and ended with Picasso's inability to buy art supplies during the Nazi occupation of France, forcing him to work with boat paint.

Relieved that he'd skipped over Solzhenitsyn's time in the Gulag, Laura reminded Nick that although she *wanted* to be able to work in the face of penury and woe, she couldn't write if the spell-checker on Microsoft Word didn't work. If she'd been Mozart, the world wouldn't have the *Requiem*, because she couldn't spell *Dies Irae*.

Unable to deny this, Nick stirred his coffee, then reached for the latest issue of *Cassandra*, which sat next to a paper bag filled with morning-glory muffins. On the cover of the magazine Cassandra Lovelace beamed in finger-waved platinum hair and a pink lamé halter-top dress that signaled a return to what some magazines were calling "Depression-era elegance." The talk-show host had her arm around the waist of one of the many members of the minor European nobility whose approval she craved. They were standing in front of a building that, a caption implied, was a castle in Burgundy, but that looked suspiciously like the Cloisters as seen from West 192nd Street.

Nick flipped to the table of contents and began to read aloud. "Cassandra and her great friend, the Bulgarian princess—" He looked piercingly across the table. "How can you think of writing about this kind of Euro-trash?"

Laura winced. Nick had an instinct for the jugular that was ready to spring to life even at ten o'clock on a Sunday morning. Her future boss's adoration for the titled and decorated was one of the few things about her new job that gave her pause, and he knew it. Cassandra had interviewed her in a pink-and-white office that resembled the boudoir of someone whose social climbing required crampons, if not a portable oxygen tank. Her desk—one of the few in New York with a ruffled skirt—brimmed with framed gilt-edged invitations to balls and pictures of herself with people who wore tiaras and sashes across their chests. Cassandra seemed to prefer friends who were unable to dress themselves without the help of people who made sure their medals were pinned on correctly.

"First of all, nobody calls them Euro-trash any more," she said calmly. "The preferred term is 'Euro-chic.'"

"A Bulgarian princess is chic?" Nick asked. "We have plenty of Bulgarian women in Cleveland. They wear shawls and babushkas while shopping for pork sausages at the West Side Market."

"She's not a Bulgarian princess." Laura cringed to hear herself making such distinctions before she'd spent a day in her new job. "You misread the caption for the photo. The woman on the cover is a Yugoslavian princess."

Nick snorted. "Did you take Shakespeare courses just to write about people like that?"

"Studying Shakespeare is excellent training for writing about displaced monarchists," Laura said, hoping that it was true. "My freshman English professor said that Shakespeare was nothing but a Tudor apologist."

Nick reddened. "Your high school basketball coach was right. You *are* a pathological optimist."

Laura wished she had never told Nick about that comment. At

St. Rose of Lima Academy, the basketball coach had urged the other players to elect her their captain—even though she didn't score as many points as Erin O'Reilly or LaVonda Shields—because she always thought the team could still win even when it was down by twenty-four points, the three best players were on the bench with torn anterior cruciate ligaments, and there were only two minutes left in the game. Some people said she'd gotten the position only because the coach told everybody, "Every team needs at least one pathological optimist."

"I do have a tendency to see the bright side of things—maybe too much of one," she said. "But that can only help me at *Cassandra*."

"You'll get eaten alive if you work with people like Cassandra Lovelace," Nick said. "You're too sweet and innocent for New York."

"Sweet and innocent?" Nick's comment cut to the quick of Laura's short, unpolished fingernails. Though she could hardly admit it, she didn't see herself as "sweet and innocent" but as Audrey Hepburn in *Breakfast at Tiffany's* without the foot-long cigarette holder. Sometimes when Nick worked late at his movie theater she stood in front of their bathroom mirror and practiced saying her favorite line from the movie with elegant aplomb: "You can always tell what kind of a person a man really thinks you are by the earrings he gives you." She was ready to stop stealing turkey eggs and to start wearing slim black dresses and sunglasses as she admired her reflection in Fifth Avenue shop windows. If Nick had any idea of the desperate fantasies that lurked in her heart, he gave no indication of it.

"That's right," Nick said. He nodded toward a bookshelf lined with novels by Edith Wharton. "Just think of what happened to Lily Bart."

"Nick!" Laura said, appalled. "Whatever happens in New York, I'm not going to poison myself with laudanum." She paused. "Anyway, laudanum is probably one of those things that dermatologists inject into people's foreheads now, like Botox."

Nick ignored the comment. "Have you thought about how

your new job will affect your mother? Who will take care of her after you move?"

Laura could see that Nick was getting desperate. Nobody knew better than he did that if anybody could take care of herself, it was her mother. Her parents had fled Budapest separately as teenagers, just before the Communist tanks rolled into the city in 1956, and later opened a Cleveland bakery known for its *dobos torta* and walnut and poppy seed strudel. Her mother had run the shop on her own after her father died and, after selling it, had assumed the role of an unofficial Red Cross feeding station. She seemed to check every visitor to the house for signs of kwashiorkor and other nutritional diseases. In her retirement she cooked tirelessly for church potluck suppers and for Laura's younger brother, Steve, who lived at home.

"I'm much more concerned about Steve than about my mother," Laura said truthfully. "He's the only unemployed twenty-two-year old I know who isn't embarrassed to spend his time reading *Juggs* instead of the classified ads."

Nick ignored the comment. "If you can't think about your mother, what about *me*? I may be about to make a major breakthrough on my screenplay. You're leaving me just when I need the support most."

By "support," Nick usually meant sex. Or, only slightly less often, her Visa card, which he used to put gas in his beat-up Mazda.

"Nick, you're not having a bone marrow transplant. You're writing a screenplay. You can finish it without my coming to visit you for ten minutes every hour while the nurses keep checking for a pulse."

Nick looked pained. Clearly he did see himself as somebody who was having all of the marrow sucked out of him, washed in a high-tech machine, and pumped back into his ravaged body. "How would you know what I can finish? You've never tried to write a script for a two-hour movie. You write articles that people read in dentists' offices."

Not for the first time, Laura felt slightly defensive about her work. At times she seemed to be the only writer in America who didn't want to write the screenplay for the next *Blue Velvet* or a novel that would make Don DeLillo seethe with envy. She *liked* working on light and amusing pieces about offbeat characters who could inhale spaghetti through their noses or sing arias from *Turandot* as they drove Zamboni machines at hockey games. Her favorite assignment had been traveling around the state to interview people for "Bowling-Trophy Wives," a cover story about the wives of Ohio's best bowlers.

"At least I'm moving up to a better grade of dentists' offices," she said flippantly. "Now I'll be writing for people having their gums scraped on Park Avenue instead of Shaker Boulevard." Not wanting to appear insensitive to Nick's concerns, she reached for a more sympathetic note. "Have you considered that you might be more productive—not less—after I move? Think of the distractions you'll no longer face. Every time I come home with a new silk camisole, it sets you back to the Bronze Age of creativity. You can't flip through one of my women's magazines without wanting to try any sex technique with a name like 'The Fire-Breathing Dragon.'"

Laura tried to remember precisely what "The Fire-Breathing Dragon" was. Was it the technique that involved wearing a kimono that stopped at the tops of her thighs? Or eating hot chili peppers before sex? Nick's inexhaustible appetites led them to try so many recipes for bliss that they were starting to run together in her mind like the chutneys at Cleveland's one good Indian restaurant.

Nick nodded glumly but said nothing, sunk in his own memories of the sexual lunch wagon that was pulling out of town. He picked up a pen and drew mustaches on the two women on the cover of *Cassandra*. Laura had once interviewed a psychologist who said that, in disturbed children, this kind of behavior often preceded pulling the wings off insects or drowning kittens.

"It isn't as though I'm moving to one of the countries where you can't eat the lettuce," she said. "New Yorkers have a lettuce fixation. Social ostracism can result from serving iceberg at a dinner party. You could search entire blocks on the Upper West Side and not find anybody who has ever tasted Thousand Island dressing."

Nick began turning the pages of *Cassandra*. Laura realized that he might start drawing erect nipples on any photos of Queen Elizabeth that he saw, as he'd done with an earlier issue, and snatched the magazine away. Nick said nothing and took another muffin.

Laura was unnerved by the silence from a man who tended to express his emotions in great Wagnerian outbursts. Lately he'd stopped just short of accusing her of turning him into an unwilling participant in a cruel sex-deprivation experiment that she had devised with the help of her best friend, Alice, who was going to let her stay at her house in Connecticut until she found a place in the city.

"Can't you try to focus on the benefits of my new job?" she pleaded. "I'll be working for such a fashionable magazine that I'll probably meet a lot of Hollywood stars who could help your career. I might run into Quentin Tarantino in the elevator." Laura stopped, remembering an article she'd read that said that celebrities used freight elevators so they wouldn't run into people like her. "I'll probably be home every other weekend," she rushed on, knowing on her salary she would be lucky to be able to take the ferry to Fire Island on weekends, let alone fly to Cleveland. "I'm planning to come back for at least three days for Tina's wedding."

Nick looked doleful. "That's not until Labor Day. Three months from now."

On hearing this reminder of how much time her cousin had to change her mind about wanting her to be a bridesmaid, Laura brightened. As Nick stood up, signaling that their last breakfast in the apartment had ended, she thought, *Thank God.*

2
Psycho Fan

Leaning on the handle of her carry-on bag, Laura stared at the line of irritable and sweating humanity that snaked toward the Continental Airlines ticket counter at Hopkins International Airport. She hadn't seen so many people trying to get out of Cleveland since the day after Bruce Springsteen had performed at the opening ceremonies for the Rock and Roll Hall of Fame. It was small comfort that, this time, half of the passengers did not appear to have survived the weekend only with the aid of Class B controlled substances.

She had arrived at the airport early enough to give baggage inspectors plenty of time to search her luggage for any lethal-looking nail files and manicure scissors that she had forgotten to remove. Now it appeared that she would spend most of that time waiting in line or, as the staff at *Cassandra* said, waiting *on* line.

Trying to figure out why so many people swarmed around the ticket counters, Laura studied the man standing behind her, who wore a baseball cap that said GO TRIBE and a blue satin jacket imprinted with the image of an Indian chief. He carried a clutch of sports magazines—*Sports Illustrated, Baseball Weekly, Golf Digest*—and a monogrammed tennis bag that said TOM.

With a feeling of dread, Laura realized that she was standing next to the sort of person whom Nick called the "Psycho Fan," someone whose support for his teams went far beyond buying season tickets or serving football-shaped cakes at Super Bowl parties. The Psycho Fan risked pneumonia by going to Browns games with his bare chest painted orange and brown in zero-degree weather. He showed up for Indians games in a headdress that made him look like an extra for *Dances with Wolves*. And he could be a she.

As the captain of the basketball team at St. Rose's, Laura had led her squad to the Parochial Athletic League championship, only to break her leg in the last few seconds of the game when a guard from Holy Innocents tripped her. She had less trouble forgiving the player who stuck out her foot—who always claimed the incident was an accident—than fans of the rival team who hooted and cheered when she fell.

Laura noticed that the Psycho Fan was studying her faded Notre Dame sweatshirt. She cast about for a way to avoid an hour of small talk about Knute Rockne and single-wing offense as their line inched toward the ticket counter.

"I've never seen so many people here on a Sunday night," she said, grasping feebly at the obvious. "It looks as though somebody had just announced over the PA system that Little Eva had turned up and wanted to lead everybody in the Locomotion."

Psycho Fan smiled. "Please feel free to put your hands on my waist and let me lead you to the departure gate. That is, if this line ever starts moving."

"I wonder what's going on. As a weekend getaway destination, Cleveland isn't exactly Nantucket in August. Do you have any idea why all of these people are here?"

"Maybe because it's Father's Day?"

"Father's Day?" In her rush to pack, Laura had forgotten that others were celebrating the holiday.

"Sure. Or the Indians game. Most likely, a combination of both. People flew home to take their fathers to the game. At least I did."

Laura could see that his explanation made sense. "You're probably right. For years my brother, Steve, could tolerate my parents' presence only if he could eat hot dogs and watch Omar Vizquel play shortstop at the same time." She thought about the trouble that she and Nick sometimes had getting good seats at games. "But you must have ordered your tickets months ago. The stadium usually sells out on holiday weekends."

"No, just a few days ago."

"Did you have to sit in the last row of the upper deck?" Laura asked. "The only time my boyfriend and I bought tickets at the last minute, we had to sit so high up the players looked like Lilliputians on steroids."

"I sat in a box. If it's any comfort, some of the players looked like Lilliputians on steroids from there, too." He set down his tennis bag and held out his hand. "I'm Tim Moran. My full name is Timothy Oliver Moran, so people tend assume that my nickname is Tom. Sometimes I think of having chiseled on my gravestone, 'It's Tim, not Tom.'"

Laura began to relax. "You might be lucky that you haven't had worse problems with your name. I'm Laura Smart, and I've spent years listening to jokes like, 'Laura Smart, who probably isn't,' or 'Laura, who's too smart for her own good.'"

"Maybe we should both be glad that we don't have a last name like Lovelace," Tim said, glancing at Laura's copy of *Cassandra.* "How would you like to have people associate you with the star of *Deep Throat?* Not that it seems to have hurt Cassandra. I just read an article about the new magazines started by television personalities. It said that the wars among them are pretty bruising right now but that *Cassandra* should do well if it can survive the shakeout."

Laura didn't know what to make of this. Her interview at *Cassandra* had left her feeling less sanguine about the future of the magazine. Simon Wright, the managing editor, told her that newsstand sales for the first few issues were soft, partly because Cassandra had insisted on hiring Euro-chic friends who had a marginal command of English. Once Simon had asked the grand-daughter of a marchesa for some page proofs and the young woman inquired whether he wanted "forty proofs" or "sixty proofs" because she had both strengths of liquor in her desk drawer. Simon had threatened to quit unless he could hire some staff members who (a) spoke English, and (b) were not incipient alcoholics. Cassandra yielded, albeit reluctantly, to the ultimatum. Laura understood from Simon that she was in the vanguard of the new group of English-speaking, nonalcoholic staff members. She could hardly say this to a man she'd just met in a ticket line, but couldn't see any harm in admitting that she worked for the magazine.

"I'm glad that *Cassandra* is getting some good publicity," she said. "Because I start work there tomorrow, or I will if my flight to LaGuardia doesn't leave before we reach the ticket counter. But I don't really know what anybody except my mother thinks about the magazine, and she has trouble remembering the name. She keeps calling it *Lolita*. When Cassandra was younger, she wore heart-shaped sunglasses, like the heroine of an old movie version of the novel. Ever since my mother found out about that, she seems to think I'm going to work for a magazine edited by a twelve-year-old nymphet."

"Maybe you'd be better off if—" Tim broke off. "What made you decide that you wanted to work for *Cassandra*?"

Laura fought the urge to say: *I have to get away from my sex-maniac boyfriend who thinks that any day now Steven Spielberg is going to call and offer him a six-figure sum and a percentage of the gross for a screenplay that he hasn't written.*

She remembered all the how-to-get-a-job books she'd read before interviewing at *Cassandra*, which recommended that you sound practically orgasmic with enthusiasm for your work at all times. Short of gasping and rolling around on the floor with your teeth clenched, you couldn't lay it on too thickly. The relentlessly chipper books she'd taken out of the Cleveland Public Library suggested that even in a crowded ticket line, you never knew when you might run into somebody who could punch a hole in the glass ceiling for you

"I've always wanted to work for *Cassandra*."

"Really?" Tim raised an eyebrow. "It's impressive that you've always wanted to work for *Cassandra* when the first issue just came out six months ago."

"What I meant was—" Laura knew that she had blundered. "Who wouldn't want to work for someone like Cassandra? She's a heroine to millions of American women."

Laura had spent so much time poring over her new boss's autobiography that she knew parts of *Don't Shoot the Messenger* by heart, and she could recite the highlights as easily as Nick's cell phone number. "Cassandra grew up poor in the red dirt hills of the Texas Panhandle and might have stayed there forever if she hadn't entered the Miss Longhorn Breeder contest for the scholarship money. After she won, a television producer saw her picture in the paper and offered her an internship at his station."

"Miss Longhorn Breeder?" A faint smile appeared at the corners of Tim's mouth. "Cassandra won a contest run by a group of cattlemen?"

"Among other pageants."

Laura knew that, in the twenty-first century, many people saw Cassandra's beauty-contest victories as silly. But she had her own embarrassing history in rhinestones that gave her a certain sympathy for her boss. In high school she won the title of Queen of the Hungarian Wine Festival after her mother submitted her photo and her father gave the customers at their bakery free almond crescents along with the ballots. By then her father was ill, and she didn't have the heart to deny him the pleasure of watching her take home a crown that he regarded as the pinnacle of success in America, at least among Hungarians in Cleveland. Steve had to escort her to the ceremony because by then she had achieved her full height of five-foot-ten and no boy wanted her to tower over him on stage.

"That's quite a story." Tim was obviously trying to weigh the credibility of what he'd heard. *Typical*, Laura thought. Men never believed that women could become fabulously successful on their own terms. They couldn't fathom someone like Cassandra, who didn't own a copy of Tom Brokaw's playbook. But even television anchormen didn't see their faces on the cover of a magazine every month. Women like Cassandra were rewriting the rules, and men could not understand.

"That kind of career must have taken a toll on your new boss's private life," Tim added. "Doesn't that concern you? You must wonder if you'll have time for a social life after you start work at *Cassandra*."

"Not at all," Laura said with more confidence than she felt. She told Tim about Cassandra's marriage to a record producer who had retired on a couple of hits of the disco era but still wore black leather pants and studded jackets. Cassandra and Irwin had become a power couple who seemed to appear every week in another photograph taken at a star-dusted benefit for the Costume Institute of the Metropolitan Museum of Art even though, Laura understood, this event occurred only once a year.

Laura had just begun to talk about their his-and-her Porsches when the line started moving again. For a few minutes, hundreds of people pushed, pulled, rolled, kicked, and carried their baggage toward the ticket counter. As the crowd shifted position, Tim watched her carefully, as though she might walk off with his three-hundred-dollar tennis racquet.

Wishing that she had changed her clothes after she packed, Laura suspected that he was wondering why *Cassandra* had hired someone who wore oxblood penny loafers and had hair that fell to her shoulders instead of finding its God-given destiny in an Anna Wintour-ish bob. She imagined that his wife—if he had a wife—spent all her time in tennis dresses, or possibly a blue satin baseball jacket that matched her husband's. To discourage unflattering attention, she reread an article in *Cassandra* about the décor in her new boss's duplex co-op, which included dozens of heart-shaped lace pillows handmade by nuns in a French convent founded in the days of Louis XIV.

She reached the ticket counter just as she got to the ads in the back of *Cassandra* for genealogy services and real estate agents who advertised fully staffed villas in Tuscany or apartments in the 16th Arrondissement. Her plane was leaving in twenty minutes, and she had to go through another line at the baggage X-ray station. After an anxious glance at the Timex watch that she'd owned since high school—a pitiful contrast to the diamond Piaget that Cassandra wore—she handed her ticket to an agent.

"I'm sorry, miss," he said. "This ticket is for next Sunday, and I can't change it without charging you an extra fee. It's subject to thirty-day advance purchase restrictions."

"That can't be right." Laura had made her reservation through a travel agent who was a friend of Steve's. The agent had assured her that he'd found a great deal. He hadn't mentioned that he'd found it for the wrong date.

"I'm afraid I'm right," the ticket agent said. "If you want to fly tonight, you have to pay—" he punched his keyboard, "—four hundred and thirty-nine dollars more."

"Four hundred and thirty-nine dollars!" Laura almost shouted the sum. The agent was asking for more than she'd been paying each month for her half of the rent on her apartment in Cleveland Heights. But she could hardly call her new bosses and say that she had to start work the following week. Even Cassandra's Euro-chic friends no doubt managed to stagger into the office on the appropriate day despite their Stoli hangovers.

Laura reached into her wallet for her Visa card and couldn't find it. She rifled through her leather shoulder bag, hoping to spot a glint of silver amid the reporter's notebooks, felt-tipped pens, and a restaurant receipt. With a tug of dismay, she realized that she'd forgotten to turn in an expense report for an interview with a man who said he could read the thoughts of rottweilers. She sifted through her pockets, then crouched down and ransacked her carry-on bag. As she rummaged through a nest of bras, she said a silent prayer to St. Anthony, the patron saint of lost objects, whom the teachers at St. Rose's had taught her to invoke in such a crisis. After a few more minutes of futile excavation, Laura felt her stomach turn over. Nick had probably borrowed her credit card again and failed to return it.

"I guess I've left the card at home," she said, close to tears. "I'll have to take another flight."

Laura was repacking her carry-on bag when Tim walked up to the counter.

"I see that you're having a problem. Can I help?"

"Thanks, but it's hopeless," Laura said, giving the zipper on her carry-on bag a furious yank. "My boyfriend borrowed my Visa card and didn't return it, so I can't pay the extra amount that I owe for my ticket. I'm going to miss my flight, which should be boarding right now."

"Can't you charge the extra fee to your company?" Tim had an odd note in his voice. "It's typical for employers to pay for relocation expenses."

"Not my employer. Simon—the managing editor—said that he couldn't afford to pay for moving expenses for the staff and for Cassandra's lunches at Le Cirque. I'll have to miss my first day at work."

"That's not a good idea when you're dealing with someone like Cassandra."

Laura, struck by the truth of this comment, said nothing. Tim asked the ticket agent to see if any seats were available on his flight to Newark, which left an hour later. The agent shook his head. Tim handed him a credit card.

"Please charge her extra fee to this as quickly as you can."

"But why are you paying for my ticket?" Laura asked as the agent processed the credit card. "You don't even know me."

"You'll miss your plane if I explain it. But don't worry," he laughed. "You may find out soon enough. I'm leaving for France tomorrow, but I'll try to get in touch after I get back. I'm sure I'll have no trouble reaching someone who works for 'a heroine to millions of American women.'"

Just before Laura broke into a sprint toward the baggage X-ray machine, Tim nodded toward her copy of *Cassandra*. "By the way, if I were you, I wouldn't walk into my new office on Monday morning carrying a magazine with a mustache drawn on the editor," he said. "Just a bit of friendly advice."

***

Laura had no time to think about the reasons for Tim's spontaneous generosity until she had boarded her flight. She wondered if he was a celebrity—maybe an actor or a rock star angling for early induction into the Hall of Fame—whom she hadn't recognized or who was traveling under an assumed name. He might have been someone whose career had received a boost from a story in *Cassandra,* or who was scheduled to appear in a future issue that promoted his new film or CD.

What else would explain why he wanted to pay for her ticket? The people she wrote about for *Buckeye* were always trying to take her to lunch or give her gifts to thank her for the publicity, even though the magazine wouldn't allow staff members to accept favors that might affect their editorial judgment. For a movie star, the cost of a plane ticket would amount to a comparable expense. And a star could pull strings to get into one of those luxury boxes at the last minute.

Laura wondered if she might have done a story about Tim for *Buckeye*—which often profiled celebrities who had grown up in Ohio—but she dismissed the idea. She wrote about ordinary people, not stars, and rarely forgot those she had interviewed. That was partly why she loved her work. So many of the celebrities she read about sounded alike—lately they all seemed to have "very simple tastes" in six-hundred-acre ranches in Montana—but you never forgot a John Belushi imitator who smashed pop cans against his forehead. Why hadn't she taken a better look at the face under that Indians cap?

By the time she arrived in New York, Laura had convinced herself that the baseball cap was part of a brilliant disguise intended to make Timothy Oliver Moran look like any other out-of-control fan. She was sure he would laugh all the way to France in his Gulfstream jet.

3
Time Warp

Simon Wright had a number of eccentricities, one of which was that he regarded the antismoking regulations in New York as rough guidelines. In his brilliant career as an editor in London he had come to believe that a direct relationship existed between the amount of nicotine he consumed and the spectacular circulation figures that he produced for his magazines, which ranged from slightly right-wing to so fanatically reactionary that they stopped just short of advocating a return to the days of Edward the Confessor. Although only in his early thirties, Simon was so conservative that even the *Telegraph*—nicknamed the *Tory-graph*—refused to hire him when he had thought for a brief period of taking his formidable talents to a newspaper. Several of the better-known British pundits had observed that the type in his magazines ought to appear only on right-hand pages.

Simon had made his faith in nicotine clear to Laura partly by offering her a Marlboro Mild during her interview, explaining that he smoked Milds while editing lighter-weight articles and Regulars while working on more difficult stories. Startled, Laura had turned down the cigarette. But when she called her best friend to tell her about her offer from *Cassandra*, she could tell that the incident troubled Alice, a Vassar graduate whom she had met when they both spent a summer studying at Oxford.

"Are you sure you want to work for somebody who has so little respect for the law, not to mention for the health of his coworkers?" Alice asked anxiously.

"Frankly, no," Laura admitted. "But I *am* sure that I want to get out of Cleveland. And *Cassandra* is the only magazine that has offered me a job."

"Why not keep looking?"

"Alice, I've been looking for months," Laura replied, excruciatingly aware of how much she'd spent on airline tickets and cut-rate hotel rooms in midtown, though "cut-rate" was always a relative term in Manhattan. "Not many New York magazines want to hire a writer who specializes in quirky stories about people who imitate John Belushi and smash pop cans against their heads."

Laura wondered how much of the truth she could bear to tell her best friend. She decided that Alice, a lifelong New Englander, had a natural tact that made her unlikely to repeat the compromising details.

"The only reason I got the offer from *Cassandra* was that I met Simon briefly during the summer you and I spent in England. One of the dons invited him back to Oxford to have dinner with the American students who were thinking of becoming writers. He and I sat so far apart and said so little to each other that I don't think I've mentioned him. Our entire conversation might have consisted of my asking him if he'd mind passing the salt. But to an Englishman, even that kind of introduction is better than none at all."

"That can't be the only reason you got the job," Alice insisted. "But if it was, just think of what a sparkling impression you must have made on Simon if he remembered you after all those years."

"I'm not sure he did remember me. Simon told me that he wanted to hire me partly because after a summer at Oxford, I'd understand all his British slang like, 'Don't get your knickers in a twist.' He said that just before I sent him my résumé, he'd interviewed an NYU graduate who thought he was talking about a Knicks game."

"But you've won so many journalism awards!" Alice said loyally. "That must count for something."

This, in fact, was a sore point with Laura. At *Buckeye*, she had won every journalism award in the state and had become a finalist for several national prizes. The judges for the contests she'd entered defined "feature writing" broadly enough to consider her idiosyncratic stories along with other articles.

But the editors of the women's magazines she approached had shown less interest in her writing than in the elusive quality they defined as "taste" or "style." Of which, Laura soon learned, she had almost none. By the time she realized that she ought to have torn herself away from her computer long enough to learn to walk over subway grates in Edmundo Castillo stilettos, she felt as depleted as her bank account. So she rejoiced when Simon called and, exhaling charm like smoke rings, said that he'd be delighted if she could start work at *Cassandra* immediately.

Laura knew she'd have trouble explaining all of this to Alice, who had so much faith in her that she didn't see why Diana Vreeland hadn't risen from the grave to offer her a job at *Vogue*. She tried to direct her best friend's attention to the results of her efforts. "My writing *does* count with Simon," she said, "and that's what matters now. He says that I'll see my byline in practically every issue of *Cassandra*."

"But I'm still worried about your working for somebody who smokes like the Rib Burn-Off," Alice said, referring to a grilling festival that she had attended when she visited Laura in Cleveland. "I don't understand why Cassandra lets Simon do something that's a fire hazard."

"Cassandra doesn't spend as much time at the office as other staff members do," Laura said, realizing that this was a considerable understatement. "She tapes her shows in the morning and comes into the office for only a few hours a day, if at all, so she doesn't have to inhale as much of the smoke. I gather that a lot of the time Simon runs the magazine while Cassandra amounts to a figurehead. As a condition for moving from London to New York, Simon made a deal with her that lets him smoke as long as he does it behind the closed door of his office. Graydon Carter at *Vanity Fair* is famous for smoking on the job—he gives out ashtrays as favors at the magazine's Oscar parties—so there was a precedent."

"If I didn't know how committed you were to Nick, I'd think a crush on Simon was affecting your view of the situation," Alice said lightly.

Laura was embarrassed by her own transparency. She *did* have a slight crush on Simon. But it was the kind of crush she had in high school on the rich boys from St. Izzy's—the nickname for St. Isidore of Seville, the most elite boys' parochial school in Cleveland—who would have asked her out only after an asteroid had wiped out every other teenage girl the city. That Simon was out of her league made it safe for her to indulge her fantasies while remaining loyal to Nick.

"Maybe I do have a bit of a crush on him. But what's the harm in working for an attractive single man instead of Ron Swoboda, my old boss at *Buckeye*, who went home to his wife and children in Strongsville at five-thirty sharp every night?"

Alice fell silent, and Laura thought she knew why. A descendant of rich New Englanders, Alice would never have to worry about finding a job. If she wanted to teach at a tiny girls' school for $23,000 a year—as she did—she didn't have to think about paying the rent. She could live with her slightly dotty father in their nineteenth-century Shingle Style mansion with a wraparound veranda overlooking the ocean in Connecticut. The Dudleys had called it their "cottage" ever since the days when it had served as a summer home.

Rose Bluffs, with its peeling wallpaper and threadbare wing chairs, was hardly luxurious, but it did have dignity. Laura loved to sit in a living room filled with items handed down by a Dudley ancestor who made his fortune in the China trade—an apricot velvet sofa, a Dutch brass chandelier, an Oriental rug, and a pair of antique jardinières flanking a stone fireplace. Her favorite item was a dark wood mantelpiece carved with AEQUAM MEMENTO REBUS IN ARDUIS/SERVARE MENTEM. Alice said that the words, her family motto, were the Latin equivalent of "When the going gets tough, the tough get going," which Vince Lombardi or some other football coach had borrowed from Horace. The closest the Smarts had to a motto was a Hungarian saying that Laura's father had liked to quote: "God favors the chef with the better recipes."

Knowing that she would inherit Rose Bluffs, Alice would never have to worry about her financial security. Nor did she have to get away from a boyfriend who seemed to believe that she was telepathically causing his writer's block. Although surrounded by female teachers during the day, Alice was always going out with bankers or stockbrokers whom she'd met years earlier at regattas or race weeks. She had turned down three proposals in as many years, insisting that she wanted to marry "someone different" from the boys she'd grown up with. If Alice didn't have such a kind-hearted nature—and hadn't kept her lovely Fragonard skin through all her windblown years on sailboats—Laura would have felt sure that they were after her trust fund.

"I know you'll do the right thing," Alice allowed at last. "But I admit that I have concerns about your working for a Marlboro Man."

"Simon may be a Marlboro Man," Laura said. "But he speaks like the Duke of Marlborough. All those plummy vowels! Cassandra said in an interview that she met him at a shooting party at a stately home in Yorkshire and hired him after learning that he wasn't just a journalistic wunderkind—he's the grand-nephew of an earl and had an ancestor who was a favorite of a Turkish vizier."

Laura was unsure of how having a vizier-friendly ancestor would benefit an American magazine edited by an afternoon talk-show host. But after years of writing stories about some of the looser marbles in Ohio, she worried less about the quirks of her new bosses than about whether she could afford an apartment in the city. That concern eased when Alice insisted that she stay at Rose Bluffs until she'd found a place.

"Our housekeeper will wait on you hand and foot," Alice said soothingly, "and after living with Nick, wouldn't you enjoy having somebody wait on you for a while?"

Laura had to think about this for only a few seconds before she realized that, when Alice put it that way, there was almost nothing she'd like more.

***

As usual, the staff meeting started late. Simon had warned Laura about this possibility soon after she started work at *Cassandra*, explaining that some of his writers and editors operated on what he called "Frog Mean Time," even if they weren't French. This meant that they wafted into meetings when they thought they should begin, not when they actually did begin.

If Simon was lucky, they showed up within an hour of the appointed time, often savoring the afterglow of a weekend in the Hamptons or St. Bart's. But sometimes their conception of when a meeting ought to begin differed by much more than that, and long after he'd resolved the issue he wanted to discuss, they would show up in his office, indignant that he had started without them. The situation had gotten so bad that Simon, in announcing meetings, said that they would begin an hour earlier than he wanted them to start.

It was obvious that he wasn't having much luck. More than an hour after the scheduled starting time of her first meeting at *Cassandra*, Laura found herself at an oval conference table with fewer than a half dozen staff members. Cassandra was on vacation, several staff members were AWOL, and the fashion and beauty editors were on location shootings or "on

Seventh"—on Seventh Avenue.

That left mainly the people from Features, including Caitlin Stearns, the only other female writer in the department besides Laura, and Ethan Naff, Simon's assistant. These two detested each other as much as their work for a magazine that, for different reasons, they regarded as beneath them. Caitlin had spent several years writing for alternate newsweeklies and liked to wear cargo shorts and a yellow bandanna around her forehead. She resembled a cross between the winner of a Pat Benatar look-alike contest and a Snake River rafting guide. Ethan had just graduated from Brown and had taken his job because he couldn't get an interview at *The New York Review of Books*. In the summer heat, he wore tweed jackets and silk bow ties, clothes that he imagined that people at the literary journal preferred, in case one of its editors called on the spur of the moment and wanted to take him to lunch at the Century Club.

All of them were sitting in an area euphemistically called "the conference room," a small section of a loft partitioned off by a burlap screen covered with production schedules, memos from Cassandra, and an occasional obscene drawing. From their spot close to a grimy window they could hear the staccato blasts of pile drivers and jackhammers a few stories below their offices on one of the less fashionable streets in Tribeca.

Monica Stryker, the copy editor, put out a box of stale and crumbling cookies in strange flavors like arugula and radicchio, nestled in red tissue paper and sent by a mail-order company hoping for free publicity. Laura took a bite of one of the cookies, winced, and felt a twinge of homesickness for the gluey apple-cinnamon doughnuts and bad coffee served at staff meetings at *Buckeye*.

Seated at the head of the conference table, Simon showed no annoyance with the absence of so many of his subordinates. Only his tumble-dried appearance suggested that their indolence was taking a toll. An hour before the noon sun struck the windows of the erratically air-conditioned offices of *Cassandra*, he had deep perspiration stains on his white shirt, and his dark brown hair fell straight forward from the back of his head. In red suspenders and a gold signet pinkie ring, he had an air of disheveled elegance—the para-doxical allure of a man at once harried and carefree.

"Let's get started, shall we?" Simon said. "I know that some of you spent the weekend at the beach," he cast a mock-despairing glance at the vacant seats around the conference table, "and others may still be at the beach. But we need to start planning for the October issue."

Though it was a sweltering summer morning, Laura tried to imagine that yellow leaves were falling from the gingko and sycamore trees on the streets of Manhattan. Working for a monthly magazine was a little like being a character in one of those science-fiction novels where the date on the heroine's calen-dar never matched that on everybody else's. The temperatures in the city were flirting with the nineties, but editors all over town were writing about new fall tweeds and testing recipes for low-fat pumpkin cheesecake.

Well-established magazines dealt with the time warp by doing some of their photography a year in advance, so they could show snow in a Christmas story without flying half the staff to Greenland in the middle of August. But new magazines like *Cassandra* had trouble with the long lead time, the interval between planning an issue and its appearance on newsstands. Their editors were always trying to find Ukrainian Easter eggs before they'd shaken off their New Year's Eve hangovers and jousting with models who disliked wearing tube tops on a sand dune when they could see their breath.

"Before we get to the October issue, I have a few announce-ments," Simon went on. "I've received a memo from our parent corporation, Carapace, asking that we keep the costs of business lunches to twenty-five dollars per person, including the drinks and tip. We'll have to pay out of pocket any expenses that exceed that amount."

"Twenty-five dollars!" Laura blurted out. "You can't get lunch at some of the better restaurants in Cleveland for twenty-five dollars.

I had the impression that twenty-five dollars was closer to what you pay for an appetizer at a good restaurant in New York."

"An astute observation," Simon said cheerily. "I can see that our newest employee is a quick study. Twenty-five dollars *is* closer to what you pay for an appetizer in New York. But one of the charms of working for a magazine like *Cassandra* is that people are so eager to appear in it that you can take them to any fish-and-chips shop instead of the Rainbow Room."

Caitlin jumped in before Laura could think of a tactful way to ask where you could find a fish-and-chips place in New York, something she had never seen. "Does this mean that the people at Carapace are also going to start questioning what we spend on office supplies?" she asked, making no effort to hide her irritation. "This is the first magazine I've worked for that makes you buy your own cassette tapes for interviews."

Laura understood why Caitlin was unhappy. The *Cassandra* supply cabinet was woefully undersupplied with basics like staplers and letter-openers, which its parent corporation seemed to regard as luxuries. Caitlin complained that you could find a five-hundred-dollar jar of skin cream at the magazine more easily than a seventy-nine-cent box of paper clips, and there was some truth to her comment. A floodtide of tinted moisturizers washed over the beauty department, but nobody sent the staff free paper clips.

"Caitlin, you can buy all the gel pens you like. Just keep in mind that we're in a period of belt-tightening."

"Belt-tightening!" Caitlin said. "If our belts were any tighter, we'd need pelvic surgery."

Monica looked up from the page proof that she had been correcting as Caitlin and Simon sparred. "Next thing you know, the people in midtown will be saying we can't take any free trips, either." The only person in Features who was over fifty, Monica had so much work that she kept threatening to take early retirement. She had walked out a month earlier, but returned after the travel editor arranged for her to take a free wine-tasting cruise that obliterated her memories of the white-knuckle deadlines.

"The corporate side hasn't sent out any memos about trips, but do I have one other bit of bad news to report," Simon said. "*Aurora*'s newsstand sales were up again last month. Ours, unfortunately, showed no improvement."

Laura felt slightly worried about this news. Aurora Starr, Cassandra's furious rival in the afternoon television wars, had launched a women's magazine that was trying to adapt the approach of reality television to a print format. Every month it ran articles with titles like "American Midol: PMS Cures Your Doctor Won't Tell You About" and "Who Wants to Be on Unemployment? The Upside of Getting Downsized." Laura hated to admit it, but she usually found its articles more interesting than *Cassandra*'s stories on subjects like "Rating the Robot-Operated Pool Cleaners" and "Is There a Finger Bowl in Your Future?"

Simon held up the latest issue of *Aurora*, which included a tongue-in-cheek report by an intern from Medill who had posed as a visitor to federal penitentiaries for a cover story entitled "Cell Food: Culinary Secrets from America's Great Prisons." "No doubt *Aurora* did better at newsstands partly because its editor appeared on the cover with a blue-eyed, blonde teenager while Cassandra stood next to a brunette. But—"

"Simon, you are so sexist," Caitlin interjected. "In this country we've moved beyond that kind of thinking."

"My comment had nothing to do with sexism," Simon said amiably. "It had to do with marketing surveys, which have shown repeatedly that—all other things being equal—blondes sell more magazines than brunettes. Of course, all other things never *are* equal, including whether readers identify with the star. So Julia Roberts outsells Sharon Stone because women want to *be* Julia but apparently find Sharon a bit alarming. At a luncheon the other day I heard an editor of *Redbook* say that she'd rather put a dead bunny on the cover of the magazine than Sharon Stone, 'Ms. Newsstand Death.'"

Laura suspected that what Simon said was true. Most successful publications did market research surveys of which of their covers sold best, and the results for women's magazines were remarkably consistent. Women sold better than men, young sold better than old, thin sold better than fat, blondes sold better than brunettes, and blue eyes sold better than brown. One of the fashion magazines had refined the formula further and found that its ideal cover showed "a blonde-haired, blue-eyed woman with two-to-five teeth showing." Even *Buckeye* did market research that found that if you did a story on pets, it was better to put a cat on the cover than a dog, because cat-lovers liked every kind of cat but dog lovers liked specific breeds. You might lose the schnauzer people with a collie.

"*I'm* a woman, and *I* don't find Sharon Stone alarming," Caitlin said in tones that made Laura think that at any moment she would jump to her feet and break into Sojourner Truth's "Ain't I a Woman" speech.

"Be that as it may, Cassandra believes that we need to rethink our plans for the August and September issues. We still have time to decide what to do about the September issue. But we don't have that luxury with August. As you know, we've been planning to do a cover story on the young interior designer Courtney Swilling. But Cassandra thinks—and I'm inclined to agree—that we ought to replace it with a piece on somebody better known outside New York."

Caitlin, who had written the cover story on Courtney Swilling, went on red alert. "You told me you liked the story. What's the problem with it?"

Ethan put down the pen with which he'd been taking notes on the meeting. "Does Cassandra object to our giving a spot on the cover to a socialite who earns her living at a strenuous profession like decorating instead of spending her time looking for a husband?" He flipped through a stack of photographs scheduled to appear in the August issue and held up a picture of a living room vertiginously decorated with flower prints and ruffles similar to those on Cassandra's desk. "Or does she object to Courtney's slogan, 'Take time to stop and smell the cabbage roses?'"

"Neither, my dear fellow," Simon said. *My dear fellow?* Laura thought. She hadn't heard those words since an emeritus professor at Notre Dame invited some of the graduating English majors to his house for tea. For all his pink-cheeked youth, Simon sounded at times as though he had come to New York directly from an assisted-living facility for geriatric members of the House of Lords. "Cassandra quite admires an ambitious woman like Courtney who works as hard as she did when she was younger, and she thinks her slogan is rather clever. She has no problem at all with our running a profile of her. She just doesn't want her on the cover."

"But the August issue has closed!" Caitlin protested. "The last story went to the printer yesterday."

"I've spoken to the printer," Simon said, "and we can remake the issue if we pay the overtime costs for it."

"It would be hard enough to line up a new cover subject in the spring or fall when half of our 'international trendsetters' weren't on vacation in Cap Ferrat or Positano," Caitlin persisted. "Who would be available at this late date?"

"Cassandra wants us to make another attempt to approach Normendie Latour."

Caitlin almost shot out of her chair. "Simon! I'm *not* calling Liz Kaiser again!"

For weeks Caitlin had been trying to reach the publicist for Normendie Latour, a Social Register stripper–turned–pop singer whose career had gone into eclipse after glowing like a halogen lamp for few minutes in the late nineties. Hoping to make a comeback, Normendie had hired Liz Kaiser, founder of the public relations firm of Shilling and Flax, to represent her. Liz was billing her client as "Britney Spears with a trust fund." That the singer was pushing thirty and known for dating a balding and overweight cosmetics tycoon instead of Justin Timberlake made no difference to her PR rep.

"Liz practically told me never to call again until Normendie is old enough to appear in Pepsodent commercials," Caitlin added. "She thinks that *Cassandra* is beneath her client 'at this point in her career.'"

"I heard that Roger Hornsley is beneath Normendie," Ethan said smugly. "They showed up at a few at Knicks games together. The rumor is that Rog paid for her navel surgery."

Any American who had ever leafed through a tabloid in a checkout line knew that Normendie had undergone an operation to change her belly button from horizontal to vertical, which plastic surgeons were promoting as a way to achieve a "more youthful" look. After the surgery, the singer had developed complications, including a belly-button lint problem, that she mentioned in almost every interview.

"I don't care who paid for her operation," Caitlin said, throwing a sullen look at Simon. "I refuse to give Liz another chance to ignore my calls."

"I'm not asking you to give her another chance," Simon said affably. "You have several other stories in the August issue, including your excellent piece on the latest studies of mammography." Simon held up the page proof of a health column in which Caitlin faulted doctors for their overuse of the technique. "I thought that writing the Normendie Latour story would be an ideal way for our newest writer to get her feet wet at *Cassandra*."

Simon turned to Laura. "Wouldn't you like to meet a Social Register stripper–turned–pop singer? Cassandra thinks that Normendie's combination of celebrity and social cachet would be perfect for us, and I think you'd be perfect for Normendie. She *does* go to quite a lot of Knicks games—whether she or Roger Hornsley pays for them—and if I remember correctly, you played on your high-school basketball team. You might have more to talk about with Normendie than most reporters would."

Laura wondered how her ability to sink a free throw could help her land an interview with a former lap dancer with a surgically enhanced navel. But she could hardly turn down her first assignment for *Cassandra*. "I learned most of what I know about strippers from the Bada Bing Club on *The Sopranos*. But if that doesn't matter—"

"Wait a minute," Caitlin said. "Normendie is *my* story."

"You just said you don't want to give Liz another chance to ignore you," Simon said. "Why not give her a chance to ignore Laura?"

As Caitlin sulked, Simon began to talk about possible articles for the October issue. But Laura had trouble concentrating as he described the food editor's plans to show baby pumpkins filled with Beluga caviar or ostrich stew. She had only the dimmest memories of Normendie Latour's career and could see that Caitlin didn't want to help her revive them. After the meeting, she would have to rush to Sam Goody's to see if she could pick up a couple of the singer's CDs.

Laura was making notes on what she had to do that afternoon when Simon ended the meeting by saying that Cassandra, who was vacationing on a friend's yacht in the Mediterranean with her husband, would return after the Fourth of July. "She called this morning from Nice, and she's eager to get back to work."

"Really?" Caitlin said. "For one hour a day or two?"

Simon ignored her. "Laura, you needn't worry," he said, giving her a pat on the arm that lingered for a beat longer than necessary. "You *will* get the interview."

Laura couldn't tell, from the ambiguous tone of his voice, whether he intended his words as a pep talk or a threat.

***

By the end of the day, Laura wondered if she had made a mistake by agreeing to try to track down Normendie Latour. If

Caitlin was right, she would have a better chance of interviewing the Three Tenors at the Baths of Caracalla than Normendie in New York. At least you could *find* the tenors' recordings. A clerk at Sam Goody's laughed when she asked if the store had Normendie Latour's best-known CD, *Junior League Dropout.*

"That one didn't exactly ship platinum. If we have any copies left—and I doubt that we do—they'll be over there." He pointed to an aisle that had CDs by the Carpenters and the Captain and Tennille. "*Junior League Dropout* is hard to find these days."

Laura hadn't imagined that there was so much demand for Normendie Latour's music that Sam Goody's couldn't keep it in stock. "Why is the CD hard to find?"

"Normendie said that she wrote the title song for *Junior League Dropout.* But I heard that it sounded so much like 'Beauty School Dropout' from *Grease* that the composers threatened to sue. So Normendie's label shipped a fraction of the number it planned and let the supply run out."

On hearing this, Laura felt a grudging respect for Liz Kaiser, who had kept the subject of plagiarism out of the interviews that she had granted Caitlin. But powerful as she was, the publicist clearly couldn't get Normendie's music into stores. After coming up empty-handed at Sam Goody's, Laura kept looking until she found *Junior League Dropout* at a used-record shop in the East Village that reeked of patchouli and did a brisk sideline in old Marvel comic books.

When she got back to the office, she returned a call from Nick, who wanted to know when she was coming home for the Fourth of July. The question caught her off guard. She had hoped that Nick might come to New York for the weekend and help her look for an apartment. But he took for granted that she would fly to Cleveland. Why should *he* make the trip when she had a higher salary? Laura was unwilling to commit to going home until she knew how much work she'd have to do on the

Normendie Latour story, so they argued until Nick allowed that he would try to find an airfare he could afford.

This conversation left Laura too unsettled to make another effort to reach Liz Kaiser, who had ignored two calls and an email message since the staff meeting. Nick was becoming more unreasonable every day. She was furious that he hadn't mailed back her Visa card and suspected that he might still be using it.

But she took some comfort in knowing that Alice was thinking of breaking up with her boyfriend, Chip, another of her well-heeled suitors who looked as though he had been born in a bank vault. As long as Alice stayed single, she wouldn't lack for company on weekends if Nick refused to come to New York. *Alice*, she thought, *why couldn't you have been born poor and homely instead of rich and lovely? I can survive anything except your wedding.*

4
Rose Bluffs

"Oh, Laura, you have no idea how glad I am that you moved to New York!" Alice said, toying with one of the Triscuits that remained a pillar of the Dudley family's cuisine long after most of their neighbors had moved on to blue-corn tortilla chips or jalapeño cheese straws. "You're so much easier to talk to than Chip."

Laura was sitting on the veranda of Rose Bluffs, watching a flock of sailboats catch the last of the day's sun on Long Island Sound. She and Alice had just listened to Normendie Latour's CD and decided that they preferred the squawking of seagulls to the lyrics of *Junior League Dropout*, which told of Normendie's transformation from a blue-blooded debutante to a lap dancer–turned–pop singer.

"But I thought you liked Chip better than some of your other boyfriends. You told me you had to admire a venture capitalist who was still a earning living instead of planning to go to law school or become an Ayurvedic massage therapist."

Alice tossed a Triscuit to a seagull on the back lawn. "I like him the same way I like Revere bowls." She cast an ambivalent glance, half affection and half resignation, at the silver bowl filled with Triscuits that Mrs. Brennan, the Dudley's housekeeper, had set out along with a warm avocado dip that had turned to a tepid mush. "They're handsome and dependable, but also safe and predictable. Most of the Revere bowls made today are like the men I go out with: they all seem to come from the same factory. I don't think I've ever gone out with a man who didn't sail or play golf, or look as though Ralph Lauren had moved into his house to coordinate his wardrobe."

Laura wasn't sure why Alice kept going out with men like Chip if, as she insisted, their similarities ended with their Sperry Topsiders and their ability to tie a figure-eight knot. At Oxford she and Alice had gravitated to each other because they were among the few students in their program who got up for church on Sunday mornings after a triathlon of parties on Saturday nights. They ran into each other on their way back from their separate services and, after they began stopping for lunch, Alice spoke of experiences that seemed as remote as cruising on a fjord—going to the Fly Club Garden Party at Harvard, watching men in drag kick like testosterone-fueled Rockettes in the Triangle Club shows at Princeton. Since then Laura had assumed that Alice wanted to go out mainly with the upper-crust swains who courted her, so she didn't know what to make of her friend's new dissatisfaction with her social life.

"Did you and Chip have a fight last weekend?"

"No, that's part of the problem. We never fight. Sometimes I think he majored in conflict avoidance at Amherst"—Alice pronounced it "AM-erst"—"or maybe took a course in anger management at the Learning Annex. He thinks that when we disagree, one of us should yield instead of trying to thrash things out. In some ways, life with him is very easy. Or it would be if I were willing to do most of the yielding."

Alice studied her father, who was taking his nightly walk on the beach with the metal detector that he carried in the hope of finding loose change dropped by sunbathers. "I just can't see spending the rest of my life with someone like Chip, who never surprises me. Some of his habits are already starting to make me want to tie him to a mast and push him out to sea. It drives me crazy that he keeps talking about the two of us in financial terms. At first he said that he saw our relationship as a 'strong buy' or 'growth stock.' Now he says that it will start 'trading down' if I don't make more time for him."

Laura tried to cheer Alice up by reminding her that if she broke up with Chip, she might find it easier than expected to meet men. Hadn't her own experience at the airport just proved it? On her last day in Cleveland she had met a man who seemed to be full of the kind of surprises that Alice craved. She brought up her theory that despite the initials on his tennis bag, Tim Moran was an actor or rock star traveling incognito.

Alice had her doubts. "It's true that celebrities travel under assumed names. I've heard that you see more aliases on the registration list at the Plaza than on a computer at the FBI. But celebrities who use assumed names have to keep changing them so that their fans don't catch on. It doesn't make sense that a star who was using an alias would have a monogrammed tennis bag. He'd have to buy a bag with different initials every week."

Laura was reluctant to give up her romantic theory of his identity. "What if he wasn't traveling under an assumed name, but under his birth name? What if Tim Moran is the name that nobody knows except the old friends who first saw him when he showed up at day care in his OshKosh overalls?"

"A lot of people know the stars' birth names, too," Alice said. "So he would need to find a better way to hide his identity. I may come from the only family in Connecticut that's never had cable TV or a subscription to *People*. But even *I* know that Tom Cruise's real name is Thomas Cruise Mapother IV."

"Even if Tim was traveling under his real name, I can't help thinking that he paid for my ticket out of something more than pure generosity."

"Maybe he was wildly attracted to you."

"In my old Notre Dame sweatshirt? Not likely. And I'm sure I'm taller than he is. In Cleveland tall women are a taste men acquire if they can't get dates with shorter ones."

"I know plenty of men who have fallen in love with taller

women. Although their trust funds were pretty tall, too." Alice, who was five-four, watched a gray-haired couple walk hand-in-hand along the beach, followed by a golden retriever. "Assuming you're right, maybe your parents helped Tim somehow. Let's say that your father gave him his first job as a stock boy at the bakery, and he's been grateful ever since. But he knew that your father died and he couldn't repay him, so he wanted to do something for you."

Laura thought about this idea. She couldn't deny that her parents might have helped Tim. After nearly starving on their flight to Austria, they were quick to share what they made at their bakery. They were always giving away free slices of honey bread to adults or sending children home with Sweet Bull's Eye cookies. On holidays they delivered more elaborate confections to immigrant families who had fared less well than theirs in America, including plum tarts, hazelnut cakes, or the Hungarian Christmas candies known as *Szalon Cukor*.

"That's a possibility. But my parents focused their attention on helping Hungarian refugees. Besides, Moran isn't a Hungarian name. It's Irish, the kind you see a lot at Notre Dame."

"Laura, I've eaten at your house. Your mother would never let the fact that somebody wasn't Hungarian stop her from trying to satisfy that person's nutritional requirements for a year. Remember the time she tried to put me on a plane with that huge goose drumstick wrapped in aluminum foil? I was afraid it would set off the metal detector. If the Morans were Irish, she might have been more likely, not less, to think they needed help. She might have felt sorry for people who ate plain boiled cabbage and sent them vats of stuffed cabbage made with more spices than some people put in five-alarm chili. You can't always judge people's nationalities by their names, anyway. Tim's mother could be Hungarian instead of his father."

Laura said nothing for a moment as lightning bugs began to blink on the veranda. "Even if Tim is Hungarian, I can't believe that every time he goes to an airport he's waiting for the opportunity to become a one-man Traveler's Aid Society or to give money to somebody he doesn't know."

"I'm not sure that he wasn't waiting for that. Maybe he has a lot of money he doesn't know what to do with. You'd be surprised at how many people have millions of dollars they can't figure out how to spend. They may give huge amounts to charity, but they still want to feel that they're making a difference in people's lives, not just paying for the upkeep of the ficus trees at the offices of a foundation in midtown."

Laura could see that she and Alice weren't going to reach to any conclusions about Tim before the last sailboat on the Sound headed back to its slip for the night. "You may be right that he doesn't know what to do with his money," she said. "But I've got a bigger problem than figuring out why Tim bailed me out. I may need to buy a ticket back to Cleveland if I can't figure out a way to interview Normendie Latour."

5

Behind-the-Back Dribbling

Laura fidgeted at her desk, trying to tune out the squeals of a group of tourists from Fort Wayne who were taking pictures of themselves next to the life-sized cutout of Cassandra near the reception desk. Although disappointed by the absence of the editor-in-chief, they had decided to snap a few photographs, and their laughter was reverberating throughout the office. Caitlin had stormed off to complain, and Ethan had made a theatrical display of clamping the headphones of his MP3 player over his ears.

But Laura didn't mind the distraction. An hour earlier, she had left another message for Liz Kaiser requesting an interview with Normendie Latour, and she couldn't make a follow-up call just yet. In journalism the line between "aggressive" and "pushy" was a chimera, often situated in different places for men and women. Every female journalist had probably heard a variation on, "He's a hard-charging reporter. She's a bitch." Or, "He's got balls. She's got an attitude problem." To have any hope of getting the Normendie Latour interview, she couldn't come on like the love child of Michael Douglas in *Wall Street* and Sigourney Weaver in *Working Girl*.

To keep her spirits up while she waited for the inevitable turndown, Laura checked to see if had any messages on her AOL account. To her disappointment she had no messages from Nick that might have eased the tension after their argument about the Fourth of July. Not that she had really expected any. Nick viewed his literary abilities as precious and in short supply, like a fine wine not be to wasted on an ephemeral medium, while she saw hers as modest and self-renewing, like a mother's milk. But she cherished the irrational hope that he would get over his aversion to email long enough to send her electronic copies of some of the love poems that he used to slip under her door in college. He had excelled at finding old romantic ballads that let you read double meanings into every line, like "My Love in Her Attire":

My love in her attire doth show her wit,
It doth so well become her:
For every season she hath dressings fit,
For winter, spring, and summer.
No beauty she doth miss,
When all her robes are on:
But Beauty's self she is,
When all her robes are gone.

Whenever she was tempted to break up with Nick, Laura reread the poems and remembered why she had felt so attracted to him. Most of the men she'd known at Notre Dame had shown no interest in poetry beyond the two-word rhyme they scrawled on bedsheets before the annual Michigan State game: "Hate State." Some of them couldn't even master the words to the "Notre Dame Victory March."

Then she met Nick, who didn't just know the words to the fight song and its racier parodies, but to a half dozen Elizabethan soliloquies. So what if he'd learned his Shakespeare by watching Olivier and Gielgud instead of from a book?

More than that, he was the first man who encouraged her to write in her own voice, not in the solemn cadences of the inverted-pyramid style that her journalism professors favored. If Nick hadn't urged her to focus on the offbeat stories she liked, she might have spent her entire time at Notre Dame dutifully compiling statistics on daily Mass attendance in the dorms. It wasn't until after college, when she began to surpass him in income and recognition, that their troubles began. She was sure these would ease when they stood again on a level plain, especially if they made a fresh start in a place spacious enough to accommodate both of their talents.

Laura cheered up when she saw that she had email from Molly Chase, her freshman year mentor at Notre Dame, who now worked as an associate at a Cleveland law firm. Molly went out mainly with lawyers, and her stories about them always provided a fresh incentive to work out her problems with Nick.

To: Laura Smart
From: Molly Chase

Hi Laura,

Congratulations! Called your apartment and heard from Nick that you have a great new job that lets you ride the elevator with Quentin Tarantino. Also ran into your brother at Blockbuster, and he said you're going to fix him up with Kate Moss. How did you get such a fantastic job that you've already met Quentin Tarantino AND Kate Moss?

If you see David Boies, would you please tell him to call if he needs help with the next Microsoft case?

I've started going out with a sixth-year associate at Soke and Bilkem—rival firm across town—named Chad Heller. On our first date, he asked if I wanted to see him suck the pimiento out of an olive. Please tell me that sophisticated New York men do NOT regard this as an appropriate way to try to impress a woman.

Molly

To: Molly Chase
From: Laura Smart

Hi Molly,
Got my job the old-fashioned way, by a fluke. Months of answering ads, in print and on the Internet, led nowhere. But a brief meeting in England a half dozen years ago led quickly to a job at *Cassandra* (where "sophisticated New York men" have yet to appear).

Unfortunately both my boyfriend and brother have seriously exaggerated the benefits of the job. Might be more likely to get hit by a tornado on Houston Street than run into Tarantino, Moss, or Boies. My only regular contact with celebrities occurs when I hear their voices urging me to buckle up in taxicabs.

Now I know why so many Midwesterners regard New York as a city filled with crazy people who hear voices in their heads. New Yorkers *do* hear voices in their heads (at least in taxis).

Cheers,
Laura

Buoyed by the note from Molly, Laura signed off AOL and switched back to the email program for *Cassandra*. She had a message from Liz Kaiser's executive assistant.

To: Laura Smart
From: B. B. Gunnerman_Shilling and Flax

Dear Ms. Smart:
Liz Kaiser asked me to respond to your request for a two-hour face to face interview with Normendie Latour for an August cover story for *Cassandra*. She would like you to know that:

1) Two hours is out of the question. I am sure you can under-

stand that a singer of Normendie's caliber needs to avoid straining her voice when she hopes to undertake a major coast to coast tour next year. We *might* be able to give you twenty minutes.

2) A face to face interview is also impossible. We believe that Normendie should do substantive interviews only with such major television personalities as Diane Sawyer, Barbara Walters, or Oprah Winfrey. We *might* be able to arrange for a phoner.

3) Similarly, we cannot agree to your request that Normendie appear on your cover in August. We would obviously want any such publicity to coincide with the release of a new CD so that our client would get the maximum benefit from it. Owing to unfortunate technical difficulties, Normendie will have nothing in stores until next spring. We *might* be able to make her available to you then.

If all of this is acceptable to you, and you would like to have a twenty-minute phoner when Normendie's CD comes out, you would need to agree in writing to our conditions. Please let me know if you would like to us to send you these.

With warmest personal regards,
B. B. Gunnerman

"With warmest personal regards?" Laura wondered what B. B. Gunnerman said when she wanted to ice out telemarketers who called during dinner. She forwarded the executive assistant's memo to Simon, who told her to ask Shilling and Flax to send the conditions for the interview. Liz or B.B. might be bluffing or irritated that he hadn't called the firm himself. If so, he might still be able to bushwhack a trail to the interview.

But Simon urged her to line up an alternate cover subject in case B.B. didn't get back to her or imposed more odious restrictions on the interview—always a risk when you were dealing with Shilling and Flax, whose staff members prided themselves on giving every journalist the freedom of somebody who wore an electronic ankle bracelet. Perhaps, Simon suggested, she could "ring a few people" and find out which celebrities were available?

Laura began calling publicists but heard only about a sitcom star of the 1980s who was doing regional theater, a troubled actor whose availability would depend on whether he could post bail, and a couple of members of washed-up rock bands who had entered their hair-plug years. She ran their names by Simon, who made clear that Cassandra would have a nuclear meltdown if anybody proposed them for a cover. Laura had just spoken to the publicist for a cable-television chef who was trying to bring back Polynesian pu-pu platters when she got another email message.

To: Laura Smart
From: B. B. Gunnerman_Shilling and Flax

Dear Ms. Smart:
Cassandra needs to agree in writing to the following if you would like to have a twenty-minute phoner with our client when her new CD comes out:

1) We must approve the writer for the story. This is in your best interest since Normendie will speak most freely with a writer she likes.

2) To approve the writer, we need you to submit a list of a half dozen journalists and samples of their work, preferably earlier interviews with Normendie or another Shilling and Flax client. We will vet your list and reject inappropriate candidates. You will then select your choice from the remaining writers. If no subsequent problems develop with your candidate, we will schedule an interview.

If you agree in writing to the terms described above, we will send you the list of our interview conditions which naturally include that we reserve the right to exclude certain topics or questions that we believe would not interest the readers of *Cassandra*.

We also would like to suggest subjects that you might pursue in addition to that of Normendie's forthcoming CD. You may not be aware that our client has some fascinating things to say about the belly-button lint problem that she developed after her courageous navel operation. We think Cassandra could build a very exciting story around these comments!

If you wish to take pictures to accompany your story, please let me know so that I can send you the photo shoot conditions.

With warmest personal regards,
B. B. Gunnerman

After reading the message, Laura worried that Simon might make her do a write-around, her least favorite kind of article, on Normendie. Anybody who saw journalism as an inherently parasitic profession might have gotten that idea from stories that had nothing new in them but "wrote around" the lack of an interview, usually by regurgitating published facts and retailing dubious quotes from "friends" of stars. She almost felt sorry for Jennifer Aniston and Brad Pitt, who gave joint interviews so rarely that magazines often made them the target of these descents into journalistic shoplifting.

As she was trying to figure out how to avoid inflicting that fate on Normendie, Laura remembered that the singer lived in the Village, a short walk from Tribeca. Why had she been fencing with a high-handed rep instead of approaching the singer directly? Every serious journalist knew that when you couldn't reach people you needed to interview, you camped on their doorstep and waited for them to enter or leave the building.

The trouble was that Laura didn't know exactly where Normendie lived. She tried without luck to find an address in the phone book, on Internet sites devoted to celebrities, and through the reference desk of the New York Public Library. She was thinking of giving up when she remembered the Social Register that Monica Stryker kept on a reference shelf above the copy desk. Stars who removed their addresses from other listings sometimes kept them in that volume for reasons of vanity or their friends' convenience.

Laura went through the Social Register until she found Normendie listed on West 12th Street under her birth name, Tower. She had heard that the phone numbers in the book were printed in a code, but she didn't know how to crack it. Her only option was to walk to the Village and take a look at her building. What did she have to lose? If she didn't see Normendie, she might pick up a few details that she could use in a write-around.

After slipping a notebook into her tote bag, Laura walked north toward the Village, trying to decide what to say if she saw Normendie. She thought of Simon's reminder that the singer liked the Knicks, but Laura followed the Cavs and the WNBA and could remember little about the New York team except that, for the past couple of seasons, it had failed to make the playoffs. Not exactly a fact likely to ingratiate her with an ardent fan.

On an impulse Laura stopped in a sporting goods store and bought a basketball before heading for West 12th Street. When she got to Normendie's block, she took up a position across the street from her building and watched for signs of life. After half an hour she hadn't seen a light go on or a visitor ring the bell. She walked around the block. Still nothing. When she got tired of waiting, she walked over to Washington Square Park and dribbled her basketball, thinking that she would return to the building later.

It was a lovely evening, and the park was abuzz with the energy of people hurrying home from work or summer classes at NYU. Everybody seemed to be taking part in a contest designed to show how many things you could do at once without breaking your stride—kissing, dialing a cell phone, eating a tuna wrap. The Memorial Arch looked very grand and Napoleonic, and it made Laura feel like a conqueror, exhilarated by the victory of moving to New York. Pausing under the arch, she reveled in a kind of scene that she never saw in Cleveland, where the work day ended at five and people drove home afterward. She tried to remember how she had allowed Nick to persuade her that Los Angeles could be as romantic as this. On the spot she decided that she would stay in the city for at least a year. If Nick sold his screenplay before then, he would have to join her in New York. She couldn't leave the city before she understood all that she saw before her and knew whether she belonged to it.

After a few minutes, she began to dribble again with a step quickened by the decision. Halfway through the park, Laura slowed her pace. A young woman was sitting alone on a bench reading the *New York Post*. She wore sunglasses and a Knicks cap low on her brow, but there was no mistaking the surgically altered navel visible below a cropped pink T-shirt. Or that waif-like body, thin enough that a breeze might have lifted it off the bench. Anybody who pulled off the Knicks cap and sunglasses was sure to see a lightning bolt of black roots streaking across a familiar cascade of white-blonde hair—not to mention sea-green eyes and lashes as long as a ski jump—that had helped to land *Junior League Dropout* briefly in the Billboard Top Forty. Normendie Latour was enjoying her solitude on a summer afternoon.

Laura knew that the singer would shrink from a blunt greeting. She decided instead that she had to make Normendie want to approach *her*. Hoping that showing off a few of her best basketball skills would do the trick, she dribbled the ball behind her back while darting right and left as though trying to elude a defender. When she knew that she had the singer's attention, she sat down on Normendie's bench. She pretended to study two intense young men who were playing speed chess against a clock on a stone table.

Normendie looked up from her *Post*. "You're really good, you know?"

Laura understood why people called Normendie a Locust Valley Girl, or somebody with the speed of a Valley Girl and the elongated vowels of a victim of Locust Valley Lockjaw. Her accent was half boarding school and half boarding pass at LAX.

"I always wondered how the guys on the Knicks did that," Normendie said. "I mean, I could figure out how they dribbled in front of them. Even with their right hand or the left. Anybody knows that you just sort of push the ball. But I could never figure out how the guys dribbled behind their backs."

"You mean like this?" Laura jumped up and dribbled the ball behind her back while running in a circle. "Or like this?" She picked up her pace. It had been so long since she had dribbled at that speed that she felt slightly dizzy.

"Wow!" Normendie said. "That is so cool."

"Want me to show you how to do it?" Laura said, trying to sound as though she might be able to spare a moment if the singer insisted.

Normendie set aside her *Post* and stood up slowly. "It looks so hard." She held out lacquered fingernails that bore the Louis Vuitton logo, a fad that was cresting in Los Angeles salons. "Especially with these."

"Catching a pass is easy. Try this one."

Laura tossed powder puff, and Normendie caught it. "Hey, I'm really good!" Normendie said, flipping the ball back. "Toss me another."

For a few minutes they passed the ball back and forth. Laura encouraged Normendie to dribble without looking at the ball, the obvious first step toward behind-the-back dribbling. When the singer broke a fingernail, they sat down and talked about other basketball techniques. After a while, Laura mentioned casually that she was a writer for *Cassandra* and wondered if Normendie would mind if she wrote a brief article about their meeting that would show a side of her that most people didn't know.

"Hey, that would be really cool!" Normendie said. "Just as long as you don't spend the whole article talking about my operation on my navel. Please! I am *so* sick of talking about my belly-button lint! Why can't reporters ever ask about anything else?"

The question confirmed what Laura suspected, that stars often didn't know the demands that their publicists made on their behalf or the demands that they could make on their publicists. One of Simon's English newspapers had reported that Naomi Campbell asked of a new biography of her, "Is it authorized?"

"You know, you can tell Liz that you don't want to talk about certain things." Laura felt as though that she had gone over to the side of the enemy, but she had to sympathize with a woman who got asked about lint in every other interview. "Liz can tell the reporters not to ask you certain questions."

"Are you kidding?" Normendie sounded amazed. "I can do that?"

"Normendie, Liz works for *you*. You don't work for her. You can tell her to do anything you want." Laura didn't want to push her luck but had to make sure *Cassandra* could run her story. "For example, if Liz tries to stop *Cassandra* from running the article I'm going to write about our playing ball, you can tell her that she has no right to do that because *you* said that the magazine could run it, and *you* don't go back on your word."

"I certainly would tell her that!" Normendie said, her brow furrowed with defiant sincerity. "She can't tell you what to do!"

If you only knew, Laura thought. She asked a few more questions for her story, then stood up. She started to slip the basketball into her tote bag.

"That's a beautiful ball," Normendie said wistfully, looking at the basketball, a regulation WNBA Spalding. "Where did you get it?"

Laura had the odd feeling that Normendie wanted the ball— that she had led a life so sheltered that she didn't know that she could walk into any Modell's and charge a basketball with her American Express card. "Would you like to have this?"

"You mean it?"

"Sure. That way you can practice that dribble."

"Maybe I can pay you back sometime by taking you to see the

Knicks," Normendie said, seemingly unaware that the cost of her Knicks tickets might have bought enough basketballs for every student at a high school in Ohio. "I can get pretty good seats."

"That would be great," Laura said, knowing that there was a better chance that Walt Frazier would come out of retirement and have a 100-point game. "In the meantime, thanks a million. I'll send you the story when it comes out." She didn't dare add, "Or *if* it comes out."

***

"Miss Laura, come quickly! Mr. Nick is on the phone. He says it's urgent."

Mrs. Brennan, the Dudley's housekeeper, burst into the guest room at Rose Bluffs, where Laura was writing her story on Normendie Latour on her laptop while stretched out on a white wicker chaise lounge with a view of the ocean. Mrs. Brennan spoke in an accent that Alice liked to call "half Irish and half television" because it combined the tones of her native County Clare with odd inflections picked up while watching *Masterpiece Theatre*.

Laura hurried to a phone on a piecrust table in the study to find that Nick was calling on his cell from the supermarket to say that he couldn't find the coffee filters.

"You're calling long-distance to ask me where the coffee filters are?" she asked. "Why don't you just ask one of the clerks?"

"I did, but I still can't find them," Nick said irritably. "You know how big this supermarket is. And the clerk wouldn't give me a straight answer."

Laura could hear someone talking about Häagen-Dazs in the background and realized that Nick was looking for coffee filters in the frozen-food section. "What do you mean, the clerk wouldn't give you a straight answer?"

"I asked her to explain where the coffee filters were in terms of north and south. But she just kept saying they were in Aisle 9. I've been wandering in circles for five minutes trying to find it. Why can't women learn to give directions correctly?"

Laura couldn't quite comprehend what she was hearing. "So you want me to explain to you—in terms of 'north' and 'south'— how to find the coffee filters?"

"Right. And don't take forever, because this call is costing me money. I'm standing next to the half-gallons of Pierre's ice cream."

Laura drew a mental map of the supermarket. "Are you facing the half-gallons," she asked slowly, "or standing with your back to them?" She was afraid that if she didn't get the spot right, Nick would lump her in with all the other women whose defects included their failure to serve as twenty-four-hour-a-day Global Positioning Systems.

"I'm sort of standing at an angle."

"Okay, if you turn so that you're *not* at an angle and have your back to the half-gallons, you'll be facing Chagrin Boulevard. Which means you'll be facing north. Then you'll have to walk north for two aisles and turn east into Aisle 9." Laura heard the wheels rolling on Nick's shopping cart. "Are you following me?"

"Wait a minute. I'm walking north with my cart right now."

As she pictured Nick sweeping past the rows of frozen catfish and corn dogs, Laura wished she had one of those boyfriends she read about in Dave Barry's columns who refused to ask for directions. Nick would ask her how to get from the right side of the bed to the left.

When he got to Aisle 9, Nick made her stay on the phone until she'd guided him to the filters and answered his questions about a) what size he needed, b) what quantity he should buy, and c) why the coffee filters were so expensive. Then came the zinger that, Laura was sure, he had hoped to bury amid talk of the coffee filters: he wasn't coming to New York for the Fourth of July. The airfares were too high, he needed to work on his screenplay, and he couldn't take time away from his work on "the Sundance of Northeast Ohio." He had to coordinate the appearances of a half-dozen independent filmmakers, including a former assistant to Robert Redford who was flying in from L.A. With speechless dismay, Laura listened as Nick reminded her that she had promised to come home "nearly every weekend." If the Fourth of July wasn't a weekend, what was? If she couldn't fly home, they couldn't see each other until Tina's wedding on Labor Day.

Laura groped for a compromise. "What about if I come home later in the month for the film festival? If I have some money left over after I find an apartment—"

"Don't bother," Nick said curtly. "You'd hate the films we're showing."

"How do you know?" Laura asked, hurt. "I sort of liked some of the films we saw at the festival last year. Like that Japanese take-off on *Four Weddings and a Funeral,* where all the brides die before the ceremony and the corpse comes to life at the end. Parts of it were hilarious."

"That just proves my point," Nick said coldly. "That film *wasn't* a take-off. It was a tragic postmodern commentary on the symbolic death of female identity that occurs when women marry. Some people were sobbing in the theater."

"Nick, I'm sure those were tears of laughter rather than sadness," Laura said, suddenly unsure of this. "But, either way, the film had its moments."

"For years you've been telling me 'it has its moments' is a publishing code for 'This manuscript is rubbish unredeemed by the moments in which the author trades his bad Hemingway imitation for a bad Faulkner imitation.' So you can't fool me with that one."

Laura knew that if she kept arguing with Nick, she might never finish her story on Normendie Latour, so she agreed to see him over Labor Day weekend. But after she hung up, she had second thoughts about not going home for the Fourth. In a patriotic town like Cleveland, Independence Day was closer to a sacrament than a national holiday, and there could hardly be a better time to return than right after interviewing a star like Normendie Latour.

Steve would have to stop carping about her failure to introduce him to models after learning that she had met someone more well known than any of this year's runway sensations. Her mother would be overjoyed by the visit, and even Molly, who often worked weekends at her law firm, would probably be able to make time to see her.

Laura logged on to the Internet, found an inexpensive flight, and decided to surprise Nick by arriving just before a barbecue that her Aunt Eva and Uncle Frank, Tina's parents, had every year. She didn't want to risk another argument with Nick by calling to say she was coming home, and she worried that her mother might accidentally spill the news, so she left a message about the visit only with Molly. Then she went back to writing her story on Normendie with new motivation to finish it quickly. If Simon liked the piece and put it on the cover, how could her family and friends back in Ohio fail to be impressed by how quickly she had begun to leave her mark on New York?

6
Horse-trading

"Brilliant! A perfect cover story for August."

Simon turned away from his computer and adjusted a red suspender that had slipped as he read the interview with Normendie Latour that Laura had stayed up until 3 AM to finish. After stubbing out a Marlboro, he lowered the volume on the short-wave radio that he kept tuned to the BBC, which was filling his office with the chorus of "Figaro's Song" from *The Barber of Seville*.

"We'll have to pay the printer a fortune in overtime costs to rip out the story on Courtney Swilling and replace it with yours," Simon added. "And we won't have time to take our own pictures for it, so we'll have to buy stock photos. But the switch will be worth it. Aurora Starr will be wild with jealousy."

Laura saw that Simon, for all his affability, burned with a competitive fire as bright as Cassandra's. From the flare in his eyes she could see that he had wanted the new cover story as much to sweep past Aurora as to please his own readers. But she didn't understand the mention of Cassandra's rival, whom she was sure would never have wanted to have Normendie Latour on one of her covers.

"Why would Aurora be jealous? She usually puts ordinary people on her covers—the winners of her talent contests and scavenger hunts—instead of celebrities. Aurora might put a Normendie Latour impersonator on her cover, but not Normendie."

"Aurora is an astute businesswoman. She'll recognize that, even if she didn't want to have Normendie on one of her covers, the interview was a coup that may help us surpass her on newsstands in August. It's the first interview that Normendie has given in months, maybe years, that wasn't scripted by Liz Kaiser."

A coup? Nobody had ever said that about anything Laura had written—there wasn't a lot of competition to interview singing Zamboni drivers in Toledo—and she thought she might start to levitate in Simon's office. She hadn't expected to complete her first assignment so easily, but she worried that something could still go wrong.

"Are you sure Liz won't try to kill the story?"

"On the contrary, I'm sure she will try to kill it."

"Then how do you know you'll be able to use it?"

"Cassandra wants Normendie on the cover so badly that if Liz complains, she'll offer her a deal that involves her show. She'll promise to devote a segment to another Shilling and Flax client if Liz drops her objections to the story on Normendie."

"How do you know Liz will accept the deal?"

"She'll accept because television trumps print every time. An appearance on *Cassandra!* is worth far more than most magazine covers. If you ask a hundred book publicists whether they'd prefer to have an author appear on *Oprah* or get a great review in the *New York Times*, you'd be hard-pressed to find three or four who would choose the *Times*. Liz may protest the story on Normendie even if she doesn't object to it, so she can use the issue as a bargaining chip to get another client on *Cassandra!* or to get Normendie on the show when her CD comes out."

"I thought you didn't like that kind of horse-trading."

"I don't. But in this case the deal won't directly involve me. I may not even know the details. Liz will call me to complain, and when I refuse to kill the story, she'll call Cassandra. The two of them will work things out on their own. My part in the deal will be limited to warning Cassandra about the call from Liz, so she'll have time to think about what she's willing to give up in return for having Normendie on the cover."

Laura's spirits frayed at the edges. Normendie was hardly Marilyn Vos Savant, that fixture in *Parade* who tapped into her genius IQ to answer wacko questions from people in Boise and Duluth. But the singer had a sweet vulnerability and, when Knicks fans were defecting in droves, an almost childlike loyalty to her team. She deserved better than to get traded on the open market like the stock of her recording company.

"Why do you look so glum?" Simon asked. "You've written a splendid piece. I'm delighted that you left out that iffy business involving Tim Moran, which could have been rather embarrassing to the company."

Laura jerked to attention. "Tim Moran? How do you know *him*?"

Simon looked puzzled. "Didn't you know? He works for Carapace, our parent company, at the corporate headquarters in midtown."

Laura wondered if, in her sleep-deprived state, she had misheard. "Tim works for *us*?"

"It would be more accurate to say that we work for him."

"We can't be talking about the same person. I'm sure Tim would have told me if we worked for the same company. It doesn't make sense that he wouldn't."

"It makes perfect sense. Every smart executive likes to see how ordinary readers react to his magazine. It gives you information you can't get from your market-research surveys. The surveys may tell you which articles people like most. But they don't tell you when people laugh or put an article aside. If I ever write a memoir, I may call it *Everything I Really Need to Know about Editing I Learned from British Rail*. Watching people read the London newspapers on trains was a marvelous education in popular tastes. I'm certain that Tim was paying far more attention to your comments about *Cassandra* than you think."

Laura suspected that Simon was right, which made her slightly nervous. She remembered the time she'd been unable to take her eyes off a patient poring over one of her articles in a doctor's office. She was so excited that she wanted grab the woman and shout, "I wrote that!"

"I wish I'd recognized Tim's name."

"There was no reason you should have. No magazine lists all of the officers of its parent company on the masthead. Those are more likely to appear in its annual report. But somehow I thought you knew Tim. He certainly seemed to know you. He mentioned it yesterday when I called to let him know that we might use a new cover story for the August issue after we had paid a ten thousand dollar day rate to the photographer who took the pictures for the Courtney Swilling story."

Laura wasn't too groggy to avoid feeling a flash of irritation that Tim, after a brief meeting at the airport, had cast himself as a friend. But she still didn't know why she might have mentioned him in her story. "What iffy business did I leave out?"

"Didn't Caitlin tell you? There's a rumor that Tim went out with Normendie a few years ago before she took up with Roger Hornsley. Never substantiated. But Tim and Normendie are both Knicks fans, and a photograph of the two of them at courtside kept turning up until Liz threatened to cut off access to her clients from any newspaper that published It. She thought it made Normendie look fat."

"Fat? Normendie is a waif. She looks like a Save the Children poster girl after surgery that might have cost enough to feed a village in Ecuador for a year. If you took away all the white-blonde hair, which gives her some ballast, you might have to put weights in her shoes to keep her earthbound." Laura saw that she was getting off the point. "But why would I want to bring up Tim's relationship with her in my story? Most magazines would see that as too incestuous for comfort."

"Caitlin thought that if we did a story on Normendie, in the interest of 'full disclosure' we ought to find out what went on between her and Tim and mention it in our piece. But any romance that Normendie had before Roger came along strikes me as old news. Even if she and Tim had a fling, they were hardly Jane Fonda and Ted Turner. Dredging up an old affair could have embarrassed Carapace given that Tim has such a high position in the company."

Laura's palms began to sweat when she remembered her coolness to Tim and how disorganized she must have appeared on her last day in Cleveland. She had practically pasted her face to *Cassandra* to avoid talking to him. "What high position?"

"I believe his exact title is deputy chief financial officer. He's one of the highest ranking financial officers in the company. He started out as the publisher of the Carapace sports magazine group and moved up. Among other duties, he acts as the liaison between the financial people in New York and the corporate headquarters in Paris. One story has it that he and Normendie met on the Concorde."

"I guess that explains it."

"Explains what?"

"Why Tim bailed me out at the airport. On my last day in Cleveland, I found out that I owed extra money for my ticket to New York, but I didn't have my Visa card with me. Tim put the cost on his card. He must have known that Cassandra wanted to do a story on Normendie and hoped to keep his name out of it. I had a feeling that he either wanted a favor or was grateful for one that he had received."

"Why would Tim have to bribe somebody in his own company for a favor?" Simon lit another Marlboro and offered one to Laura, who shook her head. "If he wanted something, he had only to call Cassandra or me and ask for it. I get calls every week from people on the corporate side who want favors, usually write-ups for their friends. An affair with Normendie doesn't strike me as something most men would hide, even if they had professional reasons for wanting to keep it out of print. I suspect that they might rather be inclined to boast about it. And people at Tim's level are rarely embarrassed to ask for what they want. You don't get to be a high-ranking officer of a company like Carapace, especially at a young age, by being timid. If Tim didn't want us to write about his affair with Normendie—if there was an affair—I would have known about it. Perhaps he wouldn't have told me directly. But the word would have filtered down through our publisher or someone else."

Laura could see the truth in Simon's explanation. The publisher of *Buckeye* was never shy about letting writers and editors know when he wanted them to honor his favorite shoe repair shop or Slovenian restaurant in the annual "Best of the Buckeye State" issue.

"Then why would Tim have paid for my ticket?"

"Perhaps he's one of the few men who still enjoys rescuing damsels in distress. He strikes me as an excellent fellow even if he *has* slashed our expense budget."

"Tim was responsible for that memo that said that we have to take our sources to falafel stands?"

"I doubt that he personally dictated the memo about expenses. But obviously somebody at his level decided that we needed to hold down our costs."

Laura was perversely glad that she hadn't been friendlier to Tim. She didn't want to get seduced, in any sense of the word, by somebody who cared more about profits than about the editorial content of the magazine. How did the brass at Carapace expect *Cassandra* to survive if they kept nickel-and-diming the staff? "I don't care who suggested it. How can *Cassandra* catch *Aurora* if bureaucrats like Tim keep us on such a short leash?"

"Why don't you ask him?" Simon said. "I'm sure you'll hear from him soon."

"What makes you say that?" Laura asked, hoping that Tim didn't intend to rebuke her for the low-keyed guerrilla tactics she'd used to interview Normendie.

"Tim is one of those executives who still believes in management by wandering around, an idea that I believe used to be quite popular in business schools in the States. But since his office is in midtown and we're down here in Tribeca, he tends to do his wandering by telephone or email. He's always dashing off notes to writers when he likes their stories. And he has a posh flat on the Upper East Side where he gives parties that sometimes include staff members. He's famous for an annual Fourth of July cookout on his terrace. I've been invited this year, and I hope to stop by. The view of the spray from fireboats on the river is apparently spectacular."

Simon studied Laura as he took a drag on his Marlboro. "Tim asked whether I thought you might like to attend, too. I told him I thought you'd be delighted to have an invitation." Simon glanced at his fax machine, which was receiving a long document on the letterhead of Shilling and Flax. "And if you care about your future at the company you'll *act* delighted even if you aren't. It never hurts to be civil to the person who, figuratively speaking, signs your paychecks."

"I'll do my best to be civil," she said doubtfully. "But I'm planning to go to Cleveland for the Fourth and would hate to cancel the trip for his cookout."

"I'm sure Tim wouldn't want that. But if you can't attend, I'd let him know you'd accept a rain check. Getting to know Tim could make a great difference to your career." Simon allowed an ash from his cigarette to fall the floor. "And to your social life."

After returning to her desk, Laura wrote captions for several pictures of Normendie that Anne Meyer, the art director, had found through a photo-research service and left on her desk while she was talking to Simon. Then she checked her email.

To: Laura Smart
From: Molly Chase

Hi Laura,

Got your message about the Fourth and wish we could get together. But I'm still seeing Chad, the associate at Soke and Bilkem, who said we could go away if I could find "a charming, rustic cottage on Lake Michigan" (my requirements) with "voice mail, a fax machine, and a DSL Internet connection" (his). Suspect he agreed only because he thought I couldn't pull it off. But I did, so we'll be away for the weekend.

Would have called you back except that, as it is, I may not be able to leave the office until after midnight unless I skip dinner, bathroom breaks, and other essentials, such as late-inning checks of the score of the Tribe game. Maybe we can catch up at the shower that your cousin Maggie is supposed to be giving for Tina later this summer? My firm has done some work for Brad's PR agency, so I might get invited.

Molly

To: Molly Chase
From: Laura Smart

Hi Molly,

No problem about the holiday. Ought to spend most of the weekend with Nick, anyway, with a pit stop at a barbecue given by Tina's parents.

Lately have noticed the striking fact that widowed mother with arthritis seems better able to function on own than young, vigorous boyfriend who lifts weights. Mother is delighted when I call (taking it as proof of my continued survival in city with threats to life on every corner) while boyfriend is sullen and reproachful (taking it as proof of my continued absence from city without threats to life on every corner unless you count shocking number of drive-by shootings, hold-ups of 7-Elevens, etc.).

Is it any comfort that Chad at least works in the same city that you do?

Cheers,
Laura

To: Laura Smart
From: Tim Moran_Carapace

Just wondered if you had plans for the Fourth. Want to come to a cookout on my terrace if you don't?

I heard from Simon that you got a great interview with Normendie. Must admit that I didn't at first believe that you had pulled it off. (Liz Kaiser strikes me as the Cerberus of PR, a three-headed dog who can't be fought, only lulled to sleep with a lyre.) So I called Normendie, and she assured me that, to her delight, you did. Have no idea what you said to her, but after months of worrying that Liz would fire her if she didn't made a serious comeback, she's now asking me if *she* should fire Liz.

Normendie will be spending the Fourth with Roger in Sag Harbor and can't join the rest of us at the cookout. But you can still bring a basketball and show off a few of your moves on my terrace.

Laura half-regretted that she had bought her ticket to Cleveland. If Simon was right, she could only benefit from accepting the invitation she had received. At a large party she wouldn't have to make much conversation with Tim, and it might be interesting to see him without his sports gear. But couldn't he have invited her sooner if he really wanted her to attend? The lateness of his invitation negated any satisfaction that she might have taken from knowing that, so far as she could tell, none of her coworkers except Simon had been invited. She would have to find a way to turn Tim down gracefully enough to have a chance of getting invited to next year's cookout.

To: Tim Moran_Carapace
From: Laura Smart

It's my bad luck to have to spend the Fourth dribbling barbecue sauce on my chin instead of a basketball on your terrace. I'm going home to see if the man who forgot to return my Visa card has developed a better memory since I left. (Not taking any chances, though—I'm soldering my credit cards to my wallet.)

Would you keep me in mind for next year's cookout? The closest I've come to attending party on a high-rise terrace is eating a hot dog on an upper deck of the Jake. In the meantime please tell Normendie that we're excited about having her in *Cassandra* (and that she has the best passing technique I've ever seen from someone with Louis Vuitton fingernails).

To: Laura Smart
From: Tim Moran_Carapace

Why wait until next year to get together? Let's have a drink after you get back. And please feel free to stop by on the Fourth if your flight gets canceled or Simon gives you so much work you can't get away. The cookout will be informal with plenty of food for an extra guest.

I'll pass along your compliment to Normendie. But was it a "compliment"? It reminded me of an author friend who says that whenever a friend asks him to give a blurb for an amazingly bad book, he has to resort to a double-edged comment like, "This book is amazing!"

After reading Tim's notes, Laura still had no idea of what kind of relationship, if any, he'd had with Normendie. But she was beginning to see how the singer might have gravitated to him in the way that Julia Roberts did to Lyle Lovett. He might be one of those men who had more appeal to women in his own circle than in others.

It occurred to Laura that she might fix Tim up with Alice, who had just broken up with Chip. Alice, though unlikely to find him more attractive than she did, desperately needed to go out with men who didn't have to be dragged by the hair out of J. Press. Laura knew that if Nick kept refusing to come to New York, she might have no romance in her life all summer. Why, she wondered, shouldn't she have the fun of hearing about someone else's sex life if she had none of her own?

7
Independence Day

Laura slipped a key into the lock of her old apartment, feeling a pang of nostalgia for the days when she lived in a place that required only one key. Everybody said that in New York you needed at least two—often three or four—locks on your door, and she suspected that some people would have gladly added moats and drawbridges. Would she ever get used to living in a city honeycombed with small-scale medieval fortresses, *if* she could find a fortress of her own?

As she stepped into the living room she used to share with Nick, Laura caught a whiff of the stale popcorn that spilled out of a red-and-white box on an end table. Looking around in shock, she half-wondered if she had entered the wrong apartment, perhaps that of a vagrant with literary aspirations who had grown tired of writing his screenplay underneath the Lorain-Carnegie Bridge. In a few weeks Nick had reduced their sunny living room to a glorified hovel sullied by a jumble of castoffs: a limp T-shirt on the floor, a cannibalized sports section of *The Plain Dealer* on the sofa, a drift of manuscript pages on the coffee table. What bothered her the most was that the leaves of the spider plant hanging in a window had turned brown—she had thought that spider plants were the cockroaches of the botanical kingdom, capable of surviving a nuclear attack—and she rebuked herself for not having reminded Nick to water them after she left.

Reaching down to pick up a chopstick from the floor, Laura heard the hiss of a shower turned on full blast and realized that Nick might be the only clean thing in the apartment. She was thinking about surprising him by taking off her clothes and jumping in the shower with him when his seductive baritone rang out from the bathroom.

"Hi, Tara! Come on in. The water's fine."

Tara? Laura froze. *Who was Tara?* Thinking that the running water might have made "Laura" sound like "Tara," she said nothing. Nick called out again.

"C'mon, Tara, baby! Wash that L.A. smog off you!"

Tara, baby?

Laura felt her fury rising. So that—or rather, *she*—was why Nick hadn't come to New York for the Fourth of July. She had a molten urge to burst into the bathroom and confront him, if not strangle him with dental floss. But lately he had been acting so irrationally that he might be insane enough deny the obvious, maybe even suggest that he'd planned to take a shower with the Tar Baby. *Forget it, Uncle Remus,* she thought.

Feeling her reporter's instincts kick in, Laura scanned the living room for tangible evidence of his betrayal. Two empty trapezoids that once held Chinese food clearly weren't good enough. Nick might try to claim that his appetite picked up, no doubt along with other body parts, during his work on the film festival.

Laura tiptoed to the sofa and lifted the cushions but found only a few more popcorn kernels and fossilized sesame noodles. She dropped to her knees, slid her hand underneath it, and struck gold in the form of a black lace push-up bra. As she pulled it out, she heard the bathroom door slam. Nick strode naked into the hallway humming a buoyant "Hotel California."

"Hey, Tara," he called. "Did you miss me while I ..."

Nick fought to arrange his face into a nonchalant expression.

"Laura, what are you doing here?" he stammered. It was ludicrous to see a naked man trying to hold on to his dignity with an erection that could pick up a radio signal from Juneau. "Wait, I'll go get a towel."

"Don't bother," Laura said archly. "I've seen it before."

Nick ignored her and, like a startled hare, bounded back to the bathroom and returned with a towel around his waist. Still dripping water on the hardwood floor in the hallway, he stationed himself several feet away from Laura. She tossed the black lace push-up bra to him.

"Not my size," she said. "Or my style, either. As you've pointed out, I have nothing to push up."

"What are you getting so upset about?" Nick's demanded, his fire returning as his embarrassment abated. "You told me you weren't coming home for the Fourth."

"So you made plans to cheat on me?"

"I didn't *plan* to cheat on you. Tara is a filmmaker who came to town to work out a few details for the festival, and it just happened."

"You can tell Tara that I just happened to break up with you while she was out."

Laura thought that she saw a flicker of relief cross Nick's face.

"It's probably for the best," Nick said with a theatrical sigh. "I can't live with a woman who's never around."

Laura didn't try to untangle his twisted logic. "Just out of curiosity," she asked, "when were you planning to tell me that you thought we ought to break up?"

"I wasn't. I knew how upset you'd get if I did. So I thought I'd do you a favor by letting you break up with me."

As she turned to leave, Laura was suddenly unsure of how she was going to get through the weekend. There was no doubt that, in a big small town like Cleveland, others knew about Nick's affair and would be whispering about her over the kielbasa they grilled along with hot dogs.

Laura calculated that, if she could get an early evening flight to New York, she could spend a few hours with her mother at her aunt and uncle's, then make it back to the city in time to catch the end of Tim's cookout. She had brought clothes for a Midwestern barbecue, not for a party on the Upper East Side that might attract power players in the publishing or broadcasting industry. But Tim said that the event would be informal, and she might be able to find something appropriate in the closet in her old bedroom upstairs. Now that Nick was out of her life, what did she have to lose by going to a party where she might meet somebody who could pay his own Visa bills?

***

As she stepped out of a cab in front of Tim's building, Laura wondered if she had made a mistake by stopping by his party. Even in the darkness, she could see that the place was more posh than she expected. The towering brick-and-glass building, overlooking the East River, seemed to have more plants in the lobby than the rain forest at the Cleveland Zoo. Why hadn't she worn something more stylish than a white pique sundress? It had looked fashionably retro when she retrieved it from a closet at her mother's house, but guests might mistake it for something made from Brawny paper towels. How had she convinced herself that flat black patent leather sandals were just the thing to complete the outfit?

Tim had left the door to his apartment open, and from the foyer Laura could hear the waves of laughter sweeping in from the terrace and smell gas from an outdoor grill. Seeing no one except a maid who was loading plates into a stainless-steel dishwasher, she rolled her suitcase to a bedroom that served as a coatroom—a few women had tossed pastel cashmere shawls onto the bed—and made her way toward a terrace aglow with tiny white lights in the branches of ficus trees.

Laura couldn't see Tim, so she headed for the bar, almost needing a compass to help her find it. It was obvious that, while the writers at *Cassandra* scavenged for paper clips, the top managers at Carapace lived like pashas and stopped just short of asking turbanned servants to fan them with ostrich plumes. After declining the bartender's offer of an imported blueberry vodka on the rocks, Laura took a bottle of Sam Adams, then settled back against a brick wall banked with red impatiens.

From the snippets of conversation that drifted toward her, she couldn't pigeonhole the crowd. Some of the guests came from the upper ranks of the broadcasting industry while others were old friends of Tim's from college or an after-work softball league in Central Park. About half of the people looked as though they had just checked out of Ian Schrager hotels and the other half looked as though they watched for "Kids Stay Free" signs on the interstate. Anybody who believed that he could make that mix work was either a deft or deranged host.

Waiting for the right moment to plunge into the crowd and find Tim, Laura turned her attention to a dark-haired woman who had elegantly tanned legs and the glassy, android features of someone who was on better terms with her plastic surgeon than some women were with their children. She was purring to a man in a double-breasted blue blazer and blue-and-white striped ascot.

"Wonder what's going on between Tim and that woman who's been clinging to him all night like wet seaweed … Gorgeous but obviously trying to use him as her ticket out of Des Moines, or wherever she works, and he's too nice too see it … At least Normendie adored him even if she did end up dumping him for Roger … Told me she did It because she was convinced that *he* would never fall in love with her … Thank God she didn't mention *that* to that nasty little twit from Cincinnati who ambushed her in the park!"

Laura felt a swig of beer go down the wrong pipe and coughed. The dark-haired woman glanced at her, as though trying to decide whether she knew her, then went on.

"That's the trouble with people from the provinces … Have no idea what the rules are in New York … Would never have happened if Cassandra had been in town … Didn't want to call her about it on the yacht … Lord knows she needed a vacation with

Aurora rolling over her at newsstands every month ... If she doesn't give me an hour of airtime for one of my clients after she gets back, I'm pulling all of them from *Cassandra* ... Just about ought to finish off the magazine given all its other problems ... Well, I have two more parties tonight to take my mind off it ... Let's go to Gramercy Park first, then Soho."

Laura simmered as the woman and her companion breezed past her, air-kissing friends on their way out. *"Nasty little twit?"* She had no doubt that she had been listening to Liz Kaiser and was thinking of leaving the party when she saw Tim hurrying toward her, trailed by a woman who had a tumble of honey-colored hair and makeup that Way Bandy might have risen from the grave to apply. Laura saw that he was better-looking than she remembered. Moonlight clearly did more for him than the stark brightness of an airport concourse. With his blue eyes and dark wavy hair, he had the kind of looks that her Notre Dame friends called Black Irish.

Still, Laura thought, he was more Alice's type than hers. He was an inch or two shorter than she was, and she had never met a man who really wanted to go out with a taller woman. But he was the perfect height for Alice. He even wore the kind of clothes that Alice liked, a navy sports jacket and khakis with Tod's loafers and one of those high-tech watches that did everything but broil hamburgers for you.

"Great to see you, Laura. I thought you'd be in Ohio, maybe spending the day on an upper deck at the Jake." Tim introduced his companion as Brandy North-Cox, who did color stories on sports for a Chicago television station, then studied Laura with concern. "You look lovely but a bit ... flushed—from the heat. If you're uncomfortable, we can go inside and see if my new air-conditioning system works."

"Flushed?" Laura thought. How could Tim think that she was flushed from heat instead of what Liz had said?

"I was just telling Brandy how you got your interview with

Normendie. We were both hoping to hear more about it."

"I hope Liz Kaiser didn't hear you. She doesn't seem too happy with the story."

Brandy flashed an enameled smile. "Don't worry," she said, smiling again and slurring her words. "After you've been in journalism for a while, you'll learn how to get interviews without alientating people."

Tim looked nervous, and Laura didn't know whether it was because of the insult to her or the mispronunciation of "alienating." "Laura didn't alienate anybody," Tim said mildly. "Normendie said she'd never had so much fun talking to a reporter."

Brandy took a sip from her drink. "Michael Jordan said he never had so much fun talking to a reporter as he did to me. But I didn't have to alientate everybody at IMG to get the interview."

"Brandy, you asked Michael Jordan one question at a press conference after a Bulls game," Tim said gently. "You didn't have time to alienate him."

"No, but he *liked* the question," Brandy said, pouting. "Since he's so tall, I asked him: if he could be any kind of tree, what kind of tree would he like to be? He said nobody had ever asked him that in a post-game interview before."

"Perhaps that's because in post-game interviews reporters usually ask about the game," Tim said. Laura couldn't be sure, but she thought she saw him wink at her. "I've forgotten. What kind of tree did Michael Jordan say he wanted to be?"

"He told me that since he'd never been asked that question, he couldn't say. But he said it was interesting to *think* about." Brandy swayed on her Capri sandals, and Tim took her drink out of her hand.

Laura had the feeling that Brandy was somebody who should definitely be kept from operating any heavy machinery in the building, possibly including the washing machine. She couldn't believe that a station would let her near Michael Jordan and wondered if she had invented the story.

"Would you excuse us?" Tim asked firmly, as he took Brandy by the elbow. "I want to see if we can find some coffee in the kitchen. Please don't go before we get back. I want to hear how you're enjoying *Cassandra*."

After they left, Laura grabbed her suitcase from the bedroom, hoping that Tim wouldn't see her dash toward the elevator. In the lobby of the building she ran into Simon, who was on his way up to the party.

"Simon!" she said, delighted to see a friendly face. "I thought you'd come and gone from the party long ago."

"I thought you were in Cleveland."

Laura poured out the story of her breakup with Nick. "The worst of it is that I should have broken up with him long ago. I don't know why I put up with his moods for so long. I must have been, to use one of your favorite words, daft."

"I don't think you were daft at all," Simon said. "But you do look a bit distraught. Let's go for a walk. The river looks so lovely from here."

As Simon slipped an arm around her shoulder, Laura admitted that she wasn't sure whether she was more upset about Nick's betrayal or about the conversation she'd overheard on the terrace. "Liz Kaiser made clear that if she has anything to say about it, I'll be panhandling in the subways by Christmas."

"Surely you aren't still worried about Liz?" Simon asked. "Not after I told you that Cassandra will find a way to calm her down when she gets back from vacation?"

"How could I not be upset? The problem goes beyond Normendie. Liz threatened to deny us access to all her clients. I'm afraid she'll do it and Cassandra will blame me for it." Laura didn't dare tell Simon that she was afraid *he* would blame her.

"Liz is the one who should be afraid. She may be one of the most powerful publicists in the entertainment industry, but she depends on the goodwill of clients who have egos the size of an aircraft carrier and who are, in some ways, more dangerous to her.

Without them, she is nothing. Believe me, the industry is full of washed-up reps who have fallen out with clients over less than a cover story in *Cassandra*. Liz is afraid that although Normendie agreed to the story, she'll change her mind after it appears and blame her for not killing it. Or that the word will spread that you can get around the Dragoon Guards at S & F with enterprising tactics such as yours, which would make it more difficult to wield the authority she wants. In either case, you should feel flattered. Not many young reporters can rattle someone of her stature."

Simon stopped walking for a moment. "Did you know that when the Brooklyn Bridge was built, the city had to get elephants to walk across it to prove to New Yorkers that it was safe? People were afraid to use it. Liz sees you—and to a lesser extent, me, because she doesn't know me well either—the way New Yorkers saw that bridge. She has to work with us to maintain good relations with Cassandra. But she would prefer to deal with writers and editors whom her elephants have trampled many times. I must say, I admire the courage that Tim showed in inviting her. Rather bold of him. Did you have a chance to speak to him?"

"For a few minutes. Then he went to get coffee for a woman named Brandy, who would never get into Harvard if it required a Breathalyzer test."

"Ah, the aptly named Brandy. I've heard about her, though not from Tim. A few years ago she had a job at a station here in New York. At the time Tim was publishing a sports magazine that predicted that she might become the first female play-by-play analyst on *Monday Night Football*. A media critic wrote that she had the potential to be 'Terry Bradshaw with bosoms.' I gather that all the pressure contributed to a drinking problem. Tim has spent a lot of time trying to talk her into joining AA."

Simon said nothing as a jogger swept past them in the darkness. "I suppose we ought to head back to Tim's building so that I can put in an appearance at the party. But before we do, I have news that might cheer you up. Cassandra was supposed to return to work this week. But she decided to spend a few days at the fall collections in Paris before coming back, which means that your work load should remain light for a while longer."

Light? Laura thought. Simon had given her several new assignments after she finished her cover story, and she was taking work home on the train almost every night. If she would have to work more after Cassandra returned, she *had* to find an apartment so that she could write without listening to commuters shriek into their cell phones or worrying that the battery on her iBook would die as the train whizzed past Westport.

Laura had just said goodbye to Simon when Tim dashed out of his building carrying a bouquet of white freesias from a vase in the foyer of his apartment.

"Laura! So glad I caught you. You stayed for a such a short time that I thought you might like to have a party favor." Tim handed her the freesias. "I also thought that, with your luggage, you'd want to take a cab to your place, and I was going to help you find one. But I ran into Simon in the lobby and he said you have to go to Connecticut. So I'll call a car service for you."

"That would cost a fortune. I don't mind taking a cab to Grand Central and waiting for a train."

"Trains are running on a holiday schedule. You might have to sit for hours at the station, and this was partly a company event. Simon was here, and so were some of the people from Carapace. The company can absorb the cost of the car service." Tim took a sprig of white freesia from the bouquet and tucked it behind her ear. "By the way, white really suits you."

As they waited for the car, Tim said that if she ever had to work too late to catch a train, she could stay in his second bedroom. "You don't have to worry that it will raise eyebrows. Some of the French executives of Carapace stay over so often when they visit that one of them calls the place 'The Moran Hilton.' It saves the company a fortune on hotel bills."

As the car approached, Tim opened his wallet and handed her fifty dollars. "You don't need to pay the driver. The service will put it on the company account. But you'll need to tip Eddie well for a long trip on a holiday weekend. This should do it."

"Do you think that, on my salary, I can't afford to tip the driver?" Laura asked, keeping her tone light. "I appreciate that you bailed me out at the airport. But I'm not always so short of cash …"

Tim laughed and rumpled her hair the way her old basketball coach used to do when she missed an easy shot. "I don't *think* that, on your salary, you can't afford to tip the driver. I *know* you can't afford it."

***

On the way to Connecticut, Laura rediscovered that female hormones abhor a vacuum. As she replayed her latest conversation with Simon, her dormant crush on him swept into the void that losing Nick had left. Why had he kept his arm around her for so long? Was he trying to say that he had a crush on her, too?

If she were dealing with an American man, she might have had answers. But she had scarcely begun to understand Englishmen when her summer at Oxford ended. She had never quite learned how to distinguish between neutral British gallantry and a more personal interest. And while the American bosses she knew tried to avoid even the appearance of affairs with underlings, Simon made no secret of his belief that sexual harassment laws grew out of an absurdly puritanical streak in the national character.

No less unsettling was her sense that if Simon *did* have a crush on her, he might be out of her emotional range. He said so little about his private affairs that nobody at *Cassandra* was sure whether he was straight or gay, and his presence fostered wishful thinking in both sexes. Trying to read him was like trying to read one of those AC/DC sonnets in which Shakespeare coyly withheld the sex of the beloved.

Tim's behavior unnerved her as much as Simon's. What did he

mean by tucking a flower behind her ear? Had he meant to do more than confirm her sense that she was underdressed?

By the time the car reached Rose Bluffs, Laura decided that she had to try to meet a few men whom she might understand better than Simon or Tim. She asked Eddie where single women met men in New York.

"Not sure, miss," he said. "I must say that I take a lot of young people home from the downtown clubs. But I hardly ever have the same two people in my car more than once. If I pick up a man and woman at a club one week, no matter what they were doing with each other in the car then, I'll see them with someone different next time."

Eddie looked gratefully at his tip. "I'll tell you one thing. I'd look into that nice young man who called for the car. Feel sort of sorry for him. I pick him up just about every week at the airport, and he's never got a girl waiting."

"You never know in cases like that," Laura said idly, thinking again about Simon. "Maybe he's gay."

Eddie burst out laughing. "Oh, no, miss, I must have given you the wrong impression. He never has girls waiting for him at the airport. But that's not the same as not having girls."

8
Bad Chi

Ever since she got her job at *Cassandra,* Laura had put off looking for an apartment, and not just because she loved living near a beach in the summer. She had the impression that finding an apartment in Manhattan resembled a cross between going on an Outward Bound expedition and getting into Harvard. You needed a certain amount of physical stamina just to keep climbing up to fifth-floor walk-ups or racing from agents' offices to vacant units before somebody rented them. If you found an apartment you liked, you had to supply the kind of references normally submitted to Ivy League admissions officers while writing a check for a sum that could buy you a degree from a community college in Geauga County, Ohio.

But Laura had never imagined living in Connecticut. She pictured herself as Audrey Hepburn in Gap jeans, coming home to an elegant brownstone on a tree-lined street and keeping an atomizer in her mailbox so she could spray her pulse points with perfume on the way to her sparkling nights on the town. And now that she had broken up with Nick, she had to get her furniture out of the apartment that he was turning into a set for *Animal House: The Next Generation*. So she began poring over the classified ads, calling rental agents, and exploring the streets of seductive neighborhoods, hoping that she'd see a "For Rent" sign in the window of a townhouse with a polished brass door knocker in the shape of a pineapple or a lion's head.

When none of it led to a place she could afford, she sent email messages to friends back home in case the word of a great apartment had somehow trickled back along the Pennsylvania Turnpike to Ohio.

To: Molly Chase
From: Laura Smart

Hi Molly,
Have discovered that looking for a place in Manhattan isn't just a full-time job—it's a full-time job working for Orson Welles in *Citizen Kane*—and wondered if you could let me know if you hear about any apartments from people in the New York office of your firm.

Am perfectly willing to give up things seen as essential by Cleveland friends, including: 1) eat-in kitchen, 2) bedroom, and 3) working plumbing. (Don't even mention the word "doorman"—it's hopeless.) Still can't find a place.

Cheers,
Laura

To: Laura Smart
From: Molly Chase

Hi Laura,
Sent an email to some of the younger associates and found most living in places like Hoboken or Weehawken, New Jersey, and commuting to city via the PATH train. Had visions of these people roaming the docks looking the way Marlon Brando would have looked in *On the Waterfront*—tight pants, black leather jackets, ripped T-shirts—if he had carried a Dunhill briefcase.

But younger associates say Hoboken and Weehawken are now chic and rents are "very affordable"—a couple of thousand a month gets you a great one-bedroom with spectacular views of Hudson River and New York skyline. One coworker said, "Even lawyers making $100,000+ a year can't afford to live in Manhattan." Feel sure that he must have been exaggerating, so will try friends at other firms and get back to you.

Molly

To: Molly Chase
From: Laura Smart

Hi Molly,
"A couple of thousand a month" is out of the question—at least while I'm working for *Cassandra*—so I'd love to know if you hear of anything else.

It seems that the general principle of glamour jobs in New York is that salaries vary inversely with those of the people you work for. (Obviously conflicts totally with the strange practices that you say exist at companies you represent, where the secretaries of top executives are presumed to have more responsibility than others and therefore to deserve more money.)

The basic idea in publishing is that of Cash Flow by Osmosis: who needs further payment when you're spending all day standing over a machine making copies of the manuscript of John Grisham's new novel? Or working for Cassandra Lovelace (who could probably have bought my parents' old bakery several times over with one week's—day's?—salary)?

Cheers,
Laura

To: Laura Smart
From: Molly Chase

Hi Laura,

Bad news. Friends at other firms say rents even in Hoboken and Weehawken now exceed reach of many young apartment-hunters.

Keep in mind that some of the Jeremiahs are litigators with a tendency to see things in the needlessly dramatic terms—unlike the cast of *The Practice*, always keenly attuned to elegant nuances of plight of less fortunate, including bug fetishist once defended by Jimmy Berlutti. (You *can* get ABC in New York, can't you?). Chad, who worked in New York for a couple of summers in law school, said to tell you that if you keep having trouble finding a place, "Jersey City is the next Hoboken."

Molly

To: Molly Chase
From: Laura Smart

Hi Molly,

Not quite ready to try Jersey City—or Staten Island, helpful suggestion made by cousin Tina, who thinks I am "too picky" about where I live—but appreciate the tip.

Fortunately, ABC is one of the few networks received by the rabbit ears television set at Rose Bluffs. Who needs a $5,000 flat screen?

Cheers,
Laura

Laura thought she had made a breakthrough in finding a place when Caitlin, after listening to her on the phone during lunch hours, gave her a tip. "Don't you know that nobody under thirty finds an apartment through the real-estate section in the *New York Times*? You've got to check the online listings posted daily by the *Village Voice*."

But Laura either couldn't respond quickly enough to the *Voice* listings or found that they involved unfathomable living arrangements, such as sharing an apartment with two roommates, both of whom were considering sex-change operations. So she began dropping in at rental agents' offices, hoping that she would hear of a place that hadn't yet appeared in a listing. At one of her first stops, an agent seemed to want to see a list of all the landlords she'd had since she was a fetus.

"How can I give you a 'list'?" Laura asked. "I've had only one apartment since I got out of college. Before that, I lived with my mother to save money."

The agent looked at her pityingly. He pointed toward a woman in an expensive pants suit who had just opened a briefcase that held a sheaf of laser-printed résumés, several letters from rabbis, and her bat mitzvah photograph. The picture was a hedge against the skepticism fostered by the fake letters of reference from clergy members that tended to turn up when desirable apartments came on the market. Attempting to soften the blow, the agent suggested that she return when she was "prepared."

Next Laura spoke to a woman who told her about a place that, though "practically in Soho," was "technically in Little Italy." The agent added that the apartment was "unrenovated" but had "a lot of character" and might remind her of "a charming *pensione* in Rome." Laura found out, when she visited it, that this meant that it had a claw-foot bathtub in the kitchen and a pull-chain toilet.

Still another agent told her that he might have a couple of places available if they hadn't been rented by the people he'd just sent over. The first apartment, though "practically in Chelsea," was "technically in Hell's Kitchen," and the second, though "practically in Washington Heights," was "technically in the South Bronx." Laura went to the place in Hell's Kitchen and learned from the building superintendent that another woman had rented it, undeterred by the sight of two men doing a drug deal on the sidewalk. She was so frightened by the South Bronx that, the moment she emerged from the subway, she turned around and went back to Manhattan without visiting the apartment.

Just when she might have despaired, Laura got a note that gave her a whiff of hope.

To: Laura Smart
From: Molly Chase

Hi Laura,
Haven't heard from you in a while, so I assume you've found a place to live. But if not, I heard about apartment just vacated by a paralegal in our New York office that's supposed to be a great deal. Want the details?

Molly

To: Molly Chase
From: Laura Smart

Yes yes yes yes yes yes yes yes yes yes yes yes yes yes yes yes yes yes yes yes yes yes yes yes yes yes yes yes yes yes yes yes yes yes yes yes yes yes yes yes yes yes yes yes yes yes yes yes

(I know that I sound like Molly Bloom but I finally understand why New Yorkers talk about apartments the way people in other places talk about sex, complete with gasps, moans, sighs, tears, squeals, and pleading.)

P.S.   Could we switch to instant messaging for this? Have irrational
fear that I may lose only possible apartment in New York owing to
few seconds' difference between speed of regular and instant email.

M: Okay, I should tell you up front that the place has a
few problems.

L: What kind of "problems"? Dictionary definition of
this term differs slightly from that of New Yorkers
looking for apartments ...

M: I don't want to prejudice you because the apartment is
such a great deal. But the gist of it is that Barbara, the
paralegal, took a course in feng shui and got interested
in the energy that the Japanese call *chi*. As I understand
it, *chi* is a little like cholesterol. There's good *chi* and
bad *chi*. Barbara decided that the apartment had the
kind of *chi* that could give you a heart attack—

L: A little bad *chi* couldn't be worse than living with the
Lake Effect.

M: It's not quite as simple as that, or so I gather from
Tony Slavin, the associate Barbara works for. Barbara
heard that hanging a wind chime just inside her door
would redistribute the energy in her apartment and
banish the bad *chi*, so she got the super to install one.

The chime fell on another tenant, Derek, when he
stopped by to borrow a can of Black Flag roach spray
and injured him. Or at least that's his story. Derek
sued Barbara, and Barbara countersued. Barbara
claims Derek was trespassing, because he didn't have
permission to enter her apartment. She also accuses
Derek of being an "insect Hitler" who caused the bad
chi through acts of "roach genocide."

The whole thing is a mess. Barbara moved out,
and Derek is threatening to. And lawyers for both
parties are taking depositions from everybody in the

building. It's like *Lord of the Flies* in there.

L: (Silence)

M: Laura?

L: Just weighing worst possible results of Lake Effect against those of living in *Lord of the Flies* building with "insect Hitler"…

M: All right, then here's the rest: Barbara also bought a small fountain to enhance the "prosperity sector" of her apartment. But she was so upset by the legal proceedings that she forgot to turn it off one day before she left for work. The fountain overflowed and damaged the floor, and strictly speaking, the landlord can't advertise the unit until the super brings it up to code again. But Tony thinks that if you wanted to rent the place unofficially on a month-to-month lease until the problem gets fixed …

L: You mean, if I offered to rent the apartment under the table?

M: Not sure I'd use that exact phrase. I'd just drop by and tell the super that you heard he might have an apartment available. If he likes you, he might put in a good word for you with the rental agent.

L: It sounds a little complicated—

M: Tony says this is nothing compared with what some people do to get apartments in New York—watching the obituaries, going up to members of grieving families at Frank Campbell's to get the inside track …

L: Frank Campbell's? The funeral home?

M: Mmm-hmm. Tony says there's one other thing you should know about the building. The super is hard of hearing, so he doesn't talk much, and he's mildly paranoid about crime. He wears a deerstalker's cap and subscribes to *Guns & Ammo*, and he sometimes carries a plastic rifle. Everybody calls him Jacko, although I'm not sure whether that's his real name or he has a Michael Jackson obsession. Tony says that the way to get on his good side is to bring any gun magazine. But don't let this scare you. In New York the supers have so much power that, to some extent, they all have delusions of grandeur …

***

Laura pounded on a door decorated with a plaque that said "Hank Jacovich: Building Superintendent" and an array of signs: DON'T BLOCK THE BOX, TRESPASSERS WILL BE VIO-LATED, and PRIVATE PROPERTY: NO HUNTING OR FISHING. She couldn't tell whether somebody had stolen the signs or bought them from one of the souvenir shops in Times Square that sold kitschy T-shirts that said: MY CHILD IS AN HONOR STUDENT IN THE STATE CORRECTIONAL FACILITY. She had no idea whether Jacko had a kinky sense of humor or was completely crazy.

After a few minutes, a man in a hat with earflaps peered out through a peephole. Laura shouted that she was looking for an apartment. Jacko opened the door, with a toy rifle clutched under his arm, and stared at her. Laura asked again if he had an apart-ment available. He squinted at her intently and remained still, as though listening for the sound of twigs snapping underfoot.

Clutching her shoulder bag tighter against her body, Laura understood why people kept trying to find apartments through the *Times* even though you might have a better chance of locating one through a Ouija board. The newspaper probably had some kind of radar that screened out the crackpots. As nonchalantly as possible, she showed Jacko a copy of *Guns and Gear* that she had bought at a magazine store.

"Would you like this? As a gift for showing me the apartment?"

Jacko grunted and snatched the magazine away. He studied her as though she were a deer that might or might not be worth the trouble of killing, then nodded and led her up four flights of stairs. After fumbling with his key ring, he opened the door to a small, dark apartment with low ceilings and bars across a window on a fire escape.

Laura's heart sank. The apartment was painted an unappetizing gray that a brochure left on the kitchen counter identified as one of the feng shui "colors of the year." A hole in the floor marked the spot where the fountain had stood. Narrow and cheerless, the apartment resembled the interior of a military transport plane in a World War II movie—the kind of place where paratroopers said their last Hail Marys before getting impaled on treetops.

Grinning, Jacko pointed to the floor and walls and made a series of grunts that Laura took to mean he would fix the hole in the floor and paint the apartment before she moved in. By the time the third cockroach had scurried out of the closet, she felt sure she couldn't live in a place that Jacko clearly expected her to accept on the spot. Hoping to think of a tactful way to edify him, she suggested that they go downstairs and talk further.

They entered the super's apartment just as a young woman was leaving an agitated message on his answering machine, saying that she'd heard from a second-floor tenant that the vacant unit was "fantastic" and that she wanted to see it right away. Laura was dumbstruck. Fantastic? Caught off guard by an unexpected rival for a place she regarded as uninhabitable, she tried to analyze the situation rationally. Instead, she spoke as though she had traded vocal chords with someone else.

"Please, Jacko! I *have* to have this apartment. I *have* to. You'll never regret it if you give it to me." Laura knew she was babbling, but she couldn't stop. She wished she had brought along her First Holy Communion photo. "I have great credit and great references and a great job working for a famous boss, Cassandra Lovelace …"

"Cassandra?" For the first time, Jacko sounded impressed. He pointed to a photo of Laura's boss on the cover of a television guide.

"Yes, I work for *that* Cassandra."

"Autographed picture?"

"Yes, if I get the apartment, I can get you an autographed pic-ture of her." Laura prayed this was true even as she realized that she was becoming a person who didn't just accept once-unthinkable perks but promised them to others.

Jacko glanced again at the photo of Cassandra, then rum-maged in a drawer for a stubby pencil. He wrote down the address of the rental agent and said he would call to let him know he could expect her. Laura rushed to the office, wrote a check for a sum larger than the cost of her first car, and was told that if her credit references checked out, the apartment was hers.

***

After boarding the train to Connecticut, Laura panicked. She couldn't imagine why she had paid so much for the apart-ment. To live there she would have to give up everything she once saw as vital, including furniture if Nick wouldn't part with most of the items in their old apartment. And because of the code violations, she could get only a month-to-month lease, which meant that she might have to endure another harrowing search when the place officially went on the market. She prayed that Alice or perhaps Mr. Dudley, a retired lawyer, would know how she could get her security deposit back. There had to be a loophole in the laws that would save her from having to live in such a deathtrap.

Laura found Alice correcting papers in a wing chair beside the fireplace at Rose Bluffs. As a soft breeze blew in from the Sound, she realized that Audrey Hepburn's Holly Golightly lacked the one thing that was indispensable to single women in New York: female friends. For all her allure, Audrey had nobody to talk after a bad day to except her cat and the men who slipped her fifty dollars for the powder room. She was a man's woman in the days when women had to choose sides—you were a man's woman or a woman's woman—and who would want to make that choice today? Even Samantha Jones on *Sex and the City* knew that you needed to have it both ways.

After taking another wing chair, Laura suspected that her best friend's day had gone no better than her own. Alice was teaching a summer school course in American history at her private school and, as she set aside a stack of papers filled with red marks, had frown lines around her eyes that resembled the faint cracks in an old fine-china teacup.

"Big test today?"

"A summer midterm, and you can't imagine the answers you get from tenth-graders whose parents have been grooming them for the Ivies since nursery school." Alice picked up a paper from the stack she had set aside and read aloud. "The South succeeded from the Union …"

Laura laughed. "I'm sorry, Alice. It just struck me as funny."

"You don't have to apologize. I thought it was funny, too, the first time I saw it on a test."

"The first time? How often do you see that?"

"A lot more than you'd think. I've also asked 'Who started the Boxer Rebellion?' and gotten back, 'Calvin Klein,' 'Jockey,' and 'Fruit-of-the-Loom.'"

Alice put the test back in her stack of papers. "The worst of it is that you can't correct students any more. My school has a policy that forbids teachers from telling students that they're wrong. Ella Foster, the head of the school, thinks it's damaging to a child's self-esteem to be told that, for example, Benjamin Franklin was not president of the United States. So you have to find other ways to introduce students to reality. Mrs. Foster sent out a memo called, 'Twenty-Five Ways to Avoid Telling Students They're Wrong.' It was a list of things you could say instead of, 'No' or, 'That's incorrect' when a student gives an answer that's completely out of the ballpark. You could say, 'That's a possibility' or 'Let's think about that.' The list is useful in some cases. But what do you say to students who think that Benjamin Franklin was president? 'That's a possibility?' You have to correct them without correcting them."

"What do you do when you get, 'Calvin Klein started the Boxer Rebellion?'"

"I might start by asking the student to define the Boxer Rebellion or where it took place. But sometimes the Socratic approach seems so inefficient that I do tell students that they're wrong. So I get into a lot of trouble with Mrs. Foster."

Mrs. Brennan walked into the living room carrying a silver tray that held a bottle of sherry, two glasses, and a plate of Carr's Water Biscuits. Alice took one of the glasses. Laura, who usually declined the housekeeper's offers of sherry, took the other. She wished that the Dudleys had a higher opinion of beer, which she occasionally craved on a hot day but hadn't had the nerve to bring into the house.

Alice didn't miss the change in her habits. "It looks as though you had the same kind of day I did. Did you lose another apartment?"

"Worse. I *got* an apartment."

Laura poured out the story of her email from Molly, her meeting with Jacko, and her impulsive decision to pay a fortune for the privilege of living out a scene from *Lord of the Flies* every day. To her surprise Alice didn't think she had made a mistake.

"Just about everybody who rents an apartment in the city for the first time has a similar reaction," Alice said. "Look at the benefits of your place. You have an apartment on the Upper East Side instead of in an iffy neighborhood, like the Bowery or meat-packing district that might horrify your parents. You don't have to live with three roommates. Your place might look better after the super fixes it up, and when you need a break, you can come here. And you might fall in love with the man downstairs the way Audrey did in *Breakfast at Tiffany's*."

"Even Audrey Hepburn couldn't give my apartment charm, to say nothing of safety." Laura told Alice the story of how she'd gotten her name.

"When my mother came to this country, she fell in love with American movies. *Breakfast at Tiffany's* was her favorite, and she wanted to name me Holly after Holly Golightly. But the priests in the Hungarian community were conservative, much more so than some of the American ones. They didn't like to baptize babies who didn't have saints' names, although girls could have female counterparts of male saints' names. My mother knew that Holly wouldn't pass the test. So she named me for the Gene Tierney character in the old movie *Laura* because priests could recognize Laura as a derivative of Lawrence. Even so, my father used to joke that he thought about taking a map of the St. Lawrence Seaway to my baptism. He said he could whip it out over the font if anybody raised an eyebrow."

Laura took a sip of her sherry. "In other words, instead of getting named after someone who was full of life, I got named after a heroine who was dead by the time the movie started. My parents might still have felt guilty about not giving me a name the priests would have liked better, such as Mary. When my brother came along, they gave him the No. 1 box-office hit among the Hungarian-Catholic clergy. St. Stephen is the patron saint of Hungary."

"But Laura is a such lovely name!" Alice said. "And you're probably much better off with Laura than with Holly. It raises fewer associations in people's minds. It might be hard to live up to a name that makes people think of Audrey Hepburn in a big hat. You don't regret not being named after Holly Golightly, do you?"

"Not really. If I had, I might have heard as many jokes about my first name as about Smart. I don't think parochial-school students could have resisted playing off the words 'holy' and 'Holly' with things like 'Holly Smokes!' Or worse." Laura's eye strayed to the Dudley family motto on the fireplace. "It's just that for so long I've fantasized about having a place with an upstairs neighbor like Mr. Yunioshi in *Breakfast at Tiffany's* …"

"I think you're missing the point of that movie," Alice said. "Holly Golightly felt drawn to New York for some of the reasons that you did. She'd outgrown her hometown and needed to live where she could expand. But she didn't move to New York to become, say, an Edith Wharton heroine. She moved to the city to become herself. If she'd tried to make herself into Lily Bart, she wouldn't have been Holly Golightly. If you try to make yourself into Holly Golightly, you'll be doing the opposite of what she did. You can only have the kind of life she had by doing it your way."

In theory Laura agreed with Alice. In reality she had so many mental images of New York from books and movies that she wasn't sure that she had any ideas about it that were her own. If she couldn't take her cues from what she'd seen or read, she'd need another sign to show her the way. She was still wishing that she had it when Wickford Dudley shuffled through the living room carrying his metal detector, after his evening walk on the beach.

Alice got up and kissed her father. "No buried treasures tonight?"

"No, just a rusty key that fell out of somebody's pocket. But I brought it home for my collection. You never know what a rusty key might open."

It wasn't exactly the kind of sign Laura had envisioned. But she decided that, in the absence of any others, she would take it. She could almost imagine that her new building superintendent looked like Mr. Yunioshi.

9

Accounting

"Simon, you said you were amazed by how *low* my expenses were for the Normendie Latour interview. You told me that I was the first writer who had produced a cover story for *Cassandra* for the cost of a WNBA basketball."

"I *was* amazed by how low your expenses were."

"Then why is Accounting refusing to pay for the basketball? It's bad enough that somebody in the department sat on my expense report for days. Now I find out that Accounting won't pay for the ball at all."

The August issue of *Cassandra* had just come out, and Laura's joy on seeing her first cover story in the magazine had given way to anger when she received a note from the corporate side, turning down her request for reimbursement. The amount that she'd paid for the basketball, which had once seemed modest, had expanded in her mind to the size of the gross domestic product of a major industrialized nation after she learned the appalling amount she'd have to pay in rent each month.

Laura handed her rejected expense claim to Simon, who was seated at his desk editing a manuscript and listening to Edward Elgar's *Enigma Variations* on the BBC. The erratic air-conditioning in the office was on the blink again, and the oppressive summer heat mingled with the smoke of Marlboros and gave his office the air of an indoor barbecue pit. He studied the form, then read aloud from an attached note:

Dear Ms. Smart,

We regret to inform you that basketballs do not fall into an approved expense category at Carapace. Please be advised that if you wish to obtain an item of this sort in the future, you must submit your request through our Purchasing Department, so that we may take advantage of any bulk-buying discounts that are available to our company.

Sincerely,
Irene Field
Accounting Manager

"Perfectly clear, isn't it?" Simon said. "If you want to buy a basketball, you have to go through Purchasing, so that somebody can decide whether it would be cheaper to buy enough basketballs for the entire NBA."

Too upset to sit down, Laura began to pace. "Do you think this is funny?"

"I didn't say it was funny. But it has an amusing side, doesn't it? For sheer comic relief, nothing beats a sprightly memo from Accounting."

Simon scanned a bookshelf above his desk. "Did you ever read a book called *A Martian Wouldn't Say That?* It's a collection of memos written by network executives to television writers and producers. The title refers to an old show called *My Favorite Martian.* A network executive once wrote to the producers to say, 'Please change the dialogue on Page 14. A Martian wouldn't say that.'"

Laura saw the disadvantage of working for an unflappable boss. She appreciated his good humor, but it was beginning to grate.

"I'm having trouble seeing the amusing side of a memo that means I'm out nearly a hundred dollars. What would you suggest I do about it?"

"Redo your expense report and bury the basketball. You don't need receipts for expenses of under ten dollars. So you can hide the cost of the ball in other categories."

After twelve years of parochial school, Laura balked at the idea of making up so many claims, having had to say a dozen Hail Marys for lesser sins. "Maybe I'll absorb the expense. I just never thought that *Cassandra* might operate, in some ways, on a tighter budget than *Buckeye*. The business manager there might have questioned me about the ball, but he'd have paid for it. He didn't blink when I handed in a bill for the knitting needles I bought as a prop for a story about women who knit with dog hair."

"If you're upset, why don't you call your friend Tim? He could overrule an accountant."

"Tim is not my friend." Laura said. "He invited me to a party at his apartment, and I accepted. At your suggestion, if you recall."

"Whether or not he's your friend, you might keep it in mind," Simon said breezily. "I'm sure that you'll hear from him again soon."

Laura looked at him sharply. "What makes you say that?"

"Tim called this morning. He was afraid that Liz Kaiser might give you more trouble about your story on Normendie now that it's on newsstands. Quite right, I'm afraid. For days Liz will be fending off calls from journalists who are angry that she 'gave' the story to you instead of them. That will put her in the infuriating position of having to admit that she didn't give you anything— that you found a way around her—or pretending that she did give it to you, which will make other writers demand similar privileges. Tim said he'd be glad to try to help, perhaps give Normendie a call, if you have problems. He said he noticed that you were a bit disturbed by your brush with Liz at his party."

"Tim seems to have forgotten that I was disturbed because *he* invited Liz to the party. He led me to think that he didn't even like her."

"He doesn't like her, and he didn't invite her. He invited Jerry Zilcher, her walker, who brought her. Tim and Jerry have known each other for years. Jerry has a boat, and Tim crews for him occasionally."

Tim likes to sail? Laura was now sure that she ought to consider introducing Tim to Alice if, as Eddie had implied, he went out with women besides Brandy. But would someone at his level be offended by the suggestion that he couldn't manage his own social life?

"This may sound a little presumptuous," Laura said tentatively. "But Brandy lives in Chicago, and I've been thinking that Tim might like to meet my best friend. Alice is kind and pretty and so well bred that she'd never embarrass him by drinking too much blueberry vodka. I wonder if there would be any harm in my fixing them up." Laura tried to arrange her afterthoughts about the party into a coherent line of reasoning. "It may sound crazy, but I have a feeling that Tim might be interested in me, and I know you think I ought to be nice to him. But he's really more Alice's type than mine. If he *were* my type, I wouldn't want to risk my job by going out with a man who worked for our company …"

Laura thought she saw Simon try to hide a flicker of disappointment. "So you thought the perfect solution would be to introduce Tim to your best friend?"

"I've considered it," Laura admitted. "They both know a lot of people who might as well have dollar signs for middle initials."

Simon leaned back in his Regency swivel chair and debated the idea. "Well, why not? It might be interesting to see Tim's reaction."

"I haven't talked to Alice about this," Laura added quickly. "And she'd probably want to marry a different kind of man. But she's really frustrated with her social life. And she's such a terrific person that I thought, what do I have to lose?"

Simon looked at her with admiration. "Laura, I knew you had self-confidence by the way you went after Normendie. But I didn't realize you had the courage to think you had nothing to lose by trying to fix up a man who may have dated her."

"Are you saying that I shouldn't risk it even though it might be 'interesting' to see Tim's reaction?"

"I think that if you tried to fix Tim up he would be as stunned as any corporate officer whom you approached with such an offer after a month on the job. I also think that, after he recovered from his amazement, he would be charmed. So, in a sense, you're right. You do have nothing to lose."

Simon studied Laura for a moment. "But I should warn you that if you're thinking of introducing Tim to your friend because you hope to discourage any interest in you, you may be acting on a mistaken assumption. Tim strikes me as one of those straight arrows who would never risk the complications of an affair with somebody in a lower position at Carapace. When one of his sports magazines did a story on Brandy, he refused to go out with her until it was off the newsstands, although they met at a promotional event just before it came out. He didn't want people to think that she had received the exposure because of him. Rather gallant, don't you think?"

All of this raised enough doubts in Laura's mind that she decided to give her idea a bit more thought before acting on it. But she was convinced that it had promise.

"I should also warn you that you'll probably have more important things to do presently," Simon went on. "Cassandra called this morning to say that she hopes to resume her normal working schedule at the magazine in a day or two, which should keep us all busy."

The phone rang before he could elaborate, and he took a call from a publicist named Bruce who offered him the use of a luxury sport utility vehicle in exchange for running an article on the car in *Cassandra*, preferably with a photo of a major star at the wheel. Simon turned down the offer by saying that even if Harrison Ford would agree to the deal, he had never mastered driving on the right.

When the phone rang again, Simon glanced at the Caller ID number. "It's Cassandra, perhaps calling back to make sure that somebody stocks the minibar in her office with white apricots before she returns. So I'll have to take it. If you decide to go ahead with your idea of fixing Tim up, do let me know what happens. I saw him trying to put Brandy to bed fully dressed after you left the party. He might enjoy meeting someone more—how shall I put it?—cooperative."

Back at her desk, Laura found that she had an email from Tim.

To: Laura Smart
From: Tim Moran_Carapace

Great story on Normendie! You "got" her in a way that no other writer has.

I sent the story to Normendie by messenger, and she loves it. She told Liz that she wants you to help her write memoirs someday. I can't tell you Liz's response now, because it's unprintable in email. If you let me take you out for a drink or dinner sometime to celebrate your first cover story in *Cassandra*, I'll tell you then.

This message left her feeling torn. She didn't want to encourage Tim, but having a drink with him might give her an opening to fix him up with Alice. And she was already beginning to dread returning to her new apartment each night.

When she moved in, she found that Jacko hadn't painted the unit and had "fixed" the hole in the floor by nailing plywood over the damaged boards instead of replacing them. She stubbed her toe whenever she got out of bed in the dark to investigate a noise on the fire escape and, at times, had the sense that the Dickensian conditions represented a twisted form retaliation by her super. Jacko was furious that she hadn't produced the autographed picture of Cassandra that she had promised him, as though it was her fault that she hadn't met the editor-in-chief, let alone had a chance to ask for a signed eight-by-ten glossy. In desperation she had sent a note to the publicity department at her network asking for a photo. But it hadn't arrived, and every delay caused Jacko to regard her with deeper suspicion.

Nor was she getting any sympathy about the situation from her downstairs neighbor, Derek, who had instead been hounding her to sign a petition asking the landlord to bar furnishings that involved "water or liquids in any form," including "waterbeds, lava lamps, goldfish bowls, and vases more than six inches wide or eight inches tall." Apparently a lawyer had told him that if he used the words "feng shui" he might be accused of discriminating against the Chinese. So he had instead listed every water-bearing item that had existed from the days of the ancient Egyptians to the present, stopping just short of monogrammed shot glasses from auto-body shops.

It hardly helped that, after their breakup, Nick had claimed both their sofa and bed. She had ordered a sofa bed, but it hadn't arrived, and the sales clerk had left her with the impression that expecting a sofa to be delivered promptly in New York was like hoping to find all of your favorite flavors of Snapple in Albania. So she was sleeping on an air mattress that she had to inflate with a bicycle pump, and she couldn't get it to work properly. She kept waking up to find that air had leaked out, so she was sleeping on what felt like a shower curtain laid over a cement block. Every day she arrived at work feeling bruised. A drink with Tim might give her a short reprieve from all of it. She felt slightly nervous about having dinner with someone so high up in her company and decided that, if she was going to do it, she might as well get it over with.

To: Tim Moran_Carapace
From: Laura Smart

This is a Hail Mary pass, but what are you doing after work tonight?

To: Laura Smart
From: Tim Moran_Carapace

Taking you to the best restaurant in New York to celebrate your first cover story in *Cassandra*. By the way, although you're too young for this metaphor, I'm the Gerard Phelan of catching Hail Mary passes. Try me anytime.

To: Tim Moran_Carapace
From: Laura Smart

I would be too young for the metaphor if I hadn't gone to Notre Dame. Have you forgotten that Boston College ranks among the most ferocious rivals of the Irish? (There are no "Irish" in Boston, only in South Bend.)

Wasn't that pass to Phelan from Doug Flutie—something like fifty yards, five seconds left in the game—in a Sugar Bowl in the 1980s?

To: Laura Smart
From: Tim Moran

Forty-eight yards, six seconds, Orange Bowl, 1984. But impressive enough. (Some women think Phelan is a grade you get in chemistry.) I'll still take you to dinner.

Good to know there are no Irish in Boston, a fact I'd missed while growing up in Wellesley. (Didn't move to Lakewood until the eighth grade.) Maybe the lack of Irish in Boston escaped me because BC— my alma mater—has an eagle for a mascot instead of a leprechaun?

Laura saw that she had somehow committed herself to dinner, not a drink, and regretted that she didn't have time to go home and change before she headed for "the best restaurant in New York." She flipped mentally through the list of elegant places where Tim might take her: Nobu? Le Bernardin? Alain Ducasse at the Essex House? Or maybe the River Café, where the view was the most alluring entrée? It was exciting to think that she would at last go to a romantic New York restaurant with a man who—if Alice was right—might be interested in her. If only she didn't put her elbow in a soup bowl trimmed with gold leaf or drop a fork as heavy as lug wrench, she thought, it would be the perfect evening.

10
Cheers

Laura had never been a restaurant snob, a status that took real effort to achieve in a gastronomically challenged city like Cleveland. If you wanted to spend your life looking for one perfectly grilled Argentine shrimp—or have your day ruined by what the chef had done to the celery sorbet or fish tartare—you would pretty much have to begin someplace else.

Even so, Laura didn't feel optimistic when Tim asked her to meet him at a restaurant on the Lower East Side called Babcia's, explaining that the name meant "Grandma's" in Polish. Apart from what she had learned from her parents, she had taken most of her ideas about restaurants from the writer Nelson Algren, who had distilled a lifetime of dining out in the Midwest to a single line, "Never eat at a place called Mom's." If Algren didn't think too much of places called "Mom's," she could only imagine what he would have said about places called "Grandma's."

So she was surprised to find that Babcia's was a fresh and pretty restaurant with what she thought of as prosperous Polish-farmhouse décor: whitewashed walls, rough-hewn beams, colorful folk art, and vases full of flowers and linden branches. Tim was sipping a small glass of plum brandy, and when she arrived, a waitress brought another for her.

"Na Zdrowie!" she said, setting the glass down. Laura recognized the toast—*Naz-DRO-veey-ay!*—from weddings she'd attended in Cleveland, which had to have at least as many Polish residents as German, Slovenian, Russian, or Hungarian.

"Sto lat," Laura replied, using another Polish toast.

"Are you Pole-eesh?" the waitress asked.

"Hungarian."

The waitress, whom Tim introduced as "Babcia's daughter, Regina," lit up. She said that since Polish and Hungarian cooking had many similarities, she did not want the two of them to order off the menu. She would bring what she thought they would like.

"Okay with you?" Tim asked, smiling. "Pierogies and grilled onions are the specialty here."

"I'd love that," Laura said truthfully. She was beginning to miss the kind of food she'd grown up with after all the lamb chops she'd had at Rose Bluffs and the mix-and-match salads she picked up on the way home after work.

After the waitress left, Tim said that he was glad she'd emailed him that day because he was leaving the next day on another trip to France.

"My job is fun, but you can imagine what it does to my social life," he said. "When other people are on Martha's Vineyard or in the Hamptons, I'm preparing for meetings by going over quarterly earnings forecasts in a hotel room on the Right Bank."

"Your social life looked fine on the Fourth."

Tim was about to say something when Regina returned with a basket of rye and poppy seed rolls. He took a roll and asked Laura if she had played basketball at Notre Dame.

"I played for St. Rose's but wasn't good enough to get recruited by Notre Dame. Or any other college except a couple of very small schools close to home. The only thing I was really better at than some of the other girls was free throws. I missed a million easy shots in the heat of the game. But for some reason, whenever I had a chance to stand on the free throw line and collect my thoughts, I was a ninety-five percenter. So my teammates were always praying that, in a close game, I'd get elbowed in the eye socket by a six-foot-three girl from Blessed Sacrament or Our Lady of Lourdes."

"Ever think of playing as a walk-on at Notre Dame? I was an occasional relief pitcher for St. Izzy's, nowhere near good enough for BC to recruit me. But I tried out for the Eagles as a walk-on. Amazingly, I ended up starting in a couple of games after one pitcher got injured and another couldn't keep up his GPA."

Laura was surprised that Tim had gone to the elite high school on the West Side of Cleveland. The boys of St. Izzy's had mostly ignored her at dances in favor of the girls from their sister school. It was gratifying to think that her stock might have gone up at last.

"I started thinking about playing as a walk-on the minute Notre Dame accepted me. But then I got tripped by a guard from Holy Innocents during the PAL championship and broke my leg during my last game for St. Rose's. I had to have an operation and sort of took that as a sign from God that my athletic career was over."

In the dim light Laura thought she saw Tim freeze. Before she could ask if anything was wrong, Regina returned with salads made from cucumbers, sour cream, and onions.

"Like Hungarian, no?" Regina asked. "*Uborkasaláta?*"

"You're right," Laura said, then asked how the waitress knew the Hungarian term for "cucumber salad."

"Many Hungarian people come to Babcia's. Always ask for the cucumbers salad."

"I would have, too, if you hadn't brought it. Cucumbers are my mother's favorite vegetable."

Regina left only to return a few minutes later with a tray filled with the house specialties—grilled onions, kielbasa with sauerkraut, pierogies filled with meat, cheese, or potatoes. Laura hadn't known she could get that kind of home cooking in the city. One of her friends in Cleveland had said that New York suffered from "pan-seared tuna blight" and that "pan-seared" was a euphemism for "raw."

As they worked their way through the huge quantity of food, Laura wished that Tim didn't work for her company. He was nowhere near as attractive as Nick, but he listened to her in a way that Nick hadn't. Basking in his interest, she couldn't bring herself to break the mood by sticking to her plan to fix him up with Alice.

After she admitted to feeling worried about whether she would get along with Cassandra, Tim offered to serve as a sounding board if she wanted to talk about changes at the magazine. This comment struck her as a non sequitur and made her uneasy. *What changes?* Unwilling to get into specifics, Tim deflected her questions by saying they had a friend in common—her cousin Tina's fiancé: Bradford Newburger, who ran a public-relations firm in Cleveland. Brad had made his name by representing clients nobody else wanted and called himself "the William Kunstler of PR" until Kunstler died. His accounts included a condom boutique called Condom and Gomorrah and a Libyan restaurant that had a party every year on Moammar Gadhafi's birthday.

"You know Brad?" Laura asked, surprised.

"Everybody knows Brad."

Laura smiled. "You're right. Brad says that he has a 'solid-gold Rolodex.' Some of his critics say 'fool's gold.' How do you know him?"

"My mother has a decorating business in Cleveland and once hired Brad to do her PR. But it seems their tastes clashed. He wanted her to redo the interior of Condom and Gomorrah to make it 'more refined.' My mother said, 'The store sells musical condoms, and he wants me to make it refined?'"

Laura was sure that Tim hadn't invented the story about her cousin's fiancé. "I wish I could say that Brad was acting out of character. But, if anything, that idea was tame for him. My cousin Maggie is supposed to sing 'Ave Maria' at his wedding. Brad may come up with a way to make her solo look like one of Madonna's music videos."

Then Tim changed the subject and suggested that she consider ghostwriting a memoir of Normendie Latour. He was sure that the book would help to revive Normendie's career and that the money from it would make it easier for Laura to support herself in the city that he gave her the singer's home phone number in case she wanted to call her to explore the idea. Emboldened by the mention of Normendie, Laura asked if he'd had an affair with her. She was shocked when he admitted instantly that he had.

"Why do you look so amazed?" Tim asked, a bit defensively. "Are you astonished that someone like Normendie would go out with me?"

"No, no," Laura said hastily, unsure of whether she believed her own words. "It's just that Simon told me your romance with Normendie was never substantiated."

"How could it have been substantiated? No reporter ever asked Normendie about it. She had all but dropped out of sight when I started going out with her. Which may explain why she did go out with me. *Rolling Stone* was hardly calling every week. And we didn't stay together for long. She'd never visited the Rock and Roll Hall of Fame, so I took her home to see it and to give my younger sister a thrill. But it was obvious that we were Felix Ungar and Oscar Madison, an odd couple better suited to going to Knicks games than setting up housekeeping. So we've stayed friends with no backsliding into bed."

Laura saw an opening to ask about his date for the Fourth. "Is Brandy just a friend, too?"

"In fact, yes," Tim said, blinking. "I went out with her when she was getting started as a sportscaster. But her problems were too big for me. Brandy needs a man who can get her to stop pushing her self-destruct buttons, which I couldn't. After we broke up, it seemed heartless to abandon somebody who was having a tough time, so we've stayed in touch."

Regina brought a dessert tray and invited them to select from it. Tim took a rum baba and Laura a slice of cherry strudel.

Laura tasted her strudel and thought it was better than her

mother's. "This is wonderful! My mother says that the secret to a good strudel is using lard, not butter, in the dough. She thinks people are too squeamish about using lard today. I'm sure the pastry chef here isn't. This strudel has to have nothing but lard in it—nature's most perfect food."

Tim stared at her. "You think lard is 'nature's most perfect food'?"

***

After they had finished eating, Laura and Tim walked to his car. In the darkness, they could see the gossamer beams of light that marked the spot where the World Trade Center towers had stood. Laura understood why people liked them so much—they looked like railroad tracks to Heaven, or extra-long angels' wings. The beams left her with such a feeling of warmth that she almost wished Tim would kiss her.

But the romantic mood evaporated when they got to her apartment and Tim saw that the lock at the main entrance to the building was broken. She practically had to restrain him forcibly from pounding on Jacko's door and insisting that he call a locksmith on the spot.

When they entered her apartment, she saw that her super had slipped a note under her door making another demand for an autographed picture of Cassandra. Jacko all but accused her of lying through her teeth by promising to give him the photo. He had used cut-out letters to spell "The picture or your life" and pasted them onto a piece of paper along with a photo of Cassandra from *TV Guide* and an ad for a .357 Magnum from one of his gun magazines. Laura hoped that this was just another example of his slightly demented sense of humor. Tim was appalled.

"Laura, you can't live in this place. You *can't*."

"Why not?"

"For one thing, your super is a lunatic."

"He's not a lunatic," Laura said with somewhat more certainty than she felt. "He's an eccentric, like Mr. Yunioshi in *Breakfast at Tiffany's.*"

"Mr. Yunioshi called the police on Audrey Hepburn! He got her arrested. Do you want to go to jail?"

"I interviewed a lot of loony people in Ohio, and none of them hurt me or got me arrested. My police sources had a phrase for people like Jacko—'sick but harmless.'"

"This isn't the Midwest. You have to be more careful here, especially when you're dealing with people who have keys to your apartment."

"A friend of mine says New York supers have so much power that they all have delusions of grandeur."

"New York supers do have delusions of grandeur. But ordinarily this takes the form of demanding exorbitant tips at Christmas, not sending ransom notes."

Laura felt a perverse desire to defend new her new home as zealously as she had once condemned it. "I've talked to Barbara, the woman who used to live in the apartment, and others in the building. They all say Jacko has been acting oddly for years. There's nothing to worry about."

"If your super has been acting oddly for years, that's all the more reason to think that someday he'll snap. You need to find a new apartment."

"Why do you have to be such a pessimist? I prefer to be an optimist in situations like this."

"I'm not a pessimist. I'm a realist. And if you were an optimist, you'd believe that you could find a better apartment."

Laura was losing patience with Tim's ludicrous assumption that you needed nothing more than determination to live in a New York apartment that didn't look like something rejected by the location scouts for *Trainspotting.* As though your salary had nothing to do with it!

"The reason I'm living here," she said levelly, "is that Carapace doesn't pay me enough to live anywhere else."

"In other words," Tim said coolly, "you're blaming me for the fact that you live in a place run by the Rambo of supers."

"I didn't say I was blaming you. I'm merely pointing out the obvious. Carapace doesn't pay its employees a living wage."

"No publishing company pays its employees a living wage. It's one of the privileges of the industry that it allows you to starve with more intellectual satisfaction than you would have in other fields. That's why I suggested that you think of working on a memoir with Normendie. You won't be earning anything close to what you deserve in publishing until you're at least thirty, maybe thirty-five, if you ever do."

Laura tried to stay calm. "I earned a living wage in Cleveland because the parent company of *Buckeye* cared enough to pay us fairly."

"You earned a living wage in Cleveland because the cost of living is half of what it is here."

"Or so you'd like to think."

Tim glanced around her apartment, then got the kind of look on his face that Jimmy Stewart had when he asked Grace Kelly in *Rear Window*, "Just how would you start to cut up a human body?"

"You can keep living here if you'd like," he said stonily. "But I'd prefer to spare Carapace the expense of having to pay your heirs the death benefit on your insurance policy. So I'll remind you of what I said at my party. You're welcome to stay in my extra bedroom if you need a place to crash, and I'd advise you to take me up on the offer immediately and begin looking for a safer apartment. I'd also urge you not to use that tone with Cassandra. She might not take kindly to it. I heard from people in the midtown office that she got back last night, so you'll see that for yourself soon enough."

Laura opened the door to her apartment for him. "That kind of advice isn't necessary. I can take care of myself."

"So I've noticed."

"There's no need to get sarcastic."

"I wasn't being sarcastic. I can see that, in some ways, you can take care of yourself beautifully. You did a terrific job with your story on Normendie. In other ways, you have a lot to learn, and I was trying to help. If you don't want my help, fine."

Laura felt a stab of remorse when she thought about how Tim bailed her out at the airport. "Tim, I appreciate what you've done for me ..."

But he was already climbing down the five flights of stairs to the door without a lock.

11
Fashion Statement

Cassandra Lovelace had two points of pride: she never let her television audiences see her in the same outfit more than once, and she changed her hairstyle twice a year when people set their clocks forward and back. She had little respect for rivals who had to distinguish themselves through trademarks such as wearing the same red glasses or chin-length bob for twenty years. If you were a genius at what you did, you didn't have to look like a fossil to make people remember you.

So Laura wasn't surprised when she stood in the doorway of Cassandra's office and saw her holding court in this year's Daylight Savings Hair, the platinum finger waves that she had adopted in April. Nor was she surprised that Cassandra wore a buttoned-up military-style jacket that looked like the United States Marine Corps dress uniform, except that it was navy blue instead of black.

The temperatures in New York were clinging to the eighties, and the city felt like the inside of a blast furnace. But the fashion pages of *Cassandra* were always saying one of the secrets of looking chic was to dress slightly ahead of the season, and the military look was beginning its long march from Seventh Avenue showrooms to the homes of women across America. Her new boss was leading the parade.

Seated at her ruffle-skirted desk, Cassandra was talking to a young fashion editor, Venetia di Lorenzo, who had changed her name from Vicki Lawrence after moving to New York from Venice, California. Venetia was showing the editor-in-chief a series of handbags shaped like cigarette cartons, trying to persuade her that they deserved to appear in the magazine. Cassandra shook her head until her finger waves approached high tide.

"Darling, they're too *Aurora!*," Cassandra said. "*Far* too *Aurora*"

Venetia looked wounded. "Too *Aurora*" was office shorthand for any idea suited to the wholesome all-American readers whom Aurora Starr was trying to attract to her magazine, not to the international trendsetters who read *Cassandra*. And Laura could see why the rebuke stung. The handbags the fashion editor set before her boss like burnt offerings, made of rich and burnished leather with jewel-like clasps, were nicer than any stuffed onto the top shelf of her closet back in Cleveland. They were just the sort of accessory that might turn her one good suit, a brown tweed, into something she could wear with pride to a job interview.

"Why are the bags 'too *Aurora*'?" Venetia asked in a hurt voice. "I thought they were perfect for us. They're beautiful. They're elegant. And they're inspired by the Fendi baguette, the most influential bag of the past decade. Except that they're more practical than the baguette because …"

"*Cassandra* is not about *practical*," Cassandra snapped. "It's about *glamorous*. It's about *exciting*. It's about *so fabulous it will make your mortal enemies gnash their bonded teeth with envy every time they think of you.*"

Cassandra picked up one of the narrow leather bags on her desk and held it at arm's length, like a dead pigeon that had ended up in her office. "Does *this* look exciting? Does *this* look fabulous?" She handed the bag back to the crestfallen fashion editor. "The baguette is dead, anyway. The latest Fendi bag is the oyster. Why aren't we showing that?"

"But we did show the oyster two months ago." Venetia pulled a magazine from a stack on an Empire-style credenza and flipped to a photo of a half dozen handbags draped artfully over a split-rail fence amid a tumble of wildflowers. A pony was nuzzling an oyster-shaped bag that had a prominent spot in the picture.

Cassandra glanced at the photo and, when she looked up, spotted Laura. "Laurie!" she said. "Please come in. We're delighted to have you on board."

Laura felt, for an instant, like a steward on the *Titanic*. She caught a whiff of Cassandra's heavy gardenia-infused perfume. If she'd worn that fragrance on her flight from Cleveland, the airport security guards would have checked her for dilated pupils and ripped out the lining of her carry-on bag.

"How was your trip to Indianapolis for the Fourth of July?"

"Well, I—" Laura began, "—actually, I went to Cleveland." Afraid that she had erred by correcting her boss, she tried to backtrack. "But I *could* have gone to Indianapolis." *I could have gone to Indianapolis if I was totally insane,* she thought, *since Indianapolis is hundreds of miles away from my hometown.* After a few weeks on the job, she was starting to sound like a parody of herself.

Cassandra didn't seem to notice. "Darling, Indianapolis is a wonderful town," she drawled with a trace of the West Texas accent that her voice coach had never banished. "We've always been number one in the ratings there. Naturally, you must stay at the Canterbury if you want to enjoy your visit. Nothing does more for your morale on the road than marble bathroom fixtures."

Laura didn't know how to respond. She had the sense that Cassandra expected her to describe one of the fantastic marble bathrooms she had used, or raise the stakes by making a remark like: *Yes, but isn't it appalling how many hotels with pink-marble bidets still lack heated towel racks and give you tiny bottles of Clairol Herbal Essence shampoo instead of a custom blend by Jo Malone?* She couldn't bring herself to admit that after her only trip abroad, her summer studying in England, she thought that nothing did more for your morale than hot and cold water coming out of the same faucet.

Cassandra didn't wait for a reply. "I don't want to keep you because I know that Simon has a lot more stories that he wants you to edit."

Edit? Laura thought. "But I'm a writer," she said tentatively. "I wrote the cover story that you had wanted on—"

Cassandra waved the hand that had passed a microphone to a thousand members of her studio audience. She seemed unaware that Laura had saved August issue from running a cover story on a decorator whose cabbage roses had caused a prominent design writer to sniff, "*Skunk* cabbage." "You and Simon can work out the technicalities later. Right now I just wanted to have a better look at our newest staff member. I know Venetia would like that, too. Isn't that right, Venetia?"

Embarrassed, Venetia looked at Laura. "Sure," she said. "By the way, I'm a fashion editor. Technically the deputy fashion editor for bags, belts, and shoes."

"I'm Laura from the features department—"

"You two can get to know each other over lunch at Nobu," Cassandra said, as though her underpaid acolytes could afford to eat at the most famous Japanese restaurant in America, which was a few blocks away. "I need Laurie to turn around for me."

Laura wasn't sure she had heard correctly. "Turn around?"

"Yes, slowly, so I see you from all angles."

Baffled by the command, Laura rotated like a side of lamb about to be carved up for gyro sandwiches at a Greek restaurant. Even under the flattering boudoir lighting of Cassandra's office, she felt her stock plummeting. She wished that she'd worn something with more dash than a plaid pleated skirt and hadn't rolled up the sleeves on her white shirt.

Cassandra and Venetia exchanged glances.

"Not exactly two apples cut in half," Cassandra said cryptically. "More like two tick bites."

"Two apples?" Laura said.

Venetia jumped in. "Cassandra believes in Colette's idea that a woman's breasts should look like two apples cut in half," she said. "But for someone as tall as you are, it can be an advantage to have less than that. Some designers' clothes may fit you better. And when you also have flat hips—"

"Or no hips," Cassandra corrected, fixing her gaze below Laura's waist.

"Or no hips," Venetia went on, "your proportions can work together."

Without responding to the fashion editor, Cassandra motioned for Laura to turn around again.

"What a shame that beautiful skin is so sallow. Are you Slavic?"

"Hungarian."

"I knew it. So many Slavs have that waxy yellow undertone."

"But Hungarians aren't Slavs," Laura said, thinking the editor-in-chief had misunderstood. "Slavs are people who speak Russian, Polish, Czech—"

Cassandra cut her off before she got to Ukrainian and Serbo-Croatian. "At least her eyes are wide-set. She'll never look cross-eyed from the wrong angle."

"You can always cut your hair," Venetia said brightly. "And you can do wonders with some of those instant leg-bronzers now that most companies have resolved the streaking problems ..." Her voice trailed off. "It's too bad the plaid isn't a Burberry, but the skirt might look a lot better if it were a little shorter."

Laura had the feeling that the two women were setting her up for a sacrificial ritual that involved a shaved head, striped legs, and a Burberry thong. "Is something wrong?" she asked. "With the way I look?"

"Not at all, dear," Cassandra said, too solicitously for comfort. "It's just that everybody makes a fashion statement, and I'm trying to understand yours. What do you think, Venetia?"

Venetia squirmed, not looking at Laura.

"Come on, Venetia," Cassandra said impatiently. "Laurie is part of the *Cassandra* family now. You can tell her the truth. What fashion statement do you think she makes?"

"Um, I'm not sure," Venetia said. "It's a little, um, different from what I'm used to."

"Naturally, it's different from what you're used to. You spend your time with foot models and shoe designers who spell the word 'croc' without a 'k.' Which is a crock in itself." Cassandra looked pleased with the small witticism. "The question is: how is her style different? I'm sure Laurie would like to know."

"I wasn't really, um, prepared for this," Venetia said. "You didn't ask me to analyze Caitlin's style when she started work here."

"That's because Caitlin *has* no style," Cassandra said. "And she doesn't want to have any. She's short, overweight, and buys all her clothes at army-navy stores. It's beyond me why Simon wanted to hire the only woman in New York who brings tangerines and PowerBars to work in the pockets of her cargo shorts. At least Laurie doesn't look as though she defines a padded helmet as a fashion accessory."

Laura cringed at this assessment. She took no pride in Cassandra's backhanded compliment and knew that Caitlin boasted of never having owned a dress or set foot in a store above 14th Street. But she sympathized with the young fashion editor and could never have pulled off her outfit: a tiny white miniskirt, a black T-shirt that fit her like a bumper sticker, and black-and-white high heeled sandals that exposed her glossy red toenails. She didn't have to look closely to know that her coworker wasn't wearing stockings, an item that fashion editors seemed determined to banish to the Smithsonian Institution, along with the bustle and the Nehru jacket.

"Cassandra's right, Venetia," Laura said with more conviction than she felt. "You can be ruthless. At my old magazine in Ohio, the style editor used to say that by the time a fashion trend gets to Cleveland, it's played itself out around the country. So I know I'll have to make a few changes."

Venetia looked relieved. "Okay, but please don't take this personally. You're not much worse than most people who come to New York from other parts of the country. I'd say that your fashion statement is: 'You can never start planning to soon for your next parochial-school reunion.'"

This comment gave Laura a jolt. She had convinced herself that years of wearing a uniform didn't have to count against her at *Cassandra*. Hadn't one of her teachers said that she was the best-dressed girl in her class because her mother insisted on starching her white blouses and ironing her pleated skirts until you could bone a duck with the creases? But Venetia had pegged her for what she was—a former altar girl who still dressed as though she would be slipping white robes over her clothes before the 8 AM mass.

"Don't worry, dear," Cassandra said. "Venetia and the others will help you pull yourself together. In the meantime, if you need to represent the magazine at any important public functions, please call it in instead of dipping into your own wardrobe."

"Call it in?"

"Call a designer and have something sent over for you to borrow," Cassandra said. "It's a privilege usually reserved for the higher-ranking editors. But we're a bit short-handed right now. So you may have to take on some assignments that normally would go to more experienced staff members. If you need clothes for these events, you can call my great friend Egotista Dominguez. She's done wonders for the image of a cousin of Queen Sofia. Her latest collection has a number of items perfect for someone your age."

"I couldn't—"

"Or ask Venetia or one of the other fashion editors to call for you. If you're lucky, you may not have to return the items."

Laura wanted to say that, even if Egotista Dominguez didn't specialize in silk slip dresses that provided as much coverage as a loincloth, she couldn't accept clothes worth hundreds or thousands of dollars. Her old boss, Ron Swoboda, had briefly suspended a staff member who took a discount from a plumber hoping to earn a spot in the "Best of the Buckeye State" issue.

Before she could speak, Cassandra stood up.

"Now run along," she said, "or I'll be late for lunch at Le Cirque."

***

A few hours later as she waved away a cloud of cigarette smoke in Simon's office, Laura wondered if she had overestimated her chances for success at *Cassandra*. First, she had gotten into an argument with Tim Moran, one of the most influential people at her company. Now, if Cassandra was right, she would have to take on editing projects in addition to her writing assignments, or risk alienating Simon, too. She hoped that Simon would ease her anxieties but found no reassurance in the chaos on his desk: a crazy quilt of manuscripts, photographs, pink message slips, copies of *Cassandra*, and packages of Marlboros. It was a bad sign that he was smoking Regulars.

Simon motioned for Laura to sit down as he carried on a transatlantic call taking place partly in German, and she distracted herself by listening to the BBC on his short-wave radio. But the orchestral starbursts of the "Jupiter" *Symphony* didn't keep her from catching fragments of his conversation. "Sacher torte … FedEx … not a business expense … just the way the Yanks do things … made redundant … terribly sorry." Then came a rush of German. *"Ja … eine Flucht nach vorn … auf Wiedersehen."*

At the end of the call, Simon apologized for keeping her waiting. "I'm afraid that one of our former staff members, an Austrian fellow named Klaus, was ordering Sacher tortes from Vienna and billing them to our Federal Express account. He seemed to regard this as a business expense. So, unfortunately, he's no longer with us."

"Unfortunately?" Laura said. "If he was trying to claim Sacher tortes as a business expense, I'd call his departure pretty fortunate—in fact, essential."

To her relief, Simon laughed. "I suppose you could think of it that way. What would we have done if he'd developed a taste for Peking Duck?"

"I tried not to eavesdrop. But I couldn't help wondering about that German phrase that sounded a little like 'a fluke not for him.'"

"*Eine Flucht nach vorn.* One of those wonderful German expressions with no precise English equivalent. It means 'a retreat forward.' I was trying to convince Klaus that leaving the magazine—although, in a sense, a 'retreat'—was a step forward in a direction that would make better use of his talents."

Simon flicked an ash into a dish that showed a white lion rampant on a blue seal. "But let's not talk about minor Austrian royalty whom you never had the pleasure of meeting. What did you want to see me about?"

"Cassandra seemed to think that you might also want me to do some editing," Laura said, trying to sound casual about it. "But I have several writing assignments from you and an apartment that needs work. I'm not sure when I'd have time for editing."

"You needn't worry. The sort of things I had in mind won't take much time. In fact, I have a story on my desk now that should be quite easy for you to edit, a sprightly column written by one of your fellow Hungarians."

Simon picked up an article on a party in East Hampton and handed it to Laura. The author was a celebrated bon vivant and society columnist who claimed descent from the royal Esterházys and often lionized his aristocratic friends in articles that appeared under titles such as "Sheik and Bake" or "Down for the Countess." An aging but debonair figure who cast himself as "the Magyar Cary Grant," Zoli had such impressive social connections that he was the only contributor to *Cassandra* permitted to write under a single name, a diminutive of his first name of Zoltán. He had modeled himself after Taki, the pen name of the society writer Taki Theodoracopoulos, without ever achieving the same level of exposure in the overseas press.

Laura began to read aloud from Zoli's column. "Walking across the lawn in the pale moonlight, the magnificent estate of J. Richard Doddering IV ..." With mild alarm, she scanned the rest of the column, unable to think of anything but Herman Melville's comment: "It's hard to get poetry out of blubber."

"This is a disaster! It isn't even written in grammatical English. There's a dangling modifier in the first sentence. The author suggests that the estate was walking across the lawn when he means that Richard Doddering was walking across it. He uses clichés like 'pale moonlight' that could have come from a bad Gothic novel. You think that he'll start talking about women with 'heaving bosoms' and men who 'laugh mirthlessly' at them."

Laura glanced at several of the bold-faced names in the column. "Not to mention that half of his facts are wrong. J. Richard Doddering IV, known as 'Big Dick,' is a third, not a fourth. The fourth is his son, 'Little Dick,' who's just been kicked out of prep school for feeding Bombay Sapphire gin to the frogs in his biology lab. Have the fact-checkers seen this?"

"I'm afraid we've got a bit of a problem there."

"Which is?"

"We don't *have* any fact-checkers. You can't count the summer interns, who help out but have no real training in that area. Cassandra thinks that fact-checkers aren't necessary. She believes that magazines are like talk shows—you get better ratings when you let people do outrageous things. So she's given Zoli a rather free hand. But we've had a few complaints from readers—nothing serious—just people unhappy that he's misspelled their names or misidentified the entrées at their dinner parties. A few months ago he wrote that a Park Avenue hostess had served 'Braised Pork with Morons' because her menus said 'Porc Braisé aux Marrons.' He said that the guests at another party included a man who had died of a heart attack at Southampton Hospital two days earlier. So we've decided to reign Zoli in a bit, perhaps send someone along with him occasionally to parties to make sure he got his facts straight."

Sensing Laura's hesitation, Simon went on. "Didn't you wonder why Cassandra called you into her office and inspected you as though you were a candidate for the Coldstream Guards? She wanted to know that you passed muster before we sent you to any parties where you might run into her friends."

"But I was sure I didn't pass. I had the sense that Cassandra saw me as one of those scrawny calves that slip into the livestock section of the Cuyahoga County Fair under the judges' radar."

"Her exact words were that 'a few glamorous New York parties' might do you some good. She seemed to think that you had potential that people in the Midwest hadn't appreciated."

Laura knew she'd love to develop any potential that a few glamorous parties might bring out. But she wondered if she had the bathysphere necessary to descend into the depths of Zoli's prose and come up with something resembling the English language.

"I just wonder if, whether or not I go to those parties, you might not want to give Zoli's column to somebody with a little more editing experience."

"You have more editing experience than most of the people in Features." This comment struck Laura as alarming given that she had no editing experience, but Simon went on before she could say so. "Just give Zoli a call if you have any questions. He's always willing to accommodate charming female staff members."

Venetia appeared in the doorway holding several tubes of instant leg-bronzer.

"Hi, Laura, don't want to disturb you and Simon, but Cassandra wanted you to have these. A small gift from Calla Norton, the beauty editor. Calla is attending a product launch at a cosmetics company uptown. She's finding out everything our readers need to know about a new fragrance that smells like 'figs with an undertone of musk and cardamom.' So I borrowed a few things for you from the beauty supply closet."

Venetia stooped down to look at Laura's legs, then gave her one of the tubes of bronzing gel. "I think you might look best in Sun-

Kissed Peach. But if you don't like it, stop by my office and I'll give you Sun-Kissed Melon or Apricot instead. You can try as many tubes as you want. The new gels are so easy to apply—much better than the old messy creams—and the result should last for four or five days. You'll be amazed by how different your legs will look."

"You make Laura's legs sound like unripened fruit," Simon said. "They look remarkably fine to me." His face, when animated by an undercurrent of flirtation, became unexpectedly handsome. "By the way, how are you getting on with your piece on shoe trees? Any luck finding celebrities who will let us photograph their closets?"

Venetia gave Simon an update on a story about shoe trees of stars that she hoped to call "Trees' Company." She burbled about an actor, "the Joyce Kilmer of shoe trees," who had written a poem about his storage system that she hoped to quote.

Just before she left the office, Venetia turned to Laura. "Almost forgot to tell you. When you put on that leg-bronzer, be sure to wash your hands afterward. Otherwise you'll look as though you have premature liver spots."

After several hours of trying to reach Zoli, Laura gave up and sifted through the red tide of press releases that arrived on her desk each day. Simon had given her a half dozen phone numbers for the society columnist in three time zones, and she had tried them all. She hadn't reached Zoli or anybody who knew where he was, and her ears hurt from a cacophony of clicks, beeps, and foreign operators' diphthongs. That she shared a cubicle with Caitlin, who had never forgiven her for getting the Normendie Latour interview, only made things worse.

"If you're having so much trouble reaching Zoli, why don't you talk to Simon?" Caitlin said, looking up from a clip file on the heir to a bathroom-fixtures fortune who was said to have the world's most valuable collection of eighteenth-century French chamber pots. "Maybe he'll replace him with somebody who has credentials beyond having gone out with one of the Gabor sisters."

"I wouldn't want to bother Simon about such a small thing."

Caitlin's eyes darted sideways. "Maybe Simon would like you to bother him. Everybody in Features can see that he flirts with you every chance he can get."

Laura could feel her ears getting warm. She had the same suspicion. But Simon was such a natural flirt that when the food editor brought her eight-month-old daughter to work, he seemed to flirt with the baby. So she tried not to read too much into the flattering comments he made about her work and her appearance—not necessarily in that order. "It's not true that Simon flirts with me, or with me alone. He flirts with all the women in the office and half the men, including the messengers. Every time Simon signs for a package, Nöel Coward could have written the script."

Ethan, who had been listening in the next cubicle, overheard her. "He doesn't flirt with me the way he flirts with you."

"You see, Laura?" Caitlin asked. "You think Simon flirts with everybody because you haven't worked here long enough to recognize the difference between how he treats you and his behavior with others. But I doubt that he means anything serious by it. The rumor is that he's moving back to England in a couple of months."

Laura set down a press release from a manufacturer of sterling-silver nose-hair clippers. "You can't be serious."

"The rumor has been popping up in the gossip columns for months."

"If the rumor has been 'popping up' for months and it hasn't panned out, maybe it isn't true. Maybe it was spread by somebody who could profit from it. Let's say Aurora Starr started the rumor hoping that it would make *Cassandra* look unstable and encourage advertisers to pull their ads. Simon says that Aurora is ferociously competitive."

"Aurora is competitive. But subterfuge isn't her style. She's too direct. When she wants to hire a producer away from *Cassandra!*, she doesn't float rumors in *Broadcasting* magazine. She just offers the person a salary that will guarantee that she gets what she wants. Aurora doesn't go in for weeks of back-room negotiations or power breakfasts at Michael's. They would let the trade press pick up the scent of the deal. She sweeps in and plucks the people she wants off the sides of buildings like Spider-Man.

"*Aurora* already has far more ads than we do, and Aurora is good at schmoozing the advertisers, too. Last week she had a volleyball party for media buyers in Central Park to 'get the ball rolling' for the redesign of her magazine."

Laura felt a stab of envy when she heard the word "redesign." Overhauling the look of a glossy national magazine could cost hundreds of thousands of dollars, far more than she could imagine anyone spending on a similar project at *Cassandra*. *Aurora* was clearly making a lot of money or expected to do so. But the success of a rival magazine gnawed at her less than the rumor that Simon might go back to England. Praying that it was untrue, she went to see Anne Meyer, the art director, who heard gossip from all departments and from her husband, Dan Meyer, one of the city's best-known plastic surgeons. Anne was also one of the few people at the magazine who was over forty and might have a mature perspective on the situation.

She found the art director perched on a stool in front of a light box, looking at slides of photographs. Anne was wearing her workday uniform of black silk pants, an open throated white silk shirt, and a black leather belt with a gold-panther buckle. She also had on a pair of the black Prada penny loafers that had become popular a few seasons earlier. One of the things Laura liked about Anne was that she wore stylish black flats instead of the break-your-neck heels that made some of her coworkers look as though they had no higher ambition than to put their podiatrists' children through college.

"Hi, Anne. Have a minute?"

"Sure. You can only look at slides for so long before you get bug-eyed."

Laura asked if she believed the rumor that Simon might leave the magazine by Labor Day.

"By Labor Day? No. By the end of the year? Possibly."

"Why?" Laura said, crushed. "Simon has a great job. He can do just about anything he wants, including things that most people can't, like smoke in his office."

"Simon can do anything he wants as long he also does everything that Cassandra wants. He can smoke in his office if he agrees to replace a cover story at the last minute even though he has to stay here until 3 or 4 AM to do it. I think he likes you partly because that's what he might have had to do if you hadn't reeled in Normendie Latour. He's pulled all-nighters writing stories that freelancers haven't turned in or rewriting pieces they've botched. The office always smells like the aftermath of a timber fire the next day. Caitlin once asked him if he had smoke-jumpers come in and keep the flames under control."

"There's something else that concerns me. Caitlin thinks that Simon, as he might say, 'fancies' me. Ethan seems to agree with her. Those two rarely agree on anything, so I wonder if it's true."

"Hmm. That's the most interesting thing I've heard about Simon in a while."

"What's the most interesting thing?"

"That Ethan thinks Simon likes women. I've had trouble deciding whether Simon is straight or gay, a problem you tend to have with well-educated Englishmen. If he's involved with anyone, male or female, he's discreet about it. But Ethan works more closely with Simon than anybody except Cassandra. And Cassandra, as we all know, spends half her time on Mars, or might as well for all we see of her. So if Ethan is implying that Simon is straight, I'd tend to believe it."

"What should I do if Simon does have a crush on me?"

"That depends on whether you have a crush on him."

Laura said nothing. She was still trying *not* to have feelings for Simon.

Anne smiled. "Aha! Then you'll have to seduce him because I don't think he'd risk his job by seducing you. He may talk a lot about 'the morally repressive American office' in contrast to the enlightened British idea that if you aren't screwing a sub-editor on top of your desk every day, you aren't living up to your boss's expectations of you. But he didn't get to be as successful as he is by spending his time sleeping with underlings. He understands the rules in America even if he makes fun of them."

Laura wondered whether she would ever have the courage to seduce a boss. At any rate it was inconceivable that she would attempt it so soon after joining the staff of *Cassandra*. Vertical seduction was something that, if she tried it, she would have to work up to. "Maybe this is all theoretical. Now that Nick and I have split up, Simon might see flirting with me as a charitable act. Who will do it if he doesn't?"

"Here's something that's less theoretical. I hear that you're Zoli's new editor. So I ought to warn you that he likes to call female staff members and ask them to meet him at a hotel that has funching rates."

"Funching?"

"A time-honored hotel-industry term. A cross between 'fucking' and 'lunching.'"

Laura hoped that she wasn't blushing, a habit she'd tried for years to overcome. "I'm not sure that term has reached hotels in the Midwest. I haven't heard it before."

Anne laughed again. "Sweetie, you have no idea what hasn't reached the Midwest. If you're going to turn as red as you are now every time you hear a word like 'funching,' you'd better get yourself some earplugs."

12
Legs

Every time she arrived at work, Laura had the sense that she'd boarded the *Queen Elizabeth II*, although she doubted that the ocean liner had a life-sized poster of its namesake near the reception desk. The *Cassandra* offices occupied two floors of a converted warehouse in Tribeca, each as large as the deck of a ship and nearly as distant from her life in the Midwest. Huge bouquets of flowers turned up almost every day—gifts from publicists and others hoping to ingratiate themselves with the editors—and gave some of its offices the air of staterooms. Laura half-expected to come across a shuffleboard or swimming pool amid the computers and ringing telephones.

For all their industrial chic, the *Cassandra* offices had something of the spirit of *Upstairs, Downstairs* about them. An informal class system determined their layout. The staff members with the least glamorous jobs, including Laura and the others in Features, worked in spartan cubicles near the reception area on the lower floor. Some of them sat at computers with screen savers displaying the sort of aggressively tranquil scenes that Lamaze instructors urged women to focus on during labor—foaming surf at Big Sur, sunlit glades full of ferns, mountaintops where yaks grazed peacefully. On most days Laura and her coworkers could hear the staccato blasts of pile drivers and jackhammers on the street below.

The staff members whose jobs had a higher gloss, including the fashion and beauty editors, had private offices on the upper floor that insulated them from the noises of the street and the fans with leatherette autograph books who sometimes showed up, hoping for a glimpse of Cassandra. Although you could take an elevator to either floor from the hallway, most staff members used the red-carpeted staircase with white hand railings resembling those of a cruise ship.

At *Cassandra* the class system also shaped dress codes, or so Laura had learned from Monica Stryker, whose copyediting duties required her to shuttle between departments. Monica said that fashion and beauty editors who worked on the upper floor and met with models, photographers, and designers were expected to look the part. The highest-ranking had salaries or expense accounts and call-in privileges that reflected that requirement. Monica said that feature writers and editors who worked on the lower floor had "more leeway" in how they dressed unless they were representing the magazine at a corporate function. She added that at most New York magazines, where freedom, like a designer dress, had its price tag, "more leeway" translated to "less take-home pay."

From her cubicle Laura could see the fashion and beauty editors gliding down the staircase several times a day, appearing to drift as effortlessly as clouds. They wore mainly black or white, and some times they held garment bags or escorted models or photographers carrying flat black portfolios. The fashion and beauty editors floated so far above her that Laura hesitated to enter their sanctuary.

But now she had no choice. The night before, she had applied her new leg-bronzer by the light of a single bulb in her bathroom, which was as badly lit as the rest of her apartment was furnished. Now her legs were full of streaks that made her look like a test pattern for a shop awning, and she was wearing her one good white shirt with a bright red skirt that made her feel even more conspicuous. Trying to avoid her coworkers in Features, she hurried up the carpeted staircase and began looking for Venetia, who might know how to undo the damage caused by the leg-bronzer.

When nobody offered to help her navigate through the hallways, Laura followed the trail of scents wafting from the upper-floor departments—the fragrances of lime-and-ginger soap in Beauty, old-rose potpourri in Interior Design, fresh woolens in Fashion. She found Venetia surrounded by thigh-high stacks of shoeboxes in the *Cassandra* shoe closet, a pantry-sized room with a wall of floor-to-ceiling cubbyholes redolent of new leather. The fashion editor was holding a high-heeled python boot against her body.

"Hi, Laura. Does this boot say 'Tenth Avenue Hooker' or 'Louche Italian Contessa' to you?"

Laura tried to remember whether she'd ever seen a Tenth Avenue hooker or an Italian contessa. All that the boot said to her was, "Orthopedic Ward at Mt. Sinai," which was where the women who wore it might end up. "It's so sleek and—" she reached for a word that the fashion editors used, "—'directional.' I just can't imagine how women who wear boots like that can avoid foot surgery."

"They can't. You have no idea how many women are walking around New York in agony. If *Sex and the City* were true to life, Carrie Bradshaw would have had bunion surgery by the end of the second season."

Venetia noticed Laura's legs. "But what happened to you? An allergic reaction to the leg-bronzer?" Venetia sounded contrite. "I guess I should have told you to try a test patch to see how your skin reacted. But you didn't strike me as the delicate type."

"I'm not the delicate type. In high school I was always getting elbowed in the spleen during basketball games. My idea of a fashion accessory was an Ace bandage." Laura didn't mention that she'd had to switch to crutches after getting tripped by the guard from Holy Innocents. "But I didn't seem to apply the bronzer correctly and wondered if you knew of anything I could do. I couldn't cover my legs with pants—" Laura remembered that the fashion editors called pants "trousers" except when talking about specific kinds of pants, such as cargo pants. "That is, trousers, because most of mine are still back in Ohio."

"You pretty much have to wait for the color to fade. But I think I can help. Follow me." Venetia led Laura through a hallway lined with framed covers of *Cassandra,* then into "merch room," or merchandise room, where the fashion editors kept the clothes they were considering for future issues or had used but not returned to their designers. The room had locked closets along two walls and a pegboard bristling with belts, scarves, and costume jewelry along a third. In a corner stood a Victorian hat rack draped with a metallic tube top the size of a cigar band.

"Feel free to borrow the tube top if you have a date after work," Venetia said. "We used it on a location shoot in Aruba. The model got No. 50 sunblock on it, so we couldn't return it, and the spot is so small it would never show in the dim light of a bar or club. All of us in Fashion wear about the same size"—Laura was sure this was heading for the negative numbers—"so we decided to share it."

Venetia opened one of the locked closet doors in the merch room and smiled. "Now isn't this better than Victoria's Secret?"

Laura saw dozens of shelves filled with beautiful silk underwear and lingerie, each of which had a label such as "Bras," "Slips," or "Teddies." She imagined that it was the kind of thing you'd find in an exclusive brothel. "What's in the other closets?"

"Almost everything. Blouses, sweaters, skirts, shorts—you name it."

"Do you have to return them to their designers?"

"A lot of them we do. But we can keep a lot, too, especially smaller things like pairs of panty hose. So you're in luck."

Venetia moved to a shelf filled with panty hose in a dozen colors, then studied Laura. "Let's see. Are you tall or extra tall? I'd guess extra tall. And with your red skirt, which is a blue-red instead an orange-red, I'd wear purple."

Purple? Laura thought. She'd never worn purple panty hose in her life. Until that moment she hadn't known they existed. Her cousin's bridesmaids weren't going to wear purple panty hose with their eggplant-colored dresses, shoes, and hats. Tina had spent days trying to decide whether her attendants should wear nude, taupe, beige, or suntan but still hadn't made up her mind.

Venetia held the package of purple panty hose against Laura's skirt and nodded in approval. "This looks perfect, and it's dark enough hide your streaks. I have a pair of red-and-purple shoes back at my office that might fit you, and maybe a purple belt, although you don't want to look too aggressively coordinated—it's 'aging.'" Venetia inspected Laura for signs of excessive coordination and, finding none, went on. "I love St. John clothes. At least, on my mother. But every time I see a woman walking down the street in head-to-toe St. John, I want to shout, 'Honey, kill the earrings!'"

Another fashion editor, Kit Cameron, entered the merch room as Laura was about to comment on how much more confident Venetia sounded when Cassandra wasn't listening. Kit wore a gray pencil skirt and a matching expression.

Venetia introduced her as the editor who booked the models for the fashion and beauty pages. "Another wedding crisis, Kit?"

"You have no idea. I came by to see if I could find a new lace bra that I could borrow for a day to cheer myself up." Kit scanned the shelves of the closet. "Why didn't we ever get that aqua Roberto Cavalli underwear that Jennifer Lopez wore on the cover of *Vanity Fair?* For fifteen minutes I wished I was a lesbian just so I could rip that bra off her. It's just what I need to improve my mood right now."

"Does Gordon still want to have haggis as the first course at the reception?" Venetia asked. She explained to Laura that Kit's fiancé was a Scottish banker, who had wanted to serve their wedding guests a dish encased in a sheep's stomach.

"No, we're going to have the waiters pass slices with the hors d'oeuvres after Gordon's best man recites Robert Burns's ode 'To a Haggis.' So we shouldn't have any more arguments about that issue as long as Ian stays away from the Glenfidditch."

"So what's the problem?"

"Perky Vano has checked into a rehab clinic."

"Again?"

"For a month this time, maybe two or three."

Venetia fell silent. Kit seemed about to burst into tears that even a D-cup bra couldn't dry.

Laura knew that Patricia Vano was a model whose name rhymed with Drano, a fact often noted by editors who disliked working with her. Photographers gave her the nickname of Perky because she was always morbidly depressed. Her gloomy nature and hollow-eyed look had caused her bookings to soar in the heyday of heroin chic, when some fashion magazines looked like house organs for a methadone clinic. But now that the national mood had changed, her career was tanking, and she was trying to make the transition from a high-fashion model to a foot model while also attempting to overcome her cocaine addiction. Designers called her "Little Blow Peep" and said that, if you wanted to work with Perky, "the lines form to the right." For all this, Laura wasn't sure why Kit was so upset. She hadn't seen Perky's photo in *Cassandra* in several months, unless she'd seen her foot and not recognized it, and she thought the magazine had lost interest in her.

"But, Kit, you haven't booked Perky for any location shoots, have you?" Venetia asked. "Not after the problems we've had with her? Calla banned her from the magazine after that disastrous trip to the Maldives where Perky forgot her stash and became so unstrung that she tried to snort the custom-blended face powder with twenty-four-carat gold flecks that Jean-Pierre had in his hotel suite. Jean-Pierre said the face powder was practically as expensive as cocaine and has refused to do makeup for us ever since."

"The problem is worse than having booked Perky for a location shoot."

"What could be worse than trying to get her through customs again?"

"I booked her for my wedding. She was one of my bridesmaids."

Venetia reacted as though she'd said that she had decided to have Mountain Dew instead of Veuve Clicquot at her reception. "You hired Perky to be your bridesmaid?"

"Yes. No. I mean, I didn't hire her. I just asked her to be a bridesmaid, and now she's moved into a last-chance clinic in some place like Idaho that you're forbidden to leave. I got a call from her agency saying that she can't make the wedding."

"I hadn't realized that she was a close friend of yours."

"She isn't. But I've known her casually for years. I met her after college when I was a production assistant at *Aurora!* working on the fashion segments. Perky modeled for an annual show that we called 'Bridesmaids' Dresses from Hell.' We asked viewers to send in snapshots of the worst bridesmaids' dresses they had to wear. Then we hired gorgeous models to display the gowns on the program. The point we were making was, 'This dress would be a travesty even on Cindy Crawford.' The bridesmaids' gowns were so bad that a lot of models who would appear on other segments refused to do the show. But Perky was a real trouper."

"That doesn't mean that you had to have her in your wedding."

"I know. But Gordon was having ten ushers, so I needed ten bridesmaids, and I thought that asking her would be a nice way to pay her back for some of the ghastly things she had to wear on the show. Some of my other attendants were models I know really well. So I figured they'd keep Perky in line—"

"More likely in *lines*—"

"Why didn't anybody tell me that a year ago?"

Venetia tried to console her coworker. "At least you don't have to find a replacement at the last minute. These days it's fine to have an uneven number of bridesmaids and groomsmen, so you won't have to ask a cousin who wears a nose ring."

"But I do have to find a replacement," Kit said disconsolately.

"The problem isn't having an uneven number of male and female attendants. It's the hand-beaded bridesmaids' dresses from Paris that are costing my father five thousand dollars apiece after the discount that Egotista Dominguez is giving us. Not to mention the shoes. My father was furious about having to pay for the dresses. He said that in his day bridesmaids bought their own gowns. I kept telling him that back then everybody went to Priscilla of Boston, where even the most expensive items cost a fraction of what they would now. It took me weeks to convince him that if you want your attendants to wear couture today, you have to help them pay for it unless you're one of the Hearst sisters and your friends are heiresses. He'll never forgive me if he finds out that he's spent five thousand dollars on a dress nobody's using."

"Can't Egotista take the dress back?" Venetia asked. "Maybe she could offer it privately to a client."

"After how I begged for a discount, I don't dare ask. Egotista thinks she's doing enough for us by giving Cassandra so many of her clothes for free. And the bridesmaids have had their final fittings, so it isn't as though the dresses will fit just anybody. I've got to find somebody who can fit into Perky's dress and shoes."

"Let me think. Perky was about five-ten and wore a nine narrow shoe—"

"Long waist, broad shoulders, no breasts, and no hips. And that dreamy Modigliani neck ..." Kit spoke in the mournful tones of a eulogist for an archbishop. "Have you ever noticed how many models today have necks like bobble-head dolls? They're practically polishing their shirt buttons with their chins."

Listening to Kit, Laura realized that she'd prefer to have her body evaluated by a half dozen Notre Dame linebackers who'd drunk too many margaritas than by some of her female coworkers.

"I could live with a short neck in my wedding party. But where am I going to find somebody who has no breasts, no hips, and no social life, so she'll be willing to spend next Friday night at a stranger's rehearsal dinner?"

Kit stared at Laura as though she had seen Jesus's female twin. "Oh, my God. What size shoe do you wear?"

Laura took a step backward. "Please. I don't want ..."

"Laura, I'm a shoe editor," Venetia said. "I can guess people's shoe sizes better than their height, weight, or penis size. I know you're a nine, probably double- or triple-A width."

Venetia turned to Kit. "Laura would be ideal, and I know she'd love to go to an East Coast reception at a yacht club. How many yachts can they have in Cleveland, Ohio?" Venetia brushed a few strands of hair off Laura's shoulder. "Don't worry about the split ends. Cassandra asked me to help fix her up, anyway."

"But we do have yachts and yacht clubs in Ohio," Laura said. "Cleveland is on Lake Erie, a very large body of water. People in the region call Northeast Ohio the North Coast of America." Laura could hear herself blithering and, hoping to correct her navigational path, drove forward like George Clooney in *The Perfect Storm*. "I have so much work that I'm not sure I have time to go to a wedding. Simon wants me to edit our next society column. And I'm having so much trouble reaching Zoli that I may have to start coming into the office on weekends to get in touch with him."

The two fashion editors traded a freighted glance. "You'll never reach Zoli," Kit said. "Give it up. Zoli calls only from Airfones or other places where the lines keep going dead in the middle of the conversations. When he calls, he usually has something in his mind besides helping you unscramble his Rubik's-cube syntax."

"And going to the wedding would be much better for your career than talking to Zoli," Venetia said. "Kit knows everybody in the company—maybe everybody in the magazine industry."

None of this persuaded Laura. "I have to fix up my new apartment on weekends. When I first started work here, I stayed with my best friend, Alice, in a beautiful but falling-down mansion in Connecticut. So I put off getting a place for a while and still feel as though I'm camping out."

Kit looked at Laura curiously. "Were you staying with Alice Dudley? At Rose Bluffs?"

"How did you know?"

"Alice and I took sailing lessons together in fifth grade. We were in the same Sunfish class. I haven't spoken to her in ages. But I sent her an invitation to the wedding and hope she's coming."

Venetia slipped an arm around Laura's waist. "Perfect! So when Laura takes Perky's place, she'll have someone she can talk to at the reception in addition to all of the people from the company who'll be attending."

"I don't know," Laura said, wavering. "I've never been a free-lance bridesmaid. I'm going to be in my cousin's wedding soon, and that experience hasn't made me eager to be in another. I don't think I can handle wearing another eggplant-colored dress."

"Eggplant?" Venetia said. "Kit has picked out beautiful black dresses for her bridesmaids. You can wear yours to any club in the city after the wedding."

Probably see-through dresses, too, Laura thought. She tried to imagine whether Kit's bridesmaids' gowns would be cut lower in the back or the front, the only question you really had about most of Egotista Dominguez's creations. She finally suggested that Kit bring in the dress to see if it fit. With any luck, it would be six inches too short or fit like a Hefty bag.

"I'll bring it in, but you'll look great." Kit glanced at Laura's streaked calves. "In the meantime, I'd cover those legs before one of Cassandra's art-collector friends drops by the office and tries to hang you on a wall next to an abstract expressionist masterpiece."

"Don't worry," Venetia assured Kit, a bit too quickly for Laura's comfort. "I'll take care of them."

***

Laura hardly recognized herself in the ladies' room mirror. Venetia had accessorized her white shirt and red skirt with purple stockings, a purple belt, and red-and-purple slingbacks with sky-high heels. Then she stood back and admired her handiwork.

"This is why I love what I do. Clothes may make the man, but accessories make the woman."

Venetia noticed that Laura had adopted a swaybacked posture to accommodate her new heels. "But you've got to stand up straighter or you'll ruin the effect of those shoes. These days the most important fashion rule is: it's not what you wear, but how you wear it. You've got to project confidence in how you look. The reason why Anne Meyer looks so great, even if she wears the same thing every day, is that she has faith in her taste. She knows what suits her and sticks with it no matter how many pages we devote to prairie skirts and blouses with broderic Anglaise." Venetia took a final glance at Laura's outfit. "Now let's see what we can do about that hair and skin. I hate to admit that Cassandra was right. But your complexion *is* a tiny bit sallow."

Laura envisioned herself with scarlet lips and purple slashes across her eyelids. "I really need to get back to work—"

"Not yet."

Venetia took a pair of tortoise-shell combs out of a small shopping bag and used them to pull Laura's hair back from the sides of her face. Then she applied cream blush, mascara, and lip gloss—none of it red or purple.

"This will have to do," Venetia said after a few minutes of effort. "We didn't have the ideal colors for you on hand. But you still look great. All of the kneeling buses in the city will kneel at your feet."

Laura didn't dislike the results of Venetia's efforts, which were more stylish than any she could have achieved on her own, but she was so decorated that she had the irrational fear that somebody might try to hang tinsel from her. Wobbling like a foal on her new heels, she hurried down the staircase to the features department and tried to slip unnoticed into her swivel chair.

Before she could turn on her computer, Caitlin and Ethan, in a rare display of unity, began snapping their fingers and singing in harmony.

I heard it through the grapevine.
Not much longer would you be mine.

Laura tried to tune them out by answering her email until she saw two senior fashion editors near her desk. Fatima Rao, the exquisite-looking descendant of a Portuguese infanta, was whispering animatedly in French to Claudine Dubuffet, who had worked for a legendary couture house before joining the staff of *Cassandra*.

As particles of their conversation floated by like dust motes, Laura considered whether to introduce herself. Fatima spoke iffy English, and Claudine spent so much time in distant fashion capitals that she was an enigmatic presence. Both women were among the remote and swanlike figures whom Laura had seen gliding up and down the staircase with models and photographers. She had just decided to approach the fashion editors when they left as swiftly as they had arrived.

A few minutes later, Claudine returned with a mirror and a clutch of scarves in shades of red, purple, and white. She studied Laura from several angles without speaking, walking back and forth next to her desk and lifting her chin. When Laura tried to question her, Claudine put a finger to her lips, as though words might break the spell she intended to cast. She selected a small square scarf and tied it into a snug horizontal knot around Laura's neck, the kind Audrey Hepburn wore with her princess-posing-as a pauper shirts and Capri pants in *Roman Holiday.*

As she stepped back and examined the result, Claudine smiled for the first time. "*Pas mal.*" She held up the mirror she had brought with her. Laura saw that Venetia, as artfully as she had tried to parse her outfit, had left it unfinished. If she resembled a walking Christmas tree, Claudine had spotted the star missing from the top.

Laura tried to thank her, but Claudine waved away her gratitude with the I-was-just-doing-my-job shrug that firefighters gave to tearful mothers whose infants they had just saved. But a note of one-upmanship of the other fashion editors, if not triumph, crept into her voice as she cast a final glance at Laura's outfit.

"*Maintenant, c'est fini.*"

Simon walked through the features department a few minutes later and, when he saw Laura, stared at her in wonder.

"Some of the fashion editors spend so little time in the office that I wonder why we hired them," he said, shaking his head. "But now I understand perfectly."

13
Breasts

Laura stood in front of a full-length mirror in the *Cassandra* ladies' room, naked from the waist up and wearing little more than a tea-length black half-slip. Calla Norton, the beauty editor, stuck a strip of pewter-colored duct tape to her breasts, then ripped it off.

"Ow!"

"Don't be such a sissy, Laura," Venetia teased, as she and Kit helped Calla rummage through a Louis Vuitton satchel for a role of narrower tape. "You're not having most of your face burned off by a chemical peel. We're just trying to get your breasts into the right position for the dress."

"Some models go through this every day during the collections," Kit added. "Haven't you ever wondered why you never see any bra straps in runway shots, no matter how many sheer organza blouses the designers show?"

"I thought models used Band-Aids."

"Band-Aids are for amateurs," Calla said cheerfully, attaching another strip of duct tape to Laura's breasts. "There. I think we've got it now."

Laura saw in the mirror that the beauty editor had used the duct tape to push her breasts together and give a slight impression of cleavage. Not certain of the purpose of this painful exercise, she turned to the future bride. "Kit, I thought you wanted me to be in your wedding because I didn't have cleavage. Why do I need the tape?"

"You'll see when you put on the dress."

"Wait, she needs the shoes first," Venetia said. "A great dress without the right shoes is like a Ferrari without the ignition key."

Venetia opened a shoebox on the sink and lifted out a pair of black silk high-heeled sandals with black satin ribbons attached. Laura stepped into them and realized that, while wearing them, she might have stood eye-to-eye with six-foot-two Nick. Venetia bent down and tied the ribbon on each shoe into a bow at the ankle.

"Gorgeous!" Calla said. "That bow at the ankle is brilliant."

"Another example of why Saint-Laurent said that 'women should always wear something that looks as though it could be undone,'" Venetia said. "Those shoes would bring out the animal instincts even in a man who'd been force-fed haggis for hours."

"Now the dress." Kit unzipped a black garment bag, imprinted in gold with the initials ED, and lifted out a sinuous black dress with a beaded halter top and straps that crossed on the back. She slipped the dress over Laura's head.

"Fantastic!" Venetia said. "Can't you get a bridesmaid my height to check into a rehab clinic, too?"

Laura could see why she needed the duct tape even if the dress didn't have the swan-diving neckline she'd expected. It was cut so low in the back and under the arms—more like a pinafore than a dress—that she couldn't wear anything underneath it except a few freckles. She might have spilled out of the garment if the tape didn't offer a hedge against the laws of motion and gravity.

Calla took a few steps sideways to see the dress from another angle. "It fits perfectly, Laura. But if you lose any weight before the wedding, you can use more tape to stick the dress to your hips." She adjusted the skirt so that it hung straighter.

Laura thought that, if she lost weight, she might prefer walking down the aisle in leg irons to wrapping herself in more duct tape. She was going to ask the beauty editor how to stop the tape from itching when Kit jumped in.

"Laura doesn't have any weight to lose. She's so thin already."

Venetia patted Laura's hips, or the lack of them. "You don't know how lucky you are not to have a weight problem. You can go home and eat a pound of chocolate truffles whenever you're depressed."

"But I can't do that, because if I did, I *would* have a weight problem," Laura said, unsure that she followed Venetia's logic. "The reason I don't have a weight problem is that I don't eat a pound of chocolate truffles when I get depressed."

"What do you eat instead?" Venetia asked. "Ben & Jerry's? Entenmann's?"

"I don't eat sweets when I'm depressed. I helped out in my parents' bakery when I was growing up. And until I was a teenager, they paid me by letting me have anything I wanted from their display cases. So I lost interest in sweets, the way they say hookers lose interest in sex. To this day when I look at a Napoleon or pastry horn I don't think 'yum.' I think 'exploited child labor in the Cleveland suburbs.'"

Laura realized that her words might leave the impression that if she were unhappy, she'd pull out one of the packages of instant udon noodles that her coworkers kept in their desks. "What I mean is, I do things besides eating to make myself feel better. I shoot a few baskets or listen to the Dixie Chicks. For some reason, it cheers me up to listen to a song about a wife who gets revenge on her no-good husband by poisoning him to death with black-eyed peas. But I don't have to do that often, because I don't seem to get depressed—at least not the way other people do."

Kit looked at her as though she'd said she didn't seem to breathe. "How can you not get depressed? Everybody gets depressed."

Laura wasn't sure how to respond to this. Back in Cleveland, people didn't get depressed unless they had a good, solid *reason*, such as that all the malls sold out of Frankie Yankovic's polka albums three weeks before Christmas, or Wendy's had replaced the Mozzarella Chicken Supreme sandwich with something with sprouts on it. And when they were upset, they didn't go on about it for weeks with their friends—they just called a drive-time radio show and sounded off. So before leaving Ohio Laura had the idea that getting depressed was something that people did mainly in Woody Allen movies. But she was beginning to realize that New Yorkers thought they had a federally protected right to get depressed just on general principles. Almost every day at *Cassandra*, she heard a rattle and saw somebody shaking a Wellbutrin or Effexor or Xanax out of a bottle.

"I don't know why I don't get depressed," Laura said. "It's just something I missed, like disco or Vietnam, because I was born too late or in the wrong place."

"How could you have missed depression?" Kit asked. "You lived in the same state as the queen of turquoise eye shadow, Mimi on *The Drew Carey Show*."

Laura was about to explain the difference between life and television when Calla looked up from the roll of tape that she was putting back into her Louis Vuitton satchel. "Don't pay any attention to Kit, Laura. She's never lived more than an hour or two away from Greenwich, Connecticut. I know what you're saying. I have a cousin who lives in Milwaukee, and she's just like you. She never gets depressed, either."

Faced with this new information, Laura tried to think of a way to explain that her life wasn't a country music song written in Ohio and that if she wasn't "depressed," this fact might help to explain it. But her coworkers' airy conversation sprinted past and lapped her until they had decided that, based on the fit of the bridesmaid's dress, she was going to replace Perky Vano in the wedding.

"So I guess we're all set. I'll ask the make-up artist for the other bridesmaids to spend some extra time with her. We'll see what Yannick can do with her hair ... legs look great now that she's solved the problem with the bronzer ... those awful streaks have gone away ... just hope she doesn't try any other experiments the night before the wedding ... still a few weeks away but you can't be too careful."

Kit was zipping up the garment bag so that she could take the dress back to her parents' house in Connecticut when Calla had an afterthought.

"I'm having a giveaway tomorrow of some of the summer beauty products that we have to discard to make room for the fall and winter items. You might be able to pick up a few things there that you could use for the rehearsal dinner or ..."

Caitlin burst into the ladies' room, out of breath from having run up the staircase to the upper floor.

"Laura! Where have you been? We've been looking for you downstairs for fifteen minutes. You've got to run back to your desk this instant! Zoli's on the phone!"

✳✳✳

"Would you call 'puce' a synonym for 'fuchsia?'"

Laura looked expectantly at Caitlin, who was eating a bagel and wearing a T-shirt that said MY REALITY CHECK BOUNCED along with her usual cargo shorts and bandanna around her forehead. "*The American Heritage Dictionary* says that puce is 'a deep-red to dark-grayish purple' and 'fuchsia' is 'a strong, vivid, purplish red.'"

"Laura, just because you missed Zoli's call doesn't mean you have to take it out on me," Caitlin said crossly. "I tried to find you, remember?"

Stung by the rebuff, Laura didn't understand why Caitlin had been so touchy all afternoon. After all, *she* wasn't the one who'd rushed back to her desk, expecting to hear the voice of the *Cassandra* society columnist, and gotten only an earful of static from the car phone of a rented Bentley on the Costa del Sol. After the incident, Laura gave up on the idea of connecting with Zoli and began editing his column without his help.

"I wasn't trying to take it out on you. I appreciate that you looked for me. I just wondered if you had an opinion."

"This is the fourth question you've asked in the past half hour, and I have my own work to do. What does it matter if 'puce' means the same as 'fuchsia?'"

"It matters because Zoli said that Eleanor Doddering looked 'majestic in puce' at the Gulls and Buoys charity benefit in the Hamptons. But when I called to make sure that she'd worn the color, she insisted that her dress was fuchsia. She said that nobody had worn puce in thirty years. She'll be furious if we imply that she'd appeared at a benefit in such an unfashionable color."

"So change the word to fuchsia."

"Simon said that Zoli isn't used to having his column edited, so I'm trying to make as few changes as possible. I've already had to make several. Zoli wrote that the Gulls and Buoys party would aid the Girls and Boys Clubs when, according to Eleanor Doddering, it raised money to save the seagulls."

Caitlin tossed her bagel back onto her desk. "Seagulls aren't endangered. They're pests. I went to the beach a few weekends ago and took a sandwich in a paper bag. A gull swooped down and stole my lunch while I was collecting shells." Caitlin glanced at Zoli's column. "If I were you, I'd call Ellie back and ask if she was pulling your leg about the gulls."

"Ellie wasn't pulling my leg. The yachts on Long Island get oil in the water, and the oil coats the seagulls' feathers. People don't want to solve the problem by giving up their boats. But there's a way to round up the gulls and clean their wings that costs a fortune. So Ellie was raising money for it. People say that she's one of the busiest environmental activists in the Hamptons."

Laura knew how improbable her explanation sounded and was glad that she'd asked follow-up questions to confirm it. "But seagulls aren't the point. The point is, I have to decide whether Eleanor Doddering wore 'fuchsia' or 'puce.'"

Caitlin rolled her eyes. "Look, Laura, if Zoli said that Ellie Doddering was 'majestic in puce,' you have bigger problems than the color of her dress. I don't know why Simon didn't tell you. But

Zoli writes his column in code. 'Majestic' is his word for 'fat' and 'helmet-headed.' I guarantee that if you look at the pictures for the column, you're going to see somebody in a tent dress and a hairstyle that you could carbon-date."

Skeptical of this claim, Laura reached for a stack of photos on her desk. She leafed through it until she came across a picture of Eleanor Doddering in a freeze-dried hairstyle and a sheet of a dress.

Caitlin looked smug. "What did I tell you? Zoli has other code words, too. 'Dapper' means 'drag queen.' 'Ebullient' means 'three sheets to the wind.' 'Exquisitely delicate canapés' means 'too cheap to serve the pyramid of caviar that we all wanted.' 'Rain didn't dampen the spirits' means, 'At least the chintzy tent didn't fall down this time.' And—watch out for this one—'Ended at a refreshingly sensible hour' means, 'The party was so bad that everybody left early and went home to watch Charlie Rose.'"

Laura couldn't understand why New Yorkers were so cynical. "Maybe Zoli is just being tactful. What's wrong with that?"

"Zoli's subjects are beginning to decode his subtext. They'll call up and say that they weren't 'ebullient' the same way so-and-so was 'ebullient' at the Top Dogs benefit for the animal shelter when he tried to dance with a Jack Russell terrier. Or they'll say, 'Zoli implied that people left my party to go home and watch Charlie Rose. Well, Charlie Rose was *at* my party.' Some people have stopped inviting Zoli to their events. Others have threatened to sue."

"But Zoli has an international following ..."

"That's part of the problem. Zoli doesn't care how many Limoges teacups he rattles here. He knows that if the magazine fires him, he'll still get invited to his friends' villas in Umbria or estancias in Argentina and get his articles published in other publications."

"What can I do about it?"

"Just be careful. Double-check everything he says, and don't take anything at face value. Delete or edit everything that might get the magazine into trouble."

"Can't we just run his columns by our lawyers? Maybe they'd catch things the rest of us wouldn't."

"If Cassandra doesn't want to pay fact-checkers to go over every line, do you think she wants to pay lawyers?" Caitlin asked, exasperated. "She likes to save the lawyers for things that are really important. Let's say we're planning a location shoot with a star who wants to bring along his pet ferret and demands a letter of agreement saying that we'll provide not just his favorite snacks but food for the ferret." Caitlin took a bite of her bagel. "So just do the best you can with the column and don't worry. If you get into trouble, you can get another job easily. That's the great thing about New York. There's always somebody willing to hire you. Every time one of my newspapers has folded, I've found another job within a month."

"Every time?" Laura asked, alarmed. "How often has this happened?"

"I've worked for more newspapers that have folded than haven't."

Laura remembered that Tim had read an article that predicted a shakeout among the magazines edited by talk-show hosts, and she wanted to ask Caitlin if she agreed with it. But she realized that she had more work to do on Zoli's column than she'd planned, so she put it off and returned to her editing. She decided to go over the society column again from the beginning and got no further than the second paragraph before she read:

"The dapper 'Big Dick' Doddering was his usual ebullient self as his guests feasted on exquisitely delicate canapés …"

***

After several hours, Laura finished editing Zoli's column and sent an electronic copy to Simon, then went for a walk. Most of the time, she left the building only at lunchtime or when she had to dash to the subway before an interview, and she was surprised by how few people she saw on the streets of Tribeca.

She liked the thrombotic parts of the city like Times Square, where even the Howard Johnson's was more interesting than its kin that she'd visited in the Midwest. Before one of her job interviews, she took a bus tour of Manhattan, and the guide explained that FBI agents had once stormed the motel and captured Angela Davis, the sixties radical who'd spent years on the lam. Since then, every time she passed the HoJo's, she half-expected to see federal agents leaving with Jimmy Hoffa, shielding his face from television cameras and wearing a souvenir T-shirt with a big red apple on it.

But Laura always felt rushed in midtown. She was afraid she'd get arrested for loitering if she dallied at crosswalks or took too long to fish a few quarters out of her purse at a newsstand. At least in the middle of the afternoon, before all the clubs opened at night, Tribeca was more relaxing, almost as low-keyed as the Warehouse District in Cleveland. She had heard that Carapace had situated the *Cassandra* offices there because the rents were lower than in midtown, and it was one of the few economies she didn't mind.

Laura came across a park—that was another thing she liked about New York, you could "come across" parks—and sat down near a cluster of pigeons that strutted in the sunlight like infant kings, the Dalai Lamas of the bird world. Now that she no longer had Zoli's column on her mind, she kept thinking about her conversation in the ladies' room with her coworkers, who seemed to see depression as a way of life.

She wondered if she was too happy to thrive in New York, where a certain paranoia was essential to survival. But she didn't see how she could be anything but a pathological optimist. Her father had told her continually how lucky she was to live in a free country that hadn't fought waves of invaders for five hundred years as Hungary had—first the Ottoman Turks, then the Nazis, and finally the Communists. Her mother said that one of the happiest moments of her life occurred when she learned that American supermarkets sold cucumbers, a vegetable that she thought grew only in Europe.

Laura didn't think her mother was joking—she once got tears in her eyes when she spoke of seeing cucumbers in Heinen's for the first time—and couldn't help absorbing some of her appreciation for their comforts. At the age of four, she first heard the story of how her parents fled to Austria with her grandparents a step ahead of the Russian tanks. Afterward Laura woke up every morning half-expecting to see gun turrets from her bedroom window. She didn't relax until she had asked how long it took to walk to Canada so often that her parents figured out that she thought the Communists might try to take over the United States. Once she realized that Cleveland Heights was safe from the Red Army, she was so relieved that she had no serious worries until her father first became ill and then passed away during her freshman year of college. All that singing of "Wake Up the Echoes" practically tore her apart until she met Nick, who helped to distract her from her grief.

But Laura knew that all of this could change in New York, where she might have a panzer division of new anxieties. When she got back to the office and saw that Caitlin was in a better mood, she decided to ask her indirectly about this possibility.

"Caitlin, are you depressed?"

Caitlin looked at her as though she'd gone to a psychiatric ward at Bellevue instead of for a walk. "Of course, I'm depressed. Who isn't?"

"What are you depressed about?"

"What am I *not* depressed about? First of all, the whole country is run by Republicans, especially in New York. We have George Bush as president, George Pataki as governor, and Michael Bloomberg as mayor. Nobody even remembers that our commander-in-chief is the man who said, 'I know how hard it is to put food on your family.'"

"We have Hillary Clinton as senator. Why not focus on that?"

Caitlin ignored the comment, and Laura couldn't tell if she disliked the senator or saw the question as beside the point.

"Every day you see something new to get depressed about. Take that new study of mammograms I wrote about. All it proved was that after hundreds of years of using women as human guinea pigs, doctors are still doing it."

Laura had read Caitlin's story and thought that, if anything, it had made the opposite point. "But you quoted three doctors who admitted that they had overprescribed mammograms and that they were recommending them less. They said that they were trying to *stop* using women as 'human guinea pigs.' And doctors use men as guinea pigs, too."

"Laura, you remind me of that girl in the children's books who was always so unnaturally cheerful no matter how many bad things happened—"

"Pollyanna?"

"No, my mother wouldn't let me rent that video. She said Pollyanna was a wimp. The one with the long red braids—"

"Pippi Longstocking?"

"Right. She was an orphan and had a deluded fantasy that her mother was an angel in heaven and her father was a cannibal king."

"But Pippi Longstocking was an anarchist! She refused to go to school, then barged into a classroom and criticized the entire educational system."

"Yes, but she wasn't depressed about how bad the educational system was, the way any normal person would be."

Laura thought about this. Caitlin's position seemed to be that it wasn't enough to do something about things that bothered you— that you also had an obligation to feel depressed about them. "But what if you don't feel depressed or see yourself as a victim of, say, the educational system? Are you supposed to pretend that you do?"

"If you don't feel depressed about something, you're not paying attention." Caitlin pointed to a small framed photo of Laura's father decorating a birthday cake in the red, white, and green colors of Hungary. "What about your parents? You must be depressed about the awful things they did to you when you were growing up."

"My parents were great. When I was in high school, I thought my father was trying to bribe people to vote for me in a teenage beauty contest by giving them cookies. I begged him to stop humiliating me. But now I wonder why I was so upset. My father gave out free cookies even when I wasn't running for something. After he died, I talked to a lot of people who said they didn't know they were being bribed. 'Oh, those almond crescents were supposed to get me to vote for you? I didn't realize it. I voted for Julia Vargas.'"

Laura sensed that Caitlin was waiting for a withering comment on her mother. "My biggest problem with my mother is that she won't kick my freeloading brother out of the house and make him get a job. She waits on him hand and foot. Whenever I try to talk to her about Steve, to get her to cut off his supply of chicken *paprikás*, she says that he can't take care of himself the way I can. He spends all his time working out or practicing his skateboarding in the driveway. He doesn't understand that for some of us 'working out' means going to the office each day."

"That's not the way I heard it. I heard from Kit that you were some kind of child slave—that your parents made you work all these horrible hours in their shop when all of your friends were hanging out at the mall."

"They did make me work there. And, naturally, they let my brother out of it because his grades were lower and he 'needed to study.' But I've sort of figured out that the reason why I've had good jobs and he hasn't is that I learned to enjoy work. At times I complained about spending Saturdays at the bakery instead of at the movies or about waiting on people whose accents I couldn't understand. But, in a way, it was fun to be treated like a mascot by a lot of Hungarian grandmothers."

"There must be something that depresses you."

Laura thought about her cousin's wedding. Having to look like an eggplant for a few hours didn't seem as substantial a complaint as living in a country run by Republicans or believing that doctors had been using all women as human guinea pigs for hundreds of years. But she had the sense that Caitlin would think less of her if she didn't come up with something.

"I do have to be in the wedding of my cousin Tina, who hates me. She works in a gift shop. Before that, she tried to start her own business that sold things that she découpaged, and she wanted me to write about her in my old magazine. I just couldn't do it. She only découpaged things that were totally impractical, like Game Boys or things you had to put in the dishwasher."

Caitlin wrinkled her nose. "Who would buy anything like that?"

"That was my question. Even if Tina had created more practical items—say, Christmas tree ornaments or pencil-holders—she couldn't grasp that nobody's made a living at découpage since the seventies. Or that it would have been a conflict of interest for me to write about my cousin. I showed Ron, my old boss, some of her sketches for things like découpaged calculators to make sure my relationship with her wasn't affecting my judgment. He thought I was insane. He said, 'Pet psychics are one thing, and your cousin is another.'"

Caitlin shook her head. "People from the Midwest are so strange."

Laura couldn't tell if Caitlin was talking about her or her cousin, but she let it pass. "Tina blamed me for the failure of her business and refused to speak to me for two years. She said that ever since I went away to Notre Dame, I'd turned into a snob who didn't care about her family. But after she got engaged, she asked me to be a bridesmaid. My father was her godfather, and her father is mine. So I couldn't turn her down."

"That is so depressing." Caitlin pinked up a pink slip. "Well, here's something to take your mind off it. I forgot to tell you. Simon called while you were out to say that he had to go to midtown to see some people from Carapace—something about cost overruns for September—but that he sent you email about the society column."

Laura switched on her computer, wishing she hadn't left the office until she had spoken to Simon. As much as she liked email, it was so blunt that it had a way of making bad news seem worse.

To: Laura Smart
From: Simon Wright

Brilliant editing of Zoli. First column in three months that doesn't include the words 'dapper,' 'ebullient,' or 'majestic.' Confirmed fully my belief in keen advantages of having articles edited by someone who has never taken an English as a Second Language class.

Please plan to edit the column regularly from now on. I'm sure you can fit it in around your other assignments.

This message rekindled Laura's mild crush on Simon, dampened only slightly by her dismay about having to edit Zoli regularly. In a month Simon had given her more praise than Nick had in years. Laura knew that dwelling on his note would heighten her crush, so she trolled through her press releases until she saw Kit racing down the staircase. Kit was breathless by the time she reached Features.

"Great news, Laura! Yannick can fit you in for a cut and color tomorrow right after Calla's beauty-products giveaway. That would give you a few days to get used to your new look before the wedding. You need to call right away to confirm."

14
Giveaway

For fifteen minutes, women had been stampeding through the halls of *Cassandra*, heading for the open boxes of beauty products on the floor near the reception desk. Laura had never seen anything like it. From her cubicle she could hear the raised voices of her coworkers.

"Trade you a Dior Kohl Pencil for Dr. Hauschka's Cleansing Milk."

"Why don't we ever get the La Prairie Skin Caviar line?"

"Which model used this Kiehl's Lip Balm? I hope she didn't have Herpes."

"Is this Pretty Pretty Face Salve for skin rashes? Or for normal skin?"

"Should I take the Bliss Half-Naked Lip Gloss or the MAC Pink Swoon Blush?"

After hearing the announcement about the giveaway, Laura debated whether to join the women who pawed through the boxes that Calla had set out in the reception area. She had vowed not to take any more freebies that assaulted her conscience. And nobody her age *needed* the items that the beauty editor was giving away—the twenty-five-dollar bars of black soap and five-hundred-dollar skin creams that had the word "defense" in their titles as though intended for a limited nuclear war against crows feet.

At last, she struck a compromise with her moral qualms. She waited until she thought that the most expensive items would have disappeared, then walked to the reception area. It looked like the scene of a ticker-tape parade at which people had thrown packaging inserts folded as tightly as origami fans.

"Laura, I'm so sorry you didn't get here sooner." Calla was holding a wedge-shaped sponge as she stood in front of a box full of liquid foundation. "We had a great Hungarian mud mask that you would have loved. But I set a limit of two items per person, so we still have some good things left. What do you need?"

Laura examined a few tubes of blue lipstick and white concealer and almost refused, but it occurred to her that Alice might like to have a few things for the wedding.

"I don't wear much makeup, and Venetia gave me some the other day. But my friend Alice is going to attend Kit's wedding, too. And she might like a couple of things for it. She has big brown eyes and dark hair that gets lighter in the summer when she goes sailing."

Frown lines rippled across Calla's brow. "Then she needs a sunblock for her hair, so it won't lighten. Otherwise she'll look like a scarecrow by the time she's thirty." She pulled a bottle of spray-on hair sunblock from a box. "Your friend might like this. Tell her that she also should put mayonnaise on her hair and cover it with a shower cap for at least a few hours once a month, preferably overnight."

"You mean Hellman's?"

"The original formula. It has miraculous effects if you wash it out well."

Calla looked to see if anybody could hear. "Nobody knows how great mayonnaise is for hair because editors can't say it. I tried to at the last place I worked, and the advertisers became enraged. The president of a cosmetics company—the president!—wrote to the magazine to say, 'Why are we spending hundreds of thousands of dollars a year to advertise hair-care products on your pages if you're telling people to use Hellman's?' I didn't even suggest that readers use mayonnaise instead of Conditioner X, just in addition to it."

Laura knew that Alice would love the idea of using Hellman's, one of the few products you could count on finding in the refrigerator at Rose Bluffs. "Thanks. I might try that myself if I spend much time on the beach this summer."

Calla looked over her shoulder again. "I really shouldn't do this because of the two-item limit. But most people who wanted something would have shown up by now, so I'm going to give you a few extras for your friend." The beauty editor began filling a small shopping bag with items for Alice: a wand of dark brown mascara, tubes of cream blush, and an eye shadow palette with a range of colors that would have satisfied Gauguin. She explained why she was enclosing some of the products.

"Your friend probably wears brush-on blush like most people your age, and you've got to make her stop. Except for the sun or soap, nothing ages your skin faster than powder. It dries it out so much, it's practically Kitty Litter for your face. You won't find a fashionable woman in the city over forty who wears anything but cream blush. Unfortunately, by that age, you may have damage you can't undo."

Calla had almost finished filling the bag when she looked up at Laura. "But you haven't taken anything for yourself. Let me see if I can find something for you."

She dipped into a box and came up with an eye mask filled with a pink gel that had white ribbons attached. "Here's something you'll love. It's a mask that soothes tired eyes. You keep it in the refrigerator so that, when you're ready to use it, it will feel cool against your skin."

Calla tied the mask around Laura's eyes. "Funny, you remind of someone in that mask. I just can't remember who …" She thought for a moment, then brightened. "Oh, I've got it! Audrey Hepburn in *Breakfast at Tiffany's*! Remember that great mask she wore when she slept?"

Calla got out a mirror. "You see?" she asked, pushing the mask up on Laura's head. "You've got the look. Now all you need is the man. Although I'm afraid that these days Audrey might have to settle for her cat."

✳✳✳

Wrapped in a black smock, Laura sat in a private room at Yannick, the exclusive Fifth Avenue hair salon, trying to remember enough French to read *Maison et Jardin*. She had just declined the offer of a papaya martini from a solicitous staff member who, unpersuaded by Laura's assurances that she needed nothing, returned with an armload of magazines. Before leaving, the young woman adjusted several dials on the wall, filling the room with the scent of lavender and the muted sounds of a Chopin *polonaise*.

Despite her inability to translate most of the French architectural terms she read, Laura relaxed now that she had met the owner of the salon. A man on intimate terms with the split ends of sheikas and countesses, Yannick flew to Los Angeles every April to aim his chrome blow-dryer at the heads of a half dozen Oscar nominees. She had worried that he would insist on lopping off half her hair and giving her one of those fashionably mussed-up styles that made you look as though you had stuck your head in a fan belt.

But she discovered that Yannick liked long hair and wore his own in a glossy black ponytail that, along with his cowboy boots, made him look more Native American than French. So he had trimmed only a few inches before handing her off to a colorist whom he instructed to make her hair look like "sunlight falling on cognac." She was now awaiting the transformation with her head abloom in foil packets. Kit said that Yannick was having his employees work on her bridesmaids' hair as a wedding gift and that she needed to leave only tips.

Setting aside her copy of *Maison et Jardin*, Laura fished her purse from one of the clear plastic bags that the salon handed out as insurance against lawsuits by women whose fifteen-thousand-dollar Kelly bags couldn't survive a dab of twenty-volume peroxide. She took out the first of several memos that she hadn't had time to read before she left the office.

To her annoyance she saw that Accounting had refused to reimburse her for two taxi fares for which she hadn't handed in receipts. *Give me a break!* she thought, balling up the memo and tossing it into a wastebasket. It was true that she had a knack, maybe a genius, for failing to turn in receipts. But what journalist didn't? If you were scribbling at the speed of light in the back seat of a taxi, taking down the words of an assistant city commissioner who would talk to you only between appointments, were you supposed to stop in mid-sentence to ask for proof of the trip? Failing to turn in receipts was almost a requirement for the job. It meant that you were paying attention to your sources, not to a running meter or restaurant tab.

Trying not to think about her dwindling bank account, Laura read a memo in which Simon praised the staff for its work on the August issue and singled out her "heroic effort" on the cover story. That unsettled her slightly, too. Every time Simon heaped his praise on her prose, her crush flared up. But he never gave her a reason to believe that he had more than a professional interest in her. Was Anne Meyer right that nothing would happen between them unless *she* seduced him? And could she gain anything by it if he might be going back to England? Why did the only two attractive men she knew—Tim and Simon—both have to work for her company?

Laura was trying not to think about men or money when a salon attendant entered the room and gave her a shampoo that smelled of almonds and honey. Then he led her to a stylist who blow-dried her hair. Yannick nodded with approval when he checked the result, a cascade of soft waves as shiny as a new penny and so bouncy that Laura wanted to toss her head like somebody in a shampoo commercial until she sprained her neck. After handing out more in tips than she might spend on food for a week, she still thought she would fly all the way home.

✱✱✱

"You look amazing!" Alice said. "Those highlights brighten your entire face. What a stroke of luck that Kate Cameron needed a last-minute bridesmaid!"

Sitting in an alcove that Mrs. Dudley had used as a dressing room, Laura put a dab of Dusky Rose cream blush on her friend's cheek and spread it with the quick upward strokes that she'd seen her coworkers at *Cassandra* use. After the beauty giveaway, she had invited herself to Connecticut to give Alice a makeup lesson. It was almost finished, and Alice was still showing more enthusiasm for the efforts of the staff at Yannick's salon than for Calla's cast-offs.

"Kate calls herself 'Kit' now," Laura reminded her gently. "I heard that she made the switch after joining an Internet dating service a couple of years ago. Kit looked at the membership list and decided that 'Kate' was overexposed among twenty-seven-year-old women seeking 'financially secure' men. She thought that 'Kit' might make her stand out. The odd thing is that Gordon likes 'Kate' better, so she's thinking of changing it back."

"But she's also hyphenating her name after the wedding!" Alice said. "That means that, in two or three years, she'll have gone from Kate Cameron to Kit Cameron to Kate Cameron-MacGregor. She was born Katherine Atkins Cameron. How will she keep herself straight?"

"It could have been worse. She wanted to call herself 'Kitten,' which she thought would make men see her as 'warm' and 'approachable.' But she backed off when a friend said it made her sound like a porn star."

Alice moved so abruptly that Laura had to ask her to hold still. "Why do women see life as a game of Twister where men spin the wheel? We think that any time a man calls out a color, we have to put a hand or foot on the floor even if it means that we crack our spines. I like Kate—Kit—but she turned into a contortionist after she began dating. You'd think that any woman who had as much money as she does would believe that she has a right to call a few shots with men, but she doesn't."

After Laura added another dab of blush, Alice went on. "When we were fifteen, Kate had a wild crush on a boy named Alexander Bradford. He always wore Docksiders without socks and expected his dates to tie his laces when they came undone. Once I double dated with Kate and Sandy, and Kate tied his shoelaces a half dozen times. The worst moment came in the popcorn line at the movie theater when she tied the laces in front of about two hundred people waiting to see *Scent of a Woman*." Alice paused. "No, the real worst moment came when Sandy dumped her even though she *had* tied the laces. He'd found another girl willing to inhale his foot odors six times a night."

Laura wondered if Alice's uncharacteristically low mood had something to do with her lack of male companionship. Her split with Chip appeared to be sapping her buoyancy.

"But all of us do things when we're fifteen that we regret. When I was that age, I let Joey Molnar—otherwise known as the Altar Boy From Hell—grope me in the sacristy before five o'clock Mass on Saturday. I was wearing my pillowy altar girl robe and figured he didn't get anything but a handful of fabric. Some people would say that I ought to have reported him to the priest, if not strangled him with the white sash around my waist. But I couldn't bring myself to turn him in. Joey was having so much trouble in school that his only moments of glory came when he carried his candles down the aisle. I was afraid he'd lose his spot. Maybe Kit fell into the same kind of situation with Sandy."

"If she did, she hasn't put it behind her. I saw Kate and Gordon from a distance at a cocktail party not long after they became engaged. One of Gordon's shoelaces came untied, and Kate dropped down and tied it in her strapless dress. I'd been planning to say hello, but after that, I couldn't face her. I was afraid I'd shout, 'Kate, you beat all the boys in the Sunfish races in fifth grade! You're pretty and smart and your father could buy you a third Connecticut as a wedding present. Gordon should be tying *your* laces.' Kate is getting married to Gordon, but she's still dating Alex."

Alice studied her reflection in a gilt-edged oval mirror. "That's why I hadn't responded to the wedding invitation. My mother would have been mortified if I didn't go. She and Mrs. Cameron were roommates at Emma Willard. So I didn't have the heart to decline. But I kept having a vision of the rector saying, 'You may kiss the bride,' and Kate responding, 'Wait! I have to tie his shoelaces first.'"

Laura picked up a wand of mascara and applied it to Alice's long lashes. She had been waiting for an opening to bring up the idea of fixing her up with Tim but sensed Alice wasn't in the mood to hear about Tim or any other man right now. So she told Alice of her own decision to meet new men and asked for her advice on how to do it.

"Why think about that now?" Alice asked. "You'll probably meet enough men at Kit's wedding to keep you busy for the rest of the summer."

15
Strip the Willow

Laura dodged a piece of haggis thrown by a small boy in one of the Grenadier Guards' uniforms that the pages had worn at Kit Cameron's wedding—a crisp red jacket with gold buttons and a plumed black fur hat. Despite the damage that a fragment of a sheep's stomach could inflict on her five-thousand-dollar brides-maid's dress, she welcomed the diversion of watching the young Scottish guests let off steam.

For half an hour, she'd been sitting at a table at the Dunsinane Yacht Club, hardly able to believe what she saw: Alice was flirting. Or more precisely, flirting with Simon. Before the reception Laura understood dimly that Alice knew how to captivate men—she certainly had the dates to prove it—but she had never actually seen her do this. Now that she had, she marveled at the results. Simon couldn't take his eyes off Alice. He seemed to believe that if he looked away for an instant he would be sent to the Tower of London, or possibly force-fed all the leftover haggis.

Laura had thought that Simon flirted with *her* at work, but he gave Alice an attention she'd never seen him pay to anyone at *Cassandra*. At the office he engaged in easy sexual banter. He wasn't bantering with Alice. Behind the lightness of his words lay a seriousness that she hadn't heard when he was talking about life-or-death matters for *Cassandra*. He was telling Alice about his school days and other experiences he never mentioned at work.

At first Laura wondered if Alice and Simon had succumbed to the free-floating exhilaration of a wedding that had gone off perfectly, or to the spell cast by a regal yacht club aglow with flickering red candles and fragrant with the scent of thistles and American Beauty roses. Nearly everywhere she looked, she could see men in Bonnie Prince Charlie jackets and kilts with the red-and-black checkerboard pattern of the Roy MacGregor tartan, one of the boldest of the designs worn by the clans. Perhaps Alice and Simon had capitulated to the force of so much romance and tradition gathered in one place?

This explanation seemed plausible. But Laura rejected it when she realized that—as seductive as the wedding was—both of her friends had attended others like it without losing their heads. The more likely reason for their infatuation was that both had shown up prepared to meet destiny halfway. Alice had worn her new makeup with a pink silk shantung dress of her mother's, now fashionably "vintage," that gave her a natural air of the '30s glamour that others put so much effort into achieving. Unlike most of the American women at the wedding, she had also arrived in a large hat decorated with a pink flower. Simon had turned up in a smart black Spencer jacket and a kilt and sporran that he had once worn to the wedding of a schoolmate. Laura had never realized how much a kilt and a haircut could improve a man's looks.

Alice and Simon appeared so enamored of each other that Laura wasn't surprised when after less than an hour, they left the wedding reception to go for a walk on the beach. In their absence she searched for Venetia and saw her talking to a female guest on the other side of the crowded room. Not wanting to interrupt, she waited until her coworker spotted her and waved.

Laura crossed the room with a step quickened by an upbeat tune played by the bagpiper who had heralded the arrival of the bride and groom with "Scotland the Brave." Venetia hugged her and admired Yannick's special effects.

"Great hair, Laura, and you don't need duct tape to keep it in place. My mother says, 'God gives you a rough draft,' and I think you have your final version now. But before I go on, I'd like you to meet someone."

Venetia turned to the woman standing next to her. "Aurora, this is Laura Smart. Laura, this is Kit's former boss, Aurora Starr."

Laura teetered on her black silk heels with the ankle bow that kept coming untied. *This was Aurora Starr?* Aurora didn't exactly look dowdy in her beige silk jacquard suit, which probably came from one of the couture powerhouses. But she also didn't look as though she was gasping for breath, as Cassandra usually did, in her race to stay ahead of her viewers. Aurora could have passed for any well-dressed mother-of-the-bride in Pepper Pike or Hunting Valley in her russet bob and stylish but sensible heels.

Faced with her boss's rival, Laura wished she'd realized that the talk-show host might turn up. Cassandra had declined her invitation by saying that she had to meet with an affiliate in Detroit. So Laura hadn't expected to have to make small talk about afternoon television. She might appear to be foraging for trade secrets if she asked about Aurora's magazine, but talking about her television show seemed safe enough.

Laura mentioned the popular "Bridesmaids Dresses from Hell" segments and asked the talk-show host about the worst bridesmaid's dress she'd ever worn.

Aurora laughed. "Oh, there are so many! I grew up in the same Indiana town as Larry Bird, French Lick, and some of my bridesmaid's dresses were as embarrassing as that name. The worst? I guess I'd pick a chartreuse silk chiffon gown with gull-winged sleeves. And as if those weren't bad enough, I had to wear a cowboy hat with them. When I walked down the aisle, I felt like Buffalo Bill riding shotgun in a DeLorean. Funny, I haven't thought about that dress in years. But I can remember every stitch."

"Did the bride tell you that she picked the dress because you could wear it again?" Laura asked. "There seems to be an inverse relation between how often the bride says that and the likelihood that you actually will wear it again."

"Of course!" Aurora said, laughing. "I wanted to tell the bride I couldn't wear that dress and hat again unless somebody asked me to appear in a vintage auto show in Laramie, Wyoming. But, unfortunately, I couldn't because she was my sister. A lot of people are happy now that some brides pick a different style dress for each attendant. My feeling is this gives you five times as many opportunities to make a mistake."

A waiter approached carrying a silver tray, and Aurora took a canapé made from salmon that Kit's father had flown in from Scotland. "But what about you? What's the worst bridesmaid's dress you've ever worn?"

Laura described what she was wearing for her cousin's wedding. "But it doesn't seem as bad now that I know about your outfit. Tina thought about asking us to wear cowboy hats, too. But she decided we needed hats shaped like melon wedges instead. Our look is 'Produce Department at Shop Rite' instead of 'Vintage Auto Show in Laramie.'"

Aurora smiled and studied Laura. "Love the dress Kit found for you. But I wonder how you could afford it given the salaries that Venetia says all of you get at *Cassandra*."

Laura was surprised that Aurora assumed she'd paid for the dress. "We're lucky. Kit's father bought the dresses, and he got a big discount. Egotista Dominguez marked down the cost as wedding gift."

Aurora almost dropped her salmon-and-dill canapé. "Cassandra let Kit accept that kind of gift?"

Laura didn't know whether Cassandra *had* approved of the gift and if she had, whether she should admit this to Aurora. "I'm not sure," she said in a halting voice. "Cassandra spends a lot of time in her studio, so the editors have a lot of freedom."

"If they can accept huge discounts on couture dresses, they have too much freedom," Aurora said curtly.

Laura felt nervous about what else Aurora might ask, so she was relieved when a handsome usher from Edinburgh asked her to do a Scottish dance called "Strip the Willow." If she didn't know the dance, he said, she could pick up the steps quickly.

"You just link elbows with your partner, turn, then go down a line of dancers and turn them, too, as though you were stripping the leaves off a willow." The usher smiled as he pointed to the dance floor, where well-dressed couples were forming long rows. "Your biggest problem will be fighting off nausea as you keep turning, not mastering the steps."

Laura turned to Aurora. "Would you mind?"

"Not in the least."

As she worked her way down the line of couples in "Strip the Willow," Laura saw that the dance amounted to a musical personals ad. She found herself thrust briefly into the field of vision of so many men that for the rest of the evening she hardly left the dance floor. One of the groom's cousins claimed her for the Britannia Two Step, and other men sought her out for a flurry of reels, jigs, waltzes, and polkas played by a high-spirited Scottish band called Fiddlers' Delight. All of the attention almost made up for all the invitations to glamorous parties that hadn't yet materialized at *Cassandra*.

Near the end of the evening, Laura decided to find Aurora and Venetia to apologize for her long absence. To her surprise they were still having a lively conversation in the corner where she had left them. Venetia was telling Aurora that if *Cassandra* had a company cafeteria, the Salvation Army would run it. "Isn't that right, Laura?"

"I'll say." With her inhibitions loosened by a glass or two of Veuve Cliquot, Laura mentioned the basketball and taxi fares that Carapace had refused to pay for. "You'd never guess from the cost of the clothes on our fashion pages that the company is so frugal."

"You're far too diplomatic," Aurora said cheerily. "If Carapace won't pay for a basketball for a cover story, that's not frugal. That's cheap."

"Who's cheap?"

Laura whirled around and saw Tim Moran, whom she hadn't spoken to since their dinner at Babcia's, standing next to her in deep tan pants and an elegantly tailored dinner jacket. She was speechless. When Venetia said that Kit knew everybody in the company, it hadn't occurred to her that this would include Tim.

"You're cheap, Tim," Aurora said good-naturedly. "Or at least your people are. Laura has been telling us all about it."

"Oh, she has?" Tim asked dryly. "I'll have to keep that in mind."

"Not that I didn't know it already," Aurora bantered. She told Laura that she and Tim had served together on a broadcasting-awards committee and disagreed about whether the winners should receive cash prizes. Aurora had plumped for checks while Tim argued that work was its own reward and Connie Chung didn't need any more money. "So it doesn't surprise me that Carapace wouldn't pick up the cost of a basketball."

"Basketball?" Tim asked, staring at Laura. "What basketball?"

Laura wished she'd stuck a piece of duct tape on her mouth instead of her breasts. "Just the basketball that I bought for my interview with Normendie."

A spark of recognition lit Tim's face. "You tried to expense *that* basketball?" he asked. "And somebody turned you down?"

Laura nodded. The incredulity in his voice made clear how petty her complaint sounded.

"Now aren't you ashamed of yourself, Tim?" Aurora said in the indulgent tone of a mother scolding a favorite son. "I'd make you write out a check to Laura on the spot if all of your cost-cutting measures weren't so good for our company. They make it so much easier for us to hire away your best employees."

"Aurora, if you wouldn't mind, I'd like to dance with Laura so that I can get to the bottom of this without forcing her to reveal privileged information in front of a rival editor," Tim said in a lightly self-mocking tone. "The next dance is a Highland schottische, which Kit said is a lot of fun."

"Dancing with Laura is the least you can do for her," Aurora said, "after making her work in an office that has vending machines instead of a company cafeteria. And I'm sure she'd love to join you. She may have a few more things she'd like to tell you about how you run the financial side of the company."

Laura could hardly contradict Aurora by saying that Tim was the last man she wanted to dance with. It was obvious that the talk-show host was used to having her own way. So she followed Tim to a dance floor full of people in Highland dress. It struck her as ominous that many of the men had daggers in their stockings.

When they were out of earshot of the others, Tim spoke in a hurt whisper. "I wanted to dance with you to apologize for what I'd said about your apartment. I was only concerned about your safety. It occurred to me that you're so new to the city that you might not know the difference between normal New York squalor and the squalor in your building. But it's obviously too late because you've been slandering me to anybody who will listen, including one of our main competitors."

The bandleader began calling out instructions.

"PLEASE TAKE PARTNERS AND FORM A CIRCLE AROUND THE ROOM FOR THE HIGHLAND SCHOT-TISCHE."

"I wasn't slandering you," Laura said heatedly. "I was just talk-ing telling Aurora about a few of our company policies—"

"—which we *try* to keep confidential."

"You're acting as though I told her about our editorial plans for the next six issues instead of a rejected expense claim." Laura wished that she hadn't followed Tim so quickly to the center of the room. Why had he asked her to dance so if he wanted only to argue? Maybe it wasn't too late to persuade him to rejoin Aurora and Venetia on the sidelines, where she could find safety in numbers.

"I have a feeling this dance is more complicated than 'Strip the Willow' and some of the others," she said nonchalantly. "I saw a couple of people doing it at the rehearsal dinner. Maybe we should sit this one out."

Tim didn't seem to hear. "If you needed the basketball for a story, it was a legitimate business expense. Unusual, but legitimate. I don't see why it got rejected, or why you told Aurora if it did. Why didn't you ask Simon about what you should do?"

Laura didn't want to get Simon in trouble by saying that he had suggested that she bury the claim. "I had the idea that, in cases like mine, people resubmitted their expense reports with the claim buried. But I didn't want to lie."

Tim was silent for a moment. "Well, your honesty is admirable, anyway. Any other rejected claims?"

Laura didn't want to tell him about the rejected claims for taxi fares after how he had reacted to the news about the basketball.

"Let me guess. You couldn't get reimbursed for the fifty cents you paid for an edition of *The Daily News* that had a story on someone you were writing about."

Laura could see that he was mocking her. Determined to keep her composure, she pretended to study the band. "No."

"Or for a dollar or two for photocopying at Kinko's?"

"No."

"Or for the cost of a subway ride to an interview?"

Laura was desperate to end the argument before the Highland schottische began. It was difficult enough to have a rational conversation with Tim when the band wasn't playing. It would be much harder if they had to talk to shout over the sound of two fiddles, an accordion, and a keyboard. *Not that it would stop him from trying*, she thought. "Okay, okay. I didn't get reimbursed for a couple of taxi rides to interviews."

"Interviews in Yonkers? Or Forest Hills?"

"In Battery Park and Murray Hill."

Tim laughed. "Irene Field is a remarkable woman. She wouldn't let the pope expense his Holy Water if he didn't have a receipt."

"You think it's remarkable that—" Laura fumed.

The band played a deafening chord, and they were swept into a whirlpool of couples who hopped around the floor to a pattern of steps that might have been devised by a deranged Scottish low-impact aerobics instructor who had consumed too many glasses of malt whisky. At the sound of the music Tim seemed to forget his anger and plunged with high enthusiasm into the dance.

"Isn't this great?" Tim shouted above the music as they swerved to avoid crashing into a man in a jabot. "I love this band!"

You love a band that might kill off any cardiac patients on the dance floor? Laura thought. She was one of the few people in the circle who couldn't do the steps of the schottische at the frenzied tempo favored by the fiddlers. Tim, who was clearly the better dancer, had no trouble mastering the sequence and found her ineptitude hilarious. She fantasized about stealing a dagger from somebody's stocking and murdering him with it.

"Slide, Laura, slide!" Tim bellowed. "You keep *hopping* when you ought to *slide* and *sliding* when you ought to *hop*."

Halfway through the schottische, Laura decided that she couldn't do the steps in her high heels, so she took them off and danced in her stocking feet. Afterward she could barely move fast enough to avoid getting mowed down by people who were careening around the room while bouncing up and down like pistons wrapped in tartans.

When the dance ended, Ted grinned. "That was fantastic! The key to enjoying a dance is just to plunge in and not worry about embarrassing yourself."

Laura couldn't believe that he had loved nearly getting trampled to death by men with daggers that could have disemboweled small animals. "I've always thought," she said levelly, "that the key enjoying a dance is knowing how to do the steps."

"You *did* know how to do the steps to that one," Tim said brightly. "It was your high heels that didn't know how. You were fine after you took them off."

"It took me half the dance to figure out the pattern of the hops."

"The other American women didn't even try to figure them out. They sat out the dance. Besides Kit, you were the only non-Scotswoman who had the courage to stand up for it." The wedding guests were hooting and cheering for a reprise. "Want to try it again and see if you can get it right from the beginning?"

Laura hesitated. Most of the men who had done the schottische looked as though they had dripped dry on a Scottish heath. Only Tim looked as cool and self-possessed as he had before the dance started. He was one of the most attractive men in the room, which unnerved her slightly. She didn't know whether she ought to be more worried about dancing with him again or *not* dancing with him again. She also knew that she ought to look for Alice, who was supposed to give her a ride home. At last, she declined reluctantly. She explained that she had to find her best friend, who had disappeared.

"Then I guess I'll ask Aurora to dance before I head back to the city." Tim looked around for Aurora, who was still talking to Venetia. "Just one more thing. Normendie told me that you hadn't called to talk about her memoir and that she'd love to hear from you. I hope you have no hard feelings about what I said about your apartment. But if you do, I hope you won't take them out on her. She doesn't deserve it."

Laura said that she would call Normendie if she had time to do a book, but that this was unlikely to occur soon. She started to walk away, and a piece of duct tape fell at her feet. Tim picked it up and held it against her dress looking puzzled until a smile of recognition crept across his face.

"I thought," he said, as he handed it to her, "that women used Band-Aids."

After Tim had gone off to find Aurora, Laura wandered among the rooms of the yacht club and, when she didn't see Alice, went out onto the terrace, thinking that she might have joined Simon when he went out to smoke. She saw neither of her friends, just flags with the Cameron and MacGregor crests fluttering from a pole as a drill team spelled out the names of the bride and groom with illuminated semaphores.

Eventually she gave up and returned to the ballroom. It was clear that, as the guests were drinking the last of the champagne and eating slices of a towering Dundee cake with white frosting, Alice and Simon were having a party, if not stripping a willow, all their own.

***

"Laura, I'm going to marry Simon."

Laura wondered if Alice had drunk too much champagne at the wedding or was too exhausted to know what she was saying. She could think of no other explanation for the unfathomable statement she had just heard.

In less than an hour the sun would stream through the windows of her best friend's bedroom at Rose Bluffs, where she had decided to spend the night after the wedding instead of returning to the city. And she hoped that daybreak would restore the good sense that Alice seemed to have lost when she saw Kit walk down the aisle in a white strapless gown and enough Botulinum E to keep her forehead as smooth as her silk dress. In the meantime, she was hoping to find out what had occurred on the beach while she was learning the steps to "The Dashing White Sergeant." She was also trying to figure out what to say to Simon on Monday morning, especially if he didn't know that he'd gotten engaged to Alice.

"Does Simon know that you're going to marry him?"

"Of course not. I could never say that to a man on the first date, especially since it wasn't a date, just a lucky meeting at a wedding."

"Then what makes you feel so sure?"

"I just know it."

Laura searched Alice's face for fault lines of doubt or anxiety and saw only the smooth brow of a woman who had never looked more serene. "How do you know it?"

"I can't describe it except by saying that when I've met other attractive men, I've always said, 'Yes, but.' With Simon, there's no 'but.' Sometimes my heart has said 'Yes' and my head has said 'but.' Other times my head has said 'Yes' and my heart has said 'but.' This time they're both saying the same word."

Alice caressed the sporran, a small fur pouch, that Simon had given her. "This sporran is an example. My mother had no use for the idea, 'It's just as easy to marry a rich man as a poor one.' She thought that the concept of 'rich' had become too elastic and that you needed to have more specific expectations. For example, a doctor might be 'rich' someday. But first you might have to live in poverty while he went to medical school and did his internship and residency. So she thought that while it was perfectly fine to marry a doctor, you had to make sure that he had the money to support you until the cash started to flow. Or, as she put it, 'Never marry a man who couldn't give you a mink coat by the age of thirty.' Thirty was really the outside age at which a mink coat was acceptable to her. She thought that you ought to aim to get it sooner."

Laura wasn't sure how this related to Simon. "A sporran is hardly a mink coat."

"In some ways, it's better. The 'mink coat by thirty' concept was a problem for me because a mink coat doesn't have the same meaning for our generation that it did for our mothers'. It isn't a trophy that you get for being a good wife or that your husband gives you because he did something wrong. For a lot of women, it's an embarrassment. They can't wear it to all of the events they could in the past, such as to an event at the school I teach at because some parents would never let you hear the end of it. So I was a little worried about disappointing my mother on that count. I didn't *want* a mink coat. The moment Simon gave me his rabbit-fur sporran, I knew it was Kismet. The sporran is my mink, and I got it long before the age of thirty. My mother would be so happy."

For the first time, Laura understood the seriousness of the situation and that if she didn't sound more excited, Alice might never forgive her. "Alice, that's wonderful! I'm so happy for both of you." It *was* exciting, if a bit unexpected, to think that two people she liked so much might spend their lives together. To her surprise, she didn't feel jealous at all that Simon had chosen Alice instead of her. She wanted to live in New York, not England. But Alice was growing restless enough with her life that she might embrace a change of scenery.

But Laura was worried that Alice didn't know about the rumor Simon might return to England or that, if she did, that she hadn't considered the implications. "I'm afraid to say this because I don't want to spoil your happiness. But you have a house that you might not want to leave, and I've heard that Simon might return to London. Did he tell you—" Laura tried to put it as gently as she could—"that he might go back?"

Alice hesitated for just long enough to make clear that he had told her and that she was debating how much to say about it. "Simon did mention something about that. He said I knew you better than he did, and that if I trusted you not to tell the news to anybody at the office, he'd have no problem with anything I said. I just wonder if you want to know, or if you'd rather I didn't ask you to keep such a secret."

"I do want to know, and I could keep the secret," Laura said truthfully, knowing that she hadn't known her coworkers long enough to breach the confidence.

"Then you're partly right. Simon probably *is* going to leave *Cassandra* but not to go back to London. He's thinking about accepting a great job as the American correspondent for an English newspaper. He's made a couple of trips to London to talk to the editors about it. The details still have to be worked out, so it isn't certain that he will leave *Cassandra*. He won't take the job unless he can spend every July in England and take his wife if he got married."

"Could you leave your father for such a long time? I know how loyal Mrs. Brennan is to both of you, but she's getting on in years."

"It's true that I'd worry if I left my father with only Mrs. Brennan to look after him. But maybe you could help with that.

You could stay at Rose Bluffs when Simon and I are in England, or just come out on weekends and check up on my father."

This idea appealed to Laura so much that she almost didn't want to bring up the last thing that she believed she owed it to her friend to say. "I hate to mention this. But there's something else I have to tell you."

Alice showed no concern. "Which is?"

"Some people think Simon might be gay."

Alice laughed so loudly that Laura was almost afraid she would wake her father, who was sleeping in a nearby bedroom. "Laura, you have good judgment about people—so good that I think I let myself trust my feelings about Simon partly because I know how much you liked him. But if you think Simon is gay, you probably still think that Andy Warhol was straight."

"Want to tell me how you know he isn't? If I promise also to keep that a secret?"

Alice opened Simon's sporran and pulled out a small foil square with a Union Jack on it. "He offered to introduce to me to his favorite brand of English condoms, which you can't easily get in the United States. I told him that, given that we needed to get back to the reception. I'd have to find out another night what he was wearing under his kilt."

16
Grilled

"Having a mammogram is *not* 'like getting your tit smashed in a panini grill!'"

Laura could hear Cassandra screeching to Simon from the hallway of the fashion department, which was crowded with coat racks full of the winter coats that were arriving daily at the magazine. The editor-in-chief was raging about the health column that Caitlin had written for the August issue. But why hadn't she done so sooner? The August issue had been on the stands for several weeks—the September issue was about to appear—and Laura's stomach tightened when she realized that Cassandra might still have a similar response to her profile of Normendie Latour.

"Even if having a mammogram *was* like getting your tit smashed in a panini grill, this language has no place in *Cassandra*!"

Laura couldn't hear Simon's muted response to the tirade, but Kit, who had returned from her honeymoon on Lake Como, had caught snatches of the conversation. Cassandra was furious about the breezy tone of Caitlin's health column, and the grapevine had it that Cassandra had suspended Caitlin for a month without pay.

As she absorbed this news, Laura felt the temperature in the hallway drop to a sub-Arctic level. She hadn't seen Caitlin all morning and had assumed that she was out of the office on an assignment. Ethan hadn't volunteered any information but had been walking around with a self-satisfied look.

Laura hurried to Anne Meyer's office. She found the art director at her computer, laying out a story on a young English chef named Zadie Fox, who was trying to revive Midlands home cooking. Anne, usually unflappable, muttered as she moved her mouse.

"Why on earth do we still use PageMaker here? We must be the only magazine in New York, if not on the planet, that doesn't have Quark."

Anne said that she'd been begging the company to replace her design program with the gold standard in magazine publishing. But Cassandra didn't do hands-on work on the layouts, so she didn't see the advantages of Quark, and Simon, although sympathetic, had his own problems trying to get the latest version of Microsoft Word for the staff. Anne set aside her mouse and confirmed that Caitlin had been suspended.

"If Cassandra didn't want *tit* in the magazine, why didn't she just take out the word instead of suspending Caitlin after the story appeared?" Laura asked. "That's like killing a mosquito with an Apache attack helicopter."

"Maybe she didn't read the story before it ran. That's the rumor."

"I know she read it. I saw Caitlin put the story in her in-box."

"That somebody put a story in her in-box doesn't mean she read it. Cassandra okays a lot of layouts that she complains about after they appear in the magazine. She assumes that Simon will take care of the details, so she doesn't have to pay close attention. And Simon, much as I love him, hasn't adjusted to all the differences between American and English journalism."

"Such as?"

"English standards are looser. The Brits don't get as upset about words like *tit*, and Simon doesn't yet understand all the things that may bother Cassandra or readers. Americans think the

English are puritanical and sexually repressed. But in a lot of ways they're much more open-minded about sex and many other things than we are."

Laura had seen many examples of this in England. But Anne's comment left her unsettled. She had hoped Simon would serve as her shield—for as long as he stayed at the magazine—in any battles she had with Cassandra. If she couldn't depend on him to help her avoid trouble, she didn't know how much longer she could last there.

"Do *you* think she should have suspended Caitlin?"

Anne picked up her mouse and turned back to her computer. "If you're upset about it, why don't you talk to Simon? I hear he's head-over-heels for your best friend. If she can do no wrong, you can't, either."

***

"Simon, you know there's no love lost between Caitlin and me. But it doesn't seem fair that she's been suspended for using the word *tit*."

"Caitlin hasn't been suspended because she used *tit*. She's on leave because she didn't show Cassandra the article on mammograms as she'd been asked to do."

"But she did show Cassandra the story. I saw her drop it in her in-box. Venetia saw her, too. Why don't you ask her to confirm what I've said?"

"Please sit down. This is too important a conversation to have while you're walking back and forth like a Buck House guard."

Laura usually enjoyed Simon's use of British slang, such as "Buck House" for Buckingham Palace. But now it annoyed her. Since she'd entered Simon's office, she'd been pacing half-consciously to the beat of the "1812 Overture" on his short-wave radio. The more she thought about Caitlin's suspension, the angrier she grew. She settled reluctantly into the leather Regency chair across from Simon's desk, prepared for a scolding.

The simulated cannon blasts in Tchaikovsky's music stoked her fury.

Simon offered Laura a Marlboro, and she almost took it. She hadn't felt tempted by cigarettes in all the time that Nick had chain-smoked Kents. Working at *Cassandra* had nearly accomplished what living with a blocked screenwriter hadn't.

"Laura, I admire your passion. But no good can come of accusing your boss—and mine—of lying. That might only get you suspended, too."

"Can any good come of putting Caitlin on leave when she did nothing wrong?"

"Perhaps. Cassandra wanted to suspend Caitlin without pay. But I persuaded her to keep her on the payroll while she's on leave. Caitlin works so hard that she's had no trouble finding jobs in the past. If she's smart, she'll use her time off to find another job that will pay her more and make better use of her talents. This could be another example of *eine Flucht nach vorn,* a retreat forward."

Laura felt slightly mollified by the news that Caitlin was getting paid. But the decision to put a human workhorse on leave, and its timing, still struck her as irrational.

"Even if Cassandra was upset about *tit,* I don't understand why she waited until the issue came out to say so. If she didn't see the hard copy, she saw the page proofs."

"Cassandra is new to the magazine business. She takes her cues from her social set. My sense is that she didn't object to having the word *tit* in the magazine until she found out that her friends didn't like it."

Laura didn't doubt that Cassandra's friends could have such an influence. All the same, she wondered how the editor-in-chief expected to put out a magazine without Caitlin. She took a back issue of *Cassandra* off Simon's desk and read aloud from the table of contents.

"Listen to this. By Caitlin Stearns ... By Caitlin Stearns ... By Caitlin Stearns. Caitlin has been writing half the magazine every month. You have your hands full, Ethan is still trying to figure out how to work the fax machine, and now that I have an apartment, I'd like to fix it up and start having a social life. Who does Cassandra think is going to do the stories that Caitlin was working on?"

"Laura, I'm afraid there's only one answer to that question."

***

Too unnerved by Caitlin's suspension to work, Laura went for a walk. But a pewter sky and the heavy air carried the threat of rain. So although she wasn't hungry, she stopped into a converted pie factory called Bubby's, where her coworkers had breakfasts of pancakes with bananas and walnuts, and ordered a slice of peach pie. The wedge that arrived seemed as big as the Flatiron Building, the triangular skyscraper that she often passed on her walks.

Laura didn't understand what she was doing until she had almost finished her pie. She was eating to make herself feel better, the way her coworkers did. As the pressures at work mounted she had at times felt tempted by Simon's Marlboros and the by tranquilizers that Monica Stryker kept offering her. Now she was eating a slice of pie so large that it once would have appealed to her only after a two-hour basketball practice.

What was happening to her? She had a vision of herself after twenty years in New York as an overweight, chain-smoking drug addict—not as Audrey Hepburn, but as a cross between Perky Vano and Goldie Hawn in that movie where she wore a fat suit. Or as an incurable cynic like Caitlin, who had just been suspended and had a dumpster full of reasons for despair. She *had* to start going out with some new men—maybe a couple of the men who'd been calling her since the wedding—who could at least provide a welcome relief from her apartment and the tensions at work.

The thought of turning into a depressed person depressed Laura so much that she hurried back to the office and the distractions of her latest assignments and her email.

To: Laura Smart
From: Venetia di Lorenzo

Tried to find you while you were out to tell you my great news. I
JUST QUIT MY JOB! Got a FANTASTIC offer from *Aurora* including a
promotion to fashion editor from deputy and a much larger salary.
Aurora Starr even said I could change my name back to Vicki
Lawrence, which I've been thinking of for a while, because nobody
at her magazine would be impressed by a "di."

Simon said I could work at home until I started my new job as
long as I finish everything I have to do for the October issue. So I'm
not sure how much longer I'll be around. I'm going to try to find a
really great bra to give you as a going-away gift.

To: Venetia di Lorenzo
From: Laura Smart

Congratulations! You deserve all the extra $$$ you'll get.

Maybe you'll also have a chance to show those gorgeous
cigarette-carton purses that you'd brought to Cassandra's office on
the day we met? I still think they were the most beautiful handbags
I've ever seen.

That her closest coworker was leaving strengthened Laura's
resolve to try to recharge her social life. In New York she had con-
fided mainly in Alice and Venetia. Now she was having fewer long
talks with Alice, who was spending a lot of her time with Simon,
and would be seeing less of Venetia, too. After years of having a
ready-made social life, she needed to make friends of both sexes.

Laura had put off getting back to the men who had called since
Kit's wedding, hoping to decontaminate her apartment before she

had them over. The last thing she needed was another lecture like the one she'd received from Tim. And weren't the women's magazines always saying that with a few Japanese lanterns, throw pillows, and bamboo shades you could turn your apartment into something fit for a geisha? But she never seemed to have enough money left at the end of the week to fix up the place, and some men might lose interest if she ignored them until she did.

Laura picked up the stack of pink slips with the phone numbers of men who'd been calling since the wedding and decided that it was time to start calling them back. There *had* to be men who, unlike Tim, wouldn't recoil in horror from her apartment.

17
September Song

The September issue of *Cassandra*, as shiny and colorful as a jewel, lay on Laura's desk. Cassandra was wearing a red sequined bolero jacket and black toreador pants that might have come from a wardrobe closet for *Carmen*. This time the editor-in-chief stood with her hand on her hip, unaccompanied by any of her friends. Laura had heard a rumor that several celebrities approached about the cover had backed out after the release of the latest disappointing circulation figures for the magazine. A publicist like Liz Kaiser could yank a star without warning if she decided that the lighting had changed and a publication no longer offered the exposure she had expected. If the editors protested, they could lose the chance to use the celebrity on a later cover if their fortunes improved or they could have their access cut off altogether. They might have to publish write-arounds for years.

Laura saw as soon as she picked up the magazine that the ad pages had declined in number again. The new issue was thin, which made even the best of its articles look less substantial. *Cassandra* had also switched from so-called perfect binding, which had a glued spine, to the stapled saddle binding that created a bubble of air in the middle of the magazine, often the last desperate resort of publications trying to look less emaciated. It was a painful contrast to the September *Aurora*, which was sleek and fat.

Even so, Laura's heart lifted when she picked up the new issue. This was a moment she loved—the day when the first bound copies arrived and months of work by writers and editors coalesced into something solid and enduring. Seeing your work on a computer screen or page proof was never the same as holding something that might exist for generations, maybe forever, in attics, libraries, and the minds of people on whom you had made an impression. The first bound copies of magazines had a distinctive smell—a mix of pulp and fresh varnish—that disappeared after shoppers began flipping through them while wearing perfume or eating M&Ms.

Laura ran her hand over the cover of the issue, eager to see the society column that she had edited without the help of its elusive author. She was delighted to find that Anne Meyer's layout gave Zoli's opaque prose a regal shimmer—Ellie Doddering almost had a glow of youth—and an air of elegance despite the saddle binding that left several party guests with staples through their navels. The axiom was true: writers and editors fed a magazine, but art directors dressed it. Laura was about to send Anne a congratulatory email note when she heard two interns talking as they walked by toward Simon's office.

"We shouldn't be getting yelled at. It isn't fair. I called Jamie Smith's apartment and got a woman."

"We couldn't be expected to know Jamie Smith was a man."

Laura felt her stomach turn. She skimmed the society column and saw that the man the interns were talking about had received the equivalent of a sex-change operation in the new issue. In every reference to Jamie Smith, somebody had changed "he" to "she." Simon had evidently tried to protect the magazine against Zoli's tendency to mix up pronouns by asking the interns to fact-check the society column after she gave him the edited version. But fact-checkers were supposed to show her the changes they made, especially if they might have resulted from a misunderstanding. The students hadn't told her that they'd castrated Jamie Smith.

Laura knew she could ignore Cassandra's tantrums, difficult as this was, and avoid getting sucked into the maw of ethical conflicts at the magazine. Cassandra had started coming into the office so infrequently that she wasn't likely to notice the mix-up. Nevertheless, this lapse tormented Laura. She never minded working hard if she could take pride in the result. But if she couldn't admire the results of her efforts, what was the point? The mistake, whether or not anybody noticed it, shouldn't have happened.

Molting with frustration, Laura waited until the interns returned to their desks, then went to see Simon, who was listening to the *Pastoral* Symphony on the BBC. She marveled at the change in him since the wedding. Despite the deepening crises at *Cassandra*, he seemed to have relaxed, as though he'd found a precious family heirloom he'd lost. He had straightened his desktop, which held tidy stacks of papers instead of a chaotic jumble, and no longer kept glancing reflexively at his fax machine. For the first time, when she entered his office, she saw no signs of Marlboro—an apparent effort to please Alice by quitting smoking. He had more buoyancy than ever, if that was even possible.

"I had a feeling you might be stopping by. If it's any comfort, the interns are full of remorse."

"Thanks, Simon. I'm afraid they sounded anything but remorseful."

"They expected me to thrash them. When I didn't, they became contrite quickly. They know they ought to have shown you the changes in Zoli's column."

Laura sat down in the Regency chair opposite his desk, grateful that he hadn't thrashed *her*. "How did you find out about the error?"

"Jamie Smith—*Mr.* Jamie Smith—called. He said that you had called and confirmed everything from the existence of his Y chromosome to the name of his corgi, so he didn't understand how the mistake had occurred."

"How did it happen?"

"I told the interns that the same word stands for 'he' and 'she' in Hungarian and asked them to verify the sex of anyone Zoli quoted. They found a number for 'Jamie Smith' on Cassandra's Rolodex and didn't realize that Mr. Smith has a daughter with the same name and that both attended the party mentioned in the column. One of the interns called the number and, on reaching a woman, asked if she had gone to the event. When she said yes, he went no further. I should have known that you would do the fact-checking when you found out that we didn't have anyone else who could do it reliably."

Laura's relief that Simon didn't blame her hardly eased her despair over the error. "The odd thing is that Zoli had made the same mistake on his manuscript. When I saw the remarks attrib-uted to 'Jamie Smith,' they didn't sound like something that someone my age would say. Women in their twenties don't usu-ally go around quoting what Winston Churchill said in *The Malakind Field Force*: 'Nothing in life is so exhilarating as to be shot at without result.' Especially while drinking Bellinis at the Maidstone Club. I called young Jamie to see if she was the excep-tion. But I couldn't reach her, so I called her father, who said that I had guessed correctly and the quotes came from him."

"You have excellent instincts in both your work and in your choice of friends."

Since the wedding Laura had tried to avoid talking about Alice with Simon, whose discretion about his earlier romances made her wonder if he might see her interest in the burgeoning romance as rude. But she couldn't resist making a comment now. "Alice hasn't come down from what she calls, 'Cloud Ten: the cloud for people who are beyond Cloud Nine,' since you met."

Simon beamed. "I must say I'm relieved to hear it. Alice seems quite enthusiastic whenever we see each other. But I wonder how her father might feel about sharing her with another man and whether that might influence her feelings."

"Mr. Dudley can be a bit—" Laura wondered how to put it, "—gruff. I thought at first he didn't like it that I had moved in temporarily. But that changed after I lost a manuscript I'd taken home from work. Mrs. Brennan moved it while she was dusting, and I tore off sofa cushions trying to find it. I was beside myself and asked Mr. Dudley if he could help. He kept walking through the rooms with his metal detector, as though that might help, until he spotted it. I was so grateful that I threw my arms around him, and we've gotten along well ever since. I think that, like most people, he wants to feel needed. If you can find a way to make him feel important, you'll have no trouble with him."

"I'll keep that in mind," Simon said, smiling. His phone rang, and he ignored it after seeing a Caller-ID number that didn't belong to Alice. "But what about you? Have any of the handsome men who flocked to you at the wedding won you over?"

"What about some of the Americans?"

"Afraid not. One man told me that his good qualities began with the fact that he was 'disease free.'"

"Forget him!" Simon said with mock despair. "Let him go out with the Surgeon General."

"Then there was the man who called while I was reading *Persuasion*. He asked if it was a self-help book, like *Seven Habits of Highly Effective People*."

"Well, I can't say I'm happy that the good luck that has settled on me has eluded you. I'll try a little harder to fix you up with one of my friends. But it may be better for *Cassandra* that you have no romantic distractions because I have a bit of bad news. Caitlin called to say that she's found a new job and won't be returning when her suspension ends. I'll try to replace her as soon as I can, but ..."

Simon didn't finish the sentence. But Laura, who knew from Alice that he had reached an agreement with the English newspaper that had offered him a job, could complete his thought.

You'll try to replace Caitlin, but you won't, because you're out of here.

18
Lost and Found

"Killer fish?" Alice asked. "Are you sure?"

Laura nodded glumly. As Simon and Mr. Dudley walked on the beach, she and Alice sat on the veranda at Rose Bluffs talking about her latest disasters with men. She was trying to explain—out of earshot of a boss who depended on her good judgment—why she had gone out with an investment banker who liked to unwind after work by watching large carnivorous fish eat the guppies in his aquarium.

"Andrew asked me to dance at Kit's wedding and couldn't talk about his hobbies during an Eightsome Reel. So I didn't find out until I went back to his place for a drink that he likes to relax by watching his red devils and Jack Dempseys eat the guppies in his tank. It's a low-maintenance hobby, perfect for people who work long hours, so it's quite popular on Wall Street. You don't have to feed the fish much because they eat each other."

"Maybe he has other redeeming qualities?" Alice said doubtfully. "Such as that great sense of humor that men all say they want in us?"

"Not unless you count that he names his fish after characters on *The Sopranos*. While we were drinking chardonnay, he told me to keep my eyes on the tank so I wouldn't miss it if Tony Soprano and Paulie Walnuts bumped off Pussy Bompensiero."

"But all of the men from the wedding can't be as bad as that."

"Some were worse. One was doctor who specialized in 'food borne and diarrheal diseases' and talked about his work over dinner. Another was a minor-league ballplayer who smelled like Desenex and wanted to meet for a second date at a sports bar in Trenton, New Jersey. There was also criminal defense lawyer whose hobby was visiting the water tanks on top of New York City buildings. He asked me if I wanted to watch the sunset from a rooftop on West End Avenue that had a really great tank."

Laura stopped to watch Simon, who seemed to have dropped something on the beach. "I had to work so hard to make conversation with a couple of those men that I thought I ought to be paid for my services. But after Nick, I wanted to get to know the kind of men I never met in Ohio. Now I have."

"Maybe Simon can still come up with a friend you'll like."

"I had the idea that most of his friends live in England."

"Simon is full of surprises."

Laura had to agree. At first, she had worried that Simon, separated by thousands of miles from his countrywomen, was dating Alice by default and might drop her for an English rose. But her friends' attachment had deepened in the weeks since Kit's wedding. Every weekend Simon went to Rose Bluffs or took Alice to the homes of friends in the Hamptons, where they went to polo matches and drank Pimm's Cups. Alice found it easier to deal with Mrs. Foster and her students after Simon told her about his nerve-jangling experiences at school, and he was talking about staying in the States indefinitely instead of returning to England in a few years. It was a match made, if not in heaven, at least in its waiting room. Perhaps the best part was that Alice and Simon hadn't shut her out of their lives, but kept inviting her to join them for drinks after work or to have picnics on the beach at Rose Bluffs. Earlier in the day they had challenged her to a game of two-on-one using a basketball hoop on one of the garages. She had beaten them so easily that they were talking about playing four-on-one with Wick Dudley and Mrs. Brennan.

"Lucky for me that one of Simon's surprises was his decision to hire me. Can you imagine how discouraged I might have become if I'd spent another year living with Nick? Even if I'd broken up with him, I wouldn't have had nearly as many dates in Cleveland as I've had here. My friend Molly says that she doesn't like going out with other lawyers but has to do it. They're so obsessed with work that they're the only men she knows who didn't get married right out of school."

"I just wish you had three more weddings to go to this summer," Alice said, watching her father and Simon walk shoulder-to-shoulder along the shoreline. "It's so much easier to fall in love when everything around you gives you permission to do it."

Laura picked up the Style Section of the Sunday *New York Times* that rested on a white wicker table. "You're probably right. A lot of the newlyweds in this section must have met at another wedding—even if they look as though they'd been 'Conjoined at Birth.'" The remark was the latest variation on a running joke between Laura and Alice about the wedding announcements in the *Times*. The newspaper had a policy that the eyebrows of a bride and groom had to be at the same level in the photos, and this made the couples look as though they'd been conjoined at birth, or surgically attached at the temple.

"Isn't there any hope that a wonderful man will turn up at Tina's wedding?" Alice asked. "Say, a classmate who kept getting expelled for short-circuiting the wiring in the teachers' lounge, but has turned into the next Bill Gates?"

"I could meet only a Wilhelmina Gates. The disadvantage of going to a girls' school is that you never get to star in your own *Romy and Michelle's High School Reunion*."

"Then I'll have to insist to Simon that he fix you up soon."

Simon loped up the wooden stairway from the beach, leaving Wickford Dudley to meander with his metal detector. After he'd settled into a white wicker chair on the veranda, Alice asked him if he could fix Laura up with any eligible men.

"Absolutely, darling. Laura has never believed that there are men who smoke more than I do, and I can prove it by introducing her to them."

"Thanks, Simon," Laura said, smiling. "I'll keep looking on my own."

"Perhaps you'll want to get to know Zoli a little better?"

"Ouch!" Laura knew—or hoped—that Simon was kidding. She had finally spoken to Zoli when he called to congratulate her on her "marvelous" editing of his September column—not having reread enough of it to see that Jamie Smith had received a sex-change operation—and invited her to join him for tea at a hotel that she was fairly certain did not serve tea. She declined by explaining, half-truthfully, that she needed to do some last-minute fact-checking on a story.

"Or perhaps Ethan could fix you up with another semiotics major from—"

Mrs. Brennan burst onto the veranda with a red face.

"Miss Laura! You have come inside! A star wants you on the telephone!"

For all the celebrities she'd tried to reach at work, Laura couldn't think of a star who might want to call her at home. "A star?" she asked curiously. "Which one?"

"I don't know, Miss Laura. She just said she's a star."

Laura suspected that the caller was an overzealous publicist who had tracked her down at Rose Bluffs. She looked at Alice and Simon. "Would you mind—"

"Not at all," Simon said. "Ten to one it's Liz Kaiser, calling to say that she'll forgive you for interviewing Normendie if you'll do a story on another musician whom she's billing as 'the Elvis of Albania.'"

"Hi, Laura, it's Aurora Starr. Am I catching you at a bad time?"

Laura wondered if someone, possibly Ethan, was playing a prank. Aurora Starr couldn't be calling her at Rose Bluffs on Saturday. But the caller was doing an excellent job of imitating of the famous Hoosier twang that Laura had heard at the wedding.

"Not at all," Laura said, realizing that she had echoed Simon's phrasing.

"Wonderful! I didn't want to call you at work, because I didn't know if you could speak freely. And Venetia suggested that I try you at Alice's. But I don't want to keep you on such a beautiful day, so I'll try to make this short. I loved talking to you at Kit's wedding and wondered if you'd heard the changes that we're planning at *Aurora*."

Laura heard enough Hoosier vowels to feel sure that she was talking to the real Aurora Starr. "I know you keep gaining circulation and newsstand sales," Laura began, hoping that this suggested the Google-like familiarity with her subject that the career guides advised. Then she remembered hearing about the redesign of *Aurora* from Caitlin. "I also know that you gave a great party in Central Park to 'get the ball rolling' for your redesign."

Aurora laughed. "I hope you didn't hear too much about how I slipped when I tried to spike a volleyball. But we *are* redesigning the magazine and adding features for which we'll need writers. We're also toning down the content to make it less like *Fear Factor* and more like *Prime Time*. I'd like *Aurora* to have more appeal for the women you might meet on the street and less for those you might meet in—" Aurora laughed again— "a mental institution. I wondered if you might be interested in talking about a job."

Laura glanced toward the veranda to see if Simon could hear, and before she had resolved the issue, Aurora went on.

"I should tell you that, although I like what you've done with Zoli's column, you wouldn't have much chance to do any editing. We're top-heavy with good editors, although there's so much mobility in this business that there's a possibility something might open up later on. But you'd certainly have a chance to do more cover stories."

Laura went into a mental tizzy. Much as she'd fantasized about a new job—especially one where she didn't have to edit "the Magyar Cary Grant"—she hadn't come to grips with the reality of making a move. She had never left a job after such a short time.

How would a fast break look on a résumé that was weak enough already? Simon wasn't leaving *Cassandra* for a few months and might have trouble putting out the magazine without her. By quitting she might seem disloyal to the only editor in the city who'd wanted to hire her. But if Simon was leaving, shouldn't she have the same right? She told Aurora that she'd love to talk about a job but, just so there were no misunderstandings, she wasn't used to writing about people like Normendie Latour.

"Thank God!" Aurora said. "There ought to be a statute of limitations on how old you can be and still wear halter tops. Why don't you send me some clips that show what you *are* used to writing about, then call my secretary to set up an interview?"

Laura agreed in a rosy haze of disbelief. She was wondering how she could explain her absence to Simon when Aurora solved the problem.

"By the way, say 'hi' to Simon for me if you see him this weekend. I hear from Venetia that's he crazy about your best friend."

"You know Simon?" Laura asked, surprised. She hadn't seen Aurora talking to Simon at Kit's wedding.

"Sure. We met through the American Society of Magazine Editors. I think he's a great guy. Please tell him I said congratulations on his new job. Cassandra must be the only person on the planet who doesn't believe he's leaving."

Laura returned to the veranda and saw Wickford Dudley racing up the path from the beach, holding his metal detector aloft like an umbrella and shouting about his latest discovery. Shielding her eyes with her hand, Alice was trying to see what he had found.

Wick Dudley was almost out of breath when he reached the veranda. "Nobody believes me!" he said. "Everybody says it isn't worth the trouble to spend so much time looking for pennies on a beach. But I knew I'd hit the jackpot someday, and now I've done it. Look what I just found on the beach."

He reached into the pocket of his windbreaker and pulled out a diamond ring that, by Laura's estimation, was at least three carats.

Alice took it from him and moved to a sunny spot on the veranda to study it. "You can't keep this ring!" she exclaimed. "It's far too valuable. It belongs to somebody whose heart will break if she doesn't get it back."

Simon, who was standing behind Alice's father, winked at Laura. "You're right," he said. "It does belong to somebody." He took the ring out of Alice's hand and put it on her finger, which it fit perfectly.

"It belongs to you."

***

It took Laura a few hours to sort out what had happened on the beach. But later that day she went for a walk with Simon in the overgrown rose garden on the estate and learned that he came up with a plan after they'd talked about Wick Dudley at the office. A week or two earlier, he'd bought a ring he intended to give to Alice. Laura's comment inspired him to come up with a plan to drop it into the path of Wick Dudley when he was sure to find it. That approach, as Simon saw it, would solve two problems at a stroke: it would give his future father-in-law a central role in the drama, and it would allow him to give Alice a ring that the frugal Wick Dudley might otherwise have seen as too extravagant.

"It's brilliant, Simon. But, in retrospect, it seems a little risky. What if Mr. Dudley hadn't found the ring? What if it had gotten washed out to sea?"

"I dropped it above the high tide line so that the waves couldn't sweep it away. And I memorized its location—I lined it up with one the pillars on the veranda—so that I could dig it out if Alice's father didn't find it. After I came back from my walk with him, I kept an eye on him to make sure he did find it. I had every intention of going back to the beach and suggesting that we walk a bit longer if he didn't."

"Does Alice know about all of this?"

"She has an idea, and she approves. It seems her father has been walking along the shoreline for years expecting something like this to happen. He was so sure he'd win the beach lottery that Alice was afraid that if he ever did find something valuable, he'd refuse to return it to the owner. So my plan solved a problem for her, too."

The conversation left Laura with so much goodwill toward Simon that her call from Aurora gnawed at her. If she was thinking of leaving *Cassandra* before he did, shouldn't she give him as much warning as possible?

"Simon, there's something I have to tell you. I hate to say it. But ..." Laura couldn't finish a sentence that might undercut her boss's joy on such an enchanted day.

Simon picked a rose off one of the half-century old bushes. "Let me guess. Aurora Starr called to talk to you about a job." Simon gave Laura the flower in his hand, and she noticed how much the colors of the roses on the estate had faded since June.

"How did you know?"

"I didn't. But I've been expecting you to start getting offers, if not from Aurora Starr, from somebody else, and to make 'a retreat forward' to a new magazine. There's more poaching in this industry than on any estate in North Yorkshire, especially when the media critics and gossip columnists keep speculating that the magazine may fold."

"You don't think I'd be disloyal to you by taking a job at *Aurora*?"

"Of course, I'd think you were disloyal. But I'd be disappointed if you weren't. It would mean that you might not be able to survive in New York. That would be a shame when you have so much to offer and to gain from it. When I hired you, I thought you had everything you needed to survive in the city, except a slight degree of cunning that you would acquire with time. But after hearing how you got the interview with Normendie, I realized that you had some of that already. And I suspect you'll acquire the rest as quickly as you made clear to Tim that, no matter what he could do for your career, you never wanted to hear from him again."

Laura cringed at the reminder of a man she hadn't spoken to since Kit's wedding. "Was I really so obvious? I tried to be as nice to him as you suggested. But he was so determined to rile me in every way, from insulting my apartment to humiliating me on the dance floor, that I had trouble staying civil."

"Let's just say that if you weren't obvious to me, you were obvious to him. Haven't you wondered why you haven't heard from him lately? He called me after the wedding to say that he had intended to offer you a ride home from the reception and try to make amends for maligning your apartment. But after he heard you talking about how cheap he was, he decided that you might slam the car door on fingers he needs to pitch in his softball league in Central Park. He may have been joking, but I think—"

"—he wasn't?"

Simon laughed. "*Aurora* would be the perfect place for you."

Laura felt slightly wounded that Simon wasn't begging her to stay at *Cassandra*. "But why?"

"Laura, there aren't many bosses in this industry who wouldn't mind if you interrupt them like that or beat them by twenty points in a basketball game. But I'm one of them, and Aurora Starr is another."

19
Aurora

The first thing that struck Laura when she walked into the offices of *Aurora* was that they had permanence lacking at *Cassandra*. It wasn't just that they occupied several floors of a midtown office building with handsome Art Deco trim—leaves, vines, and fish—that had existed since the days when Zelda Fitzgerald jumped into the fountain at the Plaza Hotel. The offices of *Aurora* also didn't look like decks of a cruise ship about to set sail for a place she had never visited. They looked like *Buckeye* on a grander scale.

Their most dramatic feature was the black marble floor in the reception area inlaid with replicas of the gold stars that flashed across screens when *Aurora* came on the air. Laura had heard that the architects borrowed the idea from one of the Condé Nast magazines—*Vogue*, or maybe *Glamour*—that once had a similar floor. If so, the device had repaid its debt with interest. When she stepped off the elevator, she had the sense that she was walking on a brilliant constellation that was sparkling for her.

Laura had taken the advice she'd seen so often in *Cassandra*—to dress ahead of the season—and worn her tweed suit with a chocolate-brown purse shaped like a cigarette carton that Venetia had decided to give her instead of a bra when she left the magazine. In the ladies' room mirror at *Aurora*, she saw how much better the suit looked now that she had lighter hair, a flair for makeup, and a silk scarf that Claudine had taught her to tie. She didn't look like somebody else but the vision of herself that she had carried in her mind's eye, which helped to give her a confidence that she didn't have when she interviewed at *Cassandra*. The enthusiastic welcome she got from Melody, Aurora's assistant, fed her hope that her next round of job interviews might go better than the last.

"She can't wait to see you," Melody said, as she bounded into the reception area.

Melody led her to an office that, though about the same size as Cassandra's, had a more relaxed tone set by its sky-blue walls and hand-painted white clouds on the ceiling. Laura remembered that Aurora had once said that her office and reception area had a day-and-night theme. It was intended to suggest her intention "to work day and night to create a great magazine for American women." Some editors at *Cassandra* derided the motif as hokey, but in context it looked magical. No less surprising was that Aurora worked at a round table topped by photos of her daughter and her husband on family vacations—at Disneyland, Yellowstone National Park, and a Caribbean resort with a moon-walk for children. For the first time it struck Laura as odd that Cassandra had no photos of Irwin in her office and, according to coworkers, never brought him to office parties.

Laura did a double-take when she saw Aurora sitting on a sky-blue banquette with her feet propped on a glass coffee table that held a stack of magazines and *Is Your Mama a Llama?*, a picture book for children of her daughter's age. Aurora was wearing a black pants suit at least two seasons old and dark stockings. She looked lovely but hadn't gotten the message, or didn't care, that panty hose were going the way of the ankle bracelet and the turtleneck dickey and might soon turn up only in country-store catalogs that sold pie safes and horehound cough drops. On her lap she had the manila folder full of *Buckeye* articles and the print-out of the Normendie Latour interview that Laura had sent her.

"Laura! Thanks so much for coming by. Please have a seat." Aurora patted a spot on the banquette near a small orange mark where, she said, her daughter had dropped a few Skittles. Laura sank onto a cushion that gave her a clear view of the staff members who hurried past her host's open door carrying manuscripts instead of garment bags.

"I've been hoping to get to know you better ever since Kit's wedding," Aurora said. "Do you know that in all the time we've been doing our 'Bridesmaids' Dresses from Hell' segments, you're the first person who ever asked me about *my* worst dresses? One of the hazards of my position is that people tend to be afraid of you. They don't try to talk to you as they would to others. They gush about how much they love your shows. Or your new hairstyle."

"But you haven't changed your hairstyle in years! They must be confusing you with Cassandra."

"Exactly. Some people are so afraid of you that they'd rather be wrong than honest. Even reporters who interview me worry about how I'll react if they deviate from stock lines like, 'Where would you like to be in ten years?' I don't know if they think I'm one of Liz Kaiser's clients, who need to have scripts, or that I have a limited vocabulary. But after a while you begin to operate on autopilot. If you did an Internet search, you could probably find a hundred interviews in which I've said, 'Where I'd like to be in ten years is thinner.' You got me to open up, which means that you can get anybody to open up."

Aurora leafed through the manila folder in her lap. "I loved your story on Normendie, who always struck me as more vulnerable than you might guess from that kewpie-doll makeup. But I liked your work for *Buckeye* better, especially 'Bowling-Trophy Wives.' That's just what we need in *Aurora,* the kind of article that mainstream American women can relate to. So I wondered if you might have any interest in a job that would involve doing similar articles for a national audience. Let's say, traveling to different cities writing about people who imitate the Shirelles instead of the

Beach Boys. Or better still, who imitate a younger group who would have more appeal for the women we're trying to attract."

"What about the Dixie Chicks? I'm sure I could find a lot of women who fantasize about singing 'Goodbye Earl' at wedding receptions, if not funerals …"

"Perfect. Maybe you could also find more women who collect quirky things—younger versions of that retired schoolteacher who liked airsickness bags—and do a group portrait. I read your articles and thought, 'If we ever do a story on a woman who collects the toilet paper in public restrooms, this is the writer I want to do it.'"

Laura wasn't sure Aurora had given her a compliment, but she didn't care. "Yes!" she said. "I'd love that kind of job. In fact, I brought along a few ideas for similar stories that I could do right away." She handed her list to Aurora.

Aurora began to read aloud. "'Revenge of the Altar Girls.' I love it. We could sell the film rights to Jodie Foster, and you and the magazine could make a fortune. She has to make a sequel to her altar-boy film someday—" Aurora broke off. "But before we get too carried away, I need to warn you about something."

This is where the fantasy ends, Laura thought. *This is where Aurora tells me that I have to bring along a Rolodex filled with unlisted telephone numbers, or that she's hired Zoli to write about sweet sixteen parties in Racine and wants me to edit the columns.*

Aurora closed the clip file. "Suppose your job included a few things you hadn't expected, such as occasional appearances on my show. We're hoping to achieve more 'synergy'—if you'll pardon that overworked word—by having some of our staff members come on the show to promote their stories. That means that we need to hire people who don't just write well but who have the confidence to appear in front of millions of viewers and the polished appearance to go with it."

Laura felt her heart to do somersaults. Aurora couldn't be offering such a glamorous job to somebody who, a few months earlier, had been interviewing a pet psychic in Cleveland Heights, Ohio.

"You have the just the mix of traits we need—the talent, the poise, and the right look with that beautiful hair and makeup and that smart scarf. I was almost sure of it when we met at the wedding. But Kit said that a hairdresser and makeup artist had worked on you, so I wasn't sure what you would do on your own. Now I see that you can pull yourself together as well as your stories."

Laura had the sense that she had developed temporary aphasia.

"Naturally, we'd pay you more if you appeared on my shows, a lot more than you're making at *Cassandra*. And assuming we did, would that interest you?"

"I have no television experience," Laura said, dizzy with excitement. "But my high-school basketball coach said I was a pathological optimist, so—"

"Wonderful! I have an idea for a segment that might be ideal for you."

Aurora picked up a glossy brochure that contained a photo of a naked woman stretched out on a massage table with fruit covering strategic points on her body—orange slices on her eyes, star fruit on her nipples, apple blossoms artfully deployed where fig leaves would normally appear. "There's a kinky new spa in the Southwest called the Blue Lemon where most beauty or health treatments involve fruit. I'd like to send a writer there with a camera crew to do a brief segment. I want to show the place from the perspective of a someone who isn't trying to go from a size two to a size zero, then publish a longer version of the story in *Aurora*. Would you mind appearing on the air while sitting in a bathtub full of 'raspberries picked at dawn'?"

"I might be one of the few women who would prefer sitting in a bathtub full of raspberries to sitting under a beach umbrella in a bikini. I have a scar from an old basketball injury on my leg, and the raspberries would hide it."

"Then why don't I call you in a day or two to talk about all of this? In the meantime, I wondered if you had any questions."

Laura asked if the magazine had fact-checkers and got such a peculiar look that she was afraid that she'd squandered any good-will she'd earned.

"That's the first time anybody has asked me that question. We do have excellent fact-checkers, including one who worked briefly for the woman who inspired the Druid in *Bright Lights, Big City*."

"I have another request that may sound a little strange."

"Laura, I hope you won't take this the wrong way. But almost everything you write about is a little strange. That's what I like about it. So ask away."

"I wonder if I could get a quick tour of the magazine and see a few things, including your office-supply cabinet."

"Melody will show you anything you like. But I've heard all about your office supply problems from Venetia, and I can assure you that we have the best letter-openers in the city at *Aurora*."

***

After accepting her new job at *Aurora*, Laura sent a letter of resignation to Cassandra, who didn't respond. Simon took her to lunch at Nobu, and Kit gave her a La Perla dive-in bra as a going-away present. Ethan began lobbying for her job, and Venetia sent her almost daily email notes under her new name.

To: Laura Smart
From: Vicki Lawrence

Hi Laura,
Just wanted to make sure Aurora has told you one of the fantastic things about your new job. Everybody on the editorial staff here has offices on the same floor, so you and I won't have to run up and down a staircase in our Manolos to see each other! No more *Upstairs, Downstairs*!

But I ought to warn you that if you have any free time before you start work, you might want to use it to look for a boyfriend. *Aurora* has even fewer single men than *Cassandra* because Aurora thinks that the most important jobs at a women's magazine ought to be filled by women. So we don't have a chance to practice flirting with somebody like Simon.

Can't Alice fix you up with a rich yachtsman?

Love,
Vicki (aka Venetia)

To: Vicki Lawrence_Aurora
From: Laura Smart

Hi ~~Venetia~~ Vicki,

Glad that we'll be neighbors! I won't have to risk a sprained ankle to see you (or feel I ought to curtsy when I do). But did you forget that those wonderful red-and-purple heels you gave me—which now feel as natural as though I'd extruded them—weren't Manolos but Chanel?

Alice is temporarily interested in talking mainly about merits of wedding in rose garden on estate versus in church where her parents married. Views garden as "more romantic" than St. Anne By the Sea (but sees church as having undeniable advantages that include better plumbing and white marble slab on wall engraved with names of ancestors).

But Alice says Simon may eventually find somebody for me. Must admit would love to spend time this summer with man who will not insult my sexual allure (Nick), my competence (Ethan), my integrity (Jacko), or everything else (Tim).

Love,
Laura

The next morning a gossip column ran an item about the swelling wave of resignations at *Cassandra*, mentioning Laura's name along with those of Caitlin, Venetia, and Simon. It also reported that Calla Norton was about to take a six-figure job with a cosmetics company. Laura was about to find the beauty editor and ask if it was true when she got an email note in response to the gossip column.

To: Laura Smart
From: Junior League Dropout

Hi!
Can't believe it's taken me so long to thank you for your AMAZING story on me! That was SO cool!

I didn't write sooner because Liz told me to ignore you "and let her go through your trash like everybody else." But I'm thinking of firing her, anyway, and I HAD to write when I read about your new job. Congratulations!

Even Tim was really happy that you're leaving *Cassandra* ... and you know how he HATES it when *Aurora* steals his employees! He said, "She and Aurora Starr really DESERVE each other."

Tim also said that he was sure you would help with my memoirs, and I wondered if I could talk to you about this. If you get any time off before you start your new job, could you call me at the number he gave you?

XXX,
Normendie

Since her interview at *Aurora*, Laura had found that there was nothing like a great new job to give you a more charitable view of the people at your company who had driven you away from it. She had almost convinced herself that Tim was right—

that Jacko might be the Rambo of building superintendents—
when she got Normendie's note. Now she was on edge again.
She could hear his sarcasm when Tim's said that she and Aurora
"deserved" each other. He was happy that she was leaving
Cassandra? Well, she was happy, too. She had a job with a company that, unlike Carapace, wasn't too cheap to keep its employees in paper clips.

Still, she couldn't bring herself to send a brusque "no thanks"
to Normendie. It *was* flattering that Tim thought she could write
a book. And if she didn't want to do the memoir right now, she
might change her mind in a year or so. What if Aurora turned out
to have an oversized ego like Cassandra's? What if her magazine
was another swamp of conflicts of interest? What if she wanted to
leave *Aurora* as much as she wanted to leave *Cassandra*? She ought
at least to find out if Normendie was serious about the memoir
and keep the possibility of working on it alive until she knew
where she stood at *Aurora*.

To: Junior League Dropout
From: Laura Smart

Hi Normendie,
Have quite a few projects to finish before I leave *Cassandra* on Friday.
But I could get together for a drink next week if you'll be in town.

If that sounds good, why don't you start thinking about the
experiences you'd like to include in your book? The juicier the better! I probably don't have to tell you that, for example, you'd need
to reveal more details about your days as a lap dancer than you
did on the liner notes for *Junior League Dropout*.

In the meantime, if you talk to Tim, you can tell him that *I* think
I deserve Aurora, too (though not in the way *he* does).

Cheers,
Laura

In her last day on the job, Laura stopped by the art depart-ment to say goodbye to Anne Meyer, the only person she would really miss except Simon, whose attachment to Alice made it cer-tain that she would see him often.

"Anne, what are you going to do after Simon leaves?"

"Take an enforced but happy vacation with my husband in the Caribbean, the perfect place to unwind after the last issue of *Cassandra* appears in November."

"What!"

"Haven't you been reading gossip columns over the past few weeks?"

"Yes, but they've been predicting the demise of *Cassandra* for months."

"This time they're right."

"How do you know?"

"Cassandra let it slip while she was talking to my husband about some plastic surgery."

"Does Simon know?"

"I'm sure he does, and that's why he took his new job."

"But Simon took me to lunch at Nobu and never said a word during the meal that the magazine was folding. If it's true, I'm not sure he's even told Alice."

"Maybe he hasn't told her. He might have known that she'd tell you and that you would have trouble keeping the secret from others in the office. Or he might have a clause in his contract that prevents him from talking about things that might hurt the mag-azine if they got out. Did he ever tell you that Cassandra wanted him to fire you after the incident with Jamie Smith?"

"Fire me?"

"Yes. Simon told Cassandra that he'd quit if he had to get rid of you—that after Caitlin's suspension, he couldn't put out the magazine without your help, and even if he could have, you didn't deserve it."

"I had no idea—"

"I told you that Simon is savvy and discreet. That's partly why he's had such a brilliant career. Alice is going to have an exciting life with him."

Laura had no doubt that Cassandra would have fired her. But it was harder to believe that after so many false reports of its impending demise, the magazine would fold. "Maybe Cassandra was joking when she told your husband that the November issue would be the last."

"Cassandra has no sense of humor about the magazine."

Laura knew this was true. "But she does exaggerate. Maybe she was overstating how bad things were."

"Dan checked out what she said with a few other media powers he knows. All of them have confirmed it. Even if they hadn't, Dan and I were convinced that the magazine was folding by the way Cassandra let the news slip."

"I'm almost afraid to hear it."

"Cassandra tried to get my husband to give her a free brow lift in return for a little publicity. Dan, bless his heart, had the wit to ask whether she would mention him on her show or in her magazine. Cassandra told him he'd have to settle for the show because the magazine wouldn't exist after the November issue. You'll be happy to know that Dan told her that—in either case—he doesn't make that kind of deal."

20

Born with a Silver Spoon in Her Nose

On a balmy August evening, Laura opened a decorative wrought iron gate and, after admiring a pair of window boxes abloom with red geraniums, waited for Normendie Latour to buzz her into an elegant brownstone with fluted white columns flanking the door. Laura felt slightly wistful as she admired its graceful proportions. She had just learned she would have to leave town in a few days to do a story about the fruit-themed spa that Aurora had mentioned during her interview. If the assignment went well, she understood, she would have others like it. She would obviously have little time for return visits to the building she was about to enter.

Perhaps it was just as well. A few hours earlier, she stopped by the Mid-Manhattan Library to leaf through a few celebrity memoirs. She marveled at how far stars had to reach—and how hard their ghostwriters had to work—to fill out their books. Vanna White had padded her autobiography with her favorite afghan pattern, and Madonna had felt the need to fill her book with photos and give it extra zing by calling it *Sex*…as though the word "sex" wouldn't be redundant in the title of any book of *hers*. Even so, most stars' books slipped from view as fast as their latest hairstyles. Did anybody under forty remember that Madonna had once written a book sold in a foil wrapper? Why should she help to write a memoir that might end up on a half-price table next to last year's travel guides to Bhutan and *The Kosher Diabetic's Fondue Cookbook*?

"Up here!"

Normendie's clear alto rang out from the third floor as she leaned over a banister in sweatpants and a pink navel-baring halter top with her platinum hair pulled into a pony tail. Looking around, Laura couldn't help comparing the huge bouquet of day lilies on a refectory table with the grim entrance to her own building and its door with a broken lock. Every night, Jacko stood in the hallway with his toy rifle, his eyes darting around the way Travis Bickle's did when he said in *Taxi Driver*, "I got some bad ideas in my head."

"Sorry I don't have an elevator, but these brownstones are so beautiful..." Normendie's voice trailed off. "Did you see Ethan or Uma on your way here?"

"Ethan or Uma?"

"Ethan Hawke or Uma Thurman. They lived nearby before they broke up, and sometimes I think that people still come to my place hoping to catch a glimpse of them." Laura felt slightly sorry for Normendie when she heard this. Most New Yorkers probably *would* prefer Ethan or Uma to a singer some people regarded as washed-up at twenty-nine.

Normendie opened the door to her apartment, where Roger Hornsley stood barefooted in a white velour robe with "RH" embroidered in gold over the breast. With a generous paunch and an inlet of receding hair, he looked like a younger Ron Perlman in Clark Kent glasses. In his snowy robe he harmonized with a sea of champagne wall-to-wall carpeting, a pair of champagne velvet sofas facing a fireplace, and a near-life-sized photo of Normendie in pastel colors above the mantelpiece.

Roger grinned broadly. "I won't bother you two. Just about to take a sauna. But I wanted to meet the writer who inspired

Normendie to put up a basketball hoop in the exercise room." He and Normendie led Laura through a stainless-steel kitchen that resembled a submarine control room, then up a circular staircase to a gym with enough equipment for a YMCA in a mid-sized American city. A sound system filled the room with the sweet vibrato of Andrea Corrs. *"C'mon, leave me ... breathless!"* Laura was taken aback by the music. Nobody could accuse Normendie of being too egotistical to play anybody's CDs but her own when a reporter stopped by to talk.

"You look surprised to hear the Corrs," Normendie said with a grin that matched Roger's. "'Breathless' is my favorite workout song. My trainer said I should play something that would remind me not to get off the exercise bike until I'm gasping." She slipped an arm around the man standing next to her. "Roger, like most people of his generation, prefers 'Mendocino.' So I have Doug Sahm on tape, too."

"Normendie refuses to believe that, if it weren't for my generation, her generation wouldn't have its best movie soundtracks," Roger said with mock despair. As he headed for the a sauna, he sang, *"Teeny bopper, my teenage lover ... Please stay here with me in Mendocino."*

After Roger left, Normendie took the basketball that Laura had given her out of a bin. "Want to see something cool? Watch this."

She ran forward for a few steps, dribbling behind her back.

"That *is* great," Laura said, as Normendie repeated the move. "You couldn't do that when we met in the park. How did you pick up that dribble up so fast?"

"I had trouble at first. Roger said I should hire one of the players or coaches for the Liberty to help me in the off-season. But I wanted to figure out the dribble on my own. So I called Tim and he came over and helped me. We had a big fight when he told me right off the bat that I'd never get the dribble right until I cut my nails. He was so high and mighty about it! I mean, why do guys think they know everything about our sports in addition to their own? After a couple of days, I figured out that, hey, he was right because every time I tried to dribble behind my back with my long nails I kept breaking them. So we made up and he bought me a great sterling silver Swiss Army knife with scissors attached to show me that he had no hard feelings about how I yelled at him."

Normendie held out her hands to show off nails no longer monogrammed with "LV." It was then that Laura noticed that something else was different. Normendie had cut a few inches from her white-blond hair and gotten rid of her lightning bolt of black roots so that she now resembled a thirties glamour queen retooled for the age of anorexia.

"You gave up your trademark!" Laura exclaimed. "Does Liz know?"

"Fired her last week. I figured that since I'll have a new CD and a book coming out, I might as well get a new rep, too. The first thing I did after I fired her was to call Louis"—her hair colorist—"and get rid of my black roots. I hated them. But Liz wouldn't let me change because it would mean that she had to get new publicity photos and fight with all the editors who wanted to use the old ones."

Normendie tossed the basketball to Laura before going on. "I'd been thinking for a while that I wanted to drop Liz and sign with somebody who would return my phone calls. When I told her you were coming over to talk about my memoir, she started giving me a hard time about it. So I fired her."

"You fired Liz because of me?"

"Not just you. Once I agreed to do an interview with a really sweet reporter for a high school newspaper in Riverdale. He had found my email address on the Internet. Just the nicest kid, maybe fifteen or sixteen years old. He knew a lot more about my music than some reporters for *Entertainment Weekly*. Liz had a fit after I made a date to let him ask me some questions. She said he probably had made a deal to sell the interview to one of the tabloids, that they weren't above playing on your sympathies by using students. So she called up his principal and accused him of stalking or harassing me or something. The poor kid got into all kinds of trouble, and I never did the interview. I wanted to, but he was too frightened by whatever the principal said. So, in a way, I've been wanting to get rid of her ever since then. You gave me an excuse. What a relief!"

"How did Liz take it when you fired her?"

"Never answered the letter. Just had B.B. send me an email reminding me I that I can't sign with a new rep until my contract with S&F ends next month. Which is fine with me. My new rep has agreed to work with me beginning in September, so I have a month to do whatever I want without anybody bossing me around. Free at last!" Normendie attempted a jump shot that missed. "Damn! Why do I always miss the jumps?"

Laura took the ball from her. "You're trying to shoot and elevate at the same time. Why don't you try positioning the ball like this"—she held the ball close to her chest with her palms out—"before you jump?" She took a few running steps, then fired a shot that swished into the net.

"Wow!" Normendie said. "Let's work on jump shots today and talk about the book next time. By then maybe I'll be as good at those shots as I am at dribbling behind my back." Laura realized that Normendie had that strange mix, so common in stars, of brazen overconfidence in some areas and pitiful underconfidence in others.

As Normendie prepared to launch another shot, Laura debated whether to conduct a basketball clinic instead of finding out what the singer might include in her memoir. She would be so busy in the next few weeks that if she was going to help with the book, she had to get started right away. But she had gotten her first interview with Normendie by pretending that it wasn't an interview. Maybe the singer was one of those stars who didn't hesitate to speak off the cuff but clammed up when you turned on your tape recorder. If so, Laura thought, she might be able to combine a few interviews with getting a little exercise.

Normendie missed another shot, then studied the basket with the touching earnestness of a four-year-old hoping to keep a shaky tower of blocks upright with the power of her gaze. Afraid that Normendie might burst into tears if she missed again, Laura didn't have the heart to drag her away from the hoop.

"I'll tell you what. Why don't we work on your basketball techniques and the book at the same time? I'll ask you a few questions, say, about your childhood or your lap-dancing days, while you're setting your shots. I'll write down what you've said during your breaks or after I go home. If I can't remember all the details, I'll call or send you an email. You can correct anything I didn't get exactly right."

"You could do that?" Normendie sounded as though Laura had said she could extract answers from her through liposuction. "Most reporters won't let their tape recorders out of their sight. Even when they have them in front of them, they keep checking them every two minutes to make sure the tape didn't run out."

"I do that sometimes, too. But reporters have to know how to improvise, the way you do during concerts when the audience isn't responding. Didn't you notice that I wasn't taking notes when we met in the park? I memorized what you said, then went to a coffee shop and wrote it down. An old reporter's trick. After we've tried that approach for a couple of weeks, we'll have a sense of whether we could work together on a book."

"But I know we could work together!" Normendie sounded panicked that Laura might not do the book. "I don't know where you found those fantastic pictures for your story. But for once I didn't look like somebody Rudy Giuliani would have swept off the streets along with the crack dealers and the people who slept under cardboard boxes. You made me look great."

Laura explained that art directors, not writers, made people look good in magazines. Normendie was unswayed. "But I liked what I said, too. You made me sound like myself on a good day, not on a bad day like other reporters."

"We'll have to try it for a few weeks and see how it goes. I have to find out how much work I have in my new job. And I need to make sure you understand how much work you'll have to do. You might have to reveal more about yourself than you think."

"How could I have to reveal more of myself than I did when I was wrapping myself around a pole every night in Bayonne, New Jersey?"

Conceding that she had a point, Laura demonstrated a few shooting techniques and asked a question whenever Normendie seemed relaxed enough give an unrehearsed answer. It was a variation on the advice she'd received in a journalism class at Notre Dame: the ideal time to interview someone was when the person was driving a car because your source always paid more attention to the road than to what he or she was saying.

Roger reentered the room just as Normendie was describing her earliest memory—the terror she felt when she dropped a Waterford crystal baby bottle on a bluestone patio at the age of two and half and cut her hand trying to pick up the splintered pieces.

"I think that bottle warped her for life," he said affectionately. "To this day she won't have Waterford in the house. You have to wonder what baby gifts people will think of next. Jeweled Bulgari diaper pins? Juice boxes full of Krug? Winnie-the-Pooh steak knives to make it easier for a child to try to stab his baby sister?"

"You can tell why Roger has only one child," Normendie said, giving him a friendly pat on the seat of his white velour robe. "He's very cynical about how spoiled kids are now. He thinks that boys ought to stab their baby sisters with broken stickball bats the way he did instead of steak knives designed by Michael Graves."

"As far as I can see, it didn't do my sister a bit of harm," Roger said. "It was perfect conditioning for her future profession. Abby is one of the best matrimonial lawyers in Manhattan, specializing in killer prenups. She pioneered the concept of stipulating in your contract how much weight your spouse can gain during the marriage, which of course everybody else has copied. It's all the rage now." He slipped an arm around Laura's shoulder. "If you ever consider getting married, you must call Abby. You'll never have a husband who will have to waddle to the divorce court."

"Thanks, Roger. I'd better leave before you tell me that teenagers are drawing up contracts that say a boy has to pay a cash settlement if he says 'I'll call you' and doesn't."

"Never heard of that. But Abby says that in some suburbs, senior-prom litigation is the next big thing. You bail out at the last minute, you have to pay for her dress, her shoes, and anything she's kicked in for the limo or after-party. Not to mention for her lifetime of emotional distress about having to stay home and watch *Heathers* on the big night."

Laura left after agreeing to meet with Normendie again when she got back from the spa in the Southwest. But she reminded her that she might not have time to do the book.

"You may think that now," Roger said. "But wait until you hear the stories that Normendie has to tell. I hear that you know at least one of the men who played a role in them. You've got to get her to tell you what she and Tim did on the Concorde—"

"Tried to do," Normendie corrected. "Tim refused. He said there are some things in life that you have to save for private jets."

"Which," she said, "is why I'm so happy I met Roger."

***

Laura didn't want to know what Normendie had done—or not done—with Tim on the Concorde. She felt guilty enough about how coolly she had treated someone who, in addition to paying for her ticket to New York, might have saved her cover story. Why wrestle with the added pangs of conscience that she would feel about serving up details of his sex life?

No doubt Normendie liked Tim too much to use his real name in her book and would identify him through one of those coy phrases that you saw in stars' memoirs. *"But even Mick Jagger couldn't compare to the top corporate executive I met while cruising at 1,350 miles an hour on the Concorde ...* " Or, *"I thought I would never get over Johnny Depp until the day I saw those blue eyes look up from a copy of* Golf Digest *in an international departures lounge at JFK.... "* But Normendie didn't hide her friendship with Tim, so his identity couldn't likely be disguised.

Still, by the time she returned to the Village for the next interview, Laura was convinced that she had no choice but to find out the lurid details. Normendie had little chance of having a bestselling memoir if she didn't toss in a few sizzling anecdotes. But she wasn't likely to risk a fight with Roger by saying anything that might upset him. Laura wanted to protect Normendie from embarrassing herself, or at least to avoid exploiting her as Liz Kaiser had. So she couldn't see any solution but to get her to talk about the men she'd gone out with before Roger.

Laura brought up the subject of Tim as gently as she could, after giving Normendie a few more basketball tips. They were sitting on a bench in the exercise room, toweling off and drinking cans of Gatorade from a minibar. "You didn't seem to want to talk about what happened on the Concorde, so I hesitate to bring up Tim—"

"Why do you hesitate? I didn't want to talk about the Concorde because nothing happened there, and you said the memoir should be juicy. Tim and I met while we were comparing those little presents you get on the Concorde with the logo of the plane on them. He got a picture frame, and I got a pen. I asked if he'd trade, and I must have had too much Dom because after he agreed I suggested exchanging a few other things, too. He said that we ought to keep it to in-flight favors while we were on the plane. But that doesn't mean that I won't talk about what happened later. Come with me, and I'll show you something."

Normendie led Laura to a bedroom that resembled a Moorish opium den updated for the age of *InStyle* and plasma TVs. At the center stood a platform bed below a gathered tent-like ceiling made from the red-and-gold fabric that covered the walls. The bed was piled with exotic throw pillows, some with tiny inset mirrors, and faced a white tribal-looking hearth on which you could have roasted a goat for a late-night snack. A stack of celebrity autobiographies rested on a night table—Normendie had been doing her homework—and a tall palm tree spread its leaves in a sunny corner.

"This room is larger than my entire apartment," Laura marveled, looking at the towering ailanthus tree visible through one of the south-facing windows that New Yorkers craved. She was so overstimulated that she wasn't sure she could ever calm down long enough to fall asleep in such a spectacular bedroom. It occurred to her that Normendie might not sleep there but use the room only as love nest.

Normendie pressed a button on a wall panel, and music flooded the room. *"Wake up, little Susie, wake up."* "Roger's idea of a joke. He said he made the Everly Brothers tape to torment me. Here's my idea of bedroom music." She pressed another button.

"Oops, I did it again!"

"You listen to Britney?" Laura had thought that Britney Spears was a sore subject with Normendie, who was often compared unfavorably with the pop idol.

"Why not learn from the competition?"

Laura had to admire her subject's candor. Normendie might never sell out the Meadowlands or steal Keith Richards away from Patti Hansen. But it was refreshing to talk to a pop singer who didn't foam like a rabid Alsatian when you mentioned a rival and who could look a reporter in the eye without pupils the size of a satellite dish. Normendie was famous for having kicked drugs after a few strung-out years in prep school at the age of nineteen. She wanted to call her memoir *Born with a Silver Spoon in Her Nose*, the title suggested by her new rep.

"But I didn't bring you here to show you the sound system," Normendie said. She picked up a silver frame with the logo of the Concorde on it, which held a picture of her and Tim on a Bateau Mouche. "Good-looking, isn't he?"

Struck by the wistfulness in her voice, Laura had to agree. Tim was younger, perhaps by five or six years, when the photo was taken. But there was something about standing next to a beautiful woman that raised a man's looks to a higher power. Tim looked like himself cubed.

"If you think Tim is attractive, why aren't you still together? I'd think he was thrilled to go out with you."

Normendie sat on the bed and motioned for Laura to join her. "Maybe he was. But I knew from the start that he would never marry somebody like me. Just as I knew that Roger, as cynical as he may seem to be about marriage, *would* marry somebody like me. After all, Roger has done it twice before. Tim has this incredibly high-flying lifestyle. So you'd think that we'd be compatible. But most men are afraid of women they see as glamorous. That's especially true of men like Tim, who aren't particularly tall or gorgeous or, by New York standards, rich. They want to go out with you but not to marry you. They're more comfortable being friends than lovers."

Laura, remembering Aurora's comment that most people were afraid of her, too, mentally filed the comment under P for "Problems, What Some People Define As." "Don't you think that most men are a little afraid of women even if they aren't glamorous?"

"To some extent. But with women they see as glamorous, it's a different kind of fear. They aren't afraid of making a commitment or being tied down so much as of feeling inadequate or being left for Benjamin Bratt."

Which in Tim's case would have been a realistic fear, since you did leave him for Roger Hornsley, Laura thought. "If you thought that Tim wouldn't marry you, maybe he also thought you would never marry him."

"If so, that just proves my point. A lot of men are so convinced that you'll never marry them that they don't try to find out. Sometimes I think that men and women are like the submarines in *The Hunt for Red October.* They spend all their time circling each other underwater, afraid that they'll be found out by the enemy. Somebody has to be the first to risk coming to the surface. And Roger, unlike Tim, didn't hesitate to do that. It's too bad, really."

Laura heard her wistfulness again. "You have regrets about that?"

"Who wouldn't? Tim was the best sex I ever had."

"The best sex you ever had?" Laura echoed, wondering if Normendie had less experience with men than she had imagined. "I mean, I'd think that one of the rock stars you've gone out with—"

"I don't even *remember* the sex I had with most rock stars, and I'm sure they don't, either. They were too stoned, and I was too wasted from the touring. But I remember every detail of what I did with Tim."

Laura listened as Normendie poured out the story of their sex life, which was far too specific in its particulars to doubt, including accounts of trysts at a caravanserai in St. Maarten and at Tim's parents' house in Lakewood after a pilgrimage to see Jim Morrison's Cub Scout uniform at the Rock and Roll Hall of Fame. To hear her tell it, Tim was a cross between Tom Hanks, William Masters, and the model for Michelangelo's David. All of it might have been ludicrous if Normendie hadn't sounded so sweetly embarrassed by much of what she said. Laura thought that her tape recorder might have spontaneously combusted from the heat of the story if she had turned it on. If what she was hearing was true, she didn't see how anybody could have left Tim for Roger.

Normendie grinned when Laura asked about this. "I could answer that question in a number of ways." She opened a bedside drawer and pulled out a strand of South Sea pearls. "Here's one of them. My six-month anniversary present." She put the pearls back in the drawer.

"But I wouldn't want Roger to think that I went out with him just for the jewelry," Normendie said, smiling. "So, for the purposes of the memoir, why don't we just say that after a few months with Tim, any woman would be exhausted?"

21
The Blue Lemon

"Laura, you really have to try to concentrate a little harder on relaxing."

Laura lay on the surface of a flotation tank filled with water and apple cider vinegar at the Blue Lemon, a spa sculpted out of the desert with citrus groves and swimming pools, trying to follow orders. To her relief, the camerawoman for *Aurora!* who was following her around had left to take a few shots of the guest bungalows draped with frangipani that perfumed the air with a faint almond scent. She hoped that Pam's departure would make it easier to follow the instructions of her personal-relaxation coach. Rudy was standing next to her in the water-and-vinegar bath, supporting her body with his arms and barking out commands. Paying attention was difficult when the orders came from a man who had sunbleached blond hair, the body of a porn star, and a Speedo that left nothing to the imagination except his sperm count.

For several days, Rudy had been urging her to relax and to "feel the apple cider vinegar drawing the toxins" from her body. "You could get a Boy Scout merit badge for the knots in your back," he said when she first showed up at the center in a yellow tankini with a small blue lemon embroidered just above the right leg hole. The acrid smell of the vinegar, which made Laura feel as though she was floating in a vat of salad dressing spiked with chlorine, had so far defeated her and frustrated her coach.

During their first session in the flotation tank, Rudy had resembled a Buddha on Paxil, a man who might have had trouble breaking into a sweat if a mushroom cloud appeared outside one of the porthole windows in the Aquatic Meditation Center at the Blue Lemon. Now he sounded more like a mullah who had forgotten to take his Lithium. Pam, who had been waiting for such signs of animation from a man who might otherwise strike viewers as lobotomized, had headed for the bungalows soon after getting some footage of his unraveling serenity. Unfazed by her departure, Rudy pressed on.

"I said, 'Inhale,' Laura! Inhale! *Not* 'Exhale'!"

"I'm trying, Rudy."

"Don't you want to get rid of the knots in your back?"

"Yes! They're killing me. But I thought they resulted from standing on cement subway platforms in four-inch heels, not from toxins that needed to be killed off by apple cider vinegar."

"We always have this problem with New Yorkers," Rudy said, sighing. "They're so used to doing six things at once that they can't do one thing at once. Too much nervous energy. The whole city has Attention Deficit Disorder."

Laura, though flattered by the implication that she had become a New Yorker so quickly, was exhausted by her efforts to relax. By the end of her session with Rudy, she was also starving. The spa served food made from fruits and whole grains that would not fill her up. She longed for meat and could suddenly understand why Babcia's was Tim's favorite restaurant. Compared with the tiny bowls of brown rice flecked with bits of mango and kumquat that were a signature dish at the spa, pierogies were the food of the gods and meatloaf a meal for minor saints.

After changing out of her swimsuit, Laura went to the dining room for lunch, which ended with a dessert that tasted like Wheatina flavored with Tang. Then she went back to her bungalow to write up her notes on the morning's activities—resting with blood-orange slices over her eyes during a facial, holding a cantaloupe between her legs in an exercise class, getting a grape seed body scrub from a staff member who had rubbed her body with what felt like shredded Brillo pads until she wanted to beg for a morphine drip.

Pam kept saying that they were getting great material—who wouldn't want to find out whether you could actually remove someone's epidermis with grape seeds?—and Laura didn't doubt it. But she realized why Aurora was paying her more to do segments for her show. Television required you to write for the ear while print is for the eye, which meant that she had to take notes for two kinds of stories at once. She was also dealing with an unavoidable hazard of out-of-town assignments—you couldn't return to the scene easily to check your facts. She was afraid that she would forget to take down a detail about the spa that she would need later, which kept her in a state of nerve-fraying hyper-alertness. The night before, she had sprung out of bed to make a note to find out whether the growls she heard outside her window came from coyotes, javelinas, or wild dogs.

On her last day at the spa, Laura visited the Fruitorium, a room celebrated in brochures as a place that allowed for "thera-peutic healing." For an hour, covered only by a sheet, she lay alone on a massage table, surrounded by orange slices and inhaling the sweet fragrance of the ropes of figs, dates, and apricots that hung from the ceiling like beaded curtains in a bordello.

This strange experience was more relaxing than listening to Rudy in his Lithium-deprived mullah phase. But it gave her a new problem. In the Fruitorium she couldn't stop thinking about sex, and specifically about sex with Tim. Laura attributed this devel-opment partly to her surroundings—how could you *not* think about sex when you were lying naked in room that might as well have been called the Fruit Brothel?—and partly to Normendie's accounts of what went on in her love nest.

Without a replacement for Nick, she was having serious sexual withdrawal symptoms intensified by spending all day with people who were walking around in bathing suits and tennis shorts. Sixty-year-olds with leathery skin, gray hairpieces, and aqua velour jogging outfits were starting to look good. If she spent much more time at the Blue Lemon, she might start fantasizing about the retired CEO from Palm Springs who showed up at meals with an acupuncture needle sticking out of his ear. Or the former state legislator hoping to make a comeback who walked around in rubberized pants that were supposed to help him sweat off the extra weight that he thought made him lose his last election.

Hoping to distract herself from her fugue of fantasies, Laura went back to her room and checked her email for the first time since arriving at the spa. The Blue Lemon didn't ban computers, cell phones, and pagers from the premises. But the staff tended to regard their use as a sign of moral weakness, a notch above smuggling in cartons of cigarettes or bags of Doritos and pop-top bean dips. So she read only a few of her messages, half afraid that a chambermaid might burst in and report her to the spa director.

To: Laura Smart
From: Molly Chase

Hi Laura,

Just wanted to warn you that Tina seemed a tiny bit upset that you didn't attend the shower that Maggie had for her and Brad last weekend. Did you get the invitation? Maggie said she sent it to your old apartment, c/o Nick, who is spending a lot of time in California. So if you didn't get the invitation, you might want to make sure someone is forwarding your mail.

I went to the shower with Chad, now desperate to make partner on schedule at S&B, who spent the afternoon talking on his Starlac in the driveway. Have you heard the joke: "Why do lawyers like Fridays? Because then there are only two working days left until Monday."

Molly

This message dealt a death blow to any "therapeutic healing" that Laura had experienced in the Fruitorium. Why had Maggie trusted the notoriously unreliable Nick to forward the invitation? If she did, why hadn't she followed up with email? Laura suspected that Tina, unhappy enough about having her in the wedding party, had been looking for a way to exclude her from the shower while claiming the moral high ground. Now she had to do some damage control by sending a gift as quickly as possible.

To: Molly Chase
From: Laura Smart

Hi Molly,
If I remember correctly, Chad tried to impress you on your first date by sucking the pimiento out of an olive. So maybe you should feel thankful that—if he sees his StarTac as his Significant Other—he didn't try to suck the hot dog out of one of Maggie's famous baby-pigs-in-a-blanket?

Any idea what I should send Tina as a shower gift? And have you considered going out with lawyers who have already made partner?

Cheers,
Laura

To: Laura Smart
From: Molly Chase

Hi Laura,

The shower had a barbecue theme, so Tina and Brad got mainly items related to the slaughter of large animals (knives, skewers, tongs) or related creatures (fish-scaler, shrimp de-veiner, oyster-shucker). Trigger-happy couple registered at Dillard's, Brookstone, Williams-Sonoma, etc.

Have tried going out with partners and found that this experience, alas, tends to confirm the old joke: "Why don't associates like to have sex with partners? Because the associates have to do all the work."

Did you know that Tina and Brad are wearing small vials of each other's blood around their necks—an idea they borrowed from Angelina Jolie and Billy Bob Thornton? This gesture apparently has nothing to do with the barbecue theme. Brad represents the distributor of the vials and intends to promote them as Halloween party favors in the fall.

Molly

Laura called stores where Tina had registered for gifts and learned that other people had bought all the items on her cousin's list except for an elaborate device for electrocuting mosquitoes and an inexpensive wire basket that let you grill hamburgers without getting black marks on them.

She hesitated to buy the insect electric chair, which made her wish there were a way to put mosquitoes to death by lethal injection. The device seemed so cruel. But something in her also rebelled against the wire basket. She *liked* black lines on her hamburgers, which seemed almost the whole point of cooking meat on a grill. And the wire basket cost a fraction of what the insect electric chair did. If she sent such an inexpensive gift, Tina might accuse her of not caring about her family again.

Hoping to avoid two more years of frigid silence, Laura bought them and had both sent to her cousin, then read another email.

To: Laura Smart
From: Junior League Dropout

Hi!

Hey, thanks for helping with my jump shots! You wouldn't believe how good I've gotten since you left for the spa! I made one shot that I'm sure would have been a three-pointer on a regular court.

Any chance that you'll be back from the spa in time to join Roger and me for a last-minute dinner party that we've having in our garden tonight? It's the only weekend all summer when we aren't going to the Hamptons. (Roger has a clause in his divorce agreement that says that Ex-Wife No. 2 gets to use their house in Sag Harbor for one week a year, and this is it, so he refuses to travel farther east than Sutton Place.) A couple of my friends in the music business are coming, including the head of A&R at my recording company, and maybe a few others you might to want interview for my memoir.

We're having grilled lobster and eating at about eight-thirty. If you're allergic, let me know and I'll ask the cook to throw on some filet mignon, too.

XXX,
Normendie

Laura checked her flight schedule. If her plane arrived on time and she took a taxi to the Village, she could just make it to the dinner party. After a week at a place teeming with fruit fetishists, she was desperate for time alone and thought about declining. But Normendie's "friends in the music business" might include two Backstreet Boys, a soundman for Christina Aguilera, and the assistant publisher of *Vibe*. And if the memoir got off the ground, she would regret having missed the chance to meet to the head of A&R at Pagoda Records, who might spend six months avoiding her. She called Normendie, gave her the details of her flight, and said she would drop by after she got into town.

Then she packed and, ignoring her sore back, picked up and her suitcase. A bolt of pain shot through her. Realizing that she might have sprained a muscle in her lower back, she dropped her bag and called the front desk to ask for a porter.

Pam, who was waiting for her in the lobby, jumped up and began taking pictures again when she limped into the room, fighting off a grimace.

"Fantastic!" Pam said without irony. "This is just what Aurora wanted—a segment that will show a side of expensive spas that you don't normally see on television."

"The side that looks like a scene from *ER*?" Laura asked.

"Absolutely." Pam kept filming. "The only way we could have a better ending for your segment would be if you'd wound up on crutches."

22
Whirlpool

Somewhere over Oklahoma, Laura learned that her flight was being diverted to Houston to avoid tornadoes and would arrive in New York at least two hours late. Her injured back, barely tolerable before she boarded the plane, felt even worse as the plane fought turbulence at 29,000 feet.

The bumpier the flight got, the more the idea of taking a taxi to the Village and sitting through a dinner party struck Laura as madness. She wanted to go home, soak in an Aveeno bath, and pop a frozen cheesesteak into the microwave. Except that she didn't *have* a microwave, an item her landlord seemed to view as a ludicrous nonessential. And she couldn't take the bath for granted after Derek had warned her to keep a couple of bottles of San Pellegrino on hand so that she could brush her teeth if the water in their building went out again.

Laura called Normendie from Houston and said she would have to miss the dinner party because her back was buckling under the strain of the plane ride. She could hear the clink of ice and a ripple of laughter among the guests as Roger reached for falsetto tones—*"down by the sea-ee-ee!"*—while singing "Under the Boardwalk."

"How did you two ever get together?" Laura asked, half-jokingly. "Roger seems to be trying to upstage you at your own party."

"He is trying to upstage me. That's one of the things I like about him. He has such a huge ego that I don't have to perform when he's around. He performs for both of us."

"You mean, performs sexually?"

"That, too. But I meant it literally. Some of the other men I've gone out with always wanted me to perform—sing, dance, play the guitar—for their friends. I kept telling them that I get paid for that. Once I went out with the lighting guy for a club who kept trying to get me to do songs from *Junior League Dropout* at parties in his loft. I asked him how he'd like it if people begged him to rewire their sockets while they were watching the Super Bowl. It's relaxing to go out with somebody like Roger who just lets me be. I let him be, too. He has such a stressful job that he needs a place where he can 'regress,' as he puts it, to the days when was the social chairman of Alpha Tau Omega at Cornell."

Normendie held out the receiver so that Laura could hear more of the comically off-key warbling: *"... on a blanket with my bay-bee ..."* "See?" she asked. "He'll be doing that for hours. So feel free to drop by if your back feels better. Roger may have moved on to 'Heat Wave' by then."

Laura tried to imagine what it would be like to go out with a man who "let her be" and, unlike Nick, didn't expect her to serve as a one-woman entertainment committee. She was tempted to drop by the party just to observe Normendie and Roger more closely. But by the time her plane arrived at LaGuardia, she had no desire to find out whether Roger sang "Heat Wave" better than "Under the Boardwalk." It hurt just to pull her suitcase down from the overhead rack—never mind dragging it up the high stoop of a brownstone.

After getting jostled painfully by passengers leaving the plane, Laura stopped short at the end of the jetway. Tim was standing at the arrivals gate with several sections of the Sunday *Times* under his arm. She wondered if he was waiting for Brandy to arrive at the same gate on a flight from Chicago.

"Tim! What are you doing here?"

"Carrying out Normendie's strict instructions to keep you healthy enough to write her memoir. I was at her party when you called, and she told us about your back. She's worried that she contributed to the problem by making you demonstrate a few of the finer points of jump shots, and Roger wanted send his car out to the airport for you. But the party was winding down, and I wasn't sure how many more times I could listen to his 'Starry, Starry Night,' so I said I'd come get you."

Laura wondered if Normendie had ordered him to pick her up. "You mean you came to get me and take me to the Village?"

"Not unless you can't live without hearing a fifty-two-year-old man impersonating a young Don McLean." Tim took her suitcase out of her hands. "I'll drive you to your place. But we've got to hurry. I'm double-parked."

It was after midnight when they reached her building and Tim offered to carry her suitcase up the five flights to her apartment. In no position to refuse, Laura braced for him to start complaining that her landlord was guilty of human rights violations. They got no further than the entrance of her building.

While she was away, Jacko had replaced the broken lock on the front door with a new one. He had also left her a note saying that "for reasons of national security" he had put her key to the lock in her mailbox. She couldn't tell whether he was joking or truly believed he was providing urgently needed back-up support for Condoleezza Rice. The mailbox, in any case, was on the other side of the locked door.

"That man is crazy!" Laura exploded. "How does he expect me to get to my mailbox if he's locked me out of the building?" She thought she saw Tim suppress a smile. "Don't you dare say 'I told you your super was crazy!'"

"I never said your super was 'crazy,'" Tim said. "I said he was 'a lunatic.'"

"May I ask what the difference is?"

"A lot of people in New York are crazy—George Steinbrenner,

the people who pay one hundred thousand dollars for a summer rental in the Hamptons, the A&R man at Normendie's party who thinks that electroclash is the wave of the future. Your super is one of the people who crosses the line into certifiable."

"In that case, would you mind keeping an eye on my suitcase while I try to get back into the asylum?"

As Tim watched with amusement, Laura began pressing the buzzers for Jacko and other tenants, hoping someone would let her in. She saw lights and thought that she saw movement in one or two apartments. But some of her fellow tenants had developed a siege mentality after receiving subpoenas from a process-serving firm called Serving by Irving that Derek's lawyers were using in his feng shui–busting case. The tenants refused to buzz in a pizza delivery boy for fear of getting hit with a subpoena hidden in a Domino's box. It might take tear gas to get them to come downstairs.

After about fifteen minutes of praying for someone to let her in, Laura gave up. All of the tenants who weren't ignoring their buzzers were evidently asleep or hadn't returned from their weekends out of town. She asked Tim if she could borrow his cell phone to call Venetia, who had an apartment in Nolita and might allow her to spend the night.

"Why go all the way down to Nolita when you can stay at my place? It's practically around the corner."

Laura wished she knew whether the offer was a veiled come-on. From the safe distance of the spa Tim had begun to look maddeningly attractive. But she was in no condition to have sex with him—or anybody else—until her back felt better. "I'm not sure I should—" she said tentatively. "My back is acting up."

"Maybe I should take you to the emergency room at Lenox Hill?" Tim asked, his brow wrinkled with sudden concern. "I guess I should have offered sooner, but when you didn't yelp as we crunched over all the potholes, I thought you were fine."

"I just need to rest my back a little."

"That's all the more reason you should stay at my place instead of going down to Nolita. Venetia might sleep on an air mattress, too. At my place you could have a bed."

Laura noticed that he didn't say *whose* bed she could have. "I just want to make sure that there are no misunderstandings."

"About what?" Tim asked, either dense or feigning innocence. "Whether somebody from Serving by Irving will accost you in the lobby? My doorman is great about getting rid of people like that."

"About what will—or won't—happen if I stay over."

Tim looked at her with mock—or perhaps real—amazement. "You don't think I'm desperate enough to try to sleep with someone who thinks I'm cheap, and probably a lot of other things that neither you nor Aurora dared to say to my face? Or someone who has so little interest in me that she tried to palm me off on her best friend?"

"But—" Laura began. "How did you know that I thought of fixing you up with Alice?"

"Simon let it slip, or maybe was trying to sound me out about it. If you come back to my place, you could explain why you wanted to subvert the role normally played by my mother, who has been trying to fix me up for years with the daughters of her friends. So you don't have to worry that I'll be unable to resist you. I've never had any trouble resisting women who remind me of my mother."

For some reason, Laura was upset by this comment. In her fantasies of Tim at the spa, she hadn't considered that *he* might have no sexual interest in her. "Even if I do remind you of your mother, if I go to your place, you could get swept away ..."

"By my fond memories of your behavior at Kit's wedding or after we had dinner at Babcia's?" Tim asked, raising an eyebrow. "Interesting what you see as sexually attractive to men."

Laura chafed under his cavalier tone of voice but didn't want to start arguing with him again with her back aching. "Not by your memories, by accident."

Tim laughed. "Laura, I don't want to take anything away from your powers of seduction. I'm sure they're right up there with your ability to show how much you dislike men who don't meet your standards. Under other circumstances, you probably *could* make me lose control. But I have a world-class headache from fighting the traffic on the Queens-Midtown Expressway. A taxi nearly sheared off my door handles while I was driving to the airport to pick you up. So you don't have to worry about my losing control."

Laura felt a pang of guilt as she realized that Tim might had spent several hours in traffic on his way to and from the airport. "Tim, I'm so sorry. You were so calm in the car. I had no idea about the headache."

"My empty stomach might have distracted me from it for a while. Didn't you hear the rumbling? Luckily Normendie sent me away with a few leftovers, a small steak and a couple of grilled lobster tails, that we can eat back at my place."

Worried about the effect of the flight on her stomach, Laura had eaten nothing since lunch except a tiny bag of pretzel sticks handed out by the flight attendants. She was almost hallucinating about food. "You have a steak?"

"Filet mignon. Roger won't eat anything else, and I have a feeling he might have liked to have it for breakfast tomorrow. But Normendie had gone to a couple of spas and said that after you leave, you want to go directly to a Dairy Queen or Ponderosa Steak House. She said to tell you that if you'll work with her on her memoir, she'll ask her cook to make you filet mignon every time you finish a chapter."

***

Laura had the sense, when she entered Tim's apartment, that she had stepped into a scaled-down version of what Rose Bluffs could be if anybody ever fixed it up. Why hadn't she noticed the resemblance when she visited his place on the Fourth of July? Most single men she knew lived in places that were a combination of sterility and squalor, a motel and the set for *Animal House: The Next Generation*. They bought one big item—an overstuffed sofa from Pottery Barn, a reproduction of a Jasper Johns flag print, a Mission-style entertainment center that could hold a Trinitron the size of bank vault. Then they called it quits unless they had girlfriends who dragged them by the hair to the lamp or pillow displays at Pier One or Restoration Hardware.

Tim's co-op had a quality that she'd never seen in a single man's apartment: warmth. Or, some people might have said, character. Everything in the living room had its place—the handsome fireplace with a brass screen, the Persian rug with the peacock border, the navy blue velvet sofa with silk pillows with gold embroidery. But it wasn't the sort of room where you had to worry that you might spoil the décor if you tossed your wet trench coat over an armchair or spilled wine on the rug. The ficus tree had shed a few of its leaves, and the coffee table held a stack of books, including a copy of *Seabiscuit* with a flurry of Post-Its stuck to its pages.

"Why do you look so surprised?" he asked as he set the steak in front of her on the coffee table. "Did you expect me to live in a glorified locker room?"

Laura didn't want to admit that he'd guessed her thoughts. "You wouldn't have been the first man who did. This is one of the few single men's apartments I've visited where you don't hear Fritos or Ripples crunching underfoot. I don't think I noticed that at your Fourth of July party."

"That's because at that party there probably *were* Fritos or Ripples crunching underfoot. I told the caterers that they couldn't serve their signature fried jasmine blossoms unless they also put out some things that the men on my softball team would eat."

"This place would probably look great after a food fight."

"Most of the credit belongs to my mother. When I bought the place, she said she'd help me fix it up on two conditions: I couldn't hang any team pennants in the living room, and I had to have a maid come in occasionally to clean. She said she'd done the homes of too many single men who ruined her work by turning their places into a cross between a gym and a snack bar."

"Your mother has great taste."

"She does have great taste. Except in the women she thinks are right for me. She's always trying to fix me up in the hope that it will lure me back to Ohio. I keep telling her that I'm a lifer here. Just because I got committed to the institution later than some people doesn't mean I'm not planning to stay. There's not much mobility in broadcasting or in magazine publishing in Cleveland."

Tim noticed that Laura kept shifting positions. "This deep sofa can't be comfortable for your back."

"The sofa is beautiful," Laura said, telling a half-truth. It *was* beautiful. But it was so plush that it gave her back little support.

"I have a great cure for a bad back that I can show you."

Laura's doubts about Tim's intentions flooded back. *This is it,* she thought. *The moment when he says, "I give a really great back rub," then tries to wrestle me into a position that could lead to five hours of spinal surgery.* "I'll be fine."

"For the record, I'm not going to offer to give you a back rub."

Laura sat up. "How did you know I was thinking that?"

"Let's just say that I've offered enough women back rubs to know when somebody is going to reject one. It has a way of turning you into a Nostradamus. So I was going to suggest that you soak in my Jacuzzi instead."

"Your Jacuzzi!" Laura sank against the sofa pillows again. She couldn't think of anything that would feel better after a treacherous plane ride than slipping into the tankini she'd received at the Blue Lemon, then climbing in a hot whirlpool bath.

"You didn't think that my decorator mother would let me skip that essential, did you?" Tim asked. "If you'd like to try out the Jacuzzi, I'll put on a bathing suit and join you. It might help my headache as much as your back."

After a few minutes in the Jacuzzi, Laura had the sense that she had entered a high-rise heaven. For the first time, she felt relaxed with Tim, who was sitting placidly across from her in the Jacuzzi, sunk up to his shoulders in the hot water. He seemed far more interested in trying to banish his headache than in reviving any of their former arguments. Leaning back with his eyes closed, he said little until she started get out of the tub. Then he noticed the faint red scar on her inner thigh.

"What's that mark on your leg?" He motioned hastily for her to sit down on the lip of the Jacuzzi. "The one that runs from your thigh to just below your knee."

"Just the scar from an operation I had on my leg in high school."

Tim slid closer to her to get a better look. He traced the outline of the scar with his index finger. "It must be eight inches long!"

"But you can hardly see it. It's faded so much. By the time I'm thirty you may not see it at all."

Tim ran his finger back and forth along the scar. Laura felt as though her body might shoot skyward like a surface-to-air missile but tried to stay calm and figure out what was going on. If another man had stroked her thigh that way, she would have taken the move as the most blatant of sexual come-ons. It was certainly having no less effect. But Tim didn't seem to be making a sexual move. He was running his finger along her leg the way a doctor or trainer might, as though he was trying to get a better sense of the dimensions of the problem. That was what was so strange about his interest. Most men were afraid of her scar—if not repelled by it—and tended to ignore it. Even Nick had avoided touching it for a while after they'd started going out. Nobody had ever focused on the scar so intently.

"How many stitches did you have?"

Laura hadn't heard that question in years, not since high school. "A few dozen, maybe more. But they weren't a problem. Everybody said the stitches would itch. But mine didn't. Only the cast itched."

Tim stood up. "Let me put some lotion on your thigh." He got out of the Jacuzzi and took some Keri Lotion from his medicine chest, then dried her scarred leg and began massaging it into her thigh.

Laura clung to the Jacuzzi, afraid she'd hit the ceiling. When Tim stopped applying lotion, he kneeled down and kissed her thigh the way her mother used to kiss her elbow when she skinned it.

"There. Now doesn't that make you feel better?"

Laura didn't think she could risk telling him how much better. "Almost as good as the Jacuzzi and the food."

"By the way, there's still some lobster in the refrigerator," Tim said, as matter-of-factly as though they'd spent the past few minutes fighting gridlock in midtown. "If you wake up before I do tomorrow, you might want to have some for breakfast."

∗∗∗

The first thing Laura noticed when she woke up in Tim's apartment was that her back no longer ached. Her pain had eased while she was soaking in the Jacuzzi. After some rest and a couple of Advils, it had almost disappeared. But a good night's sleep hadn't banished her confusion about what had gone on the night before. She still had no idea whether Normendie and Roger had forced him to pick her up at the airport or whether he had wanted to see her again and seized the excuse. If he had wanted to see her, why tell her she reminded him of his mother?

Laura was still trying to figure out what had happened when, after she called Derek and arranged for him to open the door, Tim insisted on driving her back to her place, a half dozen blocks south of his. She had almost convinced herself that he had no interest in her when she saw a couple kissing at the 86th Street subway stop.

"Don't you just love seeing all the couples kissing each other in the morning in New York?" she asked. "All those people who can't resist each other! In twenty-five years in Cleveland I never saw a couple kissing at a Rapid stop. But now I see at least one or two a week. Don't you think that tells you something about the difference between people in Cleveland and in New York?"

"I think it tells you something about the difference between the weather in Cleveland and New York," Tim said, smiling. "Such as

that your lips might freeze if you spent too much time kissing out-
doors in a Midwestern winter."

"You're so unromantic," Laura said playfully. "You're confusing
love and the Lake Effect. If Midwesterners were as passionate as
New Yorkers, they'd kiss at subways, too."

"You think Midwesterners aren't passionate? That's interesting
to know." Tim glanced over at her. "By the way, how is your back
feeling today?"

"Much better, thanks. Your Jacuzzi really helped."

"Good." Tim switched on a directional signal and turned
left instead of continuing down Lexington Avenue toward her
apartment.

Laura stared at him uncomprehendingly. "Where are you
going? You're heading for the East River instead of my apartment."

"I'm not heading for the river. I'm driving around the block to
give you time to think about whether you want me to kiss you
when I get back to the 86th Street subway stop."

"I didn't mean that I wanted you to kiss me—"

"I know you didn't. I'm just giving you a chance to decide
whether you do want it that now that I've raised the possibility. I
didn't want to bring up the idea while your back was bothering
you. I wasn't sure you could focus on any other parts of your body.
But your back is better now. So there's nothing to stop us from
kissing, is there?"

Flustered, Laura watched him as he slowed his car to a crawl.
Tim seemed amused that she hadn't anticipated his move.

"Made up your mind yet?" Tim asked as 86th Street came into
view again. He sounded like Regis Philbin checking to see if a
contestant had come up with a final answer on *Who Wants to Be
a Millionaire?* "You'd better think quickly because I'm about to go
on a trip, and by the time I get back, you might have fallen in love
with somebody who thinks that kissing at subway stops is embarrassing. Maybe one of those unromantic Midwesterners who
thinks that New Yorkers are born exhibitionists—"

Laura tried to make sense of what was happening. Her fantasies of Tim—which flared up in the Fruitorium, then subsided when she hurt her back—had roared back when he stroked her thigh in the Jacuzzi. But she couldn't be sure that he wasn't mocking her, or taking advantage of the opportunity provided by Normendie and Roger to settle a score or two. She didn't know if he really wanted to kiss her, or was trying to rattle her by pretending that he was.

"Maybe I can help," Tim said. "Imagine yourself on your deathbed. You're telling your grandchildren how much you loved seeing couples kissing at subway stops in New York, and they ask you if you ever did. What are you going say?"

"Please don't talk about death."

Tim stopped his car at the 86th Street stop. "Okay. I'll just ask you again. *Do* you want to tell your grandchildren that you never kissed anybody at a subway stop?"

"By the time I have grandchildren, people will won't be kissing at subway stops. They'll be having orgies on the platforms. They'll get permits from the city, the way street musicians do now, and ask passengers to toss coins at their writhing bodies."

"I'm going to take that as a 'yes.'"

Tim unbuckled his seat belt and, in front of dozens of people who were dashing into the mouth of the subway, kissed her until a bicycle messenger almost slammed into the car. When he stopped, he seemed as amused as he had while driving around the block.

"That wasn't as bad as you thought it was going to be, was it? On a scale of one to ten, maybe a five instead of a two or three?"

Laura was speechless. All she could think was: *on a scale of one to ten that was the score of a basketball game.*

"You might want to take a while to decide whether or not you liked it. But, as you can see, somebody approved." Tim pointed to two men in orange hats and tool belts who'd been watching them in the car.

The construction workers were clapping.

23
Sorority House

Like most women's magazines, *Aurora* was a cross between a sorority house and a Gay Pride parade, a place where the only employees who weren't women were men who wore earrings or thigh-high boots. In that sense, it confirmed what Venetia had told Laura—that *Cassandra* was unusual in having an eligible man like Simon so high up on the masthead. On the nights when an issue closed, the magazine took on the atmosphere of a sleepover with better nightgowns. At times Laura smelled popcorn in the hallways or finished off a slice or two of pizza left behind by the copy editors.

All of this made it easy for her to settle in at *Aurora*, where none of her bosses flirted with her and nobody read sexual innuendoes into the interoffice memos. It also left her with time to help Normendie with her memoir after work. To her surprise the singer hadn't lost interest in the project but treated *Born with a Silver Spoon in Her Nose* as a key to her comeback. Laura was having so much fun playing basketball in her gym—the equivalent of a free membership in a four-figure-a-year health club—that she turned down Normendie's offer to pay her out of pocket for her work until they found a publisher.

The problem with the lack of men at *Aurora* was that it threw her sexual doldrums into high relief. Most of her female coworkers were married or needed hydraulic lifts to raise the yellow diamonds that they wore with their pale square-oval—or "squoval"—manicures.

Laura wondered if the sorority-house atmosphere helped to explain why Tim had begun to look so perversely alluring. It was ridiculous to think of going out with someone who had gone out with Normendie Latour, a woman who regularly received bouquets of white orchids flown in from Ecuador by her cosmetics-tycoon boyfriend. Why didn't she raise the bar a few inches and go after Matt Damon? Or, come to think of it, skip right over Matt and try to steal Brad Pitt away from Jennifer Aniston?

But after soaking in his Jacuzzi, she couldn't stop second-guessing how she had acted with Tim. Why had she made that flip comment about how New Yorkers would someday have orgies at subway stations? Now, when she waited for the IRT, she fantasized that Tim might appear and make her feel that the third rail had started running through her body as she protested weakly that they ought at least to wait for an empty car.

Unfortunately, she knew this was how she had once felt about Nick. Hadn't their behavior behind the Center for Social Concerns at Notre Dame given new meaning "social concerns"? Just look where *that* had gotten her. After Nick behaved so caddishly, she had vowed to listen to her head instead of her hormones. Yes, she needed a man whose clothes she would want to tear off with a blowtorch. But did that have to clash with the respect that her parents had always had for each other? Or with the upstanding character that the nuns of St. Rose's held out as the Holy Grail of Holy Matrimony? She hated to admit it, but what was most upstanding about Nick was definitely *not* his character.

The trouble with Tim, as Laura saw it, was that she could never get a fix on him. Nobody could deny that he had been generous with his time and his credit card, or that she might have spent her best half-hour in New York in his Jacuzzi. But if he had a sexual interest in her, his lavish gestures might have been nothing more than a shrewd business investment. He had hardly been as generous to the staff at *Cassandra*. Might he be one of those men, like Roger, who thought that if money couldn't buy you love, it could rent it for a while? Was he trying to determine her asking price?

Then there were Tim's baffling love affairs. Why did he go out with women who saw their faces on CD cases and sportscasts when he cast himself as a down-home Midwesterner who liked pierogies and after-work softball? For all she knew, he was carrying a torch for Normendie and was encouraging her to write a memoir as clever way of trying to win back a singer who had dropped him.

Laura put aside these thoughts long enough to write her story about the Blue Lemon for *Aurora*. But after she had finished, she was afraid that if a new man didn't turn up soon, she would find herself in danger of falling in love with somebody she wasn't even sure she liked. So she was grateful when Melody burst into her office one day and said that Aurora wanted to see her right away.

"Is there a problem with my stories on the spa?" Laura asked, worried that her boss hadn't liked her writing or Pam's tapes.

"Oh, no. Aurora and I watched the tapes the other day, and you looked hilarious in that weight-training session where you had to bench-press a watermelon. Pam said you held onto your melon twice as long as most of the other guests before it splattered all over the floor, so you don't have to worry about embarrassing yourself on the air. And viewers will love that shot of you in the bathtub full of 'raspberries picked at dawn,' which was sort of an *American Beauty* with fruit. The scene couldn't have worked better if we had flown Kevin Spacey out to the spa to jump into the tub with you."

Laura didn't find these comments reassuring—she had rather hoped that the watermelon scene wouldn't make the cut—but grabbed a notebook and followed Melody down the hall. "Any idea why Aurora needs to see me if the tapes turned out well?"

"She'll tell you the details herself," Melody said. "But she has an assignment for you that you're going to love."

***

"You want me to sell myself to the highest bidder?" Laura asked. "On national television?"

"Don't think of it as selling yourself to the highest bidder," Aurora said cheerily. "Think of it as raising money for your favorite charity. All you have to do is to let some of the most eligible men in the city bid for a date with you. The more they pay, the more money your charity gets. We'll be taping the auction and your date for my show, so the group might get more money when the segment airs and viewers send donations."

Laura was sitting next to Aurora at the round table in the editor-in-chief's office, which held a pile of manuscripts, several of Bethany Starr's finger-paintings, and an open box of Godiva chocolates shaped like tennis racquets. "Sometimes I worry that since moving to New York, I've become my own favorite charity. Every night when I go home to my apartment, I think that the people from Habitat for Humanity ought to come in and fix it up. It would be a real challenge for them."

"All the more reason to auction yourself off. You might meet a man you'd want to marry. Then you'd have a second income and could buy a co-op, which is tough to do at your age unless you have parents willing to spring for the downpayment."

On the way to the editor-in-chief's office, Laura had fantasized that Aurora might want to send her on another quirky trip—say, to climb an extinct volcano on Rarotonga or to swim with manatees off the coast of Florida. She hadn't expected to have to appear on television with an imaginary price tag pasted to her forehead. Not that this was particularly strange by the standards of what people saw on *Survivor* or *Joe Millionaire,* or that she minded the assignment. How could she object to meeting some of the city's most eligible men when she hadn't had a date since returning from the Blue Lemon? If nothing else, the event would take her mind off her runaway fantasies about Tim.

"A charity auction sounds like fun," Laura said with as much spirit as she could muster on a moment's notice. "How could it be more bizarre than lying naked on a massage table in fruit bordello?"

"That's what I like about you," Aurora said. "You have a sense of perspective."

Aurora offered her some of the chocolate tennis racquets. "The auction is coming up next week. So you won't have much time to prepare or pick a charity. But that shouldn't concern you. You might know one of the other women in the auction, a model named Perky Vano. She's participated a couple of times in the past. You could call her if you have questions."

Laura blinked. "Perky Vano is a notorious drug addict."

"That's why we haven't used her in *Aurora*. I had her on my show a few times, and that was enough. One of my producers swore that she tried to snort the pollen in her bouquet when she modeled a bridesmaid's dress for us."

"I thought Perky was in rehab."

"Apparently the auction gave her an extra incentive to stick to her detox program. She loves the event because, now that she's a foot model, it's one of few ways she can show her whole body on TV."

"But—" Laura began uncertainly. "Are you sure you want me to sit on the same stage with someone known as Little Blow Peep?"

"You'll look that much better next to Perky. And I've been hoping for weeks that I could send someone to the auction. It's good PR for the show and the magazine to get involved with events that benefit charities. But I didn't want to send a staff member only to have her raise a few thousand dollars. It might be easier for the company to write a check. I wanted to get a segment for *Aurora!* out of it, too. But I didn't think we had the right writer until I saw Pam's tapes of the spa and read what you'd written."

Aurora pushed a button on a remote so that Laura could see herself lying on a massage table with blood-orange slices over her eyes, on a TV near her desk. "You're a natural—not for every show, but for ours. You have no self-consciousness on camera."

Laura felt relieved that she had passed her first test in her new job. She hadn't looked for another apartment partly because she wasn't sure that her extra income for appearances on *Aurora!* would last beyond the first Nielsens of the fall. It seemed that the charity event would give her another shot at proving herself on the air.

"Who's sponsoring the auction?" Laura asked. "A dating service?"

"A wonderful nonprofit that aids charities too small or unusual to come under the umbrella of the United Way or the other big groups. So the organization will love it if you pick a charity that doesn't get much attention."

"Do you want me to get Venetia—Vicki—to help me fix myself up for the auction so that I don't embarrass you?"

Aurora studied the red mandarin-collared jacket that Laura had bought to celebrate her new job. "Shanghai Tang?"

"No, a tiny shop in Chinatown. I went there because I'd read that a lot of the stores there were failing because they lost so much business after 9/11. So I wanted to try to help them out. I can't really afford to shop on upper Madison Avenue."

Aurora glanced at a pair of black canvas flats with straps that Laura had also bought in Chinatown, hoping they would keep her back problems from flaring up again. "You can use Vicki as a wardrobe consultant if you like, but you don't need her as much as you think. The best thing most women can wear on television is a solid red dress or jacket with clean lines. Red really pops on camera. It gets you noticed in exactly the right away. And a mandarin collar looks much better than lapels that are three seasons old. It could be pure genius to wear that jacket when most of the other women will be wearing black."

"You don't think that I ought to try for a bit of high glamour? If you don't want Vicki to call something in for me—"

"—which I don't—"

"—I could wear the Egotista Dominguez dress I got for Kit's wedding."

Aurora laughed as she took the last chocolate tennis racket.

"Laura, I'm not going to tell you what to wear. You might accuse me of jealousy because I could never fit into your bridesmaid's dress after eating so many of these chocolates. But you might be forgetting that you're no longer writing for women who might as well have been born in an elevator at Bendel's. Your bridesmaid's dress might have cost as much as six months of mortgage payments for some of my viewers. That said, you did look spectacular at Kit's wedding. So, if you want to wear the dress, you have my blessing. I'd just like to ask one favor."

Laura looked at her quizzically. "Which is?"

"You've got to find a way to keep the duct tape from falling off in the middle of the auction. We've shown a lot of strange things on *Aurora!,* but even I have my limits."

∗∗∗

Every time Laura thought about being sold on the open market like a pork belly future, she reminded herself of the things she loved about her new job—her higher salary, her down-to-earth boss, and her chance to do the quirky stories that she liked. Then there was the pleasure of not having to keep trying to track down Zoli and his Euro-chic friends. She didn't know whether to feel flattered or insulted when people told her just before she left *Cassandra* that he hadn't given up hope of coaxing her into a mid-town hotel suite.

Through her work on Normendie's memoir, Laura had a modest continuity from one job to the next. Aurora didn't mind if she took on freelance projects that didn't interfere with her magazine and television assignments. In fact, she suggested that if Normendie made a comeback, she might have her on the show along with some ordinary women who had pulled their careers out of a slump. So Normendie could hardly object when Laura called her to cancel a basketball session that conflicted with the auction.

"Hey, no problem," Normendie said. "We can work on the book later in the week. The auction sounds like fun."

"Are you sure?" Laura asked. "I might be able to get down to the Village to work with you on my lunch hour—"

"No way you should do that. You need to get a manicure and pedicure on your lunch hour so that you'll look perfect for the auction."

Cradling the telephone under her chin, Laura was sitting cross-legged on her air mattress, which was leaking again. She tried to find a more comfortable position. "I don't need a manicure or pedicure. I'm just doing the auction for Aurora's show. I'm not trying to get Donald Trump's bid if he happens to show up. I'm just trying to get a good story."

"What's wrong with trying to get a high bid and a good story?"

"Too tough to do. A lot of the women in the auction are models or actresses who look as though Steve Meisel just photographed them for *Vogue*. David Bowie would leave Iman for these people. Men are going to pay a fortune for them. So I'm just hoping to get an amount that will look respectable by comparison. It would be so embarrassing if the models brought thousands of dollars and somebody tried to pay for me with a coupon from the *Newark Star-Ledger*. All of my friends back home would see it."

"If all of your friends back home are going to see it, that's all the more reason to make sure you get a high bid."

"Normendie, I told you, this is an assignment. I'm doing it because Aurora wants me to, and she doesn't care how much money I get. Anyway, there's no way to 'make sure' that I get a high bid. I have to take my chances like everybody else."

"Why don't you set a floor bid for yourself? That's what I did when I sold one of my guitars and some Peavey amps through an auction house. Tell the auctioneer that you won't accept less for yourself than a certain amount—say, five thousand dollars."

"Five thousand dollars! Nobody's going to pay that much for a date with me—not unless he expects to get more than dinner. Richard Gere paid only three thousand dollars for a *week* with Julia Roberts in *Pretty Woman*."

"You have to adjust for inflation and remember that the amount is tax deductible. A lot of the men who bid on you will think of dinner with you as a business expense. Maybe they'll get their employers to pay if they get some publicity for their companies on *Aurora!*. You just have to pray that you don't end up with a retired solid-waste hauler from Fargo who wants to spend his last years with you in North Dakota. If you do end up with somebody like that, you should make sure that your charity gets something out of it. You definitely shouldn't settle for a penny less than five thousand."

Laura fished an emery board out of a cosmetics case and began filing her nails. "The sponsor would never let us name our own prices. If we set them too high and nobody bid, our charities would get nothing. The group has set low minimum for each of us—a hundred dollars—so that every woman will get bought by somebody."

"Then you have to find a way to drive your price up on your own. For example, you could plant some of your friends in the audience and get them to bid up the price."

"My friends don't have that kind of money."

"What about if I ask Roger if some of his business associates could bid up your price? Some of his friends will drop five grand on a bottle of wine for dinner with a client. One of them might think nothing of paying that much for you."

"I'll be thrilled if somebody paid five hundred dollars for me, and if any of Roger's friends has five thousand to blow on a date, I'm sure he would rather spend it on a night with gorgeous model."

"Why don't you ever listen to me?" Normendie moaned. "I keep telling you that men are afraid of gorgeous women."

"Not the men I know. My brother has been begging me to fix him up with a model ever since I got my job at *Cassandra.*"

"That's because he's never gone out with a model. If he went out with one, he wouldn't know what to do with her."

Laura realized that this was probably true, especially if her brother didn't get a job. Steve couldn't afford to take women anywhere except to Fuddrucker's or Pita Piper's sandwich shop in Tower City. He seemed to have deluded himself into thinking that this was irrelevant because models didn't eat. "But Steve doesn't realize he wouldn't know what to do with models. So he fixates on them, which keeps him from getting to know women who would be better for him, like the adorable Stacy Fazekas down the street who has had a crush on him for years. He can't even remember her name."

Laura stopped filing her nails. "If only I could stand out a little! I thought that wearing my Egotista Dominguez dress might do it. But Aurora wants me to stick with a red mandarin-collared jacket that doesn't even come from Shanghai Tang."

"If you don't want your friends to bid up the price, and you don't want Roger's business associates to do it, and you can't wear a knockout dress—" Normendie thought aloud as she walked into another room to avoid a car alarm shrieking on the street. "Wait a minute! I know exactly how you can get noticed! Oh, this is brilliant!"

Laura was suspicious of the tone of Normendie's voice. "What's brilliant?"

"I'll have a few of my freelance lesbian friends bid for you."

"Freelance lesbians?"

"Women I knew from my old strip club who basically like men but have no problem with a little girl-girl if the money is right. I'm sure some of them would love to have the exposure on national television and I could—"

"Normendie!"

"Think about how great it would be! All the other women will have men bidding for them. You'll upstage everybody if women bid for you. And it will drive up the men's bids, too, because they'll think they're getting a threesome."

"That is not a good idea."

"Why not?"

"Because I'm not a lesbian."

"That's a technicality. Nobody would be saying that you are a lesbian, just that lesbians find you attractive."

"But that wouldn't be true, either, because the whole thing would be a set-up."

"Maybe some of my friends *would* find you attractive, so it wouldn't be a set-up. I could suggest that they drop by the auction, see what they think."

"I'd rather get a low bid honestly than a high bid by putting somebody up to it—my friends, Roger's business associates, any freelance lesbians you know."

"If you don't want me to put anybody up to it I won't, but—" Normendie sounded crushed. "—you've helped so much with my book that I'd love to do something for you. Maybe I'll think of an idea you'd like better."

"You have to promise that you won't ask a couple of Goth guys in spiky black hair to bid for me, or track down Roger's favorite Motown stars and suggest that they use hand jives to get the auctioneer's attention—"

"Let me think about it. After all, I know the entertainment industry a lot better than you do."

"You *do* know it better, and that's what I'm afraid of. This event is not just about entertainment. It's also about preserving my self-respect."

"Nothing preserves your self-respect better than a row of zeros on a check. At the very least you'll get a great dinner out of the auction. The man who buys a date with you might take you to a world-class place you could never afford on your own."

"I'm not the sort of woman men take to world-class places. After my cover story on you came out, Tim said he was going take me to 'the best restaurant in New York' to celebrate. I fantasized about going to, say, Ducasse or the Rainbow Room. He took me to a pierogie place called Babcia's that specializes in grilled onions."

"But Babcia's is great! Tim and I go there a lot. I love it because it's one of the few places in New York where people treat me like family instead of a star, and where no man has ever pulled up his shirt in the middle of the meal and said, 'Sign my chest.' Babcia's daughter, Regina, would throw him out if he did. How could you not like that place?"

"I did like it. I was just expecting something a little different, such as—"

As Laura slipped her emery board back into her cosmetics case, she saw a cockroach clamber over the eyelash curler that Kit had given her for the wedding. "Sorry, Normendie. Have to go. I've got to get the cockroaches out of this apartment."

"But every New York apartment has cockroaches, including mine. My mother used to tell a joke when we lived at 72nd and Park. How do you know when you're visiting the apartment of somebody who's in the Social Register?"

"How do you?"

"The cockroaches wear white uniforms."

24
Auction Block

It was hard to feel sorry for a foot model who saw her crimson toenails in every fashion magazine in America. But Laura still wished that the bids were a little higher for Perky Vano, who was sitting next to her on the stage of a hotel ballroom packed with men who had shouted offers in the thousands of dollars for a nurse on *General Hospital.* Perky's eyes, which looked sunken in the best of her photographs, had turned cadaverous under the merciless overhead lights and were shining with tears.

"Do I hear *two* hundred dollars for Miss Patricia Vano?"

Perky and Laura were the last two women to have their services auctioned off—Perky because her availability had been uncertain until she got out of rehab, Laura because Aurora had decided to send her only after seeing the tapes of her trip to the spa. So they had found time to chat as men jousted for dates with lingerie models and understudies for roles in *Les Miz* and *Mamma Mia!* Perky had made it clear that she was expecting a high offer despite a nasty item in a gossip column that morning, which had suggested that she was running out of parts of her body that she could model and might start offering to display her liver and spleen on MRI scans. Her face caved in when she saw that she would have trouble drawing more than the one-hundred-dollar minimum set by the sponsor. After a few minutes, she grew so despondent that Laura had to squeeze her hand as though they were the final two Miss America candidates waiting to hear the name of the first runner-up.

As the auctioneer was about to close the bidding on Perky, there was a buzz at the back of the ballroom. Flashbulbs popped as several late-arriving guests took seats partly obscured by a pillar. Laura couldn't see their faces, which seemed a football field away, but guessed that a celebrity or two had shown up with an entourage. A deep male voice boomed as soon as they had settled into their gilt chairs.

"Two hundred dollars!"

Laura recognized the voice before the flashbulbs cooled. How could she not? It was difficult to forget an off-key bass that careened recklessly toward falsetto in "Under the Boardwalk." She craned her neck and spotted a pair of Clark Kent glasses. But why was Roger Hornsley bidding on Perky? He adored Normendie as much as he could adore any woman after his honey-blond first wife had sent their bedroom sheets to a lab for a DNA analysis that made clear that he had a weakness for redheads. His bid had to be related to Normendie's determination to drive up her prices. Was he sitting so far back in the ballroom, Laura wondered, that he couldn't see the stage and imagined that he was bidding on her instead of Perky? A female voice rang out.

"Two-fifty!"

Inexplicably Normendie had topped Roger's bid. Laura was now sure that they had arrived so late they thought they were bidding on her instead of Perky. She tried to catch the eye of either member of the couple without making a movement that the television cameras might pick up. At the sound of the female voice, the auctioneer removed his half-moon glasses. He looked uncertainly at the executive director of the sponsoring organization, who was sitting in the first row of gilt chairs. Roger's voice boomed again.

"Three hundred!"

"Three-fifty!"

By now people had realized that the bids were coming from Roger Hornsley and Normendie Latour and were turning around to stare. Somebody pushed a CNN camera closer to the couple. Normendie whispered to Roger, who bellowed again.

"ONE THOUSAND DOLLARS!"

Several people in the audience tittered as though the bid had come from a prankster who hoped to see if anybody would believe it. Still convinced that Normendie and Roger thought they were buying a date with her instead of Perky, Laura was becoming frantic to get their attention when the auctioneer spoke up again.

"Do I hear eleven hundred?"

He swept the ballroom with his eyes, seeking a bid, then slammed down his gavel.

"SOLD FOR ONE THOUSAND DOLLARS!"

Gasps rippled though an audience stunned not by the size of the bid—a dozen models or actresses had gone for three- or four-thousand dollars—but that anyone had offered it for Perky. Overjoyed, Perky left the stage after announcing tearfully that her money would go to a foundation hoping to "stamp out foot disease."

As the auctioneer announced her name, Laura stood up, feeling as though fire ants had colonized her stomach. For days she had been reminding herself that she was participating in a charity event, not an index to her self-worth. Her money would help to fund a scholarship that she had received at St. Rose's—an award given annually to a female athlete who, although a good player, didn't have enough star power to get recruited by a basketball powerhouse.

But she found little comfort in the early bids for Perky. Some of the men had left the ballroom after failing to win dates with women they wanted, and others had retreated to the cash bar. Perhaps half the original number of bidders remained in their seats, many with bloodshot eyes or the bored expressions of connoisseurs who would settle for nothing less than Gwyneth or Nicole. These were men for whom even the photos on Udate or Match.com provided an insufficient hedge against the caprices of the market. Watching several flip open their cell phones or laptops during her introduction, Laura mentally thanked Aurora for urging her to stick to her modest red silk jacket and a black silk skirt. This way she would be less conspicuous if she drew lower bids than Perky.

Laura imagined that, after realizing that they had paid for an evening with the wrong woman, Normendie and Roger would quickly remedy the mistake when she came up for bids. So she was startled when they remained silent as men with jaded expressions tossed out tepid offers that, though higher than most of Perky's, bespoke a similar lack of enthusiasm.

"Six hundred."

"Seven-fifty."

"Eight."

As the bidding neared the one-thousand-dollar mark, a silver-haired man in a dinner jacket hurried to the front of the ballroom. He was holding a champagne flute and tucking a silver pen into his pocket. Unlike Normendie and Roger, who were trying to deflect attention by sitting next to a pillar at the back, he stationed himself by a potted palm near the stage. He took a sip of champagne, then called out in heavily accented English.

"TWO TOWSAND DOLLAR!"

Either because of the size of the bid or because the person who made it was twice the age of any woman in the auction catalog, murmurs of surprise ran through the ballroom. Laura had no idea who the man was, though his voice sounded familiar. Suddenly Normendie's voice sailed over the buzz of the crowd.

"Twenty-five hundred!"

Twenty-five hundred dollars? Laura thought. *Does Normendie think that the price matters more than whether I'll want to have dinner with the winner?*

Still standing next to the palm, the man in the dinner jacket looked nervously around the ballroom, then tipped his flute toward the auctioneer.

"TWENTY-SIX HUNDRED DOLLAR."

Laura still didn't know who the man was when two female sponsors of the event, who were sitting behind her on stage, began to whisper.

"… no idea where his money comes from …"

"… second or third wife fantastically rich …"

"… calls himself the Magyar Cary Grant …"

Laura whirled around, and the women stopped talking. "Zoli?" she mouthed. One of the women nodded. To her horror Laura realized that Zoli hadn't accepted defeat when she refused to meet him at a hotel in midafternoon and that he was now trying to buy what he couldn't get for free. Normendie was oblivious to her desire to go out with someone other than the potential star of films with titles like *Zoli Does the Pierre Hotel.*

"Three thousand dollars!"

As she called out the bid, Normendie made eye contact with Laura for the first time, wearing the stern expression of a bailiff dealing with a prisoner who was eyeing a jailbreak. From her position near the pillar, she held up the five fingers of her right hand. Laura understood that Normendie was ordering her to do nothing that would diminish her chances of stepping down from the stage with five thousand dollars for her charity.

Zoli wiped his brow with a handkerchief when he heard the three-thousand-dollar bid. He finished his champagne and slipped out by a side door as smoothly as he had dodged calls from the staff at *Cassandra.*

The auctioneer asked the crowd for thirty-one-hundred dollars. When Roger bid four thousand, he looked over his half-moon glasses and smiled, recognizing the pattern.

"Do I hear five thousand?"

Laura expected to see Normendie leap up on the word "five." Instead a man who had arrived with the couple stepped away from his position next to a pillar. He was wearing sunglasses and a blue Devil Rays cap that hid his face from the lights of the cameras. To catch the auctioneer's eye he raised his hand slightly, then spoke calmly.

"Five thousand dollars."

Several people gasped, and a few others clapped. The man had spoken quietly, but authoritatively enough for his voice to carry throughout the ballroom. Normendie grinned and flashed him an "OK" sign.

The auctioneer smiled and raised his gavel. "Do I hear six?"

There was a collective intake of breath as the crowd seemed to realize that no one had yet brought in more than four thousand dollars. A hush crept over the ballroom.

The auctioneer raked his eye over the crowd, allowing it to linger on the man in the Devil Rays cap, then brought down his gavel with a crash.

"SOLD FOR FIVE THOUSAND DOLLARS!"

Normendie jumped up and hugged the high bidder, and Roger leaned over and shook his hand. Laura's relief that she had dodged an evening with Zoli gave way to her embarrassment over a set-up that the television cameras no doubt had caught. How many gossip columnists would portray her as a woman so desperate for dates that friends had to bankroll her social life?

Laura didn't know who had bought her until the crowd in the ballroom thinned out and the camera crews for *Aurora!* and *CNN* had left. As she hurried toward the back of the ballroom to speak to Normendie and Roger, the high bidder pulled off his sunglasses and Devil Rays cap. She felt as though somebody had welded her feet to the floor with an acetylene torch.

The man who had ransomed her was Tim Moran, and as Laura approached, he and Normendie and Roger couldn't stop laughing.

***

Laura's mind whirled as her taxi sped up Park Avenue on the way home from the auction. She didn't know whether she wanted to weep or to shout her good news from the observation desk of the Empire State Building. At last she had a serious date with the man she had been fantasizing about ever since her trip to the Southwest—except it was the kind of date no woman wanted, a date that the man had paid for under pressure from friends who did everything but hold a revolver to his head.

After the auction, Laura had joined Normendie and Roger and Tim for a drink at the hotel bar and tried to get a straight answer about what had happened in the ballroom. Normendie swore on the wine list, after declining Roger's offer to track down a Gideon Bible, that she hadn't "forced" Tim to bid. She had merely "suggested" the idea. She had no choice but to call Tim, explain the situation, and see if he wanted to help. Which, the two of them insisted with infuriating grins, he did.

Ha! Laura thought. Tim was recruited by a fast-talking smoothie. She was certain that Normendie or Roger had put up some, if not all, of the money for the date, though, they denied this, too. Did they really expect her to believe that a man who skimped on letter openers would pay five thousand dollars for a dinner with her? At least she had the consolation of knowing that she and Tim would go to a great restaurant this time, because Normendie, in addition to "suggesting" that he bid on her, also "suggested" that he take her to Ducasse and that Roger give up a reservation he'd had for months so that they could get a table. Normendie insisted that all of it was the least she could do after Laura had refused to take any money for helping with her memoir.

Laura asked about their other bids when she saw that the three of them had no intention of letting her in on the specifics of their private joke. Were they also going to tell her that buying Perky wasn't part of some kind of plot they wouldn't reveal?

"Absolutely we're going to tell you that," Normendie said indignantly. "Our bids on Perky had nothing to do with Tim's date with you. It had to do with your brother."

"With Steve?" Laura asked. "Is he in on this, too?"

"He isn't 'in on' anything," "Normendie said. "We bid for

Perky because you said that your brother keeps begging you to fix him up with models. I thought that if Tim bought a date with you for a lot of money, it would keep you from getting embarrassed on television by a low bid that all your friends in Cleveland would see. But I know that things between you two have been a little, um, tense—" Normendie looked nervously at Tim, who still had the Cheshire-cat grin that he'd been wearing after the auction. "—so I was worried that you would be a little, um, upset about the date even though I was trying to do something nice to thank you for all the help you've given me with my book." Normendie glanced again at Tim, who was looking at his nails. "I thought that, you know, you might not even agree to go *out* with him. So I needed a back-up plan. My idea was that if you weren't too happy about having to go out with Tim, you'd be thrilled that somebody bought a date with Perky for Steve. Then he'd forget the models and go out with that Stacy Fuzzy—"

"Fazekas," Laura said. "Stacy Fazekas."

"Right. That girl down the street. But, obviously, I didn't want to spend much money on a man I don't even know. So I decided that I would only bid for a date for Steve if I could get somebody really cheap—say, for less than Roger would spend on a dinner for four at a good restaurant, a thousand dollars or so."

Only people like Normendie and Roger, Laura thought, *would see a thousand-dollar price tag as "really cheap."* But the two of them *had* solved a problem for her. Her brother pestered her so much about the models that sometimes she could hardly bring herself to call home to talk to her mother. "Steve will be thrilled. I'll call him as soon as I get back to my apartment to let him know."

"Then everything has worked out perfectly," Normendie said triumphantly. "You're going to go out with Tim, and Steve's going to go out with Perky."

"But not on the same night," Tim said hastily. "I didn't pay five thousand dollars to go out on a double date with you and your brother. For my money, I expect an intimate evening—just you, me, and the millions of people who will watch our dinner on national television."

"How could it be an intimate evening when a camera crew from *Aurora!* will be following us around the whole time?" Laura asked.

"We'll just have to find that out," Tim said, smiling, "won't we?"

25

On the Menu

Laura could make no sense of many of the entrées on the menu at the most expensive restaurant in New York. After working in a Hungarian bakery, Laura thought that she had a sense of adventure about food. Of course, she was grateful for the chance to try the restaurant that she seemed to read about every time she opened *New York* magazine. But as she tried to parse a menu full of items like "silken woodcock," she almost wished that she and Tim had gone to Babcia's again.

Perhaps, the waiter said as she pored over the menu, she might prefer the "halibut with sea-urchin custard" to the "'half-wild' duckling"? When Laura found the sea-urchin part a bit scary, he suggested the "spiny lobster with Château Chalon sauce," which further confused her. She had never seen a lobster with spines. Rick, the cameraman for *Aurora!*, was getting impatient—eager to move on to action shots of rolling pastry carts or the uncapping of domed silver trays—so Laura looked imploringly at the man who had paid five thousand dollars for their date.

Tim, who had decided quickly that he would have pheasant, seemed to find it highly entertaining to watch her wrestle with her pangs of indecision. "What about the 'Pennsylvania roasted lamb on a spit'? Even though you have to wonder if it was roasted in Pennsylvania and brought to New York in a car trunk—"

"Yes!" Laura said instantly, relieved that he had spotted a comprehensible dish on a menu that read like the Rosetta Stone. "The Pennsylvania roasted lamb sounds perfect."

The rest of the meal went as smoothly as the camera near their salad forks would permit. Laura stumbled briefly when a waiter came to their table with a wooden box filled with a lumpen object and she asked if it was a white grapefruit—it turned out to be a truffle. But she had no trouble selecting from the celestial array of baked goods at the end of the meal—a constellation of madeleines, financiers, and tiny tarts that arrived at their table along with glass bowls filled with nougats and caramels. And she was relieved that Rick's presence made it impossible for her or Tim to bring up awkward subjects such as the meaning of that less-than-platonic kiss in his car.

The problems began when Tim drove her home after dinner, trailed by a van from *Aurora!*. Laura knew from Jane, her producer, that the camera crew would follow them to the door of her apartment as though they were appearing on *Blind Date*, then leave them on their own. She also understood that the most visually compelling ending for the evening would consist either of a jaw-dislocating kiss or a volcanic argument that would recap the night's disasters.

"If there's one thing television viewers don't want," Jane had warned Laura, "it's ambiguity."

Unfortunately, when Laura explained this to Tim on the way home, he wouldn't consider either of the options envisioned by her producer.

"We can't argue about the disasters that occurred earlier tonight, because there were no disasters, unless you count our total lack of privacy during the evening," he said. "We didn't have a moment to ourselves. When the waiters weren't hovering around us, the cameras were."

Tim kept his eyes on the uptown traffic on Park Avenue as he went on matter-of-factly. "Vesuvian outbursts aren't my style, anyway. I prefer to try to work things out in reasonable way. I have no problem with writing a five-thousand-dollar check to a charity, but I do have a problem with your producer asking us to act like some of those idiots on *Blind Date* who have screeching fights at the door about who cheated at laser tag or moved the ball out of the pirate's mouth in miniature golf."

Laura saw that she was in a bind. The ending of her segment would be anticlimactic after the drama of the auction if Tim wouldn't agree either to a scene from a blue movie or the Book of Revelation on the doorstep. "But the segment needs a great walk-off. Maybe we could get by with a small argument about how much I embarrassed you by asking if that truffle was a white grapefruit."

"You didn't embarrass me. From a distance that truffle looked to me like a souvenir baseball in a box, which I might have said if you hadn't offered your view first."

"You must be irritated with me about something."

"Actually, I'm not irritated, at least not about anything that happened tonight. If I had been, I'd forgive it because of the pleasure you've given me by allowing me to look at you in that ravishing dress. I didn't expect to see it again after Kit's wedding. If you're determined to have a fight at the door, why don't you bring up the things you dislike about me? There are obviously plenty of them."

Tim said this calmly, but Laura still felt a stab of guilt. There *were* things she disliked about him—she could hardly forget his earlier insults just because he'd written a five-thousand-dollar check—but none of her grievances seemed to provide a sufficient reason to humiliate him on national television. She was still trying to figure out how to give some drama to the final scene when they reached her building. The van from *Aurora!* had gotten there first and double-parked in front.

Jane was scurrying about in the darkness, shouting orders to Rick and others in the crew. "This is fantastic! Better than anything we could have scripted!"

"What's fantastic?" Laura asked.

She saw the body before the producer could respond.

A young woman lying face down on the sidewalk with her blond hair in disarray and a pool of blood beneath her face. The heels of her Nikes were pointing up.

"Hallelujah! Young and in great shape!" Jane yelled. "Get those quads and the Spandex shorts in the pictures!"

Laura spun around to face Rick, who was standing behind her, shooting the scene. "Are you out of your mind?" she shouted. "That's a body! How can people in television be so insensitive? Somebody is dead and you just—"

Tim silenced her by putting a hand on her arm and pointing toward the ground.

The woman who had been sprawled on the sidewalk had just sat up. Dazed, she used her forearm to wipe away the blood that was running from her nose. When she saw Jacko standing near the building with his air rifle, she jumped up.

"You should be arrested!" she screamed. "You have no business frightening people that way! I'm going to tell the police about this! Don't think I won't!"

After calming down, the woman said that she jogged past the building every night, usually without incident. But lately Jacko had been watching her and seemed to regard her unvarying route as suspicious. Tonight as she went by, he stepped outside with his toy rifle and shouted, "Halt in the name of the law!" The woman was so petrified by the sight of the gun that she broke her stride and fell, although she didn't seem to have more than nosebleed and a swollen kneecap.

Tim knelt down and looked at her knee. "You need to put some ice on that. Maybe wrap it in—"

"The only that I want to wrap is that guy's brains around a telephone pole!" the jogger shouted. "Just give me the address of the nearest police station so I can report that joker, and I'll be fine."

Tim wrote the address of the precinct house on one of his business cards, and the woman loped off toward it, limping slightly. After a few steps, she turned back to hurl a final insult at Jacko, who had retreated into the vestibule of the building.

"You're a real sicko, you know that? You're not going to get away with this!"

Tim took Laura's elbow and steered her out of earshot of the camera crew before he whispered, "At least somebody agrees with me."

Laura said nothing, wondering by now if perhaps "sicko" wasn't too charitable a word for her super. When the hubbub had died down, she took Jane aside and explained apologetically that Tim wouldn't agree to either jaw-dislocation or Mt. Etna at the door. "So I don't really know what to do—"

"Are you crazy?" Jane said. "We got that whole incident on tape. We don't need a kiss or an argument now. We just need the two of you to walk right by your super as he points the gun at you with your heads high and big smiles on your faces. You'll show all of our viewers in other parts of the country that New Yorkers think nothing of living in a city filled with creeps, losers, and weirdos. They don't give it a second thought."

"But I do give it a second thought," Laura protested. "Having a nut for a super is really starting to make me nervous."

"Laura, if you're nervous, go into therapy like everybody else," Jane said in a resigned tone. "Or take some Paxil. Right now, we just need to get this shot in the bag."

✳✳✳

Ever since the auction, Laura had known that she had to invite Tim in for a drink after their dinner, the least she could do after he had paid a more than a thousand dollars an hour for their dinner date. But she wished that the glamour of Ducasse hadn't thrown its defects into such high relief. The sofa that she had ordered still hadn't arrived, so she and Tim would have nowhere to sit, except on the air mattress or at the folding table where she ate meals. And although she had stuck a bunch of daisies in a tall juice glass to brighten the place, this feeble display only reminded her of those impromptu memorials that sprang up at roadside spots where people were mowed down by sixteen-wheelers or slain by serial killers. The contrast between Tim's warm and bright co-op and the gloom of her apartment made her all the more reluctant to bring him back to it.

As they climbed the five flights of stairs, mercifully free of a camera crew for the first time all evening, Laura wished that Tim would give her an easy out by declining her invitation for a drink. Instead he accepted instantly and seemed to take a perverse enjoyment in the discomfort that the situation caused her.

"How could I say 'no'?" he asked. "You might have more hate mail from your super, which would be highly entertaining to read. Everybody at Ducasse takes food so seriously that I could use the light diversion of one of his sprightly letters."

"Jacko stopped sending me hate mail after I gave him an auto-graphed picture of Cassandra," Laura said. "He was so happy to have the photo that he put a lock on the downstairs door to show his gratitude."

"More likely to show his willingness to accept a bribe—"

"Would you mind if we didn't talk about my super?" Laura asked, as they entered her apartment. "I admit that you were right about him. But seeing him in the vestibule with that toy gun tonight gave me the creeps. So if it's okay with you, I'd like to talk about something else."

"Certainly. Let's talk about your dental plan at *Aurora* because you said you wanted me to dislocate your jaw, and I don't want to disappoint you."

Tim had backed up against the wall of her apartment and, before she could respond, began kissing her as he had in his car after her night at his co-op. Laura had the impression that he was trying to dislocate a few additional body parts along with her jaw. He def-initely hadn't lost his touch since he'd stopped the car at 86th Street.

Afterward he led her over to the air mattress and sat her down on it. "Now wasn't that better than anything we could have done on television, except maybe on cable?"

"Could be," Laura said, trying to sound indifferent. "But you didn't *have* to do it now that the camera crew has left."

"I know I didn't have to. I wanted to all night. I just thought it would be more romantic to wait until it was just you and me—" Tim flicked a bug that was crawling across the air mattress. "—and the cockroaches."

"Then why don't you come into the kitchen with me while I open bottle of wine? It's the cockroaches' favorite spot in the apartment." She started to stand up, but Tim took her hand and drew her back down onto the air mattress.

"We've been drinking hundred-dollar-a-bottle wine all night. I didn't come here for a drink."

"Then why did you?" Laura realized that it was an absurd question given that they were sitting on a mattress, but wondered what he'd say, anyway.

"To do all the things to you that I couldn't do when we were working for the same company. Or when you had a bad back. I figured that I had about a three-day window of opportunity between now and when you get hired back by another Carapace magazine or when you injure yourself again."

On hearing this, Laura felt as though her head might split apart. She needed an Advil. Half of her wanted to fling herself at Tim and show him how much five thousand dollars would buy for your money these days. The other half didn't want him to think he was entitled to it—that he could sleep with her just because he had paid for a date with her. All of Normendie's stories about him flooded back. Was it possible that Tim saw a night with her as another casual adventure, like sex at a caravanserai in the Caribbean? "I need to think about this—"

"Let me help. Why do you think I paid five thousand dollars for a date with you?"

"I know why you did. Normendie put you up to it."

"She did not. Normendie called me because she was thinking of having a few of Roger's business associates or her freelance lesbian friends bid on you and wondered what I thought of that idea. She said that you had vetoed those options but that she thought you might be worried they couldn't afford it. I told her that if you didn't like her ideas, she should forget them and let me buy the date."

Laura tried to decide whether or not she believed him. "You mean, buy a date that she would pay for?"

Tim looked offended. "No, that I would pay for. Does that seem so implausible to you?"

Spending five thousand dollars on a date frankly did strike Laura as out of character for him, but she didn't want to start a fight by saying so. "It's just that Normendie was so determined that I take home five thousand dollars that it wouldn't surprise me if she or Roger offered to write you a check if you put in the bid—"

"Normendie did offer to write me a check. I turned her down. She also suggested that five thousand dollars would be 'fair market value' for you, or at least for the work you've done on her book so far. Apparently Roger talked to some of his friends in publishing and realized that five grand was a tiny fraction of what you might eventually earn for ghostwriting her memoir. I agreed. Some of our magazines have paid ten thousand or more just for the one-time rights to an excerpt from a star's memoir. The price Normendie suggested for you struck me as entirely reasonable."

"All of that explains why she might have paid five thousand, not why you did. I've done work for her, not for you. Why did you pay so much?"

Tim hesitated for a beat or two. "Everybody at my level needs a few tax deductions, and Normendie told me that your money would help to fund a scholarship for an athlete at St. Rose's. One of my second or third cousins played girls' basketball in Cleveland, so I figured that it was a good cause."

"How can you have any respect for my skills as a reporter if you expect me to believe that?" Laura asked. "What was your second or third cousin's name?"

The apartment became so quiet that Laura could almost hear the cockroaches scuttling in her closet. "It doesn't matter—"

"It does to me."

"Mary Beth Pulaski," he said slowly. "But—"

"Mary Beth Pulaski!" Laura exclaimed. "Mary Beth was the guard from Holy Innocents who tripped me. I got the scar on my leg because of her. That's why you were so interested in it when we were in the Jacuzzi. And why you got such a strange look on your face when I mentioned my accident at Babcia's."

"In a sense, yes. I'd been hearing about the incident for years from my family. The accident happened at such a big game that a lot of my relatives attended. Some of them were furious with Mary Beth because they thought she tripped you on purpose, although she always said it was an accident. She was crying because she knew her team lost the game. But I never knew who got hurt. People always spoke of you as 'that forward that Mary Beth tripped' or 'the girl who had to go to the hospital.' So I was shocked when I realized in the Jacuzzi that you were the one who got injured. I felt terrible that someone in my family had done that."

Laura could see that for once Tim wasn't trying to rile or tweak her. He looked so stricken that she had to console him. "The accident did seem pretty awful at the time. But Mary Beth wrote me a sweet note while I was in the hospital and said she was saying a rosary for my recovery. And as you saw, the scar has faded so much, it's almost disappeared. I've hardly thought about it since college, when it seemed to spook a few men. Some of them flinched when they saw it for the first time."

"I thought your scar was beautiful."

For the first time, it occurred to Laura that Tim might have paid for the date because he had a romantic interest in her. Swallowing hard, she tried to respond casually. "It's a relief that it doesn't bother you because I've been a little worried about how New York men might react. They seem to reject women for the smallest imperfections."

"Who would reject you?"

In an instant Tim was kissing her again and sliding his hand under her dress toward her scar, but she pulled away.

Tim looked startled. "You liked that in the Jacuzzi."

Actually, I loved *it in the Jacuzzi,* she thought. "This is different."

"Why?" Tim sounded more hurt than angry. "Because you think that there might be a cameraman lurking on the fire escape?"

Pained by his expression, Laura groped for a way to describe the tug-of-war raging in her brain. "It's different because you paid five thousand dollars for our date, and I don't want to think you can buy sex with me."

There was a terrifying silence in the room. Tim's face went dark with anger and, when he finally spoke, Laura thought he would explode. "Is *that* what you think? That I have to *pay* for sex with women?"

"No, but—"

"I paid for a date with you because I kept hearing from Simon and Aurora—and you—about how cheap you think I am even after I bought your plane ticket. Which, by the way, I did *not* charge to the company. I thought if I bought the date, you might be gracious enough to admit that you'd misjudged me. But I see that I was wrong. You're incapable of accepting an act of generosity without reading sinister motives into it."

"That's completely untrue. I am grateful that you paid for my ticket."

"You have a peculiar way of showing your gratitude."

"Because you want me to show it by sleeping with you on demand."

"I do not want you to sleep with me on demand. I just thought that even with the camera in our face, the evening had been so romantic with that table overlooking the rose garden and you in the fantastic dress—" Tim broke off. "Was I supposed to wait to try to sleep with you until you had just walked off a basketball court with your hair and your jersey drenched in sweat? Should I have avoided trying to sleep with you just because I'd written a five-thousand-dollar check for a basketball scholarship?"

"You might have given a little more thought to how I might react if you did. You don't need to get so uptight about it."

Tim stood up. "Laura, I have no idea what's going on, except that it's *not* about the five thousand dollars. So I'll just tell you what I think: you got so used to living with somebody who exploited you that you expect every man to be like your old boyfriend. You think I'm going to try to take advantage of you just the way he did. In a sense, you're right. I'd love to 'take advantage' of you if you'd also like to 'take advantage' of me. I have a sense of adventure with women, a willingness to take a few risks. But I like to take risks with people who want to take them. I've never tried to force them on a woman. And I don't intend to start now."

Laura tried to scramble to her feet to gain the advantage of an eye-level view in the argument. As she did, she stumbled over the piece of plywood that Jacko had nailed over the hole in the floor and landed on her knees with a painful thump, tearing a stocking.

Tim softened after she fell and held out a hand to help her up. "I'm sorry, but I don't see what more I can do to convince you that I'm not one of those slippery types, like Zoli, who collects women the way other men collect Bavarian beer steins or baseball memorabilia. I know that it's tough for young writers in the city and that you blame me for some of your problems. That's why I suggested you help Normendie with her memoir, which might bring in some extra money. That's also why I said that, if you want to move out, you could stay at my place for a while. After I saw that scene on the street tonight, I was going to tell you could stay there as long as you like. But I'm not going to plead with you to move in, or even to have dinner again. If you want to see me, you're going to have to get in touch with me. And you can name any terms you like except for one."

Laura, fighting alternating waves of guilt and fury, tried to play it cool. "Oh, really. What's that?"

"You can't ask me to wait for you for years the way you waited for Nick. I'm thirty-one and getting tired of waking up alone in hotel rooms on another continent. It was fun for a while. But I'd like to spend a lot more time here in New York and to have someone to share it with me. So if you'd like to jump naked into my Jacuzzi someday, you don't have forever to decide, and you'll have to let me know if you do. I'm not going to keep trying to reach you when you'd rather not hear from me."

This comment threw Laura into tailspin. She hadn't wanted to plunge into a scorched-earth romance with Tim or anybody else so soon after splitting up with Nick. But the idea of losing Tim forever was unsettling. And if she was reading him correctly, he was telling her that if she didn't throw herself at him before a buzzer went off in his head, he might find another Normendie or Brandy. Why did people always talk about women's "biological clocks" instead of the game timers—complete with two-minute warnings—that men had in their heads? Tim seemed to see himself as playing in a ball game that was about to go into extra innings while her game was in the bottom of the third and the pitcher had just left the field to "Hit the Road, Jack."

Laura was convinced that she could never make up her mind as quickly as Alice, who had much more experience with men than she did. Still, she had a morbid desire to find out how much time she had before Tim took himself off the market.

"Just out of curiosity, how long would you be willing to wait for me to make up my mind?" she asked with as much nonchalance as she could muster. "Or to decide that I might want to try that Jacuzzi again?"

"Oh, at least until Labor Day."

"Labor Day!" Laura said, nearly choking on the words. Tim had to be joking. Maybe he *was* joking, but he had turned toward the door, so that she couldn't see his face and lacked the visual cues that might have confirmed it. "That's in two weeks. I won't even be here that weekend. I'm going home for my cousin's wedding. So if I decided at one minute before midnight on Monday that I wanted to take you up on the offer, I couldn't."

Tim laughed. "Why not think positively, Laura? That kind of pessimism is hardly worthy of a pathological optimist."

26
At the End of the Jetty

As her social life sputtered out, Laura spent most of her free time working on *Born with a Silver Spoon in Her Nose*. She hated to admit it, but Tim had been right that even with the fatter salary she was earning at *Aurora* she might need the extra money from the book to move into an apartment that wouldn't get condemned by the fire marshals or health inspectors.

On a late-summer Saturday, Laura put aside Normendie's memoir to go to Connecticut to help Alice look for a wedding dress. Her brief time at *Cassandra*, it appeared, had conferred on her the status of a fashion expert. They visited a half dozen bridal salons, where Alice peppered her with questions: did ecru flatter her more than ivory? Would ruching have gone out of fashion by next June? Was her mother's *point d'esprit* dress too fragile and yellowed, as Mrs. Brennan insisted, to consider?

In the late afternoon, Simon came out from the city to join them, and, as Alice helped the housekeeper clean up after dinner, he asked Laura to join him for a walk. The moon was almost full and the scent of fading roses hung in the air as they headed down the wooden steps toward the beach in sweaters that the nippier evenings now required. Simon began by apologizing for failing to keep the promise that he had made earlier in the summer to fix her up with one of his friends.

"I'm afraid that, between seeing Alice and trying to put out the last issues of *Cassandra*, I haven't given that project as much thought as I ought to have. Alice insists that I must do it soon. She thinks it might hard for you to attend two weddings—hers and your cousin's—without a dashing man for an escort."

Laura told Simon that, although she'd love to meet his friends, her moribund social life had left her with time to help Normendie with her memoir. "I have no idea if the book will ever get published. But even if it doesn't I'm having fun getting to know somebody who has nothing in common with anybody I knew at home. Even pet psychics aren't as surprising as Normendie can be at times."

"Why do you say 'if the book will get published'?"

"Normendie and I haven't tried sell it yet because she doesn't need the money and I haven't really written much of it. I've mostly taken a lot of notes on her life."

"Normendie may not need the money. But you do."

Laura was beginning to realize that one of the unwritten laws of life in New York was that there was no such thing as a single woman who didn't need money. Everybody assumed, more or less correctly, that she was chronically short of cash.

"In New York, needing money is relative. Donald Trump declared bankruptcy. You need money even if you have your name on a casino."

"Send me what you've written on Normendie's memoir along with some information about how you got involved in the project."

"I'll try, but I might not have time for a while. I have a lot to do at *Aurora*, and my cousin's wedding is coming up. And there's nothing really to tell about how I got involved. Tim had the idea that Normendie ought to do a memoir as part of her comeback, and that I ought to write it, so he put the two of us in touch."

Simon debated whether a jetty that they had reached provided a safe path after dark. He took a few steps, testing the solidity of the rocks, then helped Laura climb onto it. "I must say I'm surprised to hear it. From the way you spoke about Tim at *Cassandra*, I had the sense that you had little regard for his ideas."

Laura was unsure of whether Simon knew about her conversation with Tim after the auction. So she chose her words carefully. "Tim has opinions about many things, including my apartment, that he expresses too strongly for my taste. But Normendie wants to write a memoir, and I thought, Why should I punish her just because Tim cares nothing about the needs of writers?"

"Surely you aren't saying that because Irene Field in the accounting department wouldn't pay for your basketball? Not when you might not even have had a cover story if it hadn't been for Tim?"

Laura slowed down, trying to get a surer footing on the narrow jetty. "What do you mean, if it hadn't been for him?"

"Don't you remember my saying that it would cost a fortune to rip the story on Courtney Swilling out of the August issue and replace it with yours?"

"What does that have to do with Tim?"

"We had already spent so much on the August issue that ripping out the cover story at the last minute meant that we would go way over budget. Remember that ten-thousand-dollar day rate we paid to the photographer who took the pictures of Courtney Swilling? I had to let Tim know, as a courtesy, that we were thinking of making a change. He told me to go ahead if I knew we had a great story that would help the magazine at newsstands."

Laura stopped walking for a moment. "Then Tim has a split personality. From what I've seen, he spends money only on things with a direct benefit for him, such as his fantastic apartment or dates with women he's involved with. Or *wants* to be involved with. He was always squeezing the staff at *Cassandra*."

"Tim doesn't have a split personality. He just has his priorities in order. He'll spend tens of thousands of dollars to replace a cover story if he thinks it will make the magazine better. But he hates to waste money on unimportant things, like lunches at overpriced restaurants. Tim thinks they don't matter nearly as much as enterprise or creativity on the part of writers and editors. He loves it when people like you prove him right by getting a great story for the cost of a basketball. After you got the interview with Normendie, he was your biggest fan at the magazine—that is, apart from me."

"You must be joking. He tried to avoid paying for my basketball."

"Tim didn't try to avoid paying for the ball. Irene Field did, and you can't fault him for delegating that authority. He couldn't run the financial side of the company if he kept getting involved in petty decisions about expense accounts. At a corporation the size of Carapace, he'd have no time left for anything else."

"Why didn't you tell me all of this?" Laura asked, more in frustration than anger. "Or why didn't Tim?"

"I didn't tell you most of it because you never asked, and I might not have told you if you had. Certain kinds of corporate financial information are best discussed with as few people as possible. As for why Tim said nothing, I would imagine that he was trying to be discreet and suppressed any inclination toward indiscretion when he realized that you didn't care to hear his views, anyway. I also think that—how shall I put it?—he had a crush on you. He called the day after meeting you at the airport and gave me a stern lecture, only half-jokingly, to the effect that he hoped I had hired you for your work, not your beauty, because he couldn't afford to have me distracted by it. I understood that to mean that he would certainly be distracted. But his sense of ethics is too keen for him to have acted on any romantic interest he had in you while he was your superior at Carapace. So he tried to hide his feelings for you from you and others at the company, perhaps even from himself, while you worked there."

Laura looked at Simon in surprise. "But Tim was involved with Brandy, who's far more attractive than I am. He might still be involved with her. He says he isn't, but he seems to find her hard to resist."

"I don't think Tim has seen Brandy since the Fourth. There

was a strange paradox in their relationship that you see often in New York. She tolerated him only because she thought he might marry her. He went along with it because they didn't see each other often and he thought she needed support. But she pushed him too far when she got drunk in front of his business associates at his Fourth of July party. He apologized later to a couple of people at Carapace and said that she was, in his words, out of the picture. Frankly, I think he was embarrassed by how she acted."

Laura's mind spun. She was now convinced that the strange idea that she'd had after their dinner at Ducasse had been right. He *had* bought the dinner with her because he was attracted to her.

"I can see why he tried to hide his feelings while I worked for *Cassandra*. But what about afterward? There was no reason for him not to have told me how he felt after I started work at *Aurora*."

"Tim was somewhat awed by the changes in you this summer. He said that you looked so ravishing at Kit's wedding, but he couldn't get near you until near the end of the evening. You were always dancing with other men. He said that he was sure you would want to have the kind of affairs with some them that he had with Normendie and Brandy, that it's a stage a lot of people go through when they arrive in New York. They need to reject their past before they can appreciate it. He said that he imagined that he could hope for no more than friendship, if that. The other day he made an offhand comment: 'She's going to be besieged by men who want her because she's become so glamorous, and I'd have taken her in the penny loafers and Notre Dame sweatshirt.'"

Having reached the end of the jetty, Simon stopped, surrounded on three sides by the dark water. "I must say that I wish you liked Tim better. I admire him quite a bit. In many ways, he understands the magazine business better than Cassandra ever will. In fact, I might have suggested that he join us tonight had I not worried that you might feel as upset as you did after running into Liz Kaiser at his party. For all his high-powered socializing, Tim strikes me as somebody who might like to have a few more friends."

"Simon, I'm so sorry that you didn't invite him. I could have tolerated his presence for a few hours—more than tolerated it. I'd have enjoyed seeing him without a producer acting as a chaperone." *More than enjoyed it,* she thought, thinking of how nice it would have been to walk with Tim in the moonlight. "Now that you've told me that he approved the costs of my cover story, I could at least have thanked him for it."

"Then we'll have to invite him to the wedding, and you can thank him next June. But for now both Alice and I are determined to fix you up with a man you'd like. Give me another couple of weeks until some of my friends come back from the annual holidays in England and I'm sure we'll come up with somebody."

Back in the city, Laura kept taking apart and reassembling the conversation she'd had on the jetty. She had no reason to doubt Simon's words, which had left her shaken. She was mortified by how little gratitude she had shown for all that Tim had done for her before and after she had left *Cassandra.* Why hadn't she allowed herself a scorch-and-burn night of passion with Tim while she had the chance? Had she come to New York to take no more risks than she would have taken in her hometown, where the word of her missteps might spread so quickly that they would haunt her forever? What if getting involved with somebody from your hometown *was* the risk?

Above all, what could she could do about it now, especially by that impossible Labor Day deadline that Tim had set? She wouldn't be in the city for the holiday, and he traveled so much that he might not be around before then. How could he expect her to resolve in a few days something that had been building since June? The wedding that she dreaded had almost arrived, and she had to prepare for it—buy a gift, fly to Ohio, try to emerge from the rehearsal dinner speaking to Tina, pray that Brad wouldn't let his clients do anything wacko.

She was making a list of the things she needed to do before Labor Day when her brother called, brimming with excitement.

"Hey, Laura! Great news! Mom said she heard from Aunt Eva

that Brad wants to have the wedding guests throw foil-wrapped condoms at the church instead of rose petals. I thought that since you were a bridesmaid you'd have the inside track on getting the extras. Could you scoop up some for me?"

Laura told her brother calmly that there had to be a misunderstanding—that the priests wouldn't allow anybody to throw condoms at the church.

"Well, the story is that the condom store offered to put Brad and Tina's names on the condoms and the date of the wedding," Steve said defensively. "So in case there isn't a misunderstanding, would you get me the extras?"

"I haven't heard anything about this," Laura said evenly, crossing her fingers. "But I'm certain that nobody is going to throw monogrammed condoms at the church."

27
Arrivals

Laura shivered at the back of the church, wishing that she were wearing earmuffs instead of a hat shaped like a melon wedge. Why hadn't she remembered that Cleveland ignored the calendar and started bracing for winter storms by Labor Day? If she had, she might have taken a few sensible precautions like finding out if the limousines for the bridal party had blankets and propane heaters. Just three months after leaving for New York, she was already wondering how she had survived for twenty-five years in a city that could make you feel that you had liquid nitrogen in your veins before your summer pass to the community pool had expired.

After a cold air mass swept in from Canada the night before, Tina and Brad told everybody that the chill was a sign that God had smiled on their wedding. It meant that nobody would get struck by a tornado during the picture-taking. Whether or not this was true, the stiff blasts that blew in though the church door added a final touch of color coordination of the wedding: all the bridesmaids had lips as purple as their dresses. It was a stroke of luck that Tina was wearing a gown that was fit for Elizabeth I and might have sheltered several of her courtiers, if not their horses, under its elephantine skirt. The bride wouldn't have to worry about frostbite, even if her guests did.

Rocking on her golf-tee heels in an attempt to stay warm, Laura studied the names of companies on the back of a silver-and-white booklet that said "Christina and Bradford." Tina and Brad belonged to a new wave of couples who had corporate sponsors for their wedding, or donors who contributed items in exchange for a listing in a booklet and brochures on the tables at the reception. Brad, as a public relations executive, wanted to embrace a fast-spreading trend known as "viral marketing" and Tina realized that the strategy would allow her to have a larger wedding than her parents could afford.

Laura saw that the wedding booklet was as thick as the programs for some of her basketball tournaments and marveled at the number of endorsements the couple had collected. In the race for corporate sponsorship Tina and Brad came in slightly behind a top-ranked driver on the NASCAR circuit. She was reading a message that said "Best Wishes from Moammar and the Gang at the Flower of Libya" when she caught wisps of a conversation between two of the bridesmaids.

"… so thoughtful of Tina to let Nick invite Tara …"

"… of course, they were together for so long that Nick was Tina's friend, too …"

"… producer loves his script …"

What?! It had never occurred to Laura that Nick might turn up at the wedding, especially with Tara. He put up such a fuss about going to any event that took him away from his work that she had assumed the issue died when they broke up. Why hadn't Tina warned her? Was her cousin so dense that she didn't understand that it might upset her to see Nick with his new girlfriend?

Furious, Laura scanned the pews, hoping to identify Nick and Tara by the backs of their heads. She would need a few minutes to adjust to their presence, and she wanted to gain the advantage before walking down the aisle. In her agitation she stepped out of the line of bridesmaids in the narthex as the organist lumbered through Pachelbel's "Canon in D" and the church grew thick with the scent of incense and white roses and lilies. Her cousin Maggie warned her in a stage whisper to get back into position. Laura ignored her and deconstructed the pews with her eyes. She had to find Nick and Tara so that if seeing them rattled her, she could look the other way as she moved down the aisle. Catching an unexpected glimpse of them could be worse than any nightmare she'd had about the wedding.

Laura was still looking for Nick and Tara when the organist took up "Jesu, Joy of Man's Desiring" and people turned toward the center aisle in anticipation of the arrival of the bride. Maggie elbowed her, and she recognized her cue.

She was halfway down the aisle when she saw the last person she had expected to see at the wedding. Only it wasn't Nick.

It was Tim, who was grinning at her.

Laura took a few more steps. Then her knees buckled and, as hundreds of wedding guests watched in horror, she crashed to the floor.

With the reflexes of a former athlete, Laura scrambled to her feet. But one of her heels had snapped off in the crash, leaving one shoe with a three-inch heel and the other with none, which made it impossible to keep walking. Several women who were wearing the female equivalent of the Full Cleveland—white shoes and a white handbag—took off their pumps and handed them to her.

Laura could tell by looking at the shoes that none would fit. Forced to choose between going ahead in her stocking feet or going back to the narthex, she decided to move forward.

The last thing she saw just before she resumed her march toward the front of the church was Tim looking at her with stunned disbelief.

✳✳✳

On her way into the reception hall, Laura saw a table with two empty seats and place cards that said "Nick Peters" and "Tara Wilder" in purple calligraphy. Tina told her that Nick had backed out so he and Tara could fly to California to attend a meeting with a producer who was thinking about buying his script. It seemed he was close to making a deal and expected to move to Los Angeles with Tara soon after he did.

Laura had scarcely recovered from seeing their place cards

when she saw two others that said "Stephen Smart" and "Stacy Fazekas." Why was her brother sitting next to Stacy instead of at a family table? She searched the hall for her brother and found him having a drink at the bar with Stacy, no longer an adorable towhead in a Daisy uniform but a woman who looked stunning in a red sequined knock-off of a low-cut Egotista Dominguez dress that she had bought at Hit or Miss. They were having a good-natured argument about the newlyweds' decision to have guests throw rose petals, after all, at the church. Steve wished that people had tossed the condoms while Stacy insisted that tossing condoms ought to rank right up there with marrying your sister on any list of the top three grounds for an annulment officially recognized by Rome. Laura couldn't help thinking that Stacy would be a good influence on her brother and took him aside.

"What's going on between you two? I like Stacy. But you keep telling me you want to go out with models. That's why Normendie bought you a date with Perky Vano. I thought that you were dying to go out with her."

Laura had called Steve after the auction to tell him about Normendie's gift and had thought that he might sprain his dialing fingers calling Perky. He had seemed enthusiastic enough about her a few days earlier.

"I *was* dying to go out with her. But when I called her, she refused to come to Cleveland. She made some kind of excuse about having to go back into rehab, but I think she just didn't want to come to the wedding."

"You asked Perky to Tina's wedding?"

"I wanted to see her right away and thought that if she came here, we might be able to have the weekend together instead of just a few hours. That way Normendie would have gotten more for her money. How else could I show Perky off to my friends? If I went to New York, none of them would believe that I'd gone out with a model."

Laura made a mental note not to renew the subscription to *Maxim* that she'd given Steve for Christmas. This was not the result she had hoped for. "I might still go out with Perky after she gets out of rehab," Steve added. "But I decided that I might as well ask Stacy to the wedding. She got this great promotion from secretary to office manager at the ball-bearing company, and she saved up enough money to get some implants."

So that was where she got her cleavage, Laura thought. She wondered if Stacy had plastered herself to the dress with duct tape. "If Stacy will go out with you after you ignored her for so long, she might be a lot better for you than Perky. If I remember correctly, she sold more Samoas than any Girl Scout on our street. Maybe she could figure out how to help you sell yourself to employers."

Steve bristled at the suggestion. "I have a job. Or I will soon. Stacy introduced me to a guy at the ball-bearing company who said I would have no trouble getting a job there if I took a few more computer courses. He said that some of the things I learned at Cleveland State were already out of date. So that's what I'm doing now."

Laura strongly doubted that Steve would have "no trouble" getting a job anywhere except in his imagination. But taking courses was enough of a step in the right direction that she congratulated him before joining the other bridesmaids at their table. After dinner, she looked for her mother, who had seemed to disappear after the ceremony. She found her supervising several women from the Sodality who were arranging slices of wedding cake on plates in the kitchen and offered to help. They shooed her away, saying that she might get buttercream frosting or an apricot glaze on her bridesmaids' dress.

Unable to discount this possibility, Laura went to look for Molly, who was sitting next to an empty seat with a place card that said "Chadwick B. Heller." Molly said that Chad had bailed out of the wedding because he had to take an out-of-town deposition and that it was almost a relief not to have to spend the reception with somebody who might pull out his StarTac while others were doing the Macarena. She added that she might ask for a transfer to the New York office of her firm so that she could have the kind of great social life Laura was having.

"Great social life?" Laura asked, astonished. "Who told you this?"

"Everybody's talking about all the exciting men you've gone out with, like that Yankees farm team member who might be the next Derek Jeter."

It was obvious that the facts of her social life had become slightly distorted as her news passed from her mother or Steve to their friends and neighbors. Not wanting to disillusion her friend all at once, Laura suggested as gracefully as she could that Molly might want to spend a few months in New York before making a decision to move.

After they agreed to get together in the city in the fall, Laura returned to her table and watched guests do the chicken dance, the cha-cha slide, and "YMCA." An oldies band, a client of Brad's, provided the music, and the lead singer was imitating Elvis' deep-pile tones in "Blue Velvet" when man in a sharkskin suit and a buzz cut bounded up.

"Remember me, Laura? Joey Molnar."

"Joey!" Laura hadn't seen the former altar boy in a decade. "What are you doing these days?"

Joey said that he was divorced—a disappointment—but had done well as the owner of one of the most successful Jiffy Lube franchises in the state. He pulled her to her feet and led her toward a dim corner of the dance floor.

Laura had been dancing with Joey for only a few bars of music when he began to grope at her as he had once done in the sacristy. When she tried to break away, he pulled her closer. In a mild panic she wondered if anybody could see him. If so, he didn't seem to care. She was trying frantically to think of a way to get rid of him without causing a scene Tim cut in.

"Mind if I take over?"

Joey backed away. "Great to see you again, Laura. Let me know if you ever need a lube job."

Laura wondered if gratitude could distort her vision enough to explain how seductive Tim looked as he led her to a spot on the dance floor far from Joey. He was wearing a dark suit and a sky-blue silk tie that matched his eyes so closely he might have bought them both at a Sherwin-Williams paint store. A shirt label that was visible when they danced said Seize sur Vingt, but the overall effect was definitely Vingt sur Vingt.

"Thank you!" she said, just above a whisper. "I was desperate to get away."

"I could see that. Hope you don't mind my cutting in."

"It was a favor, the latest of many you've done for me."

Tim studied her face as though checking for black-and-blue marks. "I'm amazed that you can dance after that fall in the sanctuary. Are you okay?"

"Everything except my ego. Tina accused me essentially of trying to upstage her at her own wedding."

"I'm afraid I didn't help by showing up without warning. You turned as white as Tina's dress when you saw me."

"I was a little surprised to see you. How did you get invited?"

"I come home for a family barbecue almost every Labor Day weekend, and when you said that you'd be in the wedding, I called Brad and asked if I could attend. As usual, he was delighted to accommodate anyone in the media. He stopped just short of asking if I could send a camera crew or arrange for the Goodyear Blimp to fly over the church and transmit photos to the networks."

"Why did you want to come at all? I thought that you and Brad didn't know each other well."

"I didn't want to come to the wedding. I wanted to see you, or, rather, to see you when I hadn't paid five thousand dollars for it. And Simon said that you had told him that you might enjoy seeing me without a camera zooming in on our fish forks. That was such a remarkable change from what I've been hearing from him all summer, and I had to see for myself if it was true."

"It *is* true," Laura said, awash with relief that he was still speaking to her. "I wanted to see you more than I realized for a long time. But you said that if I wanted to see you again, I'd have to get in touch with you."

"One of my many mistakes this summer."

"I thought I made the mistakes. What were yours?"

Tim nodded toward the oldies band, which was playing loudly enough to rattle the sherbet cups on the tables at the front of the reception hall. The Elvis imitator had just performed the remarkable feat of moving from "Blue Velvet" to "Love Me Tender" without rupturing his spleen with his tectonic pelvic thrusts or poking himself in the eye with the microphone that he clutched.

"One of my mistakes might have been thinking we could talk above this music. Let's get out of here."

Outside the reception hall, the air had grown cooler than it was before the ceremony. Tim suggested that they talk in his car in the parking lot, and after turning on the heater, fished a piece of paper out of his pocket.

"Before I forget, I have a message for you from Simon. He called me on my cell phone this morning and asked if I knew where he could reach you in Cleveland. I wasn't sure where you were staying, so I told him that I'd pass along his message."

"Did something happen to Alice or Mr. Dudley?" Laura asked, alarmed.

"No, it's only good news. But you're shivering." Tim took off his jacket and slipped it over her shoulders. "Simon's news might give you a different kind of shivers, so you might want to wait until you warm up to hear it."

"Please tell me. I can handle it with blue fingertips."

"He didn't go into much detail. But he said that he sent your cover story on Normendie to a friend of his at a publishing house and told her that you were expanding it into a memoir. The editor read it on the Jitney on her way to the Hamptons and wants to see anything that you've written for the book as soon as you get back to the city."

"But I haven't written anything! Simon must have given her the wrong idea."

"Apparently not. Simon told her you were still doing research and didn't know when you could begin writing the book. He said that he thought that an editor's interest might jump-start the project and that you worked fast enough to pull a sample chapter together quickly. Whether you've written anything might be a technicality. It seems that the editor might offer you a contract based on your cover story."

"How could anybody offer a contract? I haven't written a word of the book."

"Happens more often than you might think. At the magazines I've published, a lot of writers have gotten offers based on great articles that they wanted to develop, or that editors saw and asked them to expand. Celebrity memoirs are among the easiest kinds of books to sell that way because your access counts for so much. If a star wants to work only with you as Normendie does, you're in a stronger position than if you had three Pulitzers but once wrote that her dress at the Oscars made her look like a fully loaded ore-hauler. So maybe you'll be able to afford to move out of your apartment sooner than you think."

Laura was still trying to digest this unfathomable news when Joey left the reception with a woman carrying a centerpiece. The sight of the former altar boy brought them both back to earth.

Tim shook his head as Joey walked unsteadily away from the church.

"Did coming to the wedding at times make you wish you'd never moved to New York? Make you feel all warm and sentimental about the place you'd left behind?"

Laura would have thought he was joking had he not spoken in such a worried tone. "Tim, it's Labor Day, and we have the heat on in the car because an Arctic air mass swept into town last night. Joey Molnar tried to feel me up, my brother showed up with a woman he seems to have noticed only because she got implants, and my cousin accused me of trying to upstage her at her own wedding. My mother was so busy helping with the cake that she scarcely said a word to me." She watched as Joey began kissing his companion behind a statue of the Virgin Mary. "So, no, I don't feel all warm and sentimental about the place I left behind. I can't wait to get back to New York. Coming home for weddings and national holidays might be about as much of my hometown as I can handle for a quite a while."

"Good."

"Why good?"

Tim didn't respond but backed his car of his parking spot.

"Where are we going?"

"You'll see."

Laura had the sense that Joey or something else had distracted him from what he had wanted to say before they left the reception. "You said that you might have made mistakes this summer—"

Tim waited until he had maneuvered the car around a traffic circle to pick up the thread of their conversation at the reception. "I did make mistakes. But I can't figure out what I could have done differently, except for not showing up at the airport in all that baseball gear. You have no idea how you reacted when you first saw me. You stared at me as though I was one of those deranged Browns fans who burned Art Modell in effigy after he moved the team to Baltimore."

"Please forgive me. But you did look—"

"As though the Indians' third-base coach was my personal dresser?"

Laura hoped that, in the dark car, he couldn't see her face. "For that day, anyway. Where did you get all of that gear?"

"A sports equipment manufacturer had a father-and-son Father's Day party in its skybox. He was thinking, correctly, that media people who wouldn't normally attend might show up if they could get free tickets on a sold-out day. All the gear that I was wearing came in the swag bag that the company handed out in the box. I don't like to take things that I don't need. But it would have been rude to say, 'I'd be glad to have the tickets because I'd like to do something nice for my father, but you can't bribe me with a blue satin jacket

with Chief Wahoo on it.' It was a case of 'in for a dime, in for a dollar.' Sometimes it's almost impossible to avoid taking gifts from
business associates trying to ingratiate themselves."

"Tell me about it. I could probably have come away from
Cassandra with enough cosmetics to do the makeup for every
female guest at this wedding."

"I wonder if, after twelve years of parochial school, both of us
don't have more guilt than some people about these things. I
know sports producers who have closets full of swag and no
qualms about going for more. They call the media relations people for teams playing in World Series and say, 'My son's birthday
falls on opening day. Could you please give me thirty tickets so he
can have his party at the stadium? His school has a rule that he
has to invite everybody in his class.'"

"They call them in the way fashion editors call in Fendi bags?"

"They try to. But I was never able to do it unless I needed the
tickets for work. I have a recurring vision of St. Peter turning me
away at the Gate after seeing me in a Devil Rays cap. He keeps
shouting, 'I draw the line at expansion teams! You should have
stopped with the Yankees caps!' You have to feel a little sorry for
the team publicists sometimes. That's partly why I can tolerate
people like Liz Kaiser. She makes writers' and editors' lives hell
because other people make her life hell."

Laura had the sense that Tim had more on his mind than
whether "journalistic ethics" had become an oxymoron. "You
aren't blaming yourself for the free gear you wore at the airport on
Father's Day?"

"Not really. But I feel bad that I didn't tell you right away that
I worked for Carapace. I didn't mention it at the airport because
it was so fascinating to talk to an employee who didn't know who
I was. What I hear from people at your level tends to reach me
through their managers. And even the good managers like Simon
can filter their comments heavily. I was appalled that he didn't pay
your moving expenses."

Tim slowed down as a driver ahead of them ran a red light. "But Simon made an innocent mistake. He hadn't picked up on some of the differences between how businesses operate in England and how they do here in the States. Other employees have done things that are less easy to forgive. For years Irene Field has been leaving people with the impression that she believes the death penalty is the appropriate punishment for paying too much for an electric pencil sharpener."

"Why don't you suggest that she take early retirement? Or move to another department?"

"Because if she'd lighten up a little, she's exactly the kind of person you want in that spot. After all her years with the company, she still reads expense reports meticulously instead of signing off routinely. Along with a few people at higher levels, she's one reason why we've never had an accounting scandal at the company. My secretary once made me a funny card that said, 'If you like Enron, you'll hate us.'"

Laura's conscience had rarely weighed so heavily on her as it did when she remembered how she had railed against the economies at *Cassandra*. "You must have been furious when Aurora and I tweaked you about being cheap at Kit's wedding."

"Some of your coworkers have put it more strongly than you did. Caitlin Stearns wrote me a scorching memo that almost blistered the paint on my walls. She was enraged that she had to make a pit stop at Duane Reade for batteries before every interview. I get the sense from Simon that Ethan Naff thinks that we ought to hire a secretary to run out to the drugstore *for* him when he needs supplies. I can't say that I never had similar feelings when I was just out of school. But it can be painful to hear because we approve a lot of major expenses that most employees will never know about."

"I do know about some of them," Laura said. "I know that you told Simon he could remake the August issue to run my cover story. He told me a few days ago, and I can't say how much I appreciate it, all the more so now that it might lead to a book."

"I wonder if he told you too late."

"Too late for what?"

"For us."

Here it comes, Laura thought. *This is where he tells me he's decided to marry Brandy or somebody else. Or that he's too angry with me to speak to me again, let alone invite me into his Jacuzzi.* "Why would it be it too late? Are you engaged to Brandy?"

"Brandy?" Tim asked, turning sharply toward her. "I haven't seen her since the Fourth and doubt that I will again. After Normendie I swore that I'd never get involved with a woman who needs Dr. Phil instead of me. But I did. I can't explain why except that traveling a lot on business can make it hard to keep a relationship going at home."

Tim drove east, in the general direction of St. Rose's. "The difference between Brandy and Normendie is that Normendie has pulled herself back together admirably. And she can do the same with her career, especially with the help you're giving her. The determination she showed in making sure you got a five-thousand-dollar bid at the auction is typical. If she applies that kind of energy to her new CD, she may not have another *Junior League Dropout*. But she can do clubs and tours, make a decent comeback. Brandy won't or can't make the effort."

"If you're not involved with Brandy, why is it too late for us?"

"Because of all the attention you're going to get from other men. I've seen it happen many times. Women from the Heartland come to New York to work for fashionable magazines and become transformed. They turn into Audrey Hepburn in *Funny Face*. Then they only want Fred Astaire and tap dancing on the Champs Elysées. Some of them would have been much better off with boys from Tulsa or Fond du Lac."

"I always thought Fred was way too old for Audrey in *Funny Face*. And as you may have noticed at Kit's wedding, I'm a terrible dancer."

"You're still going to have to fight men off. And you'll probably have a wonderful time doing it."

"I had a wonderful time with *you*."

Tim swerved abruptly off the road that would have taken them to Saint Rose's and began following the Rapid, the main subway line, though the eastern suburbs. "Then why did I have the impression that I've been setting your teeth on edge all summer? Simon predicted—correctly—that we would lose you to *Aurora* if we couldn't keep you happier, including by loosening up the salary schedule at *Cassandra* enough to give you a raise."

"I had a couple of—" Laura searched for the right word, not wanting to lie too blatantly in retrospect.

"Concerns?" Tim said, smiling. "That seems to be the preferred euphemism today."

"Yes, concerns," Laura said, embarrassed that he had seen through her. "But it was because I was viewing them through the lens of my own inexperience. I thought you took me to Babcia's because you were too frugal to take me anywhere else. Now I think that I'd prefer it to the most expensive restaurant in New York. I didn't like *going* to Ducasse as much as I like having *gone* to Ducasse. It's a great place to eat. Once."

"All the new men in your life will be delighted to hear that."

Laura couldn't tell from the tone of his voice whether he was serious. "But I don't want new men in my life. I want you."

Tim pulled off the road and into a park-and-ride spot along the Rapid line that they were following. For a few minutes, he said nothing. "I was sure," he said carefully, "that I was the last man in New York you thought you wanted."

"In the beginning, you probably were the last man I wanted. First, I was involved with Nick. After I broke up with him, I wanted to go out with other men. I think that started to change when I went to a spa and stood far back enough from life to gain some perspective on it. But I tried to convince myself that my attraction to you was irrational."

"When did you start to think that the attraction was rational?"

"I don't know," Laura said truthfully. "Some people say that they can date the moment as precisely as though they had carried a stopwatch. But I think that for some of us, falling in love is more like crossing the International Date Line. You can't see it when you're right on top of it. Maybe I saw it in a hazy outline when I was in your Jacuzzi and I realized that you were the only man who wasn't afraid of my old basketball scar on my thigh—"

Tim slipped his hand under her dress. "You mean this scar?"

"Mmm-hmm."

Tim took his hand away and reached for hers. "I was going to drive to St. Rose's to see if we could shoot a few baskets on the spot where my donation will end up. You're the only woman I know who could and would try a jump shot in that dress. But something you said made me think we should stop here."

He pointed to the subway tracks in front of their park-and-ride spot. "You said that couples never kiss each other goodbye at subway stops in Cleveland. Why don't we sit here and see if you're right?"

For a while, they talked about the wedding and the reception. They agreed that when two people got married they should not invite Joey Molnar, encourage the bridesmaids to look like vegetables, or ask the guests to throw condoms with the names of the bride and groom on them. Eventually, Laura understood why Tim had pulled into the stop even though it was so late that the subway had stopped running.

"Imagine that I'm on my deathbed," she said, "and my grandchildren ask me if I ever kissed a man goodbye at a subway stop in Cleveland."

Tim looked at Laura with delight. "I hope you're not planning to die while I'm alive, but I'd still like to know what you'd tell them."

"I'd tell them that I kissed a man at a subway stop in Cleveland," Laura said, "but it wasn't goodbye."

"And what would you say if your grandchildren asked you why you wanted to kiss the last man you thought you would ever fall in love with?"

"I would tell them," Laura said, smiling, "that I've always been a pathological optimist."

Acknowledgments

Not long after I began writing this book, my brother Jack died of injuries suffered in a major highway accident caused by a drunk driver operating a car on a suspended license. My brother Bill never fully recovered and, fifteen months later, died by his own hand.

To lose both of your siblings under sudden and violent circumstances is a life-shattering experience that requires heroic support. I received that and more from Mary Clarity, Jim Hutchison, Don Murray, Jane Reed, Tim Page, Nan Winterbotton, Judsen Culbreth and Walter Kirkland, Erich Hoyt and Sarah Wedden, Marianne Jacobbi and Barry Lydgate, Rick Hampson and Lindy Washburn, Helene and Larry Lynch, Pauline and Roger Mayer, and all the Heilbronners: Hans, Phyllis, Warren, Joan, Rob, and Sarah.

For years my aunt, Lois Lipka, has shown another kind of heroism though her tireless efforts to record the genealogy of our family. My brothers' deaths have deepened my appreciation for her meticulous account of generations of Frasers, MacDonalds, Boyers, Steeles, Shaws, and Sharplesses. Julius Harajda, one of New Jersey's great accordionists, keeps alive the musical heritage of the Hungarian side of our family. My wonderful godchildren, Ned Samuelson and Jasmine Hoyt, have added topspin to my life.

My beloved English teacher, Eunice Davidson, died just after Jack did, and I cherish my evergreen friendships with her students: Steve Csontos, Dennis Frenchman, Steve Goldin, Randy Goodman, David Powers, John Romano, Steve Schneider, Judy Trundt Oakley, and Chuck Ziegler. I am also grateful to Meg Torbert and Beth Salzman at the University of New Hampshire alumni magazine and to all of the classmates who have made it a such pleasure to be a UNH class secretary. If the National Book Award Foundation ever starts honoring people for their efforts to ease the isolation of novelists and others, the first prize should go to Pam Satran, founder Montclair Editors and Writers (MEWS), who understands that the correct answer to the question "What do writers want?" is "Parties!" Betty Grimmer Cronin and I once shared a fourth-floor walk-up not much more luxurious than my heroine's, and then, as now, her good cheer is inspiring.

For other acts of kindness, I would like to thank Molly Delano, Leslie Goldberg, Ed Lawrence, Mike Shulman, and the Rev. Phyllis Zoon and the members of congregation of Central Presbyterian Church in Montclair, particularly Marilyn Stone. Gina and Mike Roscilli of the Tania Guest House in Edinburgh were exemplary hosts who brought the warmth of their native Italy a restorative visit to the land of my Scottish ancestors. Back in the United States, I put the finishing touches on this book at the lovely home of Tasmin, Graeme, Daniel, Darcey, and Buffy Morrison, who went out of their way to provide all the comforts that a writer could want.

Many others also kept this novel moving forward amid a cascade of losses. Maisy Samuelson patiently answered questions about girls' basketball and provided an awe-inspiring demonstration of behind-the-back dribbling. Dominique Raccah, Heather Otley, and Kelly Barrales-Saylor came to the rescue at Sourcebooks. And in an age in which cynicism has become the occupational disease of literary agents, Carol Mann's unfailingly sunny professionalism is a joy.

Finally, Susan Samuelson deserves a line all her own. I have never known anyone who has enriched more people's lives, mine among them, with her friendship. It is all the more remarkable that she has done this while teaching full time, writing a trailblazing business law textbook, raising three admirable children, staying married to the man she wed at the age of nineteen, and keeping up her tennis game. She is the sort of person that William Butler Yeats was describing when he wrote: "Think where man's glory most begins and ends, / And say my glory was I had such friends."

Janice Harayda
Montclair, New Jersey

About the Author

Janice Harayda is an award-winning journalist whose articles have appeared in many national magazines and newspapers. A former vice president of the National Book Critics Circle, she was a staff writer and editor for *Glamour* and spent more than a decade as the book editor of *The* (Cleveland) *Plain Dealer*. She is the author of a nonfiction book about being single and the comedy of manners, *The Accidental Bride*.